PROMISES KEPT

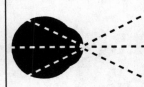

This Large Print Book carries the
Seal of Approval of N.A.V.H.

PROMISES KEPT

SCARLETT DUNN

THORNDIKE PRESS

A part of Gale, Cengage Learning

GALE
CENGAGE Learning·

Farmington Hills, Mich • San Francisco • New York • Waterville, Maine
Meriden, Conn • Mason, Ohio • Chicago

GALE
CENGAGE Learning·

Copyright © 2015 by Barbara Scarlett Dunn.
The McBride Brothers #1.
Thorndike Press, a part of Gale, Cengage Learning.

ALL RIGHTS RESERVED
Thorndike Press® Large Print Clean Reads.
The text of this Large Print edition is unabridged.
Other aspects of the book may vary from the original edition.
Set in 16 pt. Plantin.

LIBRARY OF CONGRESS CATALOGING-IN-PUBLICATION DATA

Dunn, Scarlett.
   Promises kept / by Scarlett Dunn.
     pages cm. — (The McBride brothers ; 1) (Thorndike Press large print
clean reads)
   ISBN 978-1-4104-8451-2 (hardback) — ISBN 1-4104-8451-3 (hardcover)
   1. Love stories. 2. Western stories. 3. Large type books. I. Title.
PS3604.U567P76 2015
813'.6—dc23   2015029725

Published in 2015 by arrangement with Zebra Books, an imprint of
Kensington Publishing Corp.

Printed in Mexico
1 2 3 4 5 6 7 19 18 17 16 15

*Dedicated with love to Hercules,
my faithful companion.
You defined courage and perseverance,
and I miss you every day.
Wait for me,
big guy,
and keep Apollo and Andjing busy.
I will see you again one day.*

ACKNOWLEDGMENTS

A big thank you to the following people that bless my life:

Michael — Much love to you, and thank you for always being on my team.

Mary Ann Morgan — The greatest cheerleader, and the very BEST person I know.

Jim Morgan — My inspiration to persevere. Never give up!

Mary Sue Seymour — You are a joy to work with, and a lovely person.

John Scognamiglio — It's a real pleasure to work with you. Better than fine.

PROLOGUE

Dear Miss Victoria,

My name is Chet Barlow. I read your need of a husband as writ in the *Daily Telegraph*. I thought I would tell you something about myself. I own a farm here in Wyoming that was passed down to me from my father. It's just me and old Bartholomew working the farm now. I won't spin a tale and say this is an easy life. My land is surrounded on all sides by cattlemen who want my land for the fair amount of water that runs through it, and that causes some problems. I can give myself a recommend by saying I work hard from sunup to sundown, and I'm honest. I don't have a formal education, but my dear mother was an educated woman and taught me reading, writing, and numbers. Her well-to-do family thought she married beneath her station, but my father was a decent, hardworking man, and he took good care of her. I expect I've forgotten a fair amount of what she tried so

hard to teach me, but I remember the important things like how to treat a lady proper. I
swear by all that's holy that I will treat you
kindly if you decide to come to Wyoming.

I read the Bible daily and Shakespeare
when time permits. In good weather I try to
make it to church on Sunday. I'm not much in
the way of cooking, and I can tell you it'd be a
real pleasure for me and Bartholomew to have
a decent meal now and again. My father
taught me all I know about working the land
and I will pass that down to your boys. I make
you a solemn promise I will be good to you
and the boys, provide a home, and make sure
you never go hungry.

More than likely you will have several replies
as there are few women in this territory who
didn't come here with their men. My mother
always said to prepare for what you want to
happen, so I am sending you fare for the
stagecoach and necessaries along the way.
Once you get to Promise, go see Bob at the
livery stable. He will see that you make it to
the farm.

Chet Barlow

P.S. It don't matter none to me if you are not
a handsome woman. No one ever accused
me of turning heads, but I don't recollect
anyone losing their breakfast at first sight of

10

me. I've drawn a map of the stagecoach route and the stops from Missouri to Wyoming so you will know where you are going. This will be a hard trip and not one without possible danger. If you know how to shoot a pistol, it would be wise to have one on your person.

CHAPTER ONE

Action is eloquence.
WILLIAM SHAKESPEARE

St. Louis, Missouri
Holding the small leather-bound parcel at arm's length, Mrs. Wellington squinted at the neat printing. Arms flapping like the wings of a ruffled goose, she was a flurry of silk motion as she burst through the boardinghouse door as fast as her legs would carry her. Scurrying the length of the hall toward the kitchen, she was met by the familiar popping and crackling hisses of a fryer hitting hot grease. Waving the parcel in her hand, she hustled to the young woman hovering over the stove.

"Victoria, you have a post from Wyoming that came by way of the noon stage." Gasping breathlessly, her ample bosom was heaving up and down from exertion, but she didn't wait for a response. Sucking in more air, she chattered on. "The print is small, but neat" — *pant . . . pant* — "I'd say written by a man" — *pant . . . pant* — "Isn't this the tenth post you've received? Do you have family out West?"

Victoria whirled around to see what Mrs. Wellington was carrying on about. When the woman was excited or nervous her high-pitched British accent became more pronounced and she was difficult to understand. Eyeing the pouch fluttering like a flag in Mrs. Wellington's hand, Victoria knew she had received another letter. Snatching the parcel from her employer's grip, she quickly shoved it in her apron pocket. "I . . . I was expecting this." She felt guilty lying to Mrs. Wellington, since she was the first person who had been truly kind to her, but it wasn't the first lie she had told her. The lies had started the very first day she showed up on Mrs. Wellington's doorstep with Cade and Cody in tow. She'd told Mrs. Wellington the boys were her brothers instead of trusting her with the truth. She justified her lie out of fear the boys would be taken from her if anyone found out they weren't even related. Four years ago she'd taken the boys with her when she left that saloon in Abilene to save them from a certain future in an orphan's home. She continued the lie to protect them from that fate now. While she couldn't say Mrs. Wellington was particularly nosy or judgmental, she had learned it was wise to keep her own counsel and not trust anyone with the lurid details of her life.

"Aren't you going to open it now?" It hadn't escaped Mrs. Wellington's notice that until the last few weeks Victoria had never received mail in the two years she had worked at the boardinghouse. She was more than curious to learn the reason for the sudden influx of correspondence.

Victoria forked more floured chicken slowly into the sizzling grease, saying over her shoulder, "It's nothing that can't wait until later when my work is done for the night."

"I can turn the chicken for you while you peek inside," Mrs. Wellington eagerly offered.

Victoria was anxious to tear into the letter, but she knew Mrs. Wellington would press her for details. "No, thank you. I would rather wait until later."

Disappointment evident on her face, Mrs. Wellington turned toward the dining room. "Well . . . then . . . I'll go prepare the dining room for the dinner hour."

■ ■ ■ ■

Colt McBride sat in the dining room across from George Milford, the banker and executor of his uncle's estate. It was Colt's last night in St. Louis, and he was anxious to head back to Wyoming. He'd made the arduous trip to St. Louis after receiving a telegram from his uncle saying that he was dying and wanted to see him. Though Colt didn't question his decision to come to St. Louis, it was difficult for him to be away from the ranch for any length of time, particularly with the problems he was having lately. The way he saw it, he didn't have a choice. He'd only seen his father's brother a handful of times, but he felt it was his duty to come. Arriving in St. Louis just in time to spend a few short hours with his uncle before he died, Colt's intention was to be on the next stage back to Wyoming after the funeral. Upon learning from banker Milford that he had inherited his uncle's estate, he was forced to change his plans. Working with Milford, they'd managed to have the details of his uncle's estate settled within a week.

"Have you eaten here this week?" Milford asked.

"No, I've only eaten at the hotel," Colt replied. He scanned the well-appointed dining room, thinking it was homey and inviting. The aromas wafting from the kitchen already had his stomach growling.

"You're in for a treat then. Mrs. Wellington, the owner, has employed a cook with exceptional culinary skills. I daresay you'll not taste better desserts in the finest restaurants in New York."

Mrs. Wellington was making her rounds with fresh coffee, and stopped by their table. "George, it's nice to see you again," she said. She recognized the tall cowboy sitting across from George as the man she'd seen at Edward McBride's funeral.

"Mrs. Wellington, I was just telling Mr. McBride about your delicious food," George said. "Mr. McBride is the nephew of Edward McBride."

"Mr. McBride, I saw you at the funeral. My condolences, sir," she said.

"Thank you, ma'am."

"George is correct. If you've been dining at the hotel, then you will soon make a change once you eat Victoria's fine fare," Mrs. Wellington assured him.

"Then I'm sure sorry this is my last night in St. Louis, since I appreciate a fine meal," Colt answered politely.

17

"I'm sorry to say that Mr. McBride is headed back to Wyoming in the morning," George offered.

Mrs. Wellington shook her finger at the banker. "Shame on you for not bringing him to dine before now! You know how bad the food is at that hotel."

"I feel so guilty that I'm buying his dinner to make up for my bad manners, so make those steaks extra special tonight," George responded, looking appropriately repentant.

Curious about the handsome stranger, Mrs. Wellington lingered at the table. "Would you like cream, sugar?" She'd only seen him at a distance at the funeral, but up close he was even more striking with his impressive size and square-jawed good looks. When he walked into the dining room with that large black Stetson on his head, every patron turned to stare at him.

"No, ma'am, black is fine," Colt replied, still smiling at how the Englishwoman had dressed down the banker.

Mrs. Wellington excused herself to hurry to the kitchen. She simply couldn't wait another second to tell Victoria about the handsome cowboy. "Victoria! Oh mercy! You should see the cowboy in the dining room. He is the biggest man I have ever seen, his shoulders are so wide he barely fit through the doorway. A stunning man. He is the nephew of Edward McBride, the owner of the sawmill, who died recently. His eyes are actually black, I've never seen anyone with black eyes, but his are as black as sin . . ." She drew in a deep breath and continued, "His hair is black as coal too, wavy and shiny, and though a bit too long in my opinion, it is quite attractive on him."

Mrs. Wellington was still prattling on, but Victoria paid little attention; she was busy preparing the orders and she didn't want to make a mistake. "Hmm," was her only response.

"George Milford — you know, banker Milford — said Mr. McBride was from Wyoming. Perhaps he knows some of your relatives. That would be an excellent way to start a conversation with him. It helps to have something in common," Mrs. Wellington added just in case the young woman had forgotten how to converse with a man. She rarely had interactions with men, other than to take their orders in the dining room.

Ignoring her running commentary, Victoria thrust two platters filled with steaks sizzling and a mountain of mashed potatoes into her hands. "This is the order for table six."

Mrs. Wellington hesitated, and pushed the

platters back toward Victoria. "Why don't you take these out so you can get a look at that cowboy? Mercy me, he is so handsome. You simply must go take a peek! It's not often a woman gets the chance to see a man like that!"

Disregarding the proffered plates, as well as Mrs. Wellington's excitement over the cowboy in the dining room, Victoria turned back to the stove. "We have a lot of orders, Mrs. Wellington, and I need to get them done." She didn't have time to waste; she had more steaks to cook and two pies in the oven that she needed to watch. Besides that, if she never saw another cowboy in her life it would be fine with her.

They'd had similar conversations before, and Mrs. Wellington knew what was on Victoria's mind. "I know what you are thinking, dear. Not all men are like some of the no-account cowboys that come in here from time to time being a nuisance. Some men are decent men who may actually want a wife." She pointed a finger in the direction of the dining room. "That cowboy out there seems particularly well mannered."

"I've seen enough cowboys to know what they are like," Victoria countered. Her thoughts drifted back to that night in Abilene when a drunken cowboy had nearly raped her in her room. She was just fifteen at the time. After the hardships she'd faced in her young life, not much frightened her. Yet she hadn't overcome her fear of most men . . . cowboys in particular. No, she didn't have an interest in any cowboy. She hoped the letter in her apron pocket was from anyone but a cowboy. "No cowboy I want to meet will walk through that door," she said with conviction.

Mrs. Wellington released an indignant huff of air. "You never know who will walk through that door. Just think how I was blessed when you and your brothers showed up on my doorstep." Seeing she wasn't going to change Victoria's mind, and not wanting the food to get cold, she took the platters and turned to the door, muttering to herself, "The Good Lord can get them in the door, but you need to help Him out once in a while and show yourself." It wasn't that she didn't understand Victoria's hesitancy to meet men. Many times she was forced to intervene when men were behaving badly toward Victoria, so her caution was well-founded. The girl drew attention simply because she was so lovely and men naturally gravitated to her.

When the dinner rush was over, Victoria set

about cleaning the kitchen. Once she finished washing the pots and pans, she walked to the dining room to help Mrs. Wellington clear the tables. It was a relief to see the dining room nearly empty; there were only three tables with diners left. After clearing off several tables, Victoria moved to a table next to one occupied by four rough-looking cowboys.

Colt spotted Victoria as soon as she walked into the room, as did the four cowboys across the room. The foursome were difficult to ignore; they had been loud and obnoxious since they'd entered the dining room. Right now their full attention was on the lovely woman in the yellow dress as she moved around the room collecting dishes.

Colt watched her fill her arms with dishes and then head back to the kitchen. He'd kept his eyes on the door until she returned again. He was watching when she moved to the table next to the four cowboys. Even though she was some distance from him, he could see that she was a sight to behold with her dark auburn hair curling past her waist. He was waiting for her to make her way to his table so he could get a closer look.

As soon as Victoria reached the table next to the four men, she recognized them. They had been drunk and disorderly in the dining room a month ago, and the sheriff had to be summoned. Even with her back to them, the distinct odor of whiskey filled the air. Quickly stacking the dishes in her arms, she turned to leave when one of the men reached out and snagged her skirt.

"Hey, honey, don't hurry off. Sit down with us," the leader of the foursome said.

Victoria ignored him and tried to move away, but he maintained his hold on her skirt. When he gave the cloth a tug, she almost fell backwards into his lap. She struggled to keep the china from falling to the floor. His three companions found his antics humorous and guffawed like misbehaving children. Victoria tried to turn back to the table to set the plates down, but the man tightened his grip. She feared if she tried to pull away from him her dress might rip.

"You can have dessert with us, honey," the man said to her. "I like what I'm seeing."

"I got a better idea. We can have her for dessert," one of his companions added.

"Yeah, that sounds even better," another agreed, wiping his mouth on his sleeve.

"Let me go!" Victoria demanded, showing a bravado she didn't feel. Her heart was fairly pounding out of her chest from fear.

She was always fearful around men who consumed too much whiskey. It was difficult to know if these men were just having a little fun at her expense, or if their intent was more nefarious. By the way they were leering at her, she assumed the worst.

Mrs. Wellington walked from the kitchen and saw what was happening across the room. She promptly set the coffeepot aside and made her way to the table. Before she had taken more than a couple of steps, the tall cowboy appeared at Victoria's side.

"You boys need to mind your manners," Colt said in a pleasant but no-nonsense tone.

Victoria's tormentor looked up at the man beside her. "You need to mind your own business," the man retorted. His companions laughed and jabbed each other in the ribs at their buddy's bluster.

Victoria thought the drunk must be crazy to challenge the man looming next to her. He was a huge, dangerous-looking man with a deep, commanding voice as ominous as his appearance. The top of her head barely reached his chest. No doubt he was the man Mrs. Wellington was going on about in the kitchen, and for once she wasn't exaggerating. Victoria may not have chosen the word *stunning* for him . . . *lethal* was the word that came to her mind.

"Let her go," Colt demanded.

The man grinned at Colt as he pulled Victoria's skirt higher, showing the men at the table her petticoat. "I don't think so. We've decided this gal is gonna join us for dessert."

Victoria shifted all of the dishes to one arm, and with her free hand reached back to tug at her skirt, to no avail. The miscreant wouldn't release her.

The largest man of the four stood. "In case you haven't noticed, cowboy, there's four of us and one of you."

Colt smiled, but it wasn't a smile that reached his eyes. "Then I guess we're about even." He made a quick mental note that the man holding the woman's skirt was wearing his gun on his right side. The same hand he was using to hold her captive. Big mistake. He leaned over and wrapped his fingers around the man's hand and squeezed until he heard his trigger finger snap.

The man yelped loudly, released the cloth, and clutched his hand to his chest. "You broke my finger!" he cried. The two men who were still seated jumped to their feet.

"I'd say that's three to one now," Colt stated.

Even though she was free to move, sheer

terror kept Victoria frozen in place. She couldn't take her eyes off the cowboy who was facing down the four men.

Seeing the woman hadn't moved, Colt stepped in front of her.

"I've told you men before I will not tolerate problems in this dining room. Now pay your bill and leave and do not come back," Mrs. Wellington instructed when she was a few feet from the table.

Colt held his hand up to halt Mrs. Wellington's progress. In case bullets started flying he didn't want her getting too close. "I think they were just leaving, Mrs. Wellington," he said, not taking his eyes off the men.

The four glared at Colt, taking measure of the man and the weapon he wore low on his hip. They glanced at each other, passing an unspoken signal.

They've done this before, Colt thought. It didn't matter, he was confident he could take them. He understood the necessity of assessing a situation quickly — a man didn't live long in this country by being careless. All three were right-handed, and they wore their holsters too high to be fast on the draw. And judging by their bloodshot eyes, they had consumed a lot of whiskey, which would make them even slower than normal. If they were anything like most bullies, they liked to taunt women, but they would back down when confronted by someone equal in size. He reasoned the man who stood first thought he was the most fearsome of the group. Watching their eyes, he instantly knew when they'd made a decision. The big man was going to be the one to draw. Another mistake.

Before the man pulled his gun halfway out of the holster, he was staring down the barrel of Colt's pistol. "I wouldn't if I were you," Colt said. "Now pay what you owe the lady and leave."

The man hesitated, his eyes flickering from Colt to the two men beside him.

To Colt's amazement, the two men looked ready to draw. *Whiskey brave.* "Don't," was all he said.

That one word was uttered in such a deadly cold voice it sent shivers down Victoria's spine.

The man released his pistol, allowing it to drop the few scant inches to the holster. The other two men held their hands in the air as they backed away.

Colt kept his gun trained on them. "Pay up."

After digging in their pockets, they threw some coins on the table and hurried toward the door. Before he left, the man with the broken finger turned back and yelled, "You'd best be leaving town, stranger."

Holstering his pistol, Colt glanced at Mrs. Wellington. "I think George and I would like some of that apple pie you mentioned, and please tell your cook that was the best steak I ever ate."

"Thank you for lending assistance, Mr. McBride. Maybe those rowdies will stay out of here now," Mrs. Wellington responded appreciatively. She smiled at him and added, "And you just told her."

Colt didn't catch her meaning at first, until he heard a soft voice behind him.

"Thank you . . . and thank you for . . . handling those men." Victoria didn't know what to make of the man standing in front of her. He'd just faced four men ready to kill him and he was ordering pie just as calm as you please.

Turning around, Colt gazed down at the woman he'd defended, and he felt like he'd been kicked by his prize bull. The most beautiful blue eyes, bluer than his Wyoming sky in summer, were staring up at him. A few seconds ticked by before he found his tongue. "You're the cook?" He'd expected that some little old lady like Helen, the older woman who cooked for him, had prepared that excellent meal. He enjoyed Helen's food, but he had to admit, even she had never served up such a perfect steak.

"Yes, I am," Victoria replied, thinking Mrs. Wellington was correct on another score. His eyes were as black as midnight.

When he'd seen her from across the room, Colt thought she was a real looker, but he hadn't expected her to render him speechless. He found himself regretting his decision to leave St. Louis in the morning. If he'd seen her when he first arrived he would have made a point of taking her to dinner.

"Victoria will get that pie for you, and I'll warm up your coffee," Mrs. Wellington offered.

Turning away from those intense eyes, Victoria half ran back to the kitchen on wobbly legs. She was still shaking from the confrontation as she carefully placed the dishes into the sink. After taking several deep breaths, she finally calmed down enough to cut the pie instead of her fingers. She couldn't decide who was the most frightening: those four drunken cowboys, or the cowboy who had intervened. Yes, she could. The man with the ominous black eyes was, by far, the most terrifying.

Victoria delivered the pie to Colt's table, and found Mrs. Wellington chatting comfortably with the two men.

"Victoria, I didn't introduce you. This is Mr. McBride from Wyoming. Perhaps he knows some of your relatives."

Colt almost laughed. Mrs. Wellington had obviously never been to Wyoming or she would have realized that it was so vast it would be a miracle if he knew the young woman's relatives. Not wanting to be rude, plus the fact that he wanted to talk to Victoria, he asked politely, "Where are your relatives located?"

"They're . . . ah . . ." Victoria stalled, trying to think of what she should say. She was saved from telling another lie when the twins appeared in the doorway, waving to get her attention. "Excuse me," she replied, and rushed over to the boys. The boys were ready for bed and they came to remind her she had promised them a story tonight. She took them by the hand and walked upstairs, without sparing a glance back at the cowboy.

Colt watched her lean over to speak with the two little boys in the doorway. He heard her say, which was difficult with Mrs. Wellington's chatter, "Of course you get your story tonight." So much for wishing he didn't have to leave tomorrow. Wasn't that just typical, he thought, all the beautiful women were already taken. Too bad.

CHAPTER TWO

Once the boys were settled for the night, Victoria trudged downstairs to finish cleaning the kitchen. Seeing Mrs. Wellington had finished washing the dishes, she spent her time making preparations for breakfast. It was after eleven o'clock by the time she climbed the stairs to her tiny third-floor room. Pulling the leather pouch from her apron pocket, she clutched it to her chest as she crossed the room to open the small window. She looked out at the thousands of twinkling stars in the night sky surrounding the full moon. It was such a clear night that the man in the moon looked like he was smiling at her. There was a time she would have said a prayer, but that time had long past. God didn't listen to her prayers.

Mrs. Wellington's curiosity about the letters was understandable. She had never received a single visit, much less a letter, since she had been at the boardinghouse.

But how could she possibly explain what she had done? From the day she arrived at the boardinghouse, she hadn't been forthcoming with Mrs. Wellington about her past. Now, two years later, she didn't know where to begin with the truth. Mrs. Wellington was a woman of some means, and she had been fortunate to have a husband of forty years who had cared for her until his death. She had never had the responsibility of supporting two young boys weighing heavy on her shoulders every day. There was no way she could possibly understand Victoria's reasons for advertising for a husband.

The idea had come to her when she'd overheard a man in the dining room relating a story about his friend in Wyoming advertising for a mail-order bride. The man had placed an advertisement for a wife in the newspaper and had received so many responses he had a wide selection of ladies to choose from. Why couldn't she place an advertisement like that? She didn't necessarily want a husband, since most men frightened her, but she would set aside her fears for the boys. She had to think of their future, and that road led to finding a husband. It wasn't as if men were beating down her door asking for her hand. Oh, plenty of the men who frequented the boardinghouse flirted with her, but not one had expressed an interest in a ready-made family. She'd received her fair share of crude offers, but Mrs. Wellington had a way with words that shriveled a man in his boots if she overheard anyone uttering a word that might be considered the least bit disrespectful. Judging by the remarks she'd heard from the women diners, she was to be pitied. They often told her no man would want to take on the responsibility of a woman with two small children. They were right, she grudgingly agreed. She needed to widen her horizons if the boys were to have a home.

In the past, it had been necessary for her to accept whatever job she could find just to keep the boys fed. Circumstances had forced them to sleep in barns, or just about any dry place they could find. Now they had a roof over their heads and regular meals, but most of her small salary was used for clothing and shoes for the boys. If it weren't for the dresses Mrs. Wellington had given her to alter for herself, she would have been parading around the boardinghouse in her birthday suit. She'd even used some of the cloth to make reticules to sell at the general store for extra cash. They now had the basic necessities, but she was no closer to being able to afford a home. While she appreciated the two small rooms Mrs. Wellington included in her compensation, she wanted Cade and Cody to have a home of their own. She wanted a place no one could take away from them.

A home wasn't the only thing the boys needed. They talked incessantly about having a father who would teach them all the things boys wanted to know. Just tonight, before they fell asleep, they'd asked her if they would ever have a pa. Many times they would end their nightly prayers asking for a pa to teach them to ride and rope. They wanted to be cowboys, and she had never even been on a horse. If she had any say in the matter they wouldn't be cowboys, but she recognized every boy needed to know how to ride a horse. Finding the right man, a good man, was the challenge. She wanted them to grow up to be honorable men, not like the men she'd seen in her young life. No matter how she circled the problem, she needed to find a man who could provide a home and teach the boys skills to survive.

She'd heard what Mrs. Wellington said tonight about needing to do her part when God provided a man. While she appreciated Mrs. Wellington's beliefs, they were no longer her own. When she was younger she'd prayed and prayed for a different life, but nothing ever changed. The time for praying and dreaming about what she wanted was over. She was determined the boys would have a home and respectability, and it was up to her to find a way to change their circumstances. She decided, as the cattlemen who dined at the boardinghouse were so fond of saying, it was time to take the bull by the horns. So she'd written the advertisement: *Lady of marriageable age with two young boys in need of husband. I am a good cook and used to hard work.* She'd finished the ad by including her name and address at the boardinghouse. She had decided it best to say straightaway that she came with responsibilities, so there would be no surprises down the road. She didn't actually state the boys were her children, but the implication was there all the same.

So far, she had been less than impressed with the responses. One man wrote that she should come out West, and if he liked the looks of her and she performed her *wifely duties* to his satisfaction, then he might send for the boys. *Well, no, thank you very much.* She'd seen enough men at the saloon in Abilene to know when they were just interested in one thing. As Mrs. Wellington so aptly stated, *They want the milk and not the cow.* Another letter she'd received was from a man describing himself as a married man of considerable wealth who wanted to hire her as a housekeeper. Of course, she would be required to share his bed because his wife was beset with headaches. *As if!* Every letter she'd received had mentioned her *wifely duties. Is that all men think about?*

After striking a match to the lamp on the table, she took a seat in the rocking chair and carefully opened the pouch. Several gold double-eagle coins dropped to her lap. Puzzled, she peeked inside and saw the folded letter with her neatly printed name on top. Tracing the letters with her fingers, she was nervous and excited at the same time.

She stared at the letter. Maybe this one would be different. She took a deep breath and slowly unfolded the letter. *Dear Miss Victoria . . .* She read the letter a second time, and questions filled her mind. *How old is Mr. Barlow? Is he a widower? Does he have children? Who is Bartholomew?* He described himself as hardworking and honest. *Good, he's not a cowboy but a farmer. He reads the Bible and goes to church. He reads Shakespeare.* Maybe that was a sign he was the right man. Since living at the boardinghouse she had access to Mr. Wellington's vast collection of books, and it seemed he'd had a particular fondness for Shakespeare. Surprisingly, she had also developed a liking for the man's writings.

Mr. Barlow offered more information than the other men had given her in their terse replies. The most telling line he'd written was his promise to provide for her and the boys. Those few words touched a soft spot in her heart. Unlike the other letters she'd received, he hadn't once mentioned her wifely duties. Of course, if they were wed he'd have every right to expect her to . . . well, she knew what would be expected. She picked up the coins from her lap. It was no small sum of money, certainly more than she needed for the stagecoach. Perhaps he didn't have to scratch out a meager existence as she had done her entire life. It must have occurred to him that she could take his money and never make it to Wyoming. That trusting gesture told her more about the man than his written words. He obviously dealt honestly with people and expected the best from them. Maybe this was the one man she could trust. A farmer.

Dawn peeked through the window, and Victoria had to force herself from the comfort of her small bed. She had tossed and turned all night, trying to decide what she should do. She walked to the window and pushed back the curtain, allowing the morning breeze to fill the room. Hearing voices from the street, she peeked out to see Mr. Mc-Bride talking to the stagecoach driver. Mr. McBride's deep voice resonated in the quiet of the early morning, and the light of day did nothing to lessen his intimidating countenance. He looked even larger than he had last night with that big, black cowboy hat on his head. She watched as he tossed his valise to the top of the coach with little effort.

The banker approached and Colt turned to him and shook his hand in farewell. The banker walked away and Colt opened the door to the coach and started to step inside, but paused in mid-motion. As if he knew she was watching, he tilted his head back and looked directly up at her window, pinning her with his dark gaze. Their eyes held for a long moment before he tipped his hat and climbed inside the stagecoach.

Colt leaned back and stretched out his long legs in an effort to find a comfortable position in such a confining space. He thought about the woman at the boarding-house window. He'd had a feeling someone was watching him, and when he caught her reflection in the window as he spoke to the banker, he was certainly surprised. He halfway expected it to be the hombres he'd tangled with in the restaurant last night. When he looked up at her, all he could do was stare. He'd never seen a more lovely sight, with her dark auburn hair cascading over her shoulder, shimmering in the morning sun. He had to force himself to get in the stagecoach and leave.

He wasn't sure why, but she'd occupied his thoughts most of the night. That was a first for him; he never lost sleep thinking about a woman. *Cattle maybe, but a woman? Never.* He told himself she was so lovely, any man would have difficulty forgetting someone like her. There were a few attractive women at home, but he couldn't think of one who equaled her beauty. He covered his eyes with his hat and let out a loud sigh. If she didn't have a family, he would have told the stagecoach driver to leave without him.

Victoria was still thinking about Mr. Barlow's letter as she rolled out the dough for biscuits. *It's a plumb crazy notion to travel clear to Wyoming to marry a complete stranger. What if he is nothing at all like his letter? What if he is the kind of man who beats women?* He said he was a church-going man, but as she had learned from her past, there were no guarantees where men were concerned. She'd seen her share of supposed Christian men who beat women, particularly when whiskey was involved. *What happens if I take the boys to Wyoming and he's mean to them? What if . . . what if . . . what if . . .* Her mind was reeling from the unanswered questions when Mrs. Wellington breezed into the kitchen a few minutes later.

"Good morning, Victoria. It's going to be hotter than blue blazes out there today."

"Yes, it is hot." Victoria tried her best to sound like her mind wasn't miles away in Wyoming. Before her mind caught up with her tongue, she blurted out, "I wanted to tell you that I'm going to Wyoming to see . . . an ill cousin. I will leave next Monday. That will give me time to find someone to help you out while I'm gone." Her own words surprised her. She had planned on taking the day to think things through. Too late for that, she told herself. Her course was set and she would not back out.

Mrs. Wellington crossed the room and put her arm around Victoria's waist. "Oh dear, I hope no one is seriously ill. Are you taking the boys?"

40

More lies. She couldn't think about that, she had to keep her focus on the future for the boys. "Yes, I will," she replied.

"That is a long trip for two young boys. Why don't you leave them here? I can look after them," Mrs. Wellington offered.

If the boys didn't go with her she would have a chance to see what Mr. Barlow was like before she introduced them. "Are you sure you don't mind?"

"I don't mind at all. They are such good boys." Mrs. Wellington eyed Victoria. She had a feeling Victoria wasn't telling her everything, but perhaps the news from her family had been upsetting. The young woman had never taken as much as one day off, so she could not in good conscience deny her request.

"I will tell them to help you with chores while I'm gone," Victoria promised.

"They are always very helpful, dear, don't you worry about that. It's too bad you couldn't leave this morning. I daresay that Mr. McBride would have made a perfect companion for the trip. You would certainly have been safe. Can you afford the fare? If not I can give you an advance on your pay."

Ignoring the comment about Mr. Mc-Bride, Victoria said, "Mr. Bar— My family sent me the money, but thank you. I haven't

41

mentioned this to the boys yet."

"I'll not say a word to them. Why don't you just tell them you are going for a short visit, so they don't worry?" Those boys were mightily attached to Victoria, and Mrs. Wellington wasn't sure how they were going to accept being away from her even for a short time. As far as she knew, they had never been apart.

Victoria tried to think of an excuse to give the boys for her sudden decision. She was hesitant to tell them the real reason she was going to Wyoming, not wanting to risk getting their hopes up when the arrangement might not work out with Mr. Barlow. There was also the possibility they would forget and reveal the true nature of her trip to Mrs. Wellington. "Yes, that's what I will say. Thank you so much, Mrs. Wellington. I don't know what we would do without you."

"Nonsense. You and the boys have done so much for me. Ann Merriweather will probably have the time to help me while you are gone. Folks won't be as happy with her cooking, but we'll manage."

Mrs. Wellington was so kind about her leaving that Victoria was momentarily tempted to tell the truth. She quickly abandoned that notion, knowing the woman would try to talk her out of going by reiterating all the fears that she'd already considered. This might be the one opportunity to make a home for the boys, and no one was going to change her mind, however well-intentioned. "I'm beholding to you." Victoria turned back to her task with tears in her eyes, her guilt piling on.

CHAPTER THREE

Wyoming Territory

"Barlow, I've made you an offer that is more than fair." Euan Wallace, flanked by four of his men, surprised Chet Barlow as he worked on a broken wheel in front of his barn.

Chet had been so lost in his thoughts about Miss Victoria Eastman that he hadn't been paying attention to what was going on around him. He hadn't even heard the riders until they were on top of him, and his rifle was on the seat of the buckboard some fifteen feet away. His woolgathering could prove fatal, he thought. He tried to appear unconcerned, and continued working on the wheel when he responded, "You're wasting your time and mine. I've told you before, my farm is not for sale."

"You're not getting any younger, Barlow. You and that old man can't work this farm by yourselves forever." Wallace surveyed the

44

old house and barn. While unimpressive in size, both buildings were well tended. It was obvious Barlow put in considerable hours keeping things in good order. The buildings didn't interest him; he wanted Barlow's prime piece of land.

With that comment, Chet met Wallace's eyes. "If you didn't scare most folks around here I might be able to get me some help. As it is, I figure I get by just fine."

When Wallace came to Promise and got his hands on the Taggart ranch, he put the word out that he would hire every available man and pay more than any other rancher. If they didn't want to work for him, he made sure they left town. He was a wealthy man, and he didn't often hear the word *no*. He'd come to expect the folks around town wouldn't challenge him. "Gordon Major at Circle M is selling out to me. Mark my words, Barlow, I'm going to have this land one way or the other."

"I don't care if Major is going to sell to you or not. But it's going to be mighty difficult to get your hands on my land, seeing as how it's paid for. I don't know how you folks do business back in England, but things are different in Wyoming. You can't steal land that's paid for. You can't steal the mortgage the way you did to get your hands on the Taggart ranch," Chet said plainly. There wasn't a day that went by that Chet didn't give thanks to his deceased father for long ago paying off the mortgage on their land.

One of Wallace's hired hands nudged his horse forward, his hand automatically going to the butt of his sidearm. "You can't talk to Mr. Wallace that way," he warned.

Chet looked at the man doing the talking. He didn't recognize him, but judging by his demeanor, he wasn't a cowboy. The young man had the look of a cocksure gunslinger, but that didn't sway Chet from speaking his mind. "Last time I checked, you were on my land uninvited. I'll say what I want, and what I'm saying is the truth." His gaze moved back to Wallace. "I've told you for the last time, I'm not selling. Now ride off my land."

"You speak mighty tough for an unarmed man," Wallace spit out, his eyes moving to Chet's rifle on the seat of the buckboard. "I bought the Taggart ranch fair and square, nobody will say different."

"I think I just did." It was a sad day when a man couldn't work on his farm without being harassed by hired guns, but that was the way of it since Wallace came to Promise. Tension filled the air. The gunslinger's hand twitched over his pistol.

Chet could see in the man's eyes that he was getting ready to draw. He thought of making a dive for his rifle but knew he wouldn't make it. In an instant, all movement stopped at the sound of riders coming up fast behind Wallace's men. Every head turned to see who was interrupting their conversation. Seeing it was Colt McBride with two of his men, Chet breathed a sigh of relief.

Reining in his horse behind the buckboard near Chet, Colt could feel the tension between Chet and his visitors. It felt like he'd ridden upon a nest of rattlesnakes, and judging from the scowl on Wallace's face, he was getting ready to strike.

"Chet," Colt said by way of greeting. He took off his Stetson and swiped his forehead with his shirtsleeve, taking time to measure the situation. His dark gaze moved to Wallace and his men, then back to Chet. "Did I interrupt something important?"

"No, they were just leaving," Chet answered.

"What brings you here, McBride?" Wallace asked.

Resettling his Stetson down low over his eyes, Colt looked at each man before leveling his black eyes on Wallace. "Nothing that concerns anyone but me and Chet."

"If you've come out here to talk Barlow into selling to you, I've already told him I'll double any offer you make him," Wallace said smugly.

Colt clamped his jaw down hard. "If that was my purpose, as I said, it would be between me and Chet."

"I told you, Wallace, I'm not selling," Chet reiterated.

Wallace took his reins in one hand as his horse began prancing, eager to run. "We'll talk again when you're more reasonable."

Chet glared at Wallace. "Save your time and breath."

"It's my time and my breath." Wallace turned his horse, giving rein to the antsy animal, leaving his men to follow. Three of them rode behind Wallace, but Hoyt Nelson, the young gun, didn't move. He stared hard at McBride, his eyes inching down to the revolver on his hip. Some of Wallace's men had told him McBride was the fastest draw they'd ever seen, and his own inflated ego was itching to find out. "Word is you're pretty fast with that .45, McBride."

Colt's hands were relaxed over the pommel of his saddle as he took measure of Nelson. They were close in age by Colt's estimation, but Nelson was a small man,

48

which made him appear younger. That fact probably accounted for him trying to gain a reputation as a fast gun. The man thought he could gain inches with a fast draw. "I guess there is only one way to find out."

Nelson grinned. "I figure I'll find out one day soon."

"No time like the present," Colt said flatly, his face completely void of emotion. Colt had heard of Nelson before Wallace hired him, and he knew he wasn't hired for his cow punching abilities.

"Soon, McBride, very soon." Nelson circled Colt's horse before kicking his own mount to a run, dust swirling in his wake.

Colt's eyes darted to Chet's rifle, well out of reach. "You'd best be keeping that rifle closer to you."

"I have to admit they caught me off guard. Things were getting a mite testy before you rode up," Chet said, shaking his head. "I was hoping Bartholomew had them covered from the barn." No sooner had the words left his mouth when Bartholomew limped from the barn with his ancient scattergun cradled in his arms.

"That I did, boss," Bartholomew told him. "I saw them ridin' in and thought I would make myself invisible for a while. I was just waitin' for that Nelson boy to twitch the wrong way."

Colt laughed at the wiry man who didn't look strong enough to hold his gun, much less pull the trigger. He'd known Bartholomew his entire life, but eyeing him now, he was surprised at how old and fragile he looked. He couldn't possibly weigh much more than a hundred pounds, including that shock of snow-white hair sticking out in every direction. But Bartholomew was still feisty, and he had a good grip on that gun he called Bessie.

"I'd say they weren't counting on you being around, Bartholomew."

"Wallace is always underestimating folks. Maybe that will be his undoing one day," Chet mused, keeping a watchful eye on the riders who had become dots in the distance. He glanced back at Colt. "So what brings you out this way? The last I heard you were back East."

"I got back a few days ago. I came out to tell you that Wallace hired on that gunslinger you just met. Hoyt Nelson. I didn't want them sneaking up on you and Bartholomew out here all alone. Nelson isn't the only man of questionable character Wallace has hired lately."

"I pegged him right off for a no-account gun hand," Bartholomew told them.

50

Chet knew Colt was the one neighbor that he could trust. He liked the younger man as much as he had liked Colt's father. Both were men who spoke their minds and had the courage to back it up by any means necessary. "What do you think Wallace is up to?"

"Nothing different, just a different tactic. He's land hungry, and yours isn't the only one he's wanting. I've had some cattle slaughtered and right now I'm dealing with rustlers. I'm sure Wallace is behind it, but I couldn't prove it in court. The Cross Bar D is having problems too, and it wouldn't surprise me if Wallace is trying to pit us against each other. We're not even into summer yet and water is scarce. If we don't get rain soon, no telling what will happen. Tempers are flaring all around."

Colt couldn't deny he would also buy Chet's land, but he wasn't going to force anyone into selling. While Chet might not be a cattleman, that didn't mean he didn't belong. His family history in Wyoming went as far back as his own, and in Colt's estimation that gave him the right to farm, if that was what he wanted.

Chet inherited several thousand acres from his father, who was a farmer, and he'd carried on the tradition. When Wallace started threatening men that refused to work on his ranch, Chet's workers left to avoid trouble. Without additional help, Chet and Bartholomew could only farm a few acres, producing just enough grain and vegetables needed for their own use. Chet had considered buying some sheep since he had plenty of land and water, and he wouldn't need men, just a couple of good dogs. But he knew that decision would create more problems with the cattle ranchers. They hated sheep ranchers more than they hated farmers.

What truly aggrieved the other ranchers was the several thousand acres Chet inherited from his uncle last year. Every cattleman around wanted that coveted piece of land for the water. It was common practice for land to go to auction to pay outstanding debts when the owner died, but Chet's uncle owned his land free and clear. He'd also hired a big-city lawyer to prepare a will leaving everything to Chet. Since Wallace couldn't persuade Chet to sell, he'd made it his mission to get his hands on his land no matter what he had to do.

"Wallace just said Major agreed to sell the Circle M," Chet said.

Colt was surprised to hear this bit of news.

"You think he was telling the truth or bluffing?"

"Hard to tell with Wallace."

"You two need to watch yourselves around Wallace and his men, particularly Nelson. I hear he's not opposed to shooting in the back. Things are heating up around here and everyone is on edge. Some of these cowboys are going around half-cocked, and range wars have been started over less."

"Wallace said I was getting too old to handle the farm." Chet looked off in the distance again, wondering if he might be wise to sell out and start over somewhere else. The thought of a range war starting because he wouldn't sell out was unsettling, particularly if there was a woman and boys he'd have to protect. "Maybe he's right. We ain't getting any younger."

Bartholomew gave a loud snort. "Now, boss, don't you go talkin' like that. I ain't gettin' old — maybe you are, but I ain't. Just 'cause I can't move as fast as I used to don't mean I can't get there sooner or later," the older man grumbled. "Anyways, when your bride gets here you can't be talkin' that way. She's wantin' a home for her and her boys, and I expect she's thinkin' this will be a fine farm for them to have one day. We'll leave Wallace to the Good

Lord to handle in his own way."

"Bride? Boys?" *Chet . . . married?* Colt couldn't have been more shocked if someone said he was getting hitched himself. Chet had been alone for as long as Colt could remember; he couldn't even recall him courting anyone. It was hard to believe a man his age would be interested in a wife, much less one with children. He'd always figured him to be a confirmed bachelor like himself. Colt enjoyed women, and he had been with his fair share, but when the fun was over, he liked to get up and go home . . . alone. Marriage was definitely not in his future. He was married to his ranch, and when he did find time for pleasure, he passed it with Maddie at L. B. Ditty's saloon. No promises, no strings attached.

Bartholomew chuckled at Colt's expression. "Yessir, she should be arriving any day now."

Colt glanced back at Chet. He looked like he wanted to dig a hole and have it swallow him up. "I guess congratulations are in order."

Chet wished Bartholomew hadn't mentioned his possible bride. While he wanted to think Miss Victoria would come to Promise using the money he'd sent her, there was no guarantee. He'd just as soon his neighbors didn't know about his plans until she was here and had said her *I dos*. "Thank you," Chet responded awkwardly.

"When is the big day?" Colt couldn't help himself from asking, even though it was obvious the groom wasn't eager to discuss his impending nuptials.

Chet glared at Bartholomew, silently telling him if he said one more word he would gladly strip a piece off his old hide. "I'm not sure when she will be arriving."

Colt caught the look Chet gave Bartholomew and he figured Bartholomew was about to get his ears chewed off once they were alone. It was the perfect time for him to take his leave. "Extend my best wishes to her. I look forward to meeting her." He backed his horse up. "We'll leave you to it. Now keep that rifle in reaching distance. You two might not be as lucky the next time."

CHAPTER FOUR

"You a new dove for L. B.?"

Victoria glanced at the man who was a few feet from her. Even if she hadn't been able to smell the whiskey emanating from him, it was obvious he was drunk by the way he was weaving back and forth. Curious to see the person he was addressing, she turned to look behind her. Seeing no one there, she turned back to find the drunken cowboy now standing directly in front of her. Still, it didn't occur to her that he was speaking to her. She looked right, then left, but there was no one near except the scrawny dog that she had rescued during her journey, and he was giving the drunk a low warning growl.

She stared at the cowboy in openmouthed disbelief. "Pardon me?"

The cowboy put his hands on his hips and looked at her like she was dim-witted. "Are . . . you . . . looking . . . for . . . the . . .

saloon?" he asked slowly, his whiskey-laced breath almost knocking her over.

The stagecoach driver tossed Victoria's valise to the ground before he jumped down and addressed the drunk. "Mister, go on about your business and leave the lady alone."

"I ain't bothering her," he slurred. "I think she's looking for L. B.'s." He reached for Victoria's arm. "Come on, honey, I'll take you over to her." He eyed her up and down, and seemed to be pleased with what he saw, if his toothless grin was an indication. "I'm Pete, and I'll sure be seeing you every Saturday when I get paid."

The mangy dog jumped in front of Victoria and snapped at the drunk's hand.

Considering how he was swaying from side to side, the cowboy's reflexes were still pretty good. He jerked his hand back just before the dog clamped down. "That's a vicious dog!" He fumbled for the pistol at his side.

Seeing the drunk's intention, Victoria grabbed the dog by the scruff and tried to pull him behind her.

Before the drunk could pull his gun, a large hand clamped down on his arm. "Now, Pete, I don't think you want to shoot the lady's dog." Bob, the owner of the livery, was walking toward the stagecoach when he overheard Pete making a pest of himself.

Pete tried to twist away from Bob's grip without success. "But he tried to bite me," he protested.

"He was just protecting the lady." Bob pulled Pete's gun out of his holster and tucked it inside his belt. "Now go on back to the ranch before you cause more trouble."

The drunk pointed a finger at Victoria. "I was just offering to take this here gal to the saloon. I didn't mean nothin' by it."

Victoria's face flamed red. "I am not a . . . I am not going to the saloon!"

Pete looked her up and down again in an altogether inappropriate manner. A frown creased his brow. "Well, you're dressed like one of L. B.'s gals."

What on earth was this lunatic talking about? She looked down at the suit she had fashioned from one of the dresses Mrs. Wellington had given her. She'd invested long hours copying the design for the suit and matching hat from one of Mrs. Wellington's catalogues. It was as fine as anything she'd ever seen, though quite dusty from her trip. The ensemble was elegant and not the least bit revealing, unlike a saloon girl's garment. She should know, she'd made plenty of dresses for the gals back in Abilene.

"I most certainly am not dressed like a . . . like a . . . I am not!" she screeched.

Bob tugged Pete's arm, encouraging him to walk away. "Now go on."

"You mean she ain't a whor—"

"Pete," Bob growled in a warning tone, clearly losing his patience. He pointed Pete in the direction of his horse. "Now go!"

Pete decided he didn't want to tangle with Bob. Everyone knew he was one of the strongest men in town. He stumbled away in the direction of his horse.

Once Pete was some distance away, Bob turned his attention on Victoria. "Are you waiting on someone, ma'am?"

"Yes, well . . . I'm supposed to see Bob at the livery. I was told he could give me transport to the Barlow farm."

"I'm Bob, ma'am, and I will be glad to take you to Barlow's." He headed back to the livery, saying over his shoulder, "Let me get the team hitched to the buckboard and we'll be off."

"Are you taking that dog with you, miss?" the stagecoach driver asked.

"Oh yes . . . yes, I am. Thank you for allowing him to ride with us. I just couldn't leave him on the road." When the stagecoach had stopped for the passengers to stretch their legs, the dog had appeared from the brush and limped to Victoria. They were still a long way from Promise, and the poor animal looked like he couldn't make it another step. She felt sure he wouldn't have survived much longer, so she asked the stagecoach driver if he could ride with them. Thankfully, the two male passengers offered what food they had left over, and she provided water from a canteen the driver provided. Once the dog devoured the offerings, he'd ridden the rest of the way to Promise on the seat beside Victoria, with his large head on her lap. Every time she stroked his head, he would look up at her with his soulful eyes as if he was thanking her for saving him. Victoria promptly fell in love with him, and before their journey ended, she'd made the decision the dog was now a member of her family.

The stagecoach driver smiled, thinking there was no way he'd ever turn down a request from a woman as pretty as she was. Allowing the dog to ride inside the coach was against the rules, but he'd broken a few of those in his time. How could he say no to a pretty face like hers? It had been worth it just to get a look at that smile of hers. "No problem, ma'am. I think the Lord put him at the right place. My guess is he'll prove to be a loyal friend. Take good care of him."

"Oh, I surely will. Thank you again." Victoria hoped she didn't start off on the wrong foot with Mr. Barlow by bringing the dog with her, but she just couldn't leave him to his own devices. His situation reminded her of how she'd felt not long ago. She leaned down and looked into his large, hopeful brown eyes. "Don't worry, you belong to me now. You will never have to fend for yourself again. And any man worth his salt would be happy to have a dog like you." A lump formed in her throat saying the very words she had longed to hear someone say to her when she had no home and no future. The dog whipped his tail against her skirt, sending dust flying in the process. "I don't know who is the dirtiest, me or . . . I must think of a name for you." She glanced over his filthy coat. His fur was a reddish-brown color with large white spots, and what looked like the makings of a big fluffy white tail. At least it might be fluffy once he had a bath. His big brown eyes encircled by white fur made him look like he was wearing a mask. "I'm thinking about Bandit. What do you think?" His tail flopped from one side to the other as if he agreed. "Bandit it is," she told him.

Straightening, she briskly smacked her palms on her skirt in an effort to knock off more dust. She wanted to be somewhat presentable when she met Mr. Barlow. Exhausted from the trip, she was running on sheer determination. She didn't look forward to the ride to the farm with a stranger, but it couldn't be helped. Having Bandit by her side made the situation feel less daunting, since he'd already proven his readiness to protect her. She stroked the dog's head before she squared her shoulders. "Okay, we can do this," she whispered, trying to encourage herself. She avoided thinking about how her life might change in a few short hours.

CHAPTER FIVE

"We'll be there in about an hour." Bob covertly eyed the young woman sitting beside him, thinking in all his years he'd never seen a prettier sight. She was a slight woman, but she sat ramrod straight, making her appear taller than she was. Her hair was pulled up in some sort of elaborate fashion at the back of her head, and her blue hat was just barely hanging on by a wish and a prayer. And she had the bluest eyes he'd ever seen. She was a sight all right, just like a delicate flower in the middle of a desert. He was nearing sixty, but the way he saw it, a man of any age could appreciate a beautiful woman.

He thought it odd that Bartholomew hadn't told him yesterday when he saw him in town that they were expecting company. As far as he could recollect, he'd never taken anyone out to the Barlow farm, at least not in the last ten years. "I haven't seen

Chet in a couple of months. Are you family?"

Forced to sit so close to Bob on the cramped buckboard, Victoria's nerves were at the breaking point. She was unaccustomed to being alone with a man, and she'd already fought her fears the entire trip with two strangers on the stagecoach. Fortunately, they turned out to be gentlemen, and she was especially thankful for their kindness to Bandit. She told herself that Bob also seemed to be a gentleman, but that did little to put her at ease. He was a large, muscular man, and just looking at those massive hands holding the reins made a shudder shimmy down her spine. She'd seen what a man's fist could do to a woman's face. She'd lived too many years in a saloon to be fooled by a man's polite demeanor. They could turn plain mean with that first drop of alcohol, and often it didn't even take whiskey to make a man cruel. Suddenly, it occurred to her that Mr. Barlow might drink whiskey. She'd be in a fine fix then. She promptly pushed the thought aside.

"No . . . no, I'm not family." She chose not to disclose that she didn't know Mr. Barlow. "Do you see Mr. Barlow often?"

"Not too often. Most of the time he sends

Bartholomew into town for supplies. I saw Bartholomew just yesterday, but he didn't mention they were expecting company."

"He wasn't certain when I would be arriving," she told him truthfully.

Seeing she wasn't going to offer an explanation for her visit, he didn't pry. Still, he couldn't help but mull over what business this young woman had with Chet. He glanced at her again, thinking she was certainly pretty, but she was also one nervous filly. *If she isn't Chet's family, who is she?*

Bob stopped the buckboard in front of Chet's home, but when no one came to greet them, he figured Chet was out on another part of the farm. He helped Victoria from the buckboard, and placed her valise on the porch. "Doesn't look like Chet's around right now, but I'm sure he wouldn't mind if you go on inside to wait for him."

Bandit scrambled down from the back of the buckboard to stand beside Victoria.

Before Bob turned to leave, Victoria pulled a rumpled piece of paper from her reticule and held it up to him. "Are you sure we are in the right place?" She didn't want him to leave and find out later she was in the wrong place with no way to make it back to town.

Bob scanned the paper before his gaze moved back to her pale face. No doubt she was as nervous as a cat with its tail under a rocker, but he didn't know why. "Yes, ma'am, this is the right place, the Barlow farm." He was reluctant to leave seeing how frightened she was, and it might be some time before Chet came back. Bartholomew had told him about the confrontation with Wallace and his men. He'd hate to have her face those gunslingers alone. Instead of leaving, he walked to the barn and yelled out Chet's name, but there was no response. Since he had no place in particular to go, and his curiosity had been piqued, he decided he would just wait with her. He strolled back to the porch and casually leaned against the railing. "Why don't I just wait right here with you until Chet gets back. If you decide not to stay, then I can take you back to town with me." Maybe he'd learn more about her while they waited.

She was still nervous to be alone with him, but she preferred that option over being left alone in the middle of nowhere. "Thank you, Mr. Bob." She was so tired and tense she didn't give a second thought to the dust covering the porch step when she plopped down. Bandit settled down right beside her.

"Just call me Bob, no mister needed," he told her.

"I'm sorry I didn't introduce myself. I'm Victoria Eastman."

Bob nudged his hat with one finger. "Pleased to make your acquaintance." He pointed to the mangy dog that sat snuggled to her side, positioned between them. "How long have you had him?"

She glanced down at Bandit and looped her arm around his neck. "Only a day. I saw him on the road, and the stagecoach driver was kind enough to let him ride with us."

Another man who couldn't say no to a pretty face, Bob figured. "He sure could use a bath."

"Yes, I think we are both in dire need after our trip. I hope Mr. Barlow doesn't mind that I brought him with me," she added uneasily. It was difficult enough for her to think of meeting Mr. Barlow for the first time. If he objected to Bandit she didn't know what she would do. But her mind was made up, and under no circumstances would she abandon the dog. Nervously, she removed her blue hat and placed it beside her on the porch. She tried in vain to repair her hair that had escaped her combs and was tumbling around her shoulders. She longed to freshen up before she saw Mr. Barlow, but she didn't dare presume to go into his home.

"Chet is a God-fearing man who cares for all creatures. I doubt he'll mind the dog." The way he saw it, if Chet was lucky enough to know this little lady, he wouldn't be upset over a dog she brought along. He didn't figure there was a man alive who could stay angry at her over anything. He for dang sure couldn't.

Victoria eyed her surroundings, taking in the condition of Mr. Barlow's home and barn. The home wasn't large, but it was well built of stone and wood and looked sturdy enough. There were no flowers around the house, leading her to think Mr. Barlow was obviously not a man for frills. The property was neat and functional, but nothing to indicate a woman's presence. She absently wondered if he would object to her planting a few flowers to bring some color to the drab surroundings. She'd helped Mrs. Wellington plant flowers at the boarding-house, and in the spring they were rewarded for their hard work with glorious color. Her gaze drifted to the barn, and like the home, it was old but in good repair. She could almost envision the boys running around with Bandit in the field. She thought they could be happy here. She might not enjoy marriage, but she could be content for the boys to have a home.

She glanced back at Bob. "Have you known Mr. Barlow long?"

"Yes, ma'am, all my life."

Just as she started to ask him to tell her something about Mr. Barlow, Bob straightened from the post and walked to the wagon to retrieve his rifle.

Victoria jumped from her perch on the step. "Is there a problem?"

"Riders," he said, pointing to a speck in the distance. "Out here you can't be too careful, ma'am." Bob cocked his rifle, and Bandit leaped from the porch, assuming his protective position in front of Victoria. When the riders approached, Bob recognized the big black horse. He relaxed the grip on his rifle and gave Victoria a reassuring smile. "It's okay, he's a neighboring rancher."

"Bob," Colt said, reining his stallion in beside Bob's wagon.

"Colt, Chet's not here. We were just waiting for him."

Looking past Bob, Colt glanced at the young woman standing behind him. Big blue eyes returned his regard. He recognized that face immediately, and he couldn't believe his eyes! What was she doing here? Was she related to Chet? Did she come for his wedding? He vaguely recalled the Englishwoman saying something about her relatives living in Wyoming. But how was it possible they lived in Promise? Giving no indication that he recognized her, Colt tipped the brim of his Stetson politely. "Ma'am."

"Colt, this is Miss Victoria Eastman. She's here to visit with Chet." Bob turned to face Victoria. "Mr. McBride's cattle ranch borders Chet's farm on the east side."

Colt wasn't sure what to say since she gave no indication that she recognized him. He swung a long leg over his horse to dismount and closed the distance between them.

Victoria couldn't believe her eyes. How could he possibly be Mr. Barlow's neighbor? Impossible! She remembered Mrs. Wellington say he was from Wyoming. What were the chances he would live here? He just couldn't be the neighbor of the man she was going to marry.

With the sun behind him, Victoria shadowed her eyes with her hand to watch as he approached, his spurs clinking with each step. For the first time, she really looked at him. From head to toe. Mrs. Wellington's words came to mind. *He is the largest man I have ever seen.* The leather bands at his wrists had to be eight inches wide, and he wore leather chaps over his jeans. Cartridges lined the circumference of the belt he wore around his trim waist. That pistol she remembered so well was in his holster. He took the time to remove his gloves and tuck them in his belt before removing his Stetson.

"Miss Eastman." His thoughts went back to the morning he saw her as he was leaving St. Louis. She was standing in the window looking so beautiful she took his breath away. She'd remained in his thoughts on the long trip home and many times since.

Victoria's hand flew to her hair, trying in vain to bring order to the tangled mass of curls. "Mr. McBride." That night at the boardinghouse she was awed by his size and his unusual black-as-sin eyes, and she hadn't really noticed his other features. Once he removed his Stetson she stared at his darkly tanned face and strongly chiseled features. The deep creases etched into his jaw were, no doubt, carved by the harsh Wyoming climate. All of his features were remarkably attractive, but she was drawn to his eyes. They were so black she couldn't tell the irises from the pupils, and framed by long, thick black lashes that seemed incongruous on such a masculine face. He'd

71

probably made more than a few men quake in their boots with his powerful stature, but there was no denying women would find his eyes . . . well . . . to borrow a word from Mrs. Wellington . . . *stunning.* It wasn't hard to imagine they would also think him ruggedly handsome with his perfect granite features. To her, he was dark and dangerous. His size alone made him one of the most intimidating men she had ever seen, and combined with the intensity of his stare, he appeared absolutely fearsome.

Recalling what Mr. Barlow wrote in his letter about the cattlemen surrounding his land, she wondered if he was one of the men who wanted Mr. Barlow's land. He didn't look like a rancher to her, with that pistol on his hips. Gunfighter, more like. Or with those black eyes, maybe even Lucifer himself, a fallen angel full of sin. When he moved closer she instinctively took a step back.

Colt noticed her retreating step and the wary look in her eyes. After what had happened at the boardinghouse in St. Louis, he could understand why she would be cautious around men. She couldn't possibly be the bride Bartholomew mentioned, since she already had a family. He hadn't seen her husband, but he'd seen her boys. *Boys.*

Bartholomew did say Chet's bride had two boys. *It couldn't be.* She was way too young for Chet — at least, to his way of thinking. He was never one for robbing the cradle, and he thought she might even be too young for him. Of course, there were many men who held a different opinion on that matter. This gal looked sweet and innocent, and way too young to be the mother of those two boys he saw at the boardinghouse.

Even with her hair hanging in total disarray, and the streaks of dust on her face, he'd never seen anyone more lovely. Just like the first time he saw her, he thought she sure had nice curves packed in all the right places.

Colt's scrutiny made her uneasy, but she was determined not to let it show. "Mr. McBride, do you know where we can find Mr. Barlow?"

Unsure of what to say, he simply said, "Excuse us a minute, Miss Eastman." He closed his hand over Bob's shoulder, urging him in the direction of the barn. Once they were far enough away so their voices wouldn't carry, Colt faced Bob and whispered, "Is she Chet's intended?"

"What?" Bob whirled around to look back at Victoria. "Chet's intended? What are you talking about?"

73

"Shh . . . not so loud. Chet told me he was waiting for his bride. Is that her?"

Bob stared at Colt in disbelief, trying to make sense of what he was saying. Collecting his thoughts, he said, "She never said that to me. But she sure is nervous about something." He shifted his eyes toward Victoria again. "Ain't she too young for Chet? Where is he, anyway? I guess he's the only one we can ask. I don't think it would be right for us to ask her if she is his intended, especially if she ain't."

"Chet's dead."

CHAPTER SIX

Bob stared, slack jawed, at Colt's grim face. Once he absorbed the impact of Colt's words, he asked, "What happened?"

"Some of my men were rounding up strays and saw Chet's horse. They figured he'd been thrown, but they found his body a few miles away. He was dead — not shot, so I'm thinking he might have had a heart attack. I don't know what he was doing; he wasn't farming that far out." Colt glanced back at Victoria. She was staring at them with a quizzical look on her face. "I told the men to take his body to town. I came here thinking I would find Bartholomew. How do we go about breaking the news to her?"

Bob wasn't listening. He was still trying to come to terms with Chet planning on marriage. "What was Chet going to do with a young thing like her?"

Colt imagined there were plenty of things he would do with her, but now wasn't the

time to let his mind wander on those particular thoughts.

"I'll tell you one thing — if she's Chet's
bride, he was going to have one heck of a
wedding night," Bob stated.

With a woman who looked like her, Colt
figured Chet's wedding night would have
been one to be remembered, but he had a
feeling that wasn't what Bob was talking
about. "What do you mean?"

"I think she's afraid of being around men.
The way she hugged the other side of that
seat on the buckboard all the way out here,
it was a plumb miracle she didn't fall off."

"She was traveling alone to a strange
place; I imagine that would be enough to
make most women nervous around a man
they didn't know," Colt replied. He'd seen
how some men responded to her, and he
figured that accounted for her nerves
around men. "I wish Bartholomew would
show up so we could ask him if she's Chet's
bride." Colt walked inside the barn and
looked around. "The buckboard is gone, so
I bet Bartholomew's in town getting supplies."

"I saw Bartholomew in town just yesterday, and he sure didn't say nothin' about a
woman visiting either. And he darn sure
didn't mention no bride." Knowing he

didn't want any part of what had to be done, Bob started walking toward his buckboard. "She'll probably want to stay out here to rest before the next stagecoach. I'll leave you to it."

Colt watched as Bob hurriedly jumped into the buckboard, all the while wishing he could ride away with him. He glanced at his men who had ridden in with him, and they both gave him a look that said, *Sorry, boss, but this is your party.* "Aw hell," Colt muttered. He walked back to Miss Victoria Eastman to deliver the sad news.

Stopping in front of her, he snagged his hat from his head and nervously resettled it again. He gazed off in the distance as he tried to form the right words, and said a quick, silent prayer that he wouldn't muck it up. Whether she was a relative of Chet's, or his betrothed, the news was sure to be devastating. Just as he was about to deliver the news, his attention was diverted by the sound of a buckboard coming down the road.

Bartholomew pulled the team of horses to a halt in front of Colt. "Colt," he said, but his old gray eyes landed on the young woman standing beside him. He set the brake and climbed down from the wagon, hurriedly yanking his hat from his head.

"You must be Miss Victoria," he said with a wide smile.

Victoria couldn't have been more shocked. This gentleman, with his wild white hair and a limping gait, had to be near eighty. What in the world was he doing trying to find a wife at his age? It took a full minute for her to find her voice, but she finally choked out, "Mr. Barlow?"

"No, ma'am, I'm Bartholomew," he replied, with a chuckle in his voice. "Chet is expecting you though. He should be back shortly." He couldn't stop staring at her beautiful face, and he knew Chet was going to be the happiest groom alive. "Let me tell you, when he gets a gander at you, he will be thanking the Good Lord all night."

He looked around nervously, trying to decide what was proper for him to do with Chet's bride. He glanced at Colt, who seemed unusually quiet. He figured he was caught off guard by the beauty of Chet's bride, too. He turned back to the buckboard. "I reckon I might as well climb back in and go fetch him now. I'm sure you two have a lot to talk about before marryin' up before dark sets in. Go on inside and make yourself comfortable."

"Before . . . dark . . . isn't that . . ." Victoria couldn't manage to finish her sentence.

She hadn't planned on Mr. Barlow wanting to get married so quickly. It seemed reasonable to her that they would take some time to get to know each other before they wed, or even agreed to wed.

Colt's eyes darted back to Victoria. That answered one of his questions. She was definitely here to wed Chet. At the moment she didn't look too keen on marrying up before sundown. Wonder how Chet met her in the first place? And what in the world was he thinking, wanting to marry such a young gal? He felt a stab of jealousy at the dead man. What was she thinking by agreeing to marry someone so much older? It wasn't that Chet wasn't a fine man, there was none better, but he had to be at least thirty years older than this gal, probably more. She wasn't a sportin' woman like so many that had come west in search of a man. He'd heard of many women lying about their past in an effort to land a husband. Then he remembered her boys. Maybe she was a widow and was forced to do what was necessary to find a way to raise her boys, he thought more charitably. But she had a job in St. Louis, he reminded himself.

In the midst of his internal dialogue, it registered that Bartholomew was scrambling back in the buckboard to leave. He placed a staying hand on the old man's arm. There was no help for it, it had to be said. "Bartholomew, I'm afraid I have bad news for you and Miss Eastman."

"No bad news today, Colt. This is a day to celebrate. You know Chet will expect you to stay for the wedding."

"There will be no wedding," Colt said, looking directly into Victoria's eyes.

Victoria's mouth fell open, but not a sound came out. She couldn't imagine why Mr. McBride thought he had a right to interfere. As intimidating as he was, she wasn't about to let him dictate her future. Granted, when she mistakenly thought Bartholomew was Chet Barlow, she'd nearly hiked her skirts and run all the way back to St. Louis. Her nerves were at the breaking point, plus she was tired, hungry, and thirsty. She couldn't take much more today, and she wasn't at all certain she could handle a man like the daunting Colt McBride, but she was going to give it her best effort. Finding her tongue along with her backbone, she said in the haughtiest voice she could muster, "Mr. McBride, what business is this of yours?"

Jerking his Stetson from his head again, Colt smacked it against his thigh in frustration. *Aw hell.* He absently raked his hand through his hair, gave a loud sigh, and blurted out, "Chet's dead." *Well, I could have gone about that better.*

Bartholomew staggered back against the buckboard as if the life had drained from his skinny body. "What? What do you mean, dead? Of course he ain't dead, he just went to look at that piece of land . . ." His words trailed off when he saw Colt's haunted expression. "What happened to him?"

Colt cursed himself for being the biggest kind of fool for spitting the words out like he did. He took Bartholomew by the arm and assisted him to the porch. "I'm sorry, Bartholomew. It looks like Chet had a heart attack. A couple of my men found him a few hours ago, some distance from here. I don't know what he was doing out there."

Bartholomew could hardly believe Chet was gone. He thought he would be the first to go, and he'd never have to face the day that he would bury his best friend. "Was he up on that grassy knoll overlooking the river?"

"Yes." Colt was surprised he knew the exact spot where his men had found Chet.

"A few days ago he told me he decided on that spot to build Miss Victoria a new home. Said the old place wasn't good enough for a lady like her. I guess he went back up there to start making plans," Bartholomew said sadly.

Colt glanced back at Victoria to see her reaction to what Bartholomew revealed. Her face turned a pasty white, and her body started to fold like every bit of starch had left her spine. He reached her just as she fell over in a dead faint. Sweeping her up in his arms before she hit the ground, he carried her inside the house. The thought occurred to him that if not for a twist of fate it could have been Chet carrying his bride over that threshold this very night.

CHAPTER SEVEN

For a woman with considerable heft to maneuver, L. B. Ditty deftly skirted the tables of the saloon, making her way to one of the gambling tables at the back of the room. Hearing the commotion across the room, she automatically knew who was causing the ruckus. Seeing Hoyt Nelson's streak of bad luck at poker, she'd kept a watchful eye on that table, expecting trouble. She reached the table just as Hoyt jumped to his feet, ready to draw down on Slim Hicks, the man who had been taking his money for the better part of the evening. She wrapped her strong fingers around Hoyt's forearm. "Cowboy, why don't you take a break? Go on to the bar and have a drink on the house."

Hoyt shrugged off her hand. "I didn't know you allowed cheating in your establishment."

"Slim wasn't cheating, it's just his night

to be lucky, that's all," L. B. responded in her take-charge tone.

Hoyt's hand hovered over his revolver. "I'd say his luck just ran out."

The other men around the table threw their cards down. Chairs scraped against the wooden floor as they quickly moved away, leaving Slim and Hoyt in a face-off. Silence filled the room as everyone turned from the bar to watch the action. Sam, the bartender, reached for the shotgun he kept under the bar for just such occasions.

Slim remained seated and turned his palms faceup. "I wasn't cheating, Hoyt. As L. B. said, I just got lucky tonight. You'll make it up next time." He'd seen Hoyt in action with his fast draw, and he wanted to be alive to spend his money tomorrow.

"Get up!" Hoyt demanded.

L. B. made another attempt to reason with the drunken gunman. "I don't want trouble in here."

Hoyt shoved her aside as he took a step back from the table, his eyes never leaving Slim. "I told you to stand," he demanded.

Before Slim could make a move, L. B. stuck a derringer into Hoyt's side. "You don't hear so good, cowboy. I said I don't want trouble in my saloon." She nudged the derringer deeper in his ribs. "This ain't too big, but it makes a nasty hole all the same. And if it ain't enough," she said, inclining her head to the bartender, "Sam can give you an even bigger hole if need be."

Hoyt looked up to see the bartender pointing a shotgun at his head. He moved his hand from his gun and turned to face L. B., hands in the air. "Okay, no trouble. I guess I'll take you up on that offer of a free drink."

"I've revoked that offer for tonight," L. B. replied, her revolver still poking his ribs. "Now you go on out of here and sleep it off. Next time you come back maybe your luck will have changed. The whiskey will still be here."

Hoyt gave her a mean look, wanting to argue, but Euan Wallace walked into the hushed saloon. He strolled to the bar and saw Sam with his shotgun pointed at one of his men. "Hoyt, what's going on here?" Wallace demanded.

"Nothing, Mr. Wallace, I was just leaving," Holt told him smoothly. He turned toward the doors, but before he walked through, he glanced at L. B. "I'll be back."

Once Hoyt left, the men at the tables took their seats and L. B. sauntered to the bar beside Euan Wallace. "Sam, give me a whiskey." Sam placed two glasses on the bar and filled them with the good whiskey that Wallace preferred. L. B. tossed hers back without a grimace, just like a hard-drinking cowboy. She stared at Wallace in the mirror behind the bar. "That man is nothing but pure trouble. Why did you feel the need to hire him? It obviously wasn't for his cowboying skills." She already knew the answer to her question, but she just wanted to see what Wallace would say.

Wallace took a drink of his whiskey before giving her an answer. "He has other talents."

"Yeah, I just bet he does," L. B. retorted. "He's going to provoke the wrong man one day. I just hope he doesn't kill some innocent man before that day comes."

Motioning for Sam to refill both their glasses, Wallace gave L. B. what he thought was a friendly smile and handed her the whiskey. "Why don't you let me buy into this business and you won't have to worry about drunken cowboys again. You could sit back and count your money without having to work."

L. B. wasn't fooled by his smile. She'd been around too long, and she knew the devil when she saw him. She turned to face him. "Now why would I take on a partner when I've run this business just fine for years?"

For a split second, Wallace thought about asking her to dinner, thinking he might find a way to ingratiate himself to get what he wanted. But then he took a good long look at her. He couldn't tell how old she was since she wore her face all painted up like some sort of doll. Her eyes were rimmed in black kohl, her lips were painted a bright red, and her hair was almost as red as her lips. Every time she moved, her red curls bobbed up and down, reminding him of coiled springs. Her ample rear end stuck out like a shelf on a wall, and he thought several glasses of whiskey could sit atop it without spilling a drop. He slugged back the rest of his drink and slammed the glass back down on the bar. Nope. There wasn't enough whiskey to get him that drunk. Not even for business. "You just might need more protection than you can handle from now on."

"Is that right? Protection from what?"

Wallace was slow to respond. He watched the bartender refill his glass and he took a sip, enjoying the feel of whiskey burning its way down to his stomach. He turned to look around the smoke-filled room. "I've always wanted to own a saloon. I guess if I was to set up my own establishment, that might cause you some concern."

L. B. narrowed her eyes at him. "So you're offering me protection from you, or some other enterprising soul, from opening another saloon in this town?"

"That's one way of looking at it."

L. B. had seen his kind before, men who wanted what other people had worked for. In another town she'd let a man like Wallace run her off. It wasn't going to happen again. Oh, Wallace concerned her, particularly since he had the sheriff doing his bidding for him, but she wasn't going to let him know that. She looked him in the eye. "I say the more, the merrier. Another business will just make my gals work harder to keep the clientele happy."

"I'll let you think about it." He leaned closer to her ear and whispered, "You know the sheriff and I have a good arrangement. I'm sure I could convince him to make sure no one caused you problems if I was to be part owner. Things are changing around here. Folks who don't change with them, well, I guess they'll just be flat out of luck." With that said, he threw some coins on the bar and left.

L. B. watched him walk away, considering what he said and what he didn't say.

Sam moved to stand in front of her. "Want another one?"

"Yeah." She turned her attention on Sam. "Did you hear that?"

Sam had worked with L. B. for a long time and they were good friends. He was loyal, and L. B. trusted him with her life, as he did her. They had their own private arrangement; no one knew Sam was her silent partner, sharing in the handsome profits from the business. "I heard." He put another glass on the bar and poured one for himself.

"What do you think he's up to?"

"That's not hard to figure out. He wants to own the whole town, and he won't be happy until he has it."

"We've seen his ilk before," she reminded him.

"Too many times to suit me. I've got a bad feeling about this one. Men like him don't even fear God Almighty." He drank his whiskey and gazed into her eyes. "Why don't we just retire and get out of here? We both have plenty of money, and we're getting old. Maybe we could go to Alaska, see something new, and try our hand at mining." Sam had suggested the same thing several times before, but for reasons he didn't understand, L. B. wasn't ready to leave.

L. B. chuckled. "I think I've heard that a time or two out of you."

"Maybe it's time you gave it serious consideration," he told her in a solemn tone.

Getting no response, he shook his head and smacked his glass on the bar with a thud before he moved away to serve a customer.

She couldn't ignore Sam's words; he had wanted to move on for a long time. There was no denying he was right — they were getting old. Maybe they should take off for Alaska before time got the best of them. She enjoyed Sam's company, more than any other man she'd ever met, and he was more than a friend to her. She loved him in her own way, but always figured if they had become more involved it would have ruined their friendship. Before she'd passed her prime, he'd hinted that he wanted more, yet he never pushed her. She hated to think that one of these days he would just walk out of her life and go to Alaska without her. What was holding her back? She'd never be able to spend all the money she'd saved up. Why hang around? She knew the answer to that. She'd stayed in the same place for so long for one reason. It was something she'd never told anyone, not even Sam. But then, maybe Sam was right. Now might be the time to move on.

CHAPTER EIGHT

Under Bartholomew's direction, Colt carried Victoria to what he assumed was Chet's bedroom, and gently placed her on the bed. He said a few choice words under his breath, not because she had fainted, but for some inexplicable reason he didn't want to see her in another man's bed. The only women he'd ever put to bed he'd been right along beside them, and they didn't have their clothes on. With that thought his eyes made a slow traverse down her body. No doubt about it, she was one beautiful woman. He didn't know what made him think about such things under the circumstances, other than the fact that he was a man. His only justification was it had been too long . . . well . . . in all truthfulness, he couldn't justify his bad behavior. He just needed to get control of his thoughts.

Bartholomew hurried to the kitchen to fetch some water and a damp cloth. Colt sat beside Victoria and noticed her wrist was dangling at an odd angle. He tried to untie the ribbons of the reticule at her wrist. Darned if he knew why ladies carried the little bags; they weren't big enough to hold anything important. He remembered his mother was never without one on her arm when she went to town. His big fingers working at those tiny ribbons were a test of his patience. When the bag finally dropped into his hand, he let out a loud sigh. He looked down at the bag and studied the intricate handstitched design. Granted, he didn't know much about women's fashion, but even he had to appreciate the workmanship of the delicately sewn white doves and flowers. The weight also surprised him; it was heavier than he expected. Palming the bag, he realized why it was so heavy. He felt the distinct outline of a derringer. His eyes shifted from the pouch to the immobile woman next to him. *Wonder why she's packing a gun? Definitely more to this little lady than meets the eye.* L. B. was the only woman he'd ever seen with a derringer. When he'd commented on it one time, she told him a derringer was easy to hide and it came in handy from time to time. Maddie told him most of the girls kept a gun in their rooms so they could protect themselves if a customer got too rough and they didn't have time to wait for Sam to handle the situation. Considering their line of work, it made sense they felt the need for protection. *But why does Miss Eastman need protection?*

Colt placed the reticule on the table next to his Stetson, and turned his attention back to the woman who posed so many questions he didn't know where to begin. Her complexion looked like fresh cream, a stark contrast to her dark auburn hair and the black lashes resting on her cheekbones. She had perfectly shaped brows, a small straight nose, and plump pink lips. She was definitely a looker. Every feature on her face was perfect, in his estimation. He gently tapped her cheek. "Ma'am, wake up." No luck. He tapped lightly again. She didn't move. He was half tempted to kiss her to see if that would awaken her.

Hearing Bartholomew's footsteps nearing the doorway, Colt said again, "Ma'am? Ma'am?" He glanced at the dog, which had jumped up on the bed when Colt tapped her cheek. He plopped down right next to Victoria, his eyes fixed on Colt.

"I'm not hurting her, buddy," he said to the grungy animal.

Bartholomew held the damp cloth out to

him. "Here you go. See if this will stir her."

Colt placed the cloth on her forehead. "I think she feels warm."

"Well, it is hotter than blazes, and she's traveled a long way in this heat. Then the poor little thing finds out her intended is dead on her arrival. I reckon if anyone has a reason to take ill, it'd be this little gal," Bartholomew replied, his own voice thick with emotion.

Colt flinched at Bartholomew's words. All he had been doing was thinking about how beautiful she was; he'd given little thought to her situation. "Where did Chet meet her?"

Bartholomew limped to the only chair in the room and plopped down. "He hadn't met her. He answered her advertisement in the newspaper."

Colt whipped his head around to look at Bartholomew, disbelief written all over his face. "Her advertisement?"

"Said she was needin' a husband," Bartholomew explained.

Colt stared at him for a minute, trying to make sense of his words. "You mean she advertised for a husband and Chet responded?"

"Yessir, that's what he did. He sent her money for her and the boys to come here."

"Are you telling me *she* advertised for a husband," he repeated, as if he hadn't heard correctly, "and Chet was going to marry her sight unseen?" He had heard of men sending off for mail-order brides, but he had never thought that women placed advertisements for husbands.

"That's exactly what he was fixin' to do," Bartholomew said. "Said he was plumb tired of not knowing what it was like to be married. It didn't bother him one bit that he was getting boys in the bargain. He said she was probably just a nice lady in a bad way." Bartholomew pulled himself up from the chair and walked to the table by the bed. He opened a drawer and pulled out a newspaper clipping and handed it to Colt. "This is between you and me; no one else needs to know how she came about getting to Promise. No need for her to be embarrassed about her situation."

Colt nodded, and started reading the few lines she had written. He finished reading and handed the paper back to Bartholomew. "Seems like a foolhardy way to make a commitment to someone. What would possess a woman to do something so foolish?"

"Men send away for mail-order brides all the time. I guess it beats the heck out of workin' at some place like L. B. Ditty's saloon to survive." He pointed a gnarled finger at Victoria. "Look at her. She's a lady, and she has boys she has to think about. I reckon it ain't that easy makin' her way with boys unless she finds a man who will take them in. Even pretty as she is, I doubt many men would want two boys in the bargain." Bartholomew choked up for a minute, then collected himself. "Chet was that kind of man, always there to help out someone in need." He stared at Colt, who was absently scratching the pitiful dog behind the ears. "He was sort of like you, except you take in stray animals."

Colt chuckled at that. "I do take in my share of strays." He'd always had an uncommon bond with animals. Everyone knew if they had an ailing animal all they had to do was bring them to him, and he'd nurse them back to health. But stray women? No, thank you, he would stick to animals.

"Anyhow, when Chet read what she had writ, he figured she needed his help. I asked him if he was worried about her being plug ugly or big as the side of that ol' barn out there. And you know what he said?"

Colt's mouth tilted in a grin, thinking he would have wondered the same thing. "He didn't worry about that?"

"He said a woman who was trying to do

96

the best for her boys had a beauty about her that wasn't on the outside. He said he thought the Lord was leading him to write her a letter." Bartholomew had to clear his throat to continue. "I'll never forget that look on his face when he said that to me."

"Chet was a good man," Colt told him and meant it. It shamed him all the more for where his own thoughts had been. He looked down at Victoria again, thinking for the umpteenth time how lovely she was. It was a shame Chet would never know how lucky he was about to be, ready-made family or not. He figured there were many men in Promise who would want her. Up until this moment, he'd never really thought about how few women there were to choose from in this part of the country. Not that he'd ever looked for a woman to wed. As a younger man he'd found out quick enough that if he even so much as danced at a church social with a rancher's daughter, everyone would be talking marriage before the sun came up over the horizon the next morning. That was just one more reason to leave the ladies alone.

"I guess there aren't a whole lot of women to choose from outside the gals at L. B. Ditty's." As Colt said the words, he realized he'd never seen Chet play poker at the saloon.

Bartholomew seemed to read his mind. "Chet never visited L. B. Ditty's, or he might have married up with one of them gals, thinking he was helping her to get out of a place like that." Bartholomew recalled the many times Chet told him that he regretted never marrying. Until he saw that advertisement, he'd never done anything about finding a wife. Now it was too late for him. "Chet was always shy around the ladies."

Colt felt Victoria stir on the bed and he glanced down at her. He pulled the cloth from her forehead and leaned closer. "Miss Eastman, are you awake?"

Slowly, Victoria opened her eyes and found herself looking directly into those unnerving black eyes. She tried to move away from him, but he held her firmly by the shoulders. "Be still. You should rest."

She glanced around the room, trying to figure out where she was. "What happened?"

"You fainted."

"Fainted?" she asked, clearly still confused. She'd never fainted in her life.

"Yes. I'm afraid I gave you a bit of a shock." Colt started to say something else, but wasn't sure what he should say. He wasn't about to repeat his earlier mistake, when he'd blurted out the news of Chet's death.

After a minute, her thoughts settled into place. Mr. Barlow was dead. The man she was going to marry was dead. Poor Mr. Barlow. Was it her? Did God want to punish her for something? It seemed that way, since nothing ever worked out for her. Tears trickled down the sides of her face, dropping soundlessly to the pillow beneath her head. She would never know Mr. Barlow, and there would be no home for Cade and Cody. She wanted to scream at the injustice of it all. She wept for the death of a man she had never met and the loss of a future for the boys. She would use the extra money Mr. Barlow sent to return to Mrs. Wellington's boardinghouse, stuff her dreams deep inside once again, and try to make do. Life had been so unfair. Couldn't something good happen for her and the boys, just once?

Seeing Victoria cry was nearly Colt's undoing. His throat felt raw when he said softly, "I'm sorry about your . . . about Chet." She looked so forlorn, he considered gathering her in his arms and holding her to his chest until she was all cried out, but he didn't think a woman as skittish as she was would welcome his attentions. The dog didn't have the same hesitation. He plopped his head on Victoria's bosom, and Colt thought *lucky dog* as he watched her wrap her arms around his neck and bury her face in his fur.

It was out of character for her to be emotional in front of strangers, but the events leading up to this moment were almost more than she could bear. She hid her face in Bandit's furry neck while she summoned every ounce of strength she possessed to get her emotions under control.

Colt figured most women would have given in to a crying spell under the circumstances, but he could see her struggling to hold it in. He didn't know if he and Bartholomew should leave the room until she was under control. "We can give you a minute to . . . rest up . . . if you need to."

Victoria pulled back from the dog and wiped at her cheeks. "I'm fine. I guess I need to get back to town and see about the next stage."

"Miss Victoria, you can stay here tonight. You've had a long trip, and if you'll pardon my saying so, you look like you could use a rest. You could probably use a good meal too," Bartholomew told her.

Victoria barely heard Bartholomew since

100

she was watching the fearsome Mr. McBride scratch her dog behind his ears. With his attention on Bandit, she had the chance to study his features up close. His darkly tanned skin didn't conceal the thin scar that ran the length of his square jaw. His nose was prominent but straight, and the perfect size for his face. His dark brows above those unusual eyes were thick, and like Mrs. Wellington mentioned, he wore his black wavy hair longer than most men, well past his collar, yet it suited him. What was the most surprising was a line in his cheek that she'd bet turned into a dimple when he smiled.

Colt glanced down at her like he was waiting for something, and she realized she hadn't responded to Bartholomew. Quickly turning her attention to Bartholomew, she gave him an appreciative smile. "I'm not sure it would be proper under the circumstances for me to stay here."

"You needn't worry about that. Out here we don't care as much about what's proper as they do in cities, ma'am. We help folks out as need be."

"Still . . ." Victoria started, but her words trailed off because she couldn't seem to think straight. Tired as she was, she couldn't even begin to get her thoughts in order, especially under Colt McBride's regard. She glanced away, trying to look anywhere but at those eyes. Her gaze landed on the two volumes of Shakespeare on the bedside table. *I read Shakespeare,* Mr. Barlow had written in his letter. She found herself fighting back tears again.

Seeing he was making her uneasy, Colt stood and spoke to Bartholomew. "I think it would be best if you and Miss Eastman came to the ranch and stayed there until the next stage." He didn't know what possessed him to make that offer; it wasn't like he was running a boardinghouse. Yet he did feel sympathy for her, coming all this way to be married only to find the man deceased, and all her plans dashed in one afternoon. Little wonder she fainted, she was clearly tuckered out. He knew firsthand how exhausting the trip was from St. Louis on a stagecoach. And, with relatively no law in Promise, he couldn't guarantee her safety if she stayed in town. There was also Wallace and his men to consider. They could show up at any time. It would only be a few days until the next stage, he reasoned, and then she would be safely on her way back to St. Louis.

Knowing Colt was trying to tell him, without scaring the life out of the young woman, that it might not be safe for her to be alone in town, Bartholomew said, "That is a fine idea. I know you have Mrs. Morris at your place to do the cooking, so that ought to be proper enough. Miss Victoria would have her chaperone."

"I think I should go back to town. I can stay in the hotel and take the next stage back to St. Louis," she said.

"There won't be another stage for a few days, and you would be safer at my ranch," Colt told her. He omitted the fact that Mrs. Morris went home after she cooked for him, so Miss Eastman would be in the house alone with him and Bartholomew in the evenings.

"Colt's right, Miss Victoria. This is wilder country than you are used to," Bartholomew added. "Things get rowdy, even in town."

One look at Colt's determined face told her it would be futile to argue with him. If that drunk she'd encountered earlier in town was any indication of what could happen, she would probably be safer at Mr. McBride's ranch, particularly since Bartholomew would be with her. "If you're sure it will not be an imposition."

"No problem. I have plenty of room; you won't be in my way."

Picking up the books on the table, Bartholomew said solemnly, "I guess Chet will no longer be readin' your books, Colt."

Colt nodded, but said nothing in response. He didn't want to think about how much he would miss Chet right now. He'd do that when he was alone.

Hearing the exchange, Victoria would never have expected a man like Colt to read Shakespeare.

"Here you go," Colt said, handing the reticule to her.

She looked at him with eyes wide, wondering if he felt the gun inside. His expression gave no hint of anything amiss, and she slipped the reticule into her skirt pocket.

After putting on his Stetson, and before she realized his intent, he leaned over and plucked her from the bed and carried her to the front of the house.

"Mr. McBride, I can walk," she protested.

"If you don't mind my saying so, Miss Eastman, you look like you're dead on your feet and I don't want you fainting again." In a few strides he was out the door and at the buckboard, where he gently deposited her on the seat.

Bartholomew decided to ride into town to see to Chet's burial, and told Colt he'd see him at the ranch before nightfall. Colt wasn't sure how he felt about Bartholomew's decision since that meant he would be driving Miss Eastman in the buckboard, but he understood Bartholomew needed to see his friend. While he was securing Razor to the buckboard, Bandit jumped in the back with Victoria's mangled blue hat clamped between his jaws. Colt chuckled and reached over to scratch the dog behind his ears. "I'm not sure that belongs to you, buddy."

Victoria turned to see the dog with her blue hat and she managed a smile. "He can have it. I'm afraid it's a lost cause."

Colt jumped into the buckboard and headed to his ranch with a nervous Victoria at his side . . . well, perhaps not quite at his side. Just as Bob had told him, she sat as far away from him as the seat allowed, clutching the side rail so tightly her knuckles were white.

She was quiet as they rode, her thoughts centered on Mr. Barlow and how fate had a way of squashing all her dreams. She was grateful Colt didn't ply her with questions; he seemed content to ride in silence. After they had ridden a few miles, she said, "I was surprised to see you here."

"I was surprised too," he admitted. "I only learned Chet planned to marry when I got back from St. Louis. He didn't tell me who he was marrying."

Smoothing her skirt with her hands, she tried desperately to think of something to say to change the subject. She didn't want to discuss what was to have been her impending marriage, but his broad shoulders crowding her made thought nearly impossible. After a long while she relaxed enough to ask, "Is your ranch far away?"

"By buckboard it will take about an hour." He didn't say he was going slower than normal since he figured she had to be tired of being jostled around after that stagecoach ride. He glanced down at the dog who was trying to nudge his nose between them. He still had the hat in his jaws like a lifeline. Colt smiled at him. "Did you bring that dog all the way from St. Louis? I don't remember seeing him at Chet's before."

"I saw him on the side of the road and the stagecoach driver let him ride with us." She placed her arm around the dog's neck. "I call him Bandit."

Colt nodded, thinking to himself that Miss Victoria Eastman might be as skittish around men as a sportin' gal in church, but anyone could see she had a soft heart for animals. That made her okay in his book.

"Mr. McBride, were you a good friend to

Mr. Barlow?"

"You can call me Colt. Chet's family was on this land as long as mine. I knew him all my life. He was a good man."

Nearly on the verge of tears again, she took a deep breath before she said, "I would like to go pay my respects to him."

"Eli . . . the man who works for Doc Barnes, he tends to the . . . deceased. He'll have Chet ready by tomorrow. I'll take you to town in the morning and we can both pay our respects. I'll send some men to tell the other ranchers the funeral will be held at noon tomorrow at the family cemetery."

Victoria felt obligated to tell him about her relationship with Mr. Barlow since it was obvious she had never met the man. Still, she hated to admit her circumstances to a complete stranger. "I came out here to see if Mr. Barlow was a man I could marry," she said softly.

Colt had to strain to hear her. It seemed to him that she had to force the words out of her mouth. He could understand how it might embarrass her to confess the reason for coming to Wyoming, particularly to marry a complete stranger. He wanted to ask her a lot of questions, that was a fact. The first one would be how a beautiful young woman like her, with a couple of

107

kids, got into such a fix. But he sure didn't want to talk about her almost marriage to Chet. He wondered what he would have done in St. Louis if he'd known she was looking for a husband. That was a question he would have to think about later. Right now, the silence was becoming uncomfortable, so he had to say something to acknowledge what she had confided. "You came a long way." *That was profound. Couldn't I have thought of something better to say?*

Not a word passed between them the rest of the way.

CHAPTER NINE

The entrance to the McBride Cattle Ranch was remarkably simple, yet unlike anything Victoria had ever seen. Two large posts, one on each side of the entryway, were topped by a huge log eight feet off the ground bearing the name of the ranch, McBride Cattle Company, etched deep. Mounted on top of the log was a large pair of horns whose former owner must have been a monstrous Texas longhorn. After they passed through the entryway, Colt glanced at Victoria. "We're on my land."

Looking around, Victoria saw nothing that resembled a structure. Every few minutes she scanned the horizon for a glimpse of his home, but nothing came into view except more cattle and more land. She was so tired she wished she could crawl in the back of the buckboard with Bandit to sleep. More time and distance passed before she asked, "Exactly how far away is your home, Mr.

McBride?"

"Colt," he reminded her. "We'll be there in a few more minutes."

"You must have a lot of land." It seemed like they had ridden as long as her journey from St. Louis to Wyoming.

Colt chuckled at that. "Yes, ma'am, it takes a lot of land for cattle."

A large home finally came into view. The massive structure was not what she expected. The magnificence of the formidable log and stone home silhouetted against the infinite expanse of blue sky took her breath away. It was a much grander home than one would ever expect in this secluded part of the country.

"Oh my," she said softly.

"The old home place burned down and I built this one a couple of years ago." Colt pulled the buckboard in front of the house and helped her down.

To her surprise, there were delicate pink tea roses climbing up one side of the house, lending a softer appearance to the expansive stone home. "It's beautiful. Do you have a large family?"

"Two brothers. Jake's a U.S. Marshal, and Lucas, well, I'm not sure what he's up to now, but he was busting broncs down in the Arizona Territory."

Once inside, Victoria followed him up the staircase. It was difficult for her to comprehend how his brothers could leave such a beautiful place. She would never leave a home like this. "Do you see them often?"

"It's been a few years."

Noting a sadness that seemed to come over him, she didn't ask more questions about his brothers. She understood the need to keep some things private.

Colt opened the door to a large bedroom, easily five times as large as her room at Mrs. Wellington's. Victoria's eyes immediately went to the tub in the far corner of the room. What she wouldn't give for a long, hot bath.

Colt caught her eyeing the tub. "You must be spent. I'll have water carried up for you, and some grub to hold you over until dinner." Glancing down at the dog that followed them up the stairs, he added, "I'll get him something to eat too. Maybe he won't eat the rest of that hat."

Smiling, Victoria said, "I'll take him outside. I didn't realize he followed us upstairs."

Moving to the door, Colt bent over to rub Bandit's ears. "He can stay in here with you. If you need anything, just yell for Mrs. Morris."

Victoria was hanging up her dresses from her valise when there was a soft knock on the door. "Come in."

An elderly white-haired woman entered carrying a tray filled with ham, biscuits, and jam. "Miss Eastman, I'm Helen Morris. I've brought you a little snack." She crossed the room and placed the tray on the table. "Colt said you probably hadn't eaten all day."

"Please call me Victoria. This is so kind of you, but you shouldn't have gone to so much trouble."

"No trouble at all. I just pulled the biscuits from the oven." Mrs. Morris turned a critical eye on Victoria. "Land sakes, you're just skin and bones." She pulled the chair out from the table. "Now sit yourself down and dig in. This is my special homemade blackberry jam. Colt is having the men bring water for your bath, so you have time for a bite."

"I have to admit those biscuits smell delicious," Victoria told her earnestly, taking a seat at the small table.

Mrs. Morris reached for a large piece of ham on the tray and tossed it to Bandit. "That ought to hold you till supper, too." Bandit seemed reluctant to release the hat, but the piece of juicy ham won out.

Mrs. Morris was still chatting away when

the two men came in the room to fill the tub. After the men left, she placed a towel and a bar of soap on the stand beside the tub. "Honey, you've had a terrible time; now, you get some rest before dinner. We eat about six o'clock, but we can make it later."

"Oh, that's not necessary. Please don't change dinner plans on my account."

Mrs. Morris left the room and Victoria eyed the steam coming from the water. She decided she wanted a bath more than she wanted food. Downing only half of her biscuit, she gave the remaining half to Bandit and started to undress.

Colt walked to his bedroom and poured himself a whiskey. Dropping into his favorite oversized leather chair, he sipped his drink and thought about Chet. It was difficult losing a friend, and even more so knowing that Chet had been looking forward to being married. He would have been spending this very night with his bride. As it turned out, his friend had waited too long to decide to marry. He had no time left.

Thinking about how quickly time passed allowed his thoughts to drift to his brothers. Talking to Victoria about them brought feelings to the surface that he didn't often like to rehash. There was a time when he thought no brothers were closer than the three of them. Their mother had been killed when Colt was twelve years old, and being the eldest, he shouldered much of the responsibility of raising his brothers. Their father, Kerrick McBride, died almost nine years ago, and his unexpected death hit the brothers hard. Everyone saw the elder McBride as the very foundation that held the McBride Cattle Company together, but Colt was particularly devastated by his father's death. He'd worked by his father's side since he was a boy, learning every aspect of running a successful cattle ranch. Even though he and his brothers shared an uncommon bond, Colt considered his father his best friend. The very day they buried the elder McBride, every cowboy on the place looked to Colt as boss. Without hesitation, he assumed that role, and out of necessity he had to forgo his grieving for his father. He threw himself into work, more times than not putting in eighteen-hour days trying to hold the ranch together. That first winter was the worst they had ever experienced, and he'd been close to losing the ranch. As it turned out, he ended up losing half his cattle, but he'd managed to hold the ranch together. He made a vow that first year that he would do whatever it took to make sure the McBride legacy would be intact for future generations. In tough times he reminded himself that his father had faced his share of hardships and made it through. There was no way he would lose the ranch, not as long as he had breath in his body. Considering his brothers hadn't been home in years, and his own lack of interest in starting a family, there were times he wondered why he pushed himself so hard. There was no guarantee there would even be future McBride generations.

Looking back, he knew it was the months following his father's death when he emotionally separated himself from his brothers. Not intentionally, he'd just lost himself in his work, the only way he knew how to deal with the loss of his father. It had never occurred to him that his brothers might feel there was no longer a place for them on the ranch. Within a year Jake took off to become a U.S. Marshal, and Lucas left with no particular destination in mind. It wasn't that his brothers didn't love the ranch; he knew they did, but his very soul belonged on this land, it was in his blood, the air in his lungs.

There was only one time in his life when he'd considered a different line of work. Gunslinger. His mind drifted back to the events that led him to that decision when he was just twelve years old. He'd taken his mother into town to shop while he picked up supplies for his father. As he was loading the buckboard, his mother walked out of the general store, chatting with the owner. Across the street, two men stalked out of the saloon, arguing over a game of cards. Creed Thomas, a known fast gun, had accused Dunc Gaines of cheating. Thomas said Gaines was dealing from the bottom of the deck. Tempers flared, and Colt thought he was going to see a fistfight. Instead, the two men squared off in the middle of the road with a few feet separating them. Within seconds, men from the saloon spilled onto the sidewalk to watch the action. Having never seen a gunfight before, Colt was spellbound. Even these many years later, he could recall the events as they unfolded, moment by moment. It was as though every movement, every blink of an eyelid was in slow motion. He saw the faces in the crowd. Some men jeered, while others scrambled out of the way, diving for cover. Looking into the eyes of Creed Thomas, Colt knew the moment he was going to draw, and he felt like he had a premonition. It was that moment of realization that propelled him into action. He leaped toward his mother as

116

he shouted for her to get down. Both men cleared leather, but Creed Thomas shot Gaines dead quicker than a man could spit. Gaines hit the dirt, and his pistol discharged when it slammed to the ground. Colt hadn't reached his mother in time. The errant bullet found her heart. In that split second, Colt and his brothers lost every ounce of beauty and gentleness in their lives. His mother was a beautiful, tenderhearted woman, loved by all who knew her. She was the polar opposite of Kerrick McBride, who was as tough and rugged as they came. But around his mother, his father was as gentle as a baby calf. Colt never really recovered from the feeling that he'd failed in his responsibility to take care of her like his father had instructed that morning. His father hadn't blamed him. He'd told Colt over and over that her death was an accident, there was nothing he could have done, but his words fell on deaf ears. Colt lost more than his mother that day. He'd lost his faith.

A few days after they laid their mother to rest, the sheriff told them Creed Thomas had been drinking and losing at cards for hours that fateful day, and he was spoiling for a fight. The men in the saloon swore that Gaines was not cheating, but it was a fair fight, so the sheriff couldn't charge Thomas with a crime. Even though the sheriff ran Thomas out of town, it did nothing to assuage Colt's anger. He wanted revenge, and he vowed he would have it one day.

Within the hour after his mother's funeral, Colt grabbed two of his father's pistols and started practicing. That first day he practiced his draw until he couldn't lift his arms. Not a day passed that he didn't practice for hours. By the third week his brothers joined him. A few months later, they were all fast draws and more importantly, deadly accurate shots. Their father hadn't discouraged them; he wanted his boys to be able to protect themselves with pistols if necessary. The way he saw it, pistols were a necessity if a man was going to survive in a land where guns oftentimes did the talking. Within months, Colt knew he had a faster draw than Creed Thomas, but he continued to practice.

The day Colt turned sixteen, it came as no surprise to his father that he left the ranch with the intention of tracking down and killing Creed Thomas. Colt traveled from town to town, but Thomas was always a few days ahead of him. He felt like he was playing a game of cat and mouse. If it hadn't been for the love of his father and brothers, and missing the ranch, there was no question in his mind that he would never have returned home until he found Thomas.

He'd been on the hunt for almost two years when one night in Texas he had an experience he'd never forget. He was sleeping out under the stars when he woke to what he thought was someone talking to him. Listening intently, he knew no one was there, but suddenly he was filled with a longing for home. He realized God was telling him it was time to go home. Even though he hadn't completed what he'd set out to accomplish, he accepted that he needed to return to Wyoming. That very night, he saddled his horse and headed back to Promise. He couldn't say he'd forgotten his hatred for Thomas, but he knew he could wait until the time was right. He was confident their paths would cross one day, just as sure as the sun would rise the next morning.

As the years passed, Colt was thankful he'd had the good sense to return home that day. The ranch was where he belonged; it was the place that gave his life meaning and purpose. It was the place where he found peace. There was no denying there were plenty of times when running an operation the size of the ranch could be downright frustrating. Like now, when he was worried about his cattle being slaughtered, unable to hold anyone responsible because of a crooked sheriff. If it wasn't the droughts, then it was blizzards, or diseases, or squatters, or rustlers. Ranching was not an easy life, and certainly not for the faint of heart. It made him respect all the more what his father had left behind.

If nature wasn't enough to deal with, there would always be men like Wallace to contend with. Even as he thought about the challenges, Colt knew he wouldn't change his life for anything. He would make only one change: His brothers would be working with him, side by side, sharing the responsibilities, the joys, and the heartaches. He'd told them they would always be welcome if they ever got the itch to become ranchers again. Secretly, he wanted that more than he'd ever wanted anything. He missed them more than he thought possible. Not a day passed that he didn't wish he would look up and see them riding in. He wished he could go back in time and change the way he handled things after his father's death, but that wasn't the way life worked out. He just hoped one day his brothers might give him another chance.

■ ■ ■ ■

Colt was leaning over the dining room table when Victoria walked into the room, followed by Bandit.

"I'm sorry if I made you wait." She noted his hair was damp, as though he just came from his bath. Her gaze went to the array of food on the table, and she realized how hungry she was.

"Perfect timing. I just finished carrying the food to the table," Colt explained. "Helen wasn't feeling well and decided to retire for the night." He thought it best not to mention that she left to go to her house on his ranch. Plus, he had his suspicions that Helen wasn't ill, she just wanted him to dine alone with a pretty lady. She was always dropping hints that he should invite some of the single women from town to dinner.

The thought of this big strapping man carrying the delicate china to the table made Victoria smile. "Everything smells delicious," she told him.

Her cheeks had more color, Colt thought, and she definitely looked more rested. "Were you able to get some shut-eye?"

"I almost fell asleep in the tub," she

admitted, taking the chair he held for her.

Colt chuckled, willing himself not to think of her naked in a tub. "That makes two of us."

"Isn't Mr. Bartholomew here?"

"I'm sure he'll be along. Bartholomew does things at his own pace. He wouldn't want us waiting for him."

"No one else is joining us?" she asked, thinking it was an abundance of food for three people.

"Just the three of us tonight. Tate Wagner — he's a sixteen-year-old boy who works on the ranch — usually eats with me, but he's visiting his family tonight." It wasn't unusual for Colt to have some of his other men dine with him, but sensing how nervous Victoria was around men, he'd asked them to eat in the bunkhouse tonight. He hoped with no one else around she might be inclined to talk more freely.

Colt reached over and placed his large palm over the top of Victoria's hand, causing her to jump. Her eyes darted to him, but seeing he'd lowered his head, she did the same. He said a quick prayer, released her hand, grabbed his fork, and stabbed the largest piece of meat on the platter. He held it to Bandit's nose and the dog gently took the meat from Colt's fingers. "Good boy,"

Colt said, then poured some water in a bowl and placed it on the floor.

Victoria was surprised at his thoughtfulness, not to mention he seemed oblivious to the fact that Bandit's water bowl was a fine piece of china. "He's probably had more to eat today than he has in weeks," she said. She thought the hopeless look in Bandit's eyes was beginning to fade the longer he was with her.

Without thinking, Colt plopped a large piece of meat and a huge spoonful of mashed potatoes on Victoria's plate. "He does look like he's had a few miles of bad road. But he's a smart dog, doesn't beg, and he has good manners."

Victoria was staring at the mounds of food he was adding to her plate. He was giving her as much as he'd stacked on his plate. As hungry as she was, there was no way she would be able to eat half of it.

Seeing her eyes glued on her plate, Colt realized what he had done. "Sorry, I guess I'm just used to piling it on Tate's plate. We have hearty appetites after a full day's work."

They ate in silence for a few minutes, each trying to think of something to say. Victoria was first to break the silence. "When did you say the next stagecoach would come through?"

"Two days from now." Colt couldn't keep himself from staring at her blue eyes. Earlier they were a bright blue, but under the candlelit chandelier they were a deeper blue, like the sky at dusk. For the hundredth time that day he wondered why a beautiful woman found herself in such circumstances that she would contemplate marrying a complete stranger. What man wouldn't be curious about her? "Bartholomew said you planned to bring your boys with you."

"I had planned to bring the boys here after . . ." She couldn't finish the sentence for fear of succumbing to tears again. Since Bartholomew had told him about the boys, she assumed he probably told him about her advertisement too. "Mr. Barlow responded to my ad for a husband," she said plainly. "I wanted to see if he would be suitable before the boys joined me. They stayed behind with Mrs. Wellington. The boys and I have rooms at the boardinghouse, but I was hoping to make a home for them here." She stared at Colt, expecting to see the condemnation in his eyes for what she had done. Most men would think only a fallen woman would consider finding a husband in such an unusual way.

Colt thought about her admission, and noted the one thing she didn't mention was what had happened to her husband. She must be widowed, he thought. He admired her for trying to find a suitable home for her boys. By his estimation, it took a woman with a lot of grit to survive with three mouths to feed. One would never expect a delicate woman like her to have what it took to travel out West by herself to find a husband. But as his father always said, *it wasn't the size of man that he took measure of, but the heart of him.* He figured the same thing held true for the fairer sex. This woman was no hothouse flower, not by a long shot. While she might be wary of men, that fear hadn't hindered her from making a trip few men relished. It was a grueling journey, well over a thousand miles, and it wasn't unusual for a stagecoach to have problems with equipment or animals, and pray that was the least of it. The accommodations along the way were ill suited for females, as privacy was a rare commodity. It didn't bear thinking what might have happened to someone like her if they had been attacked by Indians or robbers. As pretty as she was, she undoubtedly had encountered several unwanted advances along the way. Now that he thought about it, the derringer in her bag made perfect sense.

He gave her a steady look, thinking she

reminded him of his mother, small and graceful but stronger than she appeared. *Don't go there,* he told himself. "It can't be easy for a woman to make a way with two boys."

From her experience, most men didn't give a thought to what it was like for a woman to make her way in the world. Without a family or a husband, there were few options for women to earn a living. As she knew so well, many young women in her situation ended up in some saloon selling drinks, or worse. The same fate had been awaiting her. Thinking of the boys, her eyes welled up again. She'd cried more today than she had in a long time. Taking a deep breath, she blinked away the tears, refusing to give in to self-pity. "Mrs. Wellington pays me as much as possible, but I've been saving for two years, and am no closer to having a home for us."

Hearing a knock at the door, Colt said, "That must be Bartholomew." *Damn,* he thought, just as she was beginning to open up they had to be interrupted. He excused himself to go answer the door.

CHAPTER TEN

Standing over Mr. Barlow's body, Victoria gazed at his serene face. She recalled how he had described himself in his letter. He wasn't a handsome man, but she thought he had a kind face. No one had mentioned his age, and she guessed he was in his sixties. That made her wonder why he'd never married.

Colt watched Victoria's face as she stared at Chet. He would have given every head of beef he owned at that moment to know what she was thinking. A few minutes passed in silence before he escorted her outside so she would be spared seeing the coffin nailed closed. Once Colt and Bartholomew lifted the coffin into the buckboard, they left to take Chet to the farm for burial alongside his mother and father.

Arriving at the Barlow farm, Colt stopped at the house so Victoria could freshen up. He stayed to greet the ranchers as they began to arrive to pay their last respects to one of their own. Bartholomew took the coffin to the cemetery where Colt's men were waiting beside the freshly dug grave.

Victoria walked outside to find Colt waiting for her. Slowly, they made their way toward the cemetery. When Victoria spotted some wildflowers in the field, Colt stood patiently while she picked them for Mr. Barlow's grave.

Two dozen people were silent as they gathered around the gravesite; the only sound came from the women's skirts whipping in the wind. Victoria glanced at the assembly, studying the solemn faces of Mr. Barlow's friends. Her gaze moved to Colt standing alone, a head taller than any man there. She could see the sadness in his dark eyes as he stared off in the distance. The only outward sign of his tenuous hold on his emotions was his tightly clenched jaw. Knowing he was struggling to maintain control gave her a glimpse into his character. A tall, handsome boy walked to his side, and Colt placed his hand on his shoulder in a comforting gesture. Victoria assumed it was the young man Colt mentioned at dinner last night. His face held such admiration when he looked at Colt that it made her wonder how the twins would react to the larger-than-life cowboy.

Colt reflected on the friend he was burying way too soon. He'd stood over too many graves, and this was a loss that was hitting him hard. It saddened him to know that the plans Chet was making for his future, plans that included a bride, would never be realized. Life had a way of getting away from a man, he thought. All the more reason for his brothers to come home before it was too late. It was days like this when the absence of his brothers hit him hardest. Most times he was too busy to ruminate about not having his family near. But burying his friend today reminded him how lonely it was not to have someone to share the times of sadness or the moments of joy.

Victoria moved to stand near him, bringing his thoughts back to the present. Her cheeks were moist with the tears she shed for the man she didn't know. The wildflowers she clutched in her hands looked as fragile as the woman holding them. He noticed she had pulled the ribbon from her hair to hold the bouquet together.

Bartholomew, standing at the head of the coffin, was the first to speak. "We all knew Chet to be a quiet, decent, hardworking man." He hesitated and pulled a folded piece of paper, yellowed and brittle with age, from his pocket. "I found these words writ by Chet in his Bible." His voice was low and raw with emotion, and everyone remained perfectly still, listening intently. With shaking hands, he unfolded the paper. He looked up at the faces gathered around the coffin. "I reckon his own words say more about the man than my words ever could." He started to read what Chet had written.

"I thank you, Lord, for giving me this life, and have some measure of hope that with Your help, I made something of it. I've not been a perfect man, but I've tried to help those in need, and I have always been grateful for the kindness of others." After taking a deep breath, Bartholomew turned his watery eyes on Colt.

Looking at Bartholomew's withered face, Colt thought he looked like he'd aged fifty years overnight. He could see in the older man's eyes that he didn't have it in him to say more, so he stepped forward.

"Chet liked to read the works of Mr. William Shakespeare, and I think these words were penned for a man like Chet." Colt started, his deep baritone voice cracking with emotion. He paused in an effort to collect himself, twirled the hat in his hands a few times, trying to swallow the large lump in his throat. " 'Men of few words are the best men.' " He wanted to say more, but too many feelings threatened his hard-fought battle for control. He'd only cried one time in his life, the day his mother was killed. He'd learned long ago to keep a tight rein on his emotions. Another reason he didn't want to let anyone too close: He didn't want to feel the pain when they died or left.

The pastor stepped forward and led them in prayer. When he finished, Colt settled his Stetson on his head, silently indicating there was nothing else to be said. Everyone started to move away until they saw Victoria step forward and gently place the flowers on top of Mr. Barlow's coffin.

"I am so sorry, Mr. Barlow," she whispered, swiping the tears from her cheeks with the back of her hand. She couldn't put into words the sorrow she felt. Seeing all of his friends gathered around his coffin, and hearing the words he wrote, spoke of his fine qualities. She wished she could have met him. There might not have been love between them had they decided to wed, but she didn't question he was a man who would have treated the boys well. She could no longer stop the tears from flowing. Dropping her face in her hands, she sobbed.

Silence ensued all around. Colt couldn't

bear seeing Victoria cry like her heart was breaking. With a nod of his head, the ranchers walked away and he pulled Victoria to his chest, enfolding her in his strong arms. Over the top of her head, he looked to his men, silently indicating they could finish their work and lower the coffin into the ground. After Victoria's sobbing subsided, he gently took hold of her elbow to lead her to the buckboard, with Bartholomew at his side. After assisting her to the seat, he turned to Bartholomew and placed his arm around his thin shoulders, conveying without words he understood and shared the old man's loss.

"I found a letter addressed to me in Chet's Bible, but I just haven't been able to read it yet," Bartholomew confided.

"All in good time," Colt replied. "It'll take some time to get your thoughts settled. Some of my men will be helping out around here so you keep them busy." Colt didn't think he should be alone on the farm right now. He knew how it felt to have nothing but your thoughts for company.

"I appreciate that, Colt, there's a lot of work to be done around here. I'll have plenty for them to do."

"I don't want you alone if Wallace pays another visit. When the men head back to the ranch, you come with them." He knew Bartholomew couldn't handle Wallace and his men by himself. "I'll expect you for dinner."

Colt walked back to the gravesite to tell his men to stay with Bartholomew, and if Wallace showed up, he wanted someone to come for him. He wasn't about to let anyone cause Bartholomew trouble, and the only one heartless enough to try would be Wallace.

Tate was waiting in the kitchen when Colt and Victoria returned to the ranch. He hadn't met Victoria at the funeral, but the men were all abuzz about the beautiful woman staying at the ranch for a few days.

It lightened Colt's mood considerably watching the teenager blush and stammer as if he'd swallowed his tongue, once he introduced him to Victoria. He'd never seen the boy so tongue-tied; he usually talked nonstop for hours on end. He could sympathize with Tate because he'd suffered the same affliction when he'd first laid eyes on Victoria in St. Louis.

Tate had worked for Colt for two years, having come to the ranch half-starved and desperate to find work to feed his mother and four siblings. They'd made their way into town in a broken-down wagon and next to nothing in the way of supplies. There was no father in sight; he'd left the family to fend for themselves long ago. Upon learning they were living in their wagon, Colt set them up in a house on his ranch. Tate's mother was not one to accept charity, so Colt gave her a job of doing the wash on the ranch, a task that was too difficult for Helen to continue.

Even though Colt was going through a rough time dealing with his own problems on the ranch, he'd taken Tate in and spent his time teaching him ranch work. He saw to it that Tate's clothes and his other necessities were charged to Colt's account at the mercantile so the boy could use his earnings for his family's needs. Tate proved to be a hard worker with a willingness to learn any new task, and Colt never regretted taking him on. In some ways the boy was mature beyond his years, most likely from shouldering man-sized responsibilities.

Tate filled an empty place in Colt's heart, and he'd made it his mission to see to it the boy became a decent, hardworking man. He insisted Tate go to church with him on Sundays in an effort to set an example like his father had done for him and his brothers. He remembered what it was like to go to church with his family, and he wanted Tate to have that experience in his life. At first, Tate resisted because his family had never attended church, but after a few weeks he was waiting for him in the buckboard on Sunday mornings.

"Where's Helen?" Colt asked him, seeing that nothing was cooking on the stove. The boy was still staring slack-jawed at Victoria, forcing Colt to nudge him for a response.

"What?" Tate asked, his eyes never leaving Victoria's face. Finally, Colt's words took hold in his brain, and his face flushed bright red. "Tom took her home when I got back from Mr. Barlow's. He said she was feeling poorly."

Tom Morris worked for Colt's dad for many years, but when an accident forced him to retire from cowboying, they were given a home on McBride land with lifetime tenancy. Helen insisted that she wasn't ready to retire, so she still did the cooking and cleaning. Despite her advanced years, she told Colt she wanted to work as long as the Good Lord allowed.

"I'll check on her while I'm out," Colt said. "I was planning to stop by for a visit with Tom."

"I'll be happy to prepare dinner," Victoria offered. It was an opportunity for her to feel useful, and to thank Colt for his kindness to her. It might even keep her mind off her problems for a while.

"Are you sure you don't mind?" Colt asked, grateful for her offer.

"Not at all, I will enjoy it," she assured him. "Would you like to take something for Tom and Helen?"

"I'm headed out now, but that would be nice. Just fix something up and give it to Tate. He can take it out to them when it's ready."

Before he left, Colt instructed Tate to help Victoria with whatever she needed. After hanging his jacket on the hook by the door, he turned to leave. Pausing, he looked back at Victoria. "You don't have to go to a lot of trouble. I'll eat almost anything. Whatever you whip up is fine by me. Tate and two of my men will be here for dinner, and I expect Bartholomew will show up sometime." He grabbed his hat and smiled at her. "Thank you."

Victoria watched from the window as Colt walked to his horse. He didn't just walk, she thought, he swaggered, like a man who was comfortable in his own skin. He had that loose-hipped gait of a cowboy, and while it didn't appear he moved in a hurry, his long legs covered a lot of ground in a few steps. Taking the reins from one of his men, he jumped on his horse in one fluid motion, easily taking control of the large, scary-looking beast. She watched him ride away, moving as one with his horse, not sure which one was the more formidable.

Tate cleared his throat, and Victoria, having forgotten that he was still in the room with her, turned quickly from the window. She retrieved an apron from the hook next to the one where Colt's jacket hung, and tied it around her waist.

"Is there anything you need before I leave, ma'am?" Tate asked, grinning at her.

Embarrassed that he'd caught her staring at Colt, she felt herself turning pink. "I think I can find everything I need. You can come back in an hour, and I will have something ready for you to take to Mr. and Mrs. Morris."

Tate tipped his hat. "Yes, ma'am." He walked out the door whistling.

CHAPTER ELEVEN

"If that food is anywhere near as good as it smells, this is going to outdo Mrs. Morris's grub," T. J. Hardin, Colt's foreman, said.

Colt nodded his agreement as he hung his shirt on a peg on the back porch. He grabbed a bar of soap and dunked his head in the water before he started scrubbing. He didn't normally go to so much trouble before dinner, but he didn't normally have a beautiful woman at his table.

Victoria glanced out the window when she heard voices. She nearly dropped the platter she was holding when she saw Colt stripping out of his shirt. His clothing didn't disguise his well-muscled form, but with his torso bare he was a sight to behold. His sculpted body reminded her more of a carved marble statue than a warm-blooded man. She told herself to move away from the window, she honestly did, but her feet felt like they had taken root to the floor.

When he turned around she couldn't help but admire his wide chest and arms, rippling with well-honed muscle.

Colt snagged a cloth off a peg and glanced at the window. When he saw two big blue eyes staring at him, his mouth tilted up in a grin. He'd just caught the prim and proper Miss Victoria Eastman ogling his body.

Victoria was mortified. Not only did he catch her staring at him, he had the audacity to grin at her to let her know he'd caught her. She whirled around and headed for the dining room. It wasn't as if she hadn't seen men without their shirts before, but they certainly hadn't looked anything like Colt McBride.

Colt chuckled more to himself than aloud. After he was relatively dry he shook the dust from his shirt and shoved his arms through the sleeves. T. J. followed his lead, making an effort to improve his appearance. Rex Womack, Colt's horse wrangler, joined them on the back porch, looking spit-shined. Colt looked him up and down and arched a brow.

"I cleaned up in the bunkhouse," Rex explained with a sheepish look on his face.

Colt figured there wasn't a man on the ranch who hadn't already heard that a fine-looking woman was staying there.

Tate opened the door for the men. "You better get to the table or I might eat all this by myself. I smelled her cooking all the way out to Mrs. Morris's, and my stomach's been growling ever since."

The men filed in and headed to the dining room. Suddenly, Colt came to a halt in the doorway, causing T. J. to slam into his back. Victoria was leaning over to place a large platter of fried chicken in the middle of the table, and seeing her perform that simple chore caught him unawares. Victoria was a lovely sight in her white dress, moving around the table making sure everything was just right. She looked very much at home, as if she was right where she belonged. A memory of his mother flashed in his mind. He'd seen her do the same thing a thousand times when he was a young man. Inexplicably, that moment stirred something deep inside him.

Victoria's face was flushed, and he wondered if she was still blushing from seeing him without a shirt, or if it was from standing over the hot stove. Whatever the reason, she looked more at ease than she had in the past two days.

She turned and saw him in the doorway and gave him a tentative smile. At least, he wanted to think it was meant for him.

"Just in time," she said.

T. J. nudged Colt from behind, forcing him to move into the room. Colt shook his head as if that would chase away his unwanted thoughts, and strolled to the table.

"Something sure smells good," T. J. said to Victoria, breaking the tension.

Victoria glanced nervously at the two men accompanying Colt, and judging by the way she was wringing her hands, Colt thought she might bolt at any moment. Before she could think about running, he pulled a chair away from the table and held it for her. Once she sat, T. J. quickly took the seat next to her, and to Colt's chagrin, he wasn't sure how he felt about that. After taking his usual chair at the head of the table, he made the introductions. Like the night before, Colt lowered his head and the men followed suit. As soon as Colt said *amen,* the men reached for the food.

"Colt, you didn't tell us she was such a looker," T. J. teased, giving Victoria a wide grin.

"Thank you, Mr. Hardin," she replied softly.

"T. J., ma'am. That's what everyone calls me." He winked at her. "I reckon you can call me anything, as long as you call me for supper."

Victoria couldn't help but smile at him. He was a tall, handsome man, with a grin that was sure to be used on a regular basis. Rex was the polar opposite to T. J., having a quiet, reserved nature. He actually blushed when Colt introduced him. She guessed both men to be a few years older than Colt, yet it was easy to see they held their boss in high esteem.

"Tate says you are a fine cook." T. J. picked up the huge bowl of mashed potatoes and proceeded to slap a huge pile on his plate.

"That she is," Tate said. "I almost stopped and had myself a picnic on the food she sent Mrs. Morris."

Colt accepted the platter of chicken from T. J., helping himself to four pieces.

Victoria was stunned by the mountain of food on the plates in front of the men. She was happy with her decision to cook enough food to feed ten people.

"How is Mrs. Morris feeling? I didn't get a chance to stop by," Colt asked Tate.

"She looked real pale. I told her Miss Victoria said for her not to worry, she would handle the cooking and cleaning as long as she was here," Tate answered.

Colt's gaze slid to Victoria. "You're a guest. You don't have to cook and clean for us."

"I enjoy cooking," she responded. "You've been kind enough to let me stay in your home; it's the least I can do."

"Well, I've never tasted anything so good," T. J. said, and shoved more potatoes in his mouth. "I hope you'll stay a long time."

The men ate their fill, and when Victoria brought the dessert to the table, they thought they had died and gone to heaven. The apple pie she placed beside Colt's plate was piled a foot high. "What did you make for them?" Colt asked, picking up the pie and placing it in front of him.

Victoria thought she should have realized that a man his size could probably eat a whole pie. It wasn't until Colt winked at her, and the other men laughed, that she realized he was teasing.

By the time dinner ended, Victoria had relaxed and was beginning to enjoy conversing with the men. Listening to them joke with Tate, she thought about what the boys were missing by not having men in their lives. Before they left for the bunkhouse they all grabbed dishes and carried them to the kitchen. When Victoria started pumping water into the sink, Colt nudged her aside and took over the chore. "You want to wash or dry?"

"You don't need to help me. I'll have this

done in no time."

"You worked hard on that fine meal, and I don't mind helping with kitchen chores. You wash, I'll dry." Truth was, he rarely helped in the kitchen. He'd normally go to the stable to take care of animals that needed tending, but tonight he'd assigned that task to Rex. After a few minutes of working in companionable silence, he asked, "Where did you learn to cook like that?"

"I've cooked since I was a young girl," she responded.

"Was your mother a good cook?" he pressed.

Uncomfortable talking about herself, Victoria scrubbed a plate longer than necessary. "Not really."

"Your grandmother?"

"Hmm . . . oh, I guess," she said softly.

Obviously a subject she didn't care to discuss, Colt figured. "What are your plans now that . . . well, that things didn't work out here?"

"I'll return to St. Louis and keep working for Mrs. Wellington."

Colt took another plate from her. "How old are the boys?"

"They will be seven soon." His question reminded her that she had hoped the boys would have a home in time to celebrate their next birthday.

He was stunned her boys were that old. If she was twenty, and he doubted that, she would have had those boys when she was what . . . thirteen? Then it registered she'd said both boys would be seven. "Both of them! You mean they're twins?" He hadn't noticed that in St. Louis; he was too busy looking at her.

She smiled at him. "Yes, they are."

Colt eyed her small frame, trying to imagine her carrying one baby. "That is a whole lot of responsibility," he said. "I can see why you came out here to meet up with Chet." Considering the forlorn look that passed over her face, he could have kicked his own rear end for bringing up Chet.

Tate burst through the kitchen door. "Mr. McBride, you best come look!"

Hearing fear in Tate's voice, Colt moved fast. He grabbed his holster from the peg and bolted for the door. Victoria rushed through the door behind them. Colt had his gun strapped on by the time he stepped off the back porch. He smelled the smoke before he saw the light in the distance that could only indicate a fire. T. J. and some of the other men came running from the bunkhouse.

"You figure that's near —" T. J. didn't finish his sentence because Colt took off at a run for the stable.

"Yeah, it's near Tom's cabin," Colt replied when T. J. caught up with him. Before they reached the stable, Rex was leading several saddled horses out. Colt grabbed the reins and jumped on Razor's back. He didn't know what he would find, but he had a nagging suspicion that this was no accident. All of his men had worked for him for a long time, and they had seen dry conditions like this before. He was confident that even if someone had a smoke they wouldn't have been so careless as to drop a cigarette butt on the ground. Colt called to his men, "Everyone grab a shovel and some buckets, and ride like the devil is behind you to get those cattle to safety." He pointed to Rex. "You, Lane, and Tate stay here with Miss Eastman in case there's trouble afoot. Be ready for anything, and no one goes in that house that you don't know. If you see trouble coming, fire three shots."

Considering all of the trouble he'd had lately, he reasoned the perpetrators might be using the fire as a ruse to get the men away from the house so they could set it on fire.

He hadn't noticed Victoria outside until that moment, and he nudged Razor toward her. "The men will be just outside. Tate will be inside with you. Stay in the house unless my men say different."

Victoria's eyes were fixed on the fire in the distance. "I heard you say it could be near Helen's house."

"It's near their house, but let's not borrow trouble. Stay here, I'll be back as soon as I can."

"What can I do?"

He knew she would sit and worry if she didn't stay busy. "Make lots of strong coffee. The men will need it when we come back. You might want to keep some of that fine dinner warmed up. A prayer wouldn't hurt."

Victoria watched as Colt rode toward the fire, recalling a night, not unlike this one, when flames fed on everything in sight, and God was silent. Tonight she couldn't find the words for a prayer.

"Tom, what happened?" Colt shouted, scrambling off Razor before he came to a full stop. Tom Morris was pumping water into buckets and Mrs. Morris was scurrying about, dumping water on every bush around the cabin. The fire was still a good distance away, but the wind was blowing in their direction. Colt could hear his men yelling in the distance as they tried to round up what cattle hadn't run off and move them a safe distance away from the fire.

"I saw them set the fire, Colt," Tom yelled, relinquishing the pumping to T. J. "Them low-down dirty sons-of-Satan tried to set the fire in a circle around the cattle, but I shot one of them out of his saddle before he could finish his evil deed. I think most of the cattle took off, so we didn't lose many. Still, it'll be days rounding them up."

Colt and his men grabbed as many buckets as they could hold and started throwing water on the cabin. He turned to face the red blaze that was inching closer as the wind whipped around them. He figured they didn't have long if the wind didn't shift, so he instructed four men to start digging a trench between the cabin and the fire. It wasn't so much the house that concerned him, but he knew Mrs. Morris would hate to lose things precious to her.

"How many were there?" he asked Tom.

"I saw six of them. Now there's only five."

Once the cabin was as wet as they could get it, everyone turned their attention to digging the trench and filling it with water.

"Thank the Good Lord there is still plenty of water in that well," Mrs. Morris said with a weariness that worried Colt.

"You go sit on that porch and rest," he told her. He looked at the fire again. "I think the wind has shifted. Let's get this trench filled in case it changes direction again."

They finished filling the trench, but thankfully, with the help of the wind, it looked as though the fire was going to burn back into itself. They all stood side by side watching the flames, praying the wind didn't shift back toward them.

"How'd you see them?" T. J. asked Tom.

"I just happened to walk on the porch to . . . to have a smoke." Tom glanced at his wife, and added sheepishly, "You know how the wife don't like the smell of tobacco."

Helen gave him a disapproving look. "I know you're still smoking, you old coot. I reckon I can forgive you this time since you saved our hides."

Colt chuckled at that. He noted Mrs. Morris was already in her nightclothes, and she looked like she was ready to drop from exhaustion. "Helen, go on inside and get what you need for the night. You two are coming to the house with us."

"We'll be fine right where we are," Tom replied, rankled that Colt made it sound like he couldn't take care of his wife.

"No argument. I don't want you two alone out here without backup until I find out what's going on, and the men will be out for hours rounding up strays." He gave Tom a long look, and could see he was about to dig his heels in. The man didn't want to face the fact that he was in his seventies and wouldn't be worth a plug nickel against killers like Hoyt Nelson. All the same, he tried to smooth the old man's injured pride. "Tom, you saw for yourself these men don't come alone, and you couldn't handle four or five of them. You have Helen to think about, and she's not looking too good right now."

"What if them no-good skunks come back to burn us out?" Tom asked.

"I'll have the men ride by here throughout the night to make sure they don't," Colt replied patiently. Colt thought about telling Tom he could stay with his men, but he knew Mrs. Morris wouldn't rest if she had to worry about her husband.

CHAPTER TWELVE

Propping his feet on his desk, Euan Wallace leaned back in his leather chair and swirled the brandy in the glass he held. This was his favorite room in his home, the place where he held meetings with his men. In his estimation, the room conveyed the powerful, wealthy man that he considered himself to be. The well-appointed study held his vast collection of leather-bound books, mostly volumes of law, medicine, and the classics. He readily boasted to any visitor that he'd read each and every book. He prided himself on being an educated man, and he had no one to credit but himself. Having been orphaned in England as a babe, everything he'd accomplished was due to his own intellect and cunning. He'd survived the harsh streets of London before making his way to America as a teenager. In America, he'd not only survived, he thrived. Before he reached Wyoming, he had already amassed considerable wealth, and now he owned more land than even he had dreamed of. But it wasn't enough. He wanted an empire. *Wallace's Empire.* He liked the sound of that. He hadn't scratched his way through life to allow these ignorant, crude cowboys to get the upper hand. Men like Barlow and McBride thought they had a right to the land because it was inherited. If they'd had to fight and claw for it like he had, he figured they wouldn't have lasted long. He was going to own every blade of grass surrounding his land, one way or the other, and he would eliminate anyone who got in his way. He didn't play by anyone's rules; he took what he wanted, lawful or not, made no difference to him. It was fortuitous that Barlow had dropped over dead. His death saved a bullet.

He took a long swallow of the warm brandy, his mind skipping in a different direction. For months he'd been thinking it was time to take a wife so he could have some sons. Problem was, he didn't want to waste time courting a woman, but he would do what was necessary to build his empire. Women seemed to find him handsome enough, still in his prime, tall and lean, and he hadn't lost any of his blond hair. Not that it made a difference; he knew it was his money that attracted the ladies. The thought of a pretty woman succumbing to his every need on a daily basis appealed to his ego. His thoughts were interrupted when Hoyt strolled into his study without knocking.

"Didn't anyone ever teach you to knock?"

Grinning, Hoyt walked to the side table and picked up the bottle. After pouring himself a generous amount of whiskey, he replied, "I didn't know I had to."

"I expect that courtesy from every man on my ranch," Wallace snapped. "Don't forget it in the future." No matter how many times he'd instructed the two Mexican women who worked for him to announce visitors, it was a task they couldn't seem to handle. He didn't want people waltzing in as they pleased.

Hoyt eyed Wallace and, for a heartbeat, considered putting a bullet between his eyes. The only thing that kept him from pulling his revolver was the fact that Wallace was paying him a lot of money, including a large bonus when he got the land he wanted. He planned to hang around Promise longer anyway, since he had unfinished business: Hearing how fast a draw McBride was supposed to be, he wanted to find out for himself. He might as well milk Wallace for as much as he could while it lasted. He'd seen his fair share of nothing towns, and there were worse places than Promise. At least in this town there were some decent-looking women at the saloon where he could play poker anytime. He heard Wallace clear his throat, indicating he was waiting for him to state his business.

"Ben Roper was shot," he said.

"Is he dead?" This wasn't the kind of news Wallace wanted to hear. He didn't want anything, or anyone, left behind to implicate him.

"Yeah. That old man at the cabin shot him."

Angered by the carelessness of his men, Wallace leaned forward and snapped, "I gave implicit instructions before you left. Now there's a way to link that fire to me!"

Hoyt laughed. "Not a chance. We sat on a knoll watching the fire; it burned right where he fell off his horse. If the bullet didn't kill him, the fire surely did. Nobody will recognize him, that's a fact. There couldn't have been anything left."

Leaning back in his chair, appeased for the moment, Wallace said, "Good, good." He swallowed another shot of whiskey, and had another thought. "Did you bring his horse back?"

Hoyt thought Wallace was almost as cold-blooded as he was. "Yeah, he's in the stable."

Hoyt finished his drink and stood to leave when Wallace said, "Next time I give instructions I expect them to be followed to the letter."

Hesitating, Hoyt wondered if the man knew how close he was to meeting his maker.

"Not much left of him to identify," Colt told Seth Parker, the sheriff of Promise. "There were six riders, and that fire was set deliberately." After the fire had burned out the night before, Colt found what was left of the man Tom shot. It was a disgusting sight, but the smell was worse. Burned flesh was a smell a man didn't soon forget. Even though the man was up to no-good on his land, Colt hoped the bullet got him before the fire. He figured the worst kind of man didn't deserve to burn to death. A bullet would have been more merciful.

Colt and T. J. had wrapped the man's remains in a blanket, and when dawn broke, Colt transported him to town in the buckboard. There was no way he would bury him on McBride land. He expected even God would understand his reasoning for that. With a bit of luck someone might come to town inquiring about a missing man. If not, they would bury him in the town cemetery as an unknown person.

"Well, if he can't be identified, how can you be sure it was one of Wallace's men that set that fire?" Parker asked matter-of-factly. "Maybe a cowboy decided to have a smoke and got careless."

"Tom saw them with the torches, and that's why he shot one of them," Colt nearly bellowed. "And we both know who's behind these *accidents*."

"I don't arrest men on assumptions. Now if you have proof . . ." The sheriff let the sentence trail off like a challenge.

Colt hadn't fooled himself into thinking that Parker would be of any help; he'd proven his incompetence as well as his allegiance, time and time again. "Judge Ross should be here in a few days. I'll talk to him."

Parker gave him a smug grin. "He'll say the same thing, ya gotta have proof before you go spoutin' off at the mouth."

Standing with his hands on his hips, Colt ground his molars together, trying to control his temper. He was sorely tempted to reach across the desk separating them and grab the thick-necked weasel and beat the tar out of him. Parker was Wallace's handpicked man, and to Colt's way of thinking, he couldn't have chosen a better accomplice. Parker was as crooked as they came, and not a soul in town would argue that he wasn't worth the bullet it'd take to blow him to Hades. "Tom and Helen could have been killed, but I reckon that wouldn't get much of a rise out of you either."

Removing his booted feet from the desk, Parker straightened. "They weren't, so I don't see what all the fuss is about. You said yourself that you didn't lose but a couple of steers."

Colt braced his hands on the desk and leaned across it until he was nose to nose with Parker. "One dead steer is one too many. You tell Wallace if I find any more of my cattle harmed, I'll be coming to see him."

Leaning back to put some distance between them, Parker's head hit the back wall. He didn't like the look in McBride's cold eyes, but he bluffed his way through his next question, even though his voice cracked with fear. "Are you threatening Wallace?"

Colt straightened and casually rested his palm on the butt of his .45. "I'm stating a fact." He stalked out of the sheriff's office and slammed the door behind him so hard it rattled on its hinges.

Reaching the buckboard, Colt saw Lucy, a

gal from the saloon, standing nearby like she was waiting for someone. He tipped his hat and said, "Lucy," before he climbed onto the seat. He couldn't help but notice the bright red dress she was wearing, but at least she had a shawl covering the low-cut bodice.

Lucy moved to stand closer to the wagon. "Colt, are you coming to play poker? We haven't seen you in a long time." Just like every woman in Promise, she thought he was the most handsome man she'd ever seen. All the gals at L. B.'s waited around every Saturday night to see if he was going to come in to play poker. The gals wanted to serve his table because he was polite and tipped generously, but it was always Maddie who had that honor. Lucy figured the best thing about Colt was the fact that she'd never seen him drunk. He'd buy the whiskey for the table, but he never drank much himself.

"It's a work day, Lucy. I've got to get back to the ranch," Colt said politely. He released the brake and looked down at her to make sure she wasn't standing too close to the buckboard. That's when he saw her black eye and swollen cheek. "What happened to you?"

Her fingers moved to the sizable lump

under her eye. "One of Wallace's men got a little rough last night."

Colt thought she responded as if it was a usual occurrence. Maybe in her trade it was. "Did you tell the sheriff?"

Lucy rolled her eyes. "What for? He won't do nothin'. Everybody knows that he's as thick as thieves with Wallace. Even if he wasn't, nobody does anything about one of us gals getting beat up."

Colt couldn't fault her reasoning. The sheriff wouldn't put himself out since it was one of Wallace's men that beat her, and even the good folks in Promise wouldn't get too riled about the troubles of one of L. B.'s girls. "Who did it?"

"Hoyt Nelson."

"Son of a —" Colt ground out. This little gal, even though she had a hard-as-nails look about her, was no match for a man like Nelson. He leveled his eyes on her. "Why don't you stay away from men like Nelson? You know he's nothing but trouble. Are you trying to get yourself killed?"

Lucy gave him a look like he had sprouted two heads. " 'Cause that's my job. That's how I make my livin', in case you forgot."

"What did L. B. say about it?"

"She saw me this mornin' and was askin' plenty of questions. I'm sure she'll have something to say to him when he comes back. She's one person around here that's not beholdin' to Wallace, or afraid of him."

"Lucy, you're too young to be in this line of work," he told her bluntly.

"I'll be nineteen my next birthday, and Maddie is just six years older. You don't have any problem with her working in a saloon," she snapped.

Colt's eyes moved to the garish red paint on her lips and cheeks, and he realized she didn't look all that young in the light of day. The alcohol, along with her lifestyle, was already taking its toll. He thought of Victoria and how easily she could have succumbed to the same profession as Lucy, and probably with more reason with two boys to feed. When comparing the two women, he respected Victoria all the more for the choices she'd made. Even though she was willing to marry a man sight unseen, it was a better life than the one Lucy had chosen.

"If you ever want out of this business, let me know. I'll give you a stake so you can go to a new town and make a fresh start."

To his surprise, Lucy laughed. "Well, if that don't beat all. You never let anyone but Maddie serve your table, and she's the only one you want to be with, but you'll give me money to leave."

"There's got to be a better way to earn a living, not to mention one that's a whole lot safer," he said, pointing to her eye.

"I like what I do."

Colt considered her admission, wondering if it was bluster or fact. "As I said, if you ever want to leave . . ."

Colt didn't finish because Lucy turned to walk away, her hips swishing to and fro. After a couple of steps she whirled back around. "I'll be leaving here when I make enough to get me to San Francisco. There's a gentlemen's club there where I can make a lot more money."

On the way to the ranch, Colt thought about the gals at the saloon, and the bruises on Lucy's face. Since that was the way those gals chose to make their way in the world, like as not they had to suffer the drunks and abusers on occasion. He'd been taken aback when Lucy admitted she enjoyed working in a saloon. Lucy had given him another surprise when she told him Maddie was only twenty-five. He'd never really asked, but he would have sworn that she was well into her thirties. Maddie was a pretty woman with long blond hair, bright green eyes, more lush curves than any woman had a right to have, and she had a

good head on her shoulders. He remembered asking her one time why she worked
in a saloon, because he thought she had options for how she chose to make a living.
She'd told him it was all she knew, and
rebuffed his suggestion that she could work
in the general store, or at the hotel restaurant. He'd made her the same offer he made
Lucy — a stake so she could find another
way to earn a living, even if it wasn't in
Promise — but she'd turned him down flat.
L. B. told him most of the gals waited for
some cowboy to come along who was willing to marry them. Even though he knew
Maddie was partial to him, he'd made it
clear he had no claim on her, and it wasn't
because of her profession. He wouldn't have
married her if she owned a dress shop. He
just wasn't a marrying man.

Colt was sure L. B. would have plenty to
say about Hoyt Nelson abusing one of her
girls. L. B. wasn't one to stand idly by when
some cowboy overstepped his bounds. Aside
from barring him from the saloon, there
really wasn't much she could do if the
sheriff wouldn't do his job. Words wouldn't
solve the problem with the likes of Hoyt
Nelson. He'd come up against men like him
before, and he knew it wasn't a question of

if, but when he would have it out with the gunslinger.

CHAPTER THIRTEEN

Colt stuck his head in the kitchen door and saw Victoria sitting at the table, her valise by the door. "I'll get the buckboard if you're ready," he said.

"Yes, I am." Victoria didn't look forward to the long journey home, but she was anxious to see the boys. "I thought Bartholomew would be here by now." She wanted to say good-bye and thank him for his kindness.

"I'm sure he will meet us in town," Colt assured her. Truthfully, he was surprised Bartholomew hadn't arrived earlier, considering how he'd taken to Victoria.

Reaching the stable, Colt found T. J. harnessing the horses to the buckboard. "What are you up to, T. J.?"

T. J. responded without looking up from his task, "I thought I would save you a trip into town and drive Miss Victoria to catch the noon stage."

"Thanks, but I have other business to attend to in town." At first, Colt didn't suspect T. J. had another motive, other than doing him a favor, until he looked at him. T. J. was wearing one of his best shirts, and his hair was neatly combed. He looked like he was going courting on a Saturday night. It hadn't escaped his notice that T. J. had been hanging around after dinner lately instead of heading to the bunkhouse to play poker, like he normally did. He'd even offered to help wash the dishes last night. How could he have missed the reason for T. J.'s change in behavior? *Victoria!* T. J. was smitten. He grinned at his foreman. "You didn't have another reason for going to town, did you?"

T. J. finished with the horses and looked at Colt. Seeing that grin on his face, he threw his hands in the air. "All right! I just thought I might get to know her a little better! There ain't no crime in that, is there? Maybe she would stay in Promise if she had a reason." His voice sounded like a frog had hopped in his throat and was beginning to croak, but to his credit, he soldiered on. "It's not like we have any women who look like her in this part of the country. It'd be a real shame if some cowboy around here didn't try to herd her into his fences."

165

Colt gave him a steady look. "I get your meaning, but she doesn't come without some baggage. You aren't forgetting she has those two boys, are you?"

T. J. shook his head at Colt. "Baggage? Now that's one interesting way to put it. What kind of dang-fool man would let that get in the way of settling down with a woman like her? She's the prettiest little thing I ever laid eyes on, and I ain't never tasted anything like her cookin'. The way I look at it, having two boys could be a fine thing."

Colt couldn't believe his ears. He was as surprised by T. J.'s confession as he had been that day Bartholomew announced Chet was going to get married. Now that he thought about it, he should have seen it coming. Usually T. J. wouldn't utter a word during dinner until he'd finished eating. At least, that was the way it had been before Victoria arrived. The last few nights, it was like T. J. had forgotten his love of food because he spent all of his time talking to Victoria, and Colt couldn't get a word in edgewise. The man was a born flirt, and it didn't matter if the women were just a step up from downright homely. T. J. fancied himself to be an expert on the subject of women, and grudgingly Colt had to admit, they flocked to him like flies to an apple pie. Colt understood his appeal to the ladies. He was all cowboy: tall and trim, every muscle honed to rock hardness, and as strong as an ox with charm to match. No one worked harder than T. J., and he was never one to complain about any task. The other men teased that he was as comfortable sleeping out in the harsh elements as he was in the bunkhouse. But he was also the one cowboy who vowed he'd never settle down. "I thought you were against settling down with one woman?"

T. J. gave a loud sigh, as though Colt was trying his patience. "I've never exactly said I was against settling down. I reckon when a man sees something he thinks is worth havin', he gives up on fool notions like raisin' a ruckus until he's Bartholomew's age. Any man in his right mind would want to be puttin' a ring on Miss Victoria's finger, real quick like."

"A ring?" Colt shouted the word.

"You're dang right! A smart man would stake his claim, if for no other reason than to tell other hombres they shouldn't be sniffin' around. You can bet I would sure put my brand on her the minute she showed just a little bit of interest. I'm thirty-six years old, that's only seven years older than you, but I sure ain't as old as Chet was, and she was considerin' marryin' up with him. I've got a few more good years left in me than he did." Now he was warming up to the subject, and he gave Colt that grin that the ladies were so crazy about. "Plus, I'm a whole lot better lookin', and I know for dang sure I could show her a better time."

Colt laughed the whole time he was pulling the buckboard in front of the house. Then he suddenly stopped. He didn't know what he found so darn funny. It wasn't enough that Victoria had Bandit looking at her like he thought she was better than a meaty morsel; she had Tate following her around like a love-starved puppy, and now his foreman was talking about putting a ring on her finger. If she stayed in Wyoming much longer, every man on the ranch would be fighting over her. It was hard for him to believe T. J. would consider putting a ring on any woman's finger, much less a woman he'd met just a couple of days before. But T. J. was right about one thing: The odds of another woman coming along anytime soon who was as beautiful as Victoria was next to nil. He couldn't deny it had been a pleasure having her at his dinner table. Over the years, he'd had dinner with women at the hotel, but he'd never invited any woman to his home. He'd never given it much thought, but now he realized what he had missed. Several times he'd found himself just watching Victoria converse with his men, enjoying the sound of her soft voice and her laughter. It reminded him of dinners with his family when his mother was alive. He'd missed the female graces over the years. The various topics at dinner were a welcome respite from the usual subjects. Even he grew weary of ranch talk at the dinner table, particularly discussing the finer points of castrating bulls.

No matter how much he enjoyed Victoria's company, the plain truth was he didn't want her staying in Promise. He wanted her to get back to St. Louis, where she belonged. The sooner the better. He told himself that if she stayed in Promise, he'd be beholdin' to look after her. It was because of his friendship with Chet, he reasoned, certainly not because he might start to care about her. He wasn't about to make that mistake. He'd had a hard enough time getting over the loss of his mother, and he wasn't willing to let his feelings run that deep for anyone ever again. He liked his life just like it was, no strings attached. He didn't want more responsibilities. Running the ranch and being responsible for the livelihood of the men who worked for him was enough on his plate. No sir, he wasn't in the market for a wife, and yet he didn't want any man in Promise having notions like T. J. was having. He was taking her to town to board that stagecoach and send her back to her boys, where she belonged. End of story.

Arriving at the same time the stagecoach came barreling into town, Colt pulled the buckboard to a halt in front of the livery. As soon as he assisted Victoria down, Bandit scrambled to the ground to stand between them.

"You're welcome to let the dog stay with me if you aren't of a mind to travel with him," Colt offered. He hadn't wanted another dog to look after right now since he still missed his dog that died a few years back. But Bandit had taken to following him around the ranch and he found himself enjoying his companionship. A dog he could handle; a wife he couldn't.

Victoria leaned down and rubbed Bandit's ears. She was crazy about the dog and wanted more than anything to take him home to the boys. What boys wouldn't love to have a dog like him? She was reluctant since she didn't know how Mrs. Wellington would feel about adding a dog to the household; plus, Bandit needed room to roam. "That is kind of you to offer. I would like to keep him, but I must confess I don't know how Mrs. Wellington would feel about having him around. She has been so good to us that I wouldn't want to take advantage of her generosity."

The stagecoach driver approached and advised them it would be at least an hour before he departed due to needed repairs.

"We'll be in the hotel dining room having a cup of coffee if you're ready before then," Colt told him.

On the way to the hotel several people stopped to speak with Colt, and he was certain they were all curious about the beautiful woman on his arm. A few feet from the hotel, Colt's attention was on Victoria, and he didn't see Maddie and Lucy until he nearly collided with them.

Colt's first thought seeing them was *Dang my luck, or lack thereof.* But he was taught to be a gentleman, so he raised his fingers to tip the brim of his hat in greeting. To his dismay, they didn't move on, but stopped in front of the door to the hotel. To say he was stunned when Lucy moved in close to him didn't say it by half.

"Hi, Colt, honey. Are you coming in to

play poker soon?" Lucy asked sweetly.

The gals from the saloon didn't make a habit of speaking to men outside of L. B.'s establishment, particularly if they were in the company of a lady. Colt was certain L. B. would not approve of her gals taking such a liberty. Not that he was one of those men who ignored the women when he saw them. He had no problem acknowledging them, but with Victoria at his side, he wasn't inclined to stop and have a conversation. Like most ladies in town, he doubted Victoria approved of being seen in the company of a sportin' woman. He'd certainly never seen a lady in Promise have a chat with one.

"No poker today," he replied.

He expected them to keep walking, and when they didn't he glanced from Maddie to Lucy, but they were both glaring at Victoria. He tipped his hat again and said tersely, "Ladies." Still, they didn't move. He wasn't sure of their game, but he knew trouble when he saw it.

"Well, maybe later tonight then," Lucy urged.

Colt remained silent, thinking that might send the message.

Victoria couldn't believe these women had stopped to talk with Colt. Their attire and painted faces told her they worked in the saloon. She thought it best for her to go inside the hotel and allow Colt to handle the situation. "I'll just be inside," she said to him.

Colt foiled her attempt to walk away by curling his arm around her waist. "If you ladies will excuse us," he said, his tone brusque.

Lucy refused to move out of the way, and he couldn't reach the hotel door without knocking her aside. Maddie had rarely seen Colt angry, but she knew from his tone that he was riled. He looked like he was ready to throttle Lucy. Maddie had been in love with Colt from the first moment she saw him. Every Saturday night she would take extra care with her appearance, and wait for him to walk through the door. Worried that Lucy was going to ruin her relationship with him, she wrapped her fingers around the girl's arm and tried to pull her away. "Lucy, mind your manners. Let's go."

Shaking off Maddie's hand, Lucy stared at Victoria with undisguised hatred. When her gaze drifted back to Colt, she didn't seem to care that he was seething with anger. She smirked at Victoria, and said, "I'd say you'll need whiskey later to thaw you out, honey. You know where to find us."

Victoria couldn't believe the audacity of

the girl. For some reason she was acting like a scorned woman. Stealing a sideways glance at Colt, she saw his jaw muscles twitching.

Lucy's rude comment aimed at Victoria made Colt furious. If she were a man he would have shoved his fist in her mouth. Seeing as how he didn't think that would be the gentlemanly thing to do, he was at a loss how to handle a woman acting like a she-cat. He reached for the door behind Lucy, and she either had to move or get hit with the door, so she finally edged out of the way. Once Victoria and Bandit walked inside, he heard Lucy say, "We'll see you later, honey."

"Lucy!" Maddie shouted, and pulled her toward the saloon. "What are you thinking? If he tells L. B., she will fire you for sure."

Colt nearly ground his molars off. He wasn't sure what Lucy was trying to accomplish, but he planned to find out as soon as Victoria was on that stagecoach.

After coffee and a piece of meat for Bandit were delivered to their table, Colt glanced around the room to see if anyone was close enough to overhear their conversation. When he was satisfied no one was listening, he said, "I'm sorry about those gals."

Victoria met his dark eyes, wanting badly

to ask questions yet unsure what would be appropriate. But it was difficult to hide her curiosity about his relationship with the women. "I gather they work in the saloon?"

"Yes," Colt replied, trying to think of a plausible explanation for Lucy's behavior, but finding none.

"The one seems to know you well . . . ah . . . I mean . . . you must be . . ." Victoria spoke before she thought about how her words would be interpreted. She didn't know how to finish.

Watching her turn pink from the neck up, Colt couldn't help but smile, and some of the tension eased from his body. Placing his brawny forearms on the table, he leaned forward and said in a low voice, "I know her, but . . . not that well . . . if that is what you are asking."

Victoria's face changed from pink to crimson in a flash. She was so embarrassed she could barely meet his eyes. "I was asking no such thing!"

One dark slash of eyebrow arched up. "Weren't you?" he teased.

"Certainly not! I didn't mean . . . I . . . well, it's none of my business, Mr. McBride." All the while she was thinking he must know that girl very well for her to act so familiar with him. The other woman

175

wasn't as obvious in her feelings, but Victoria saw the way she looked at Colt. She had the look of a woman in love.

The waitress refilled their coffee, and Colt lounged back in his chair, his long legs to the side of the table. It amused him to see Victoria blushing to her toes, looking everywhere but at him. It had taken four days before he got her to call him by his given name; now she was back to Mr. McBride. When she finally met his eyes, he grinned. "Well, I didn't want to give you the wrong idea. I'm not rightly sure why she acted the way she did."

Victoria sipped her coffee, and without thinking she gazed at his wide chest and muscled forearms. Remembering how he looked without his shirt, she wondered if those women had seen him that way. She knew exactly why they'd acted jealous; they both thought Colt McBride was quite a catch. Well, that was not her concern. She was leaving Promise, and it was none of her business if he went to the saloon every night. She glanced up to see him smiling like he knew what she was thinking. She was surprised she didn't burst into flames. "As I said, it's none of my business," she told him primly.

His smile widened, and he wasn't about

to let it drop. He'd watched her gaze drop to his chest and he knew she really wanted to know how well he knew Lucy. "Now, I'm not saying I don't visit the saloon. I'm not married, and just like every other red-blooded man in Promise, I go to the saloon to play poker, and I even —"

"Mr. McBride!" She interrupted before he said more than she should hear. She was all too familiar with things that happened in a saloon. "This is not a conversation we should be having," she whispered emphatically.

Colt gave a deep chuckle, the sound reverberating around the room, garnering stares from some of the patrons. He was enjoying her reaction. "I was just going to say sometimes *I drink whiskey,*" he went on to say, grinning. He sat back and sipped his coffee, his black eyes watching her like the devil ready to pounce on a sinner.

She knew he was teasing her, and this was a side of him she had seen when he joked with Tate. Seeing that dimpled smile of his did funny things to her insides. Goodness, he was a handsome man when he smiled; it almost made her forget how formidable he was. *Almost.* Unlike most men she encountered, he didn't flirt with her. The men who came to the boardinghouse flirted with her all of the time. But Colt was different. At first, she thought he had a woman in his life, or perhaps a fiancée, though he hadn't mentioned anyone. The few days she was at his ranch, he'd been up before dawn and worked until dinnertime, then finished up chores late at night, so it didn't seem likely there was anyone special in his life. If there was, he certainly didn't leave much time to devote to her. Was it possible he cared for one of those women from the saloon? He obviously found the time to frequent that place. She'd seen many God-fearing men who forgot their religion as soon as they stepped through the swinging doors of a saloon.

"Did you make a decision about the dog?" he asked, pulling her from her reverie.

Taking a deep breath, Victoria thought of Bandit and how she hated to leave him behind, but she was forced to consider her situation, and what was best for him. He wouldn't have room to roam like he would on Colt's ranch. Every dog needed that. "I think it would be best if he stayed with you. He'd have the whole ranch to run and play, and he's become very attached to you."

He could hear in her voice that she hated to leave the dog behind. "I give you my word he will be well cared for," he promised.

CHAPTER FOURTEEN

The stagecoach was ready to depart when Colt and Victoria made their way without incident back to the livery.

Colt waited as Victoria said good-bye to Bandit, listening to her softly explain to him why he had to stay behind. The forlorn look on the dog's face made Colt think he knew what was happening. He'd always thought animals were smarter than people, and Bandit's response was more evidence of that fact.

"You ready, ma'am?" the driver asked.

Victoria leaned down and planted a kiss on Bandit's snout. "Be a good boy," she whispered, tears filling her eyes. Composing herself, she faced Colt. "Thank you for everything, Mr. McBride."

Colt reached for her hand to assist her inside the coach. He had to admit it was difficult to put her in that coach knowing he would never see her again. It reminded him of that morning in St. Louis when she was standing at the window of the boarding-house when he'd ridden away. He told himself it was for the best because he wasn't a man that wanted to commit to a woman.

"Colt, hold up!" Bartholomew yelled, hurrying toward them.

"Just a minute," Colt told the driver. He turned to Bartholomew, relieved he had finally arrived. "I was worried you weren't going to get here in time to see Victoria off."

"I wouldn't miss saying good-bye," he replied, smiling at Victoria. He held out a piece of paper to Colt. "But I think you best read this first. This was inside the letter Chet left for me. I just read it this morning."

Giving him a quizzical look, Colt took the paper and read the contents. After he finished reading, he passed the paper to Victoria. "It looks like you've just inherited a farm."

Victoria's brows drew together. "What do you mean?"

"Read," Colt said, nodding at the paper.

Seeing Mr. Barlow's handwriting made her think of the day she received his letter in St. Louis. After she finished reading, she looked from Colt to Bartholomew. "Does this mean what I think it means?"

"It does. You now own the Barlow farm," Colt said.

As much as she wanted a home for the boys, she didn't feel right about receiving one this way. She looked at Bartholomew to gauge his reaction. "I don't understand. You deserve to have the farm. Mr. Barlow didn't even know me. Why would he leave the land to me?"

"Chet's letter explained how he came to the decision. He wrote this after he sent his letter to you, and it was the smart thing to do. We were both getting on in years, and neither one of us had family left. Even if you married another fellow, you could leave the farm to the boys one day. He left me some money, and the right to live on the farm until I die. That would be my preference, seein' as I don't have any place I would rather be, if that would be agreeable with you."

Her eyes filled with tears. "Of course you would stay at the farm. But I still don't feel right about this, Bartholomew. He didn't even know if I was going to come to Wyoming. What about distant relatives?"

Bartholomew moved to her and patted her gently on the back. "He was the last Barlow. Somehow I think the Good Lord told him you were going to come, and he arranged everything." Bartholomew choked up remembering how his friend was planning to build a new home for his bride. "Just think, you and the boys have your own home now. Isn't that what you wanted? We'll keep the farm going, and then one day it will belong to them."

"Is this the lovely lady that everyone has been telling me about?" a voice said from behind them. Colt, Victoria, and Bartholomew turned in unison to see Euan Wallace standing there.

Wallace reached for Victoria's hand. "I'm Euan Wallace. I understand you were a friend of Chet Barlow's."

"I'm Victoria Eastman," she replied.

Wallace gave her a half bow and looked her up and down before he brushed the back of her hand with his lips. "I see the gossips did not do you justice."

Like Mrs. Wellington, the man had a heavy British accent and a polished manner. He was tall and thin, with pale blond hair, icy blue-gray eyes, and a long, dark blond mustache. Victoria thought he was quite handsome in an aristocratic way. She also thought he looked vaguely familiar, though she wasn't sure why.

Pulling her hand from Wallace's grip, she nervously glanced up at Colt and was startled to see him glaring at the man with what could only be described as a look of contempt. Glancing from one man to the other, she couldn't help but notice the differences between them. Colt's darkly tanned skin and his black eyes and hair provided a stark contrast to Wallace's light, almost angelic appearance. Colt's muscled shoulders and chest strained the seams of his shirt, and his well-worn jeans hugged his powerful thighs. Wallace was well-dressed, his suit tailored perfectly for his lithe frame. Colt's loosely flowing, wavy black hair almost reached his shoulders, while Wallace's pale hair was cut neatly above his collar, each strand in place. Colt's large calloused hands spoke of his long hours laboring outdoors. The soft white hands of the stranger told her he was a man unaccustomed to manual labor, more likely a man who gave the orders. Of course, there was Colt's ever present pistol; she couldn't imagine the seemingly genteel Mr. Wallace armed.

Colt didn't like the way Wallace was eyeing Victoria. "Did the sheriff give you my message?" he asked, hoping to take his attention off Victoria.

"He did," Wallace responded smoothly. "You don't actually believe I had anything

183

to do with a fire on your property?"

Colt pinned him with a black glare. "The thought did occur to me."

"I assure you I don't resort to such tactics. The sheriff said you were waiting to speak to the judge, but that is a waste of your time."

"We'll see," Colt ground out.

Wallace turned to Bartholomew. "Actually, it was you I wanted to speak with, but I was sidetracked by this lovely creature," he said, smiling again at Victoria.

Wallace was smooth, Colt had to give him that. Even though he knew the man was lying through his teeth, he did need more proof than the hairs on the back of his neck standing on end whenever Wallace was around.

"What did you want with me?" Bartholomew asked.

"Since Chet didn't have family, I assume the farm will be sold," Wallace stated.

Bartholomew's eyes widened and he glanced at Colt before he responded. He couldn't help but smile at Wallace when he replied, "I reckon not, seeing as how he left all of his property to Miss Victoria."

Wallace was surprised by this piece of news. "I was of the understanding this young woman was of no relation to Barlow."

"Relation or not, he left her the land," Colt ground out.

"Miss Victoria was Chet's betrothed," Bartholomew added, and Colt bristled at the comment. He reminded himself to tell Bartholomew to keep that piece of information to himself in the future.

Wallace recovered quickly, turning back to Victoria with a sympathetic smile plastered on his patrician face. "My condolences then, Miss Eastman. I was not aware of your engagement."

Victoria simply nodded, and Wallace questioned further, "So Chet had a will?"

Colt was about to say it was none of his business, but Bartholomew spoke up again. "Yes, and it was properly witnessed."

Annoyed that he hadn't been aware of Barlow's will, Wallace planned to go right to the bank to hear an explanation from Mr. Ford. He paid Ford a tidy sum to keep him informed of any situation where he might profit. He surmised McBride was already ingratiating himself with Victoria so he would have first chance to purchase the farm when she sold. His eyes swept over Victoria again. It would be no burden to spend some time with her. He might be persuaded to marry her since she obviously wanted a husband if she was engaged to a man old enough to be her father. That thought made him wonder why she had settled for Barlow. She was beautiful enough to grace his table, and she appeared to be a lady of breeding. "Would you be available to —"

He was interrupted by the approach of the stagecoach driver. "You ready to leave, ma'am?"

"Are you leaving Promise?" Wallace inquired.

All eyes moved to Victoria, but before she could form a response, her attention was diverted by a plump, red-haired woman scurrying across the road hailing the stagecoach driver.

"Wait! Tom!" the woman yelled. "I've a letter I need you to take."

Victoria glanced back at the men and saw they were still awaiting her response to Wallace's question. "I'm not leaving now. My plans have changed," she answered.

Wallace gave her a wide smile. "That is good news. Might I ask to escort you to dinner this evening at the hotel? Since you are already in town, it will give us the opportunity to become better acquainted. There are some matters I would like to discuss with you."

Bartholomew didn't like the idea of Victoria going anywhere with Wallace, so he spoke up, thinking to apprise her of Wallace's intentions. "Mr. Wallace has a ranch on the other side of the farm. He wanted Chet to sell to him."

The situation between Colt and Wallace became clear to Victoria and explained Colt's acrimonious attitude toward Wallace. Both men wanted the land, and because of that they were most likely enemies. But why Colt thought Wallace was involved with the fire on his land was another question. Obviously, there were many things going on here that she was not privy to, but she wanted to live on the Barlow farm. Her farm. Home. These men could settle their differences; their feud didn't have anything to do with her. She would never sell Mr. Barlow's land. And she wouldn't waste one minute worrying about men wanting to argue over buying property that was not for sale. This was a fresh start for her and the boys, and she wouldn't allow these two men to interfere with their future.

"I'm sorry, Mr. Wallace. As it happens, I have business to attend to today. Perhaps another time. But be assured, sir, that the Barlow farm is not for sale," she told him politely but plainly.

"Your farm," Bartholomew corrected. He

was so pleased with her response to Wallace he wanted to give her a big hug.

Victoria gave him a teary-eyed smile. "That may be, but we will always call it the Barlow farm." That would be her only way to honor Mr. Barlow. She glanced at the stagecoach driver, who was pulling her valise from the roof. She missed the look that passed over Wallace's pale features, but Colt didn't.

"I will hold you to that promised dinner. It was a pleasure meeting you," Wallace said, bowing politely before he walked away.

Colt watched him cross the road in the direction of the bank. He knew it wouldn't be long before Wallace made Victoria an offer on the land, or tried to find a way to steal it. He expected him to be a gentleman about it at first, but if Victoria refused to sell, he'd resort to other tactics.

"I need to send a telegram to Mrs. Wellington and tell her the news. I will get everything settled here and take the next stage out," Victoria said. She leaned down to Bandit and wrapped her arms around his neck. "You are going to get a family after all, and you will have a farm to run on," she told him.

"Ruby? Is that you?" The redheaded woman who had hailed the stagecoach driver approached them.

Victoria quickly straightened to face the woman. "I'm Victoria Eastman," she replied anxiously.

L. B.'s hand flew to her chest and she staggered backwards. Her ashen face looked like she had just seen an apparition.

Colt grabbed her arm to keep her from falling over, and Bartholomew hurried to her other side to help Colt support her weight.

"L. B.? Are you ill? Do you need the doc?" Colt inquired. He'd never seen her in such a state.

"No no, just give me a minute," she uttered on a ragged breath, her eyes never leaving Victoria's face. "I'm sorry, you look very much like someone I used to know," she uttered by way of explanation. "Someone I haven't seen in a long time."

The color drained from Victoria's face and her heart started pounding. She was certain she had never seen this woman before. She tried to maintain a calm demeanor when she responded. "Think nothing of it, these things happen."

"Let's get you over to the doc's office," Colt offered.

Taking a deep breath, L. B. straightened, brushing aside Colt and Bartholomew's support. "Nonsense, I'm as fit as a fiddle. I was just startled. This gal looks so much like . . . well, no matter. I made a mistake."

Colt released her arm but hovered near her in the event she had another spell. "Victoria, this is L. B. Ditty. She owns the saloon."

"L. B.?" Victoria questioned.

L. B. chuckled wryly. "That's all anyone around here calls me. I never tell anyone my real name; only Sam, my bartender, knows that. I've never seen you around here before. Are you visiting Colt?"

"Miss Victoria was going to marry Chet, but now we just found out he left her the farm," Bartholomew informed her.

Colt rolled his eyes. Bartholomew couldn't seem to keep a thought in his head, finding it necessary to tell everything he knew. He guessed the news would spread around town soon enough anyway.

Glancing at Colt, L. B. said, "Well, there's another hitch in Wallace's plans for that land."

"I don't think he will give up easy," Colt replied flatly.

"That's the truth of it," L. B. agreed, the color coming back to her plump cheeks. Her gaze moved back to Victoria. "You have the most unusual eyes. I've only seen one other

190

person with eyes that blue."

"I'm told that often." Victoria was uneasy with the way the woman was staring at her. She had never met this woman, of that she was sure. She couldn't imagine anyone forgetting such a character.

"Where do you hail from?" L. B. inquired.

"St. Louis. I work in Mrs. Wellington's boardinghouse there."

"Chet was a fine man," L. B. told her. Realizing how her statement might be interpreted, she gave Victoria a level look and added, "Now don't go thinking he visited the saloon — he didn't. But me and him had conversed a time or two. He was a smart man, and that's a nice piece of land out there. It should make you a fine home." Ready to make her departure, she nodded to Victoria and Bartholomew, then said to Colt, "I'll be seeing you tonight, I reckon."

Colt wished the road would open up and swallow him right there and then. Was there one woman left in that saloon who hadn't made it clear to Victoria that he was a fairly regular customer?

CHAPTER FIFTEEN

Colt escorted Victoria to the bank so she could discuss Chet's will with the banker before he took her back to the farm. Once he dropped her off at the farm he momentarily considered turning the buckboard around and going back to town to have a talk with Lucy. Maddie hadn't behaved as rudely as Lucy, but he intended to ask her about that stunt in front of the hotel. He hadn't seen Maddie since . . . *How long has it been?* Now that he thought about it, he hadn't been in the saloon since he returned from his uncle's funeral in St. Louis. That meant he hadn't seen Maddie in a long time. That in itself was unusual, since he'd seen her on a fairly regular basis for several years. But he decided he wasn't going to be seeing her tonight either. He'd already been away from the ranch too long today and he had a lot of work waiting for him. Since tomorrow was Saturday, he'd go to town with the men and play some poker, and he'd have that talk with Lucy and Maddie.

In her meeting with the banker, Victoria learned that Chet had left her a substantial amount of money as well as the land. At least, it was more money than she had ever seen. She couldn't fathom why Mr. Barlow had been so kind to a woman he didn't even know, but she was thankful. No one had ever been so generous to her. Having the money meant she wouldn't have to depend totally on the income from the sales of her reticules. Before Victoria left St. Louis, Mrs. Wellington had suggested she send samples of her hand-sewn reticules to shops in San Francisco and London. Mrs. Wellington assured her that the shops would place orders for her designs. She hoped Mrs. Wellington was right because she could use the extra income.

It wouldn't be an easy life for a woman and two small boys on the farm. But no matter what, there was no way she would sell that land. She had Bartholomew to help her, and together they'd find a way to make it work.

"Victoria," Bartholomew yelled from the door.

Victoria and Bandit walked from the

kitchen to greet him. "Come in. Can I get you some coffee?"

"Yes, ma'am, a man could get used to your fine coffee." He followed her back to the kitchen. "I wanted to tell you that tomorrow I'll go to town to get some supplies so I can build beds for those boys."

"Oh, Bartholomew, that would be wonderful! Thank you so much," she exclaimed. "If you don't mind, I'd like to ride with you and pick up some things."

"I'd love the company," he told her sincerely. Without her, he would have been terribly lonely with Chet gone. He couldn't wait for those boys to arrive; it had been a long time since he'd been around children. "I bet you're missing your boys."

"Very much, and I miss Mrs. Wellington too. I've grown very fond of her."

"Tell me about Mrs. Wellington," he said, taking a drink of the coffee she poured him.

By the time Colt got to the ranch, his mood hadn't improved. Tate met him at the stable while he was unhitching the buckboard.

"Tom and Helen went back to their house," Tate said.

Colt was surprised that Helen felt up to leaving. "Why did they do a fool thing like that?"

"I told Tom you wouldn't be happy about it, and you wanted them to stay until you found the culprits who set that fire. He said Mrs. Morris would feel better at home, but I don't think she wanted to leave." Tate was very fond of Mrs. Morris and he was obviously worried about her.

"Aw hell," Colt mumbled. Like he didn't have enough to worry about. Sometimes Tom was just too dang proud for his own good. Now he had to send a couple of men over to watch after Tom and Helen, and a couple of men to Victoria's place. At this rate, he wouldn't have enough men to work the ranch. He walked to the stall to saddle Razor.

Hours later, Colt and T. J. were tying their horses to the railing in front of the saloon when Colt glanced up and saw Victoria leaving the mercantile across the street. He glanced around, but Bartholomew was nowhere in sight. He wondered what she was doing in town by herself. Just as he told himself to mind his own business, he saw a cowboy walking toward her. Thinking of the encounter with the drunken cowboys at the boardinghouse that night in St. Louis, he thought he would just make sure she didn't have any problems. "I'll meet you inside," he told T. J. as he headed across the street.

T. J. saw what had caught Colt's attention. "Okay, boss."

"Delilah?" Colt heard the cowboy say as he approached.

Victoria ignored him and turned to walk away.

"I know that's you, Delilah," the cowboy said. He reached out and grabbed her arm to keep her from walking away.

"Let go of me!" Victoria screeched. She tried to pull away and dropped her packages in the process. "I don't know you!"

"Honey, I'd know those eyes anywhere. You're Delilah, sure enough," the cowboy insisted. "Don't you remember me? Gage Hardy."

She tried to dislodge his fingers from her arm. "I'm not . . ." Her words trailed away when she saw Colt behind the cowboy.

"Let go of the lady," Colt demanded, his tone hard.

The persistent cowboy half turned toward Colt. "Mind your own business, cowboy."

Eyes narrowed, Colt's voice took on an even more ominous tone. "I said let her go." The cowboy didn't appear to be drunk, but Colt thought he smelled whiskey.

"Delilah and I go way back," Gage Hardy said before turning back to Victoria. "Tell him. I know you remember me, honey. How can you forget a man who was with you back in Abilene?"

Colt's eyes slanted from the cowboy to Victoria. Her face had paled to a ghostly white and her eyes were wide. *Is it fear? Definitely fear.* Surely she had to know that he wouldn't allow this cowboy to hurt her.

Finally, her gaze skittered over Gage's shoulder and met Colt's eyes. "Mr. Mc-Bride, I'm afraid this gentleman has me confused with someone else."

Hearing her voice tremble, Colt realized it was more than fear. She was terrified, and that made him angry. "I'll not tell you again to take your hands off her."

The cowboy reluctantly dropped his hand from Victoria's arm and turned his full attention on Colt. He raised his palms in the air in a placating gesture. "Mister, would you ever forget a woman who looked like her?" he asked reasonably.

The cowboy did have a point; Colt had to give him that. He didn't know how two people could have mistaken her for someone else in as many days. It wasn't as if she was common looking; he'd call her a rare jewel, certainly not a face he would ever forget.

When Colt didn't respond, the cowboy eyed Victoria again, but wisely kept his hands by his side. "Honey, I don't know what game you're playing. I know you're Delilah, and you know I know you're Delilah. I've searched this country for you for four years." He inclined his head toward the saloon. "Are you working here now? If you are, I'll be seeing you later." He gave her a sinful grin, his eyes roving over her insolently. "I've never forgotten you."

Victoria was so frightened her whole body was shaking, and she couldn't have uttered a sound if her life depended on it.

Fortunately, Colt didn't suffer the same problem. "You're mistaken. The lady said she didn't know you, so I'd suggest you walk away while you're able."

Gage's eyes moved to the pistol on Colt's hip, but it wasn't until he looked into Colt's eyes that he tagged him as a man he didn't want to tangle with. He'd lived this long by being smart enough to know when to walk away, and this was one of those times. He'd found Delilah, and that meant she lived nearby. Someone would know where she lived if it wasn't in the saloon. Either way, he'd find her again. He tipped his hat mockingly at Victoria. "I'll be seeing you, Delilah." He crossed the street in the direction of the saloon.

Victoria's eyes remained glued to Hardy's

back until he disappeared behind the doors of the saloon. Once he was out of sight she released a shaky breath. "Does that man live here?"

"Never seen him before. Must be passing through." Colt bent over to pick up the packages she'd dropped, and noticed she had a tight grip on her reticule. He remembered that derringer she had tucked in there. "Seems like everyone is confusing you with someone else," he said to ease the tension. *What was the name L. B. had called her? It wasn't Delilah. Ruby? Yeah, that was it. Ruby. And now this cowboy called her Delilah.* What were the odds that there would be two other women who looked like her? One woman being her double was hard enough to conceive, but two? Coincidence? Not a chance. He didn't believe in coincidences.

"Where's Bartholomew?" he asked, shoving his errant thoughts to the back of his mind.

Victoria wanted him to go away; she needed to think. "Bartholomew should be along any minute." She tried to pull the packages from his hands. "I can handle these, Mr. McBride." Seeing he wasn't going to relinquish her packages, she folded her hands at her waist. "Thank you for your

199

help . . . again, Mr. McBride. It seems you are always rescuing me."

"Colt, remember?" She was flustered, no doubt about it.

"Please don't let me keep you. I know you have things to do." Her eyes shot toward the saloon. "I will wait right here for Bartholomew."

Colt didn't know if she was implying she'd seen him about to enter the saloon, or if she was simply trying to get rid of him. Either way, it riled him.

Bartholomew chattered all the way back to the farm, but Victoria hardly heard a word he said. She was thinking about what she should do about Gage Hardy. That was another prayer that had gone unanswered. God wouldn't even take a cruel man like Hardy from her life. It was almost too much to comprehend that he had turned up in Promise. She had recognized him, all right. She didn't even have to see his face to know it was him. That voice had been in her nightmares for four years. He was a man she would never forget. How could she? She'd never felt fear like she did that night four years ago, a mind-numbing fear so palpable she could taste it today. He would have raped her in that Abilene brothel had the bartender not come to her aid. At times, it seemed like a lifetime had passed, but the memories hadn't faded; they were as clear as the night Hardy stumbled into her room.

The very night she was attacked by Hardy, she had grabbed the boys and left Abilene for good. It never occurred to her that anyone would even bother to look for her. Certainly not Gage Hardy, or her own mother, Ruby. She'd covered a lot of miles and suffered unimaginable hardships since that night in the Lucky Slipper, trying to get as far away as possible, physically if not mentally. It seemed she had lived in fear most of her life, but when she took the boys and lit out with no destination in mind, it was no longer a matter of being afraid just for herself. She hadn't taken the time to consider the consequences of stealing the boys. Even if she had, she wouldn't have changed a thing. Knowing they were destined for an orphanage, she'd had no other option than to take them with her when she left Abilene. Their mother, Kitten, hadn't wanted them any more than her mother had wanted her. At least she was old enough that she could earn her keep by sewing and cooking. The boys were too young to be anything but a burden to Kitten, and she would have sent them away without an ounce of remorse. Kitten and Ruby didn't have it in them to show kindness, much less the loving affection of a mother. She couldn't imagine those two precious boys growing up without knowing there was one person in the world who loved them.

Hardy's words played in her mind. *I've been searching the country for you.* She had prayed the years would change her appearance enough so that no one would ever recognize her. Just one more prayer that went unanswered. It would be a blessing if Colt was right, and Gage Hardy was just passing through Promise. If she was lucky she wouldn't have to face him again. Problem was, she'd never considered herself particularly lucky, and now that something good had happened for her and the boys, she was sure something bad was about to happen. That was the way her life had always worked.

By the time Bartholomew pulled the team to a halt at the farm, Victoria had come to the decision that Hardy wouldn't force her to run. After all, she was a respectable landowner now and she could go to the sheriff and force him to take action if Hardy continued to harass her. She was determined no one would drive her from her home — not the ranchers who wanted her land, and certainly not some drifter no-account cowboy like Gage Hardy. Terrified as she was of him, she was no longer a helpless child. She had protected herself and the boys for a long time now and would continue to do so. She would never run again, even if she had to kill Gage Hardy.

That decision made, her mind drifted to Colt McBride. He was obviously headed into the saloon when he saw her. No doubt he would have a conversation with Hardy before the night was over and hear the sordid details of her life. That is, if those women from the saloon, Maddie and Lucy, didn't have other plans for him.

CHAPTER SIXTEEN

Wrapping his fingers around Lucy's arm, Colt ushered her to the far end of the bar, where they would have some privacy for their conversation.

"What was that about yesterday?" he snapped.

Sliding her hands over the front of his shirt, Lucy batted her eyelashes at him. "Well, hello to you too, handsome. Whatever do you mean, darlin'?"

Jerking her hands from his chest, he held her firmly by the wrists. "You know darn well what I'm talking about."

She tried to pull away, but he held her in his viselike grip. "Did your girl get mad?" she asked in a spiteful tone.

He released her before he did something he would regret. "You pull a stunt like that again and I will have a talk with L. B."

"Go ahead, tell her. I make that old woman a lot of money. She won't fire me for talking to a paying customer."

"I don't think she would like you being rude to customers on the sidewalk," Colt said firmly. "So if there is a next time, mark my words, I'll see L. B."

"See L. B. about what?" L. B. said from behind him. She'd seen Colt when he stalked into the saloon with murder in his eye, heading directly for Lucy. The look on his face told her he was loaded for bear about something. She wondered if Lucy had caused trouble between Maddie and Colt, since he hadn't been in the saloon in a long time.

Lucy glared at Colt, and in turn he arched a brow at her. "Do you want to discuss this with L. B.?"

Lucy smirked. "No need, nothing to discuss." She flipped around and strolled down the bar to cuddle up to a cowboy.

L. B. watched her go. "What was that all about, Colt?"

"We just had a disagreement, nothing to worry about." He motioned for Sam to pour them a drink.

L. B. cast him a skeptical look. "That gal can be trouble, I'll tell you. But the men drink double when she's around. She's in high demand."

Sam poured two whiskeys, and Colt

downed his and nodded for a refill. "Isn't she too young for this business?"

L. B. chuckled and tipped the glass to her lips, gulping back her whiskey. "Colt, I learned a long time ago not to ask a fool question like that. Most times they lie to you about their age anyway. The younger ones say they're older, and the older gals say they're younger so you'll think they have some good years left." She glanced around the room at the women hustling the cowboys for drinks and tips. "Once the cowboys have enough to drink, it makes no difference anyway. They all look the same through whiskey-colored eyes."

Colt gave her a measuring look. He could understand her low opinion of men. "I guess I can see your point."

She glanced back at him. "I know you've offered to help some of the gals get out of this business." Before he could make a comment, she held up her hand to silence him. "I admire that about you, Colt. You don't have to defend yourself to me. As a God-fearing man, I know you're trying to do what your conscience tells you." She picked up the bottle and poured them both another drink. After draining her glass in one gulp, she continued. "But let me tell you, it's the younger ones who take to this business like a cowboy takes to the saddle. They think they hold the power. Even when they've been smacked around by some no-account cowboy, they know he'll still come back." She paused, staring into her empty whiskey glass as if she would find answers in the remnants of the golden liquid. "It's the older gals who want out because they know their days are numbered. Most of them don't come to a good end."

Colt absorbed that bit of insight from the woman who was certain to have seen it all and then some. "I reckon we all make our own choices," he responded.

L. B. put her glass back on the bar. "Now that is a fact."

Colt looked around the room and spotted the drifter, Gage Hardy, playing poker. In the next moment, Maddie snuggled up beside him, curled her arm through his, and whispered, "I haven't seen you in here for quite some time."

"I've been busy," he replied. He thought about asking her to have the cook rustle up some steaks so he could talk to her over dinner. But after his encounter with Lucy, he wasn't in the mood for more talking. He needed a few hours' reprieve from the worries of the ranch, the eventual range war, and thoughts of Victoria. It had been his plan to spend some time with Maddie, but when he looked at her made-up face, his mind conjured up another beautiful woman. *What is wrong with me?* He took a sip of his whiskey and glanced at the table where Hardy was seated. "I think I'll play a few hands of poker." He extricated his arm from Maddie, grabbed the bottle, and walked to Hardy's table. "Mind if I join the game?"

Gage Hardy looked up to see the man who had interfered when he was outside with Delilah. He thought this cowboy might know where she was living. "As long as you have money to lose," Hardy replied in a friendly tone. "My luck seems to be running good tonight."

Colt stuck out his hand. "Colt McBride. Mr. Hardy, right?"

"That's right." Hardy accepted the proffered hand.

Colt held the bottle over Hardy's glass. "No hard feelings, I hope."

Hardy nodded and Colt poured. "No hard feelings, but I don't care what she is calling herself now, she *is* Delilah."

"Well, that's neither here nor there. Let's play poker." Colt put his bills in the center of the table.

"Do you know where she lives?" Hardy found himself asking too quickly.

"Actually, I've just met the lady in passing. Can't say I know much about her at all," Colt hedged.

Neither man mentioned Victoria or Delilah again. They played poker while Colt provided the whiskey.

Hardy easily consumed every glass that Colt poured. The more he drank the more talkative he became, and the more money he lost to Colt. After two hours the conversation finally got around to Victoria, but Hardy continued to call her Delilah. Fortunately, no one else at the table had the slightest notion who he was talking about.

"I'm telling you that was Delilah. She might have been a young little thing back in Abilene, but she was a looker even then." He was slurring his words, but Colt had no problem understanding him.

"You say she worked in a saloon?" Colt prompted, filling his glass to the brim.

"The Lucky Slipper. She was the prettiest gal I ever laid eyes on."

Colt clenched his fist, wanting more than anything to give the guy an uppercut that would land him in the next town without teeth, just for the way he looked when he talked about her. "Wouldn't she have been pretty young to work in a saloon?" He fairly barked the question, causing the other men at the table to pause in their card playing to see if they needed to back away from the table.

Hardy had consumed so much whiskey he didn't see the dangerous glint in Colt's eyes. "Yeah, she was young, but I like 'em like that anyways."

"You say that was four years ago?" Colt picked up the last card dealt to him and threw some bills on the table, trying to show interest in the hand when he couldn't have said what cards he held. "I'll raise."

Throwing his cards to the table, Hardy leaned toward Colt and lowered his voice. "I walked into the wrong room. Best mistake I ever made." His eyes took on a faraway look. "That's when I saw her. She was . . . in a tub . . . she was so beautiful . . . sitting there in the water. I forgot all about . . ." His words trailed off, his mind going back to that night four years ago. He leaned back in his chair and rubbed his whiskered face with both hands. He'd replayed the events of that night in his mind thousands of times over the years. He had been drunk that night, but not so drunk that he didn't remember most of what happened before the bartender knocked him out.

He'd seen Delilah several times in the kitchen of the Lucky Slipper, but he'd never been able to talk to her. One night he asked Ruby who she was and she told him Delilah had been a surprise that she hadn't gotten rid of in time. Ruby bragged to anyone who would listen that Delilah was going to be her ticket out of Abilene; she was planning on selling her to the most exclusive gentlemen's club in San Francisco. Ruby was a fine-looking woman in her day, but she didn't have a decent bone in her body. He always thought she hated her own daughter because she was more beautiful, and her own beauty was fading.

Kitten told him that night that she was leaving Abilene the next day with Ruby. They were headed to San Francisco, and he figured they meant to take Delilah with them. When he walked into her room it was like fate smiled on him. After all this time he couldn't shake thoughts of her; she'd become his obsession. Every man who laid eyes on Delilah knew there was something special about her. She was all wide-eyed innocence, the kind of face men dreamed about.

Watching Hardy's eyes take on a glazed appearance, Colt knew the man was lost in his own thoughts, blocking out everything but his memories.

Colt had never wanted to hit a man so

badly; sheer willpower kept him pinned to his seat. Throwing his cards down with such force they skittered across the table, he grabbed the bottle instead of Hardy's throat, and poured himself a generous portion. He had a bad feeling the man was telling the truth, or at least the truth as he thought it to be. Hardy was convinced Victoria was Delilah. As fixated as he was on the woman, it wasn't likely he wouldn't recognize her. Was Victoria truly this Delilah? It made no difference to Colt if he was telling the truth or not; he wanted to punch him anyway. At least he wanted to beat the memories of Victoria-Delilah from his brain.

Moments ticked by before Hardy started talking again, telling the end of his story. "The bartender cracked my skull with the butt of a shotgun. Next thing I know I'm in the middle of the street with one heck of a headache. The Lucky Slipper was on fire."

"On fire?" Colt repeated. He wasn't sure he'd heard correctly, since his mind was numb after hearing Hardy had obviously tried to take advantage of a young girl. Thank goodness for that bartender.

"Yeah, the saloon burned to the ground that night." Hardy leaned back in his chair and whispered, "That was the last time I saw her. Until tonight. I thought she might have died in that fire. But she's been right here waiting for me."

Colt didn't comment because Maddie leaned over his shoulder. "Are you winning, honey?"

"A few hands," he replied.

"Would you like me to get you a steak?" she asked, trying to keep him in the saloon as long as possible.

"No, thanks. I'm getting ready to call it a night." His mind was still chewing on the story Hardy told him, and he couldn't summon up the interest to spend time with her. He knew she wanted him to stay, and he wondered if she needed money since he hadn't been around for a while. She didn't make any tips off his table tonight because Colt had poured the drinks, trying to get Hardy loosened up and talking. When he stood and stuffed his winnings in his pocket, he discreetly passed a handful of bills to her.

"You don't have to give me this, Colt. I didn't earn it." She tried to put the bills back in his hand.

He leaned down and whispered, "Yes, I do."

She watched as he walked out the swinging doors. Something had changed between them, but she didn't know what or why.

CHAPTER SEVENTEEN

Judd Detrick from the Cross Bar D ranch was walking into the saloon as Colt exited. "What are your men doing on my range, Colt?"

"We're just rounding up strays, nothing unusual about that. And it's open range," Colt reminded him as he released Razor's reins from the post.

"Your men are crossing my land to get there. My men will round up any strays and bring them to you. We're finding enough dead cattle without letting cowboys ride to and fro as they please."

Colt clamped his teeth together, swallowing what he really wanted to say. "What's this really about, Judd? We've never had a problem before."

"That was before. Now I've got enough problems, and until I find out who's rustling my cattle, and sending squatters, no one is coming on my land that don't work for me.

I've burned out three squatters just this week."

Colt stared him in the eye, forcing himself to keep his temper under control. "As I said, it's open range. I'm dealing with rustlers same as you. We never once had a problem until Wallace showed up, and we don't need to be fighting each other now. That's playing right into his hands."

"We don't know if Wallace is behind this," Detrick countered.

"Let's call it a strange coincidence then," Colt replied, grim faced. Detrick wasn't the kind of man who made friends, but they had always been able to work out any differences in the past in a peaceable manner. "I'll be speaking to the judge when he gets here, let him know what's been going on with the sheriff. Maybe he knows something about Wallace that we don't. At least he'll be aware we're having trouble."

"Judge Ross?" Detrick snorted. "I guess you haven't heard then."

Colt pushed his Stetson back on his head. "Heard what?"

"Ross was ambushed on the trail into town. A couple of my boys found him dead last night. Shot in the back."

Colt rubbed his hands over his face. "Aw hell." He hated to hear that news. He'd always been fond of Judge Ross. Last time he was in town, Colt invited him to the ranch for dinner. The Judge told him he was planning on retiring in a year, moving back to Texas and teaching law to one of his nephews.

Detrick walked into the saloon without further comment, and Colt stood with his arm braced on a post, thinking over everything that had taken place since Wallace came to town. Nope, not a chance in hell it was a coincidence.

He was so preoccupied thinking about the Judge being ambushed that when he drew Razor to a halt at the front porch of the Barlow farm, he surprised himself. Obviously Miss Victoria Eastman had also been on his mind. After listening to Hardy's story, he wasn't sure what he believed about her. But, Delilah or Victoria, the gal sure had a storehouse full of secrets.

He barely made it out of the saddle before Bandit began barking from the other side of the door. He rapped soundly on the door, though he doubted Victoria could hear him above the dog's raucous yelping.

"Who is it?"

"Colt McBride." He envisioned her with that derringer aimed at the door. That

216

thought made him smile.

The door cracked open a few inches. "Mr. McBride, what are you doing here?"

Colt eyed her through the opening as Bandit tried to inch his nose through to sniff Colt's leg. "I thought I would stop by and make sure everything's okay."

"Oh . . . everything is fine," she answered cautiously. Bandit wedged his nose through the small crack and Colt caught a glimpse of her clutching her robe together with one hand while trying to keep a firm hold on the door with the other. Bandit had other ideas; he managed to poke his head through the opening, forcing Victoria to release her grip on the door. The dog jumped on Colt like he'd hadn't seen him in months. Colt squatted down to rub his ears. "You smell a mite better than the first time I saw you." He glanced up at Victoria. "The dog, not you."

She pressed her lips tightly together in an effort not to smile, but she failed. She liked the way he treated Bandit, and the dog clearly adored him. Surely if Bandit trusted him she shouldn't be afraid of him. "I scrubbed him down earlier. I have to bathe him nearly every day since he's always getting into something. Generally it's water and mud."

"Where's Bartholomew?"

"He went back to his own cabin."

After a few minutes of lavishing attention on Bandit, Colt stood and discreetly eyed her apparel. Under that yellow robe she was holding in a death grip, he saw a hint of white nightgown touching the floor underneath. "Do you think you could offer a neighbor a cup of coffee?"

Smelling whiskey on him made her clutch her robe tighter. "Umm . . . well, I just had a bath and I'm afraid I'm not dressed for company."

He knew he made her nervous, but if she was determined to stay in Promise she needed to find out who she could trust. He stepped over the threshold. "Bartholomew told you we don't stand on ceremony out here. You look fine to me." *Did she ever.* Her robe was some sort of silky fabric, the kind of thing a man just wanted to touch. Even though she had a gown on underneath, both garments were clinging to her in all the right places.

Looming over her like he was made her feel claustrophobic. He was too tall . . . too muscled . . . too . . . everything. And she definitely smelled whiskey. She stepped back. *He was headed to the saloon when I last saw him. Why had he left so early? And why is he really here? Had he talked to Hardy?*

Colt had the feeling she thought he was ready to jump on her, and she couldn't make up her mind whether to push him out the door or run. She was right about one thing: He wouldn't mind jumping on her because she smelled so good, like flowers on a spring day. He hadn't been the least bit interested in Maddie tonight, but one look at this woman and his mind started going down roads that he shouldn't travel. He removed his hat and gave her what he hoped was a friendly smile. "I won't bite." *Not hard anyway.*

Her eyes flashed up to his and he grinned at her. That grin. That was the second time he'd grinned at her like that, and just like the first time, it was disarming. His smile totally transformed his face and he didn't seem nearly as threatening. She could just imagine ladies falling into a puddle at his feet when he grinned at them. Definitely Lucifer himself. She told herself to relax, he didn't appear drunk, and he'd proven himself to be a man she could trust. So far. Although she hadn't been around him when he'd been drinking, she reminded herself. Earlier tonight she made a vow to overcome her fears, so there was no time like the present to stop acting like a simpering fool.

"There's some coffee left over from supper. It's still on the stove."

When she turned and headed for the kitchen, Colt closed the door and followed behind with Bandit on his heels. He tried to take his mind off how good she smelled. He managed to do that, but then he focused on her hair cascading down her back past her hips. *Aw hell. So much for good intentions.*

Stopping at the doorway of the kitchen, he leaned against the doorjamb and looked around the room. He spied the tub in the corner still filled with soapy water. "Were you finished with your bath?" The devil in him was saying *Please say no, I promise not to look.*

Victoria reached for two cups. "I was just finishing when I heard your knock."

Tossing his Stetson on the table, he moved to the tub and hoisted it in the air. "Would you open the door?"

She turned to see him holding the tub of water like it weighed nothing at all. It was all she could do to wrestle the thing off the hook on the back porch when it was empty. She hurried to the door. "Thank you so much, Mr. McBride. I knew I would spill half of the water trying to drag it to the door."

"Colt," he reminded her.

After tossing the water out, he came back into the kitchen and took a seat at the table. He noticed some papers on the table, and he thought it looked like someone had been drawing, so he picked them up to see what they were. They were beautiful drawings of various kinds of flowers and birds. One drawing looked like the roses at the side of his house. It had been his mother's favorite flower, and Helen had saved them when the old home burned down and planted them at his new home. "Did you draw these?"

"Yes." She saw the drawing he held in his hand. "I saw those roses at your house."

"It was my mother's favorite," he said. "These are really good." Actually, better than good, he thought.

"Thank you. Cream, sugar?" she asked.

I'd like some sugar. "Black." Forcing his eyes and his mind away from her night-clothes, he turned his attention to the kitchen. He'd been in Chet's kitchen before, but he didn't remember it feeling so comfortable. Like her, the room smelled delicious with the aroma of cooked apples lingering in the air. She'd added feminine touches that made the room more inviting. There were flowers in the center of the table and on the windowsill. Pretty white curtains with yellow daisies hung in the window. A colorful needlepoint hung on the wall with the words *God Bless Our Home* beautifully stitched. She'd placed a pallet for Bandit beside the stove where he now rested on his back with his legs in the air, her tattered blue hat underneath his head. He even had his own food and water bowls. He figured a man could be as content as her dog, and she'd probably have him following her around, lapping at her heels just like Bandit. Lucky dog.

"It smells good in here," he commented.

"I baked an apple pie. Would you like a slice?"

He was making headway; she'd offered him pie without looking like he was sending her to the hangman's noose. He gave her that heart-stopping grin again. "That sounds great. I didn't have dinner."

"Then let me fix you a sandwich," she offered. If he hadn't eaten dinner she knew he must be starving; she'd seen how much food he could consume. It was the least she could do for him after the kindness he'd extended her since she arrived in Promise.

"Don't go to any trouble." He hoped she knew he was just being polite. He wanted to stay right where he was for as long as possible.

"No trouble." Within minutes Victoria

placed a plate holding two large sandwiches in front of him along with a steaming cup of coffee.

"Thanks." Polishing off one sandwich quickly, he said, "I must have been hungrier than I thought." After finishing the second, Victoria gave him a huge slice of pie and refilled his coffee before she took a seat across from him. Nervously, she fiddled with the buttons at her neck, making sure she was buttoned up over every square inch of skin.

Colt watched her run her fingers over the buttons as if she feared one might pop open while she was sitting still. He really wanted to ask about Gage Hardy. Was she running from Hardy, or someone else? Was that the reason she was looking for a husband so far from St. Louis? He didn't think she would trust him enough to tell him. Hardy was convinced Victoria was Delilah, and if he was right, and he'd tried to rape her, he could understand her fear of men. At the same time, she had obviously overcome her fear at some point since she did have two children. That circled him back to the notion that maybe she was on the run from an abusive man. Could she be running from the father of her boys? With men like Hardy lurking about, he really didn't want her staying alone with no protection. He had two men riding her property at night, but if something happened at the house, they might not be able to get there on time.

"Why don't you have Bartholomew move in here with you for a few weeks?"

Logically she told herself that Bartholomew was not a threat, but she didn't want any man living in the same house. "That wouldn't be proper for an unmarried woman to live in a house with a man. What would everyone think?"

"Nobody would think anything about Bartholomew living here, because he's an old man. Besides, there's been some trouble around here, and I'm worried things might get worse. I'd rest easier knowing you had someone close in case trouble comes calling."

"Is this about the land?"

"Yes." He hesitated before he added, "If things don't settle down there's going to be a range war."

"Range war?"

He didn't want to frighten her any more than she already was, yet he wanted her to be aware of what was happening around her. He wouldn't be helping her by keeping her in the dark. "Some of the ranchers are hiring gunslingers instead of cowpunchers.

The other ranchers will be forced to defend what's theirs when trouble starts."

She found the courage to ask, "Are you one of the ranchers who want this farm?"

"Every rancher around wants this land because of the water," he told her honestly. "I'm no different. But if you don't want to sell, I wouldn't force you."

"How could anyone force me to sell if I didn't want to?"

"The Taggart ranch was sold for taxes after Ken Taggart was found dead," he told her honestly. "Wallace bought the place."

"But doesn't that mean he got it legally?"

"It would have been legal, if other ranchers had been informed of the sale. Taggart had no family to contest the sale, and then there's the fact that the banker and Wallace have a *special arrangement.* He was the only one who knew about the sale."

"You think Mr. Wallace is behind all of the trouble?"

Colt gave her a steady look. "We didn't have problems before he came here. It seems likely. He's made no secret he wants as much land as he can get."

She left the table and grabbed the coffeepot to refill his cup. "Does the sheriff suspect Mr. Wallace?"

"Let's just say Sheriff Parker is on Wallace's payroll."

Victoria didn't like the sound of that. Was she bringing the boys to a place where they wouldn't be safe? "What do you mean?"

Colt finished his pie and put his fork down. "Just before Wallace bought the Taggart place, the previous sheriff was killed. Wallace gave Seth Parker a recommendation, said he'd known him for several years, and no one had reason to be suspicious of him at that time. It wasn't long after that when the ranchers started having problems with rustlers and with cattle being shot. Parker has done nothing to find the culprits. Things have escalated, like the fire the other night. To make matters worse, I had planned on talking to the territorial judge about what's been happening, but I just found out he was killed on his way into town. Shot in the back."

"Has Mr. Wallace had any problems on his land?"

Leaning back in his chair, Colt stretched his long legs in front of him. "He says he has. Nobody but his own men can vouch for that."

"Couldn't it be coincidence that these things happened after he came here?"

It was a long moment before he responded. Gage Hardy's words flashed

226

through his mind. He said he knew Delilah from Abilene. He remembered Wallace mentioning a ranch he owned in Abilene. Seth Parker had been in Abilene. *Interesting. Coincidence?* Colt gave her a long look with those coal-black eyes. "I can't say I've ever believed in coincidences."

A moment later he stood and reached for his hat. "I think you should let me get Bartholomew."

"There's no need, I'll be fine with Bandit. He lets me know when someone is coming." She stood and led the way to the front door with Bandit trotting beside her.

Colt made a detour to the fireplace, where he spotted a rifle resting on a rack. It was so high off the ground that if she needed a gun in a hurry she wouldn't be able to reach it. He pulled it down and checked to make sure it was loaded. "Do you know how to handle a rifle?"

"I've never used one."

He gave her a quick lesson in the basics. "Keep it by the door in case you need it. But don't let a man get too close or he'll more than likely take it from you." He placed the rifle to the side of the front door and turned toward her. One side of his mouth tilted in a grin. "It's sure to do more damage than that derringer."

Her blue eyes widened. So he had felt the derringer in her reticule that day. "But I know how to use that," she retorted.

Colt chuckled. "You sure you aren't afraid to stay here alone?"

"I'll be fine." She felt anything but certain, but she managed to give him a reassuring smile all the same.

He looked into her eyes before he took a step closer. He was crowding her again and he wasn't sure of the reason. To her credit, she didn't step back this time. He expected his next move was going to shock her to her toes. Picking up a long curl dangling over her shoulder, he wrapped it around his long forefinger and tugged her closer to him. He leaned to her ear and whispered, "You can trust me, Victoria. If you ever need anything, all you have to do is let me know."

Her heart felt like it might pound right through her chest. The man had an uncanny way of moving too close for comfort, and those piercing eyes of his seemed to worm their way into her thoughts. She pulled her hair from his finger and turned to open the door. "Thank you," she stammered. Her nerves were so frazzled she was surprised she managed to say a word.

Colt leaned down to give Bandit a good-bye rub. "Take care of her, boy."

CHAPTER EIGHTEEN

With some maneuvering Victoria managed to position herself between Bandit and the front door. She knew by the dog's low growl that it wasn't Colt knocking hard enough to chip wood. Cracking the door open a few inches, she was surprised to see it was Euan Wallace standing on her front porch. "Mr. Wallace, what are you doing here so early this morning?"

Wallace took his hat off and bowed politely, but kept a wary eye on the dog she was holding by the scruff. "Miss Eastman, I've come to invite you to the church picnic this afternoon."

She had never been to a social event in her life, and she hardly knew what to say. Even though Colt's suspicions about Wallace had been on her mind all night, she couldn't find any reason to rebuff him. The immaculately dressed man on her porch, who was so obviously afraid of her dog, appeared perfectly harmless. Actually he was not nearly as threatening as Colt McBride with his powerful form, wearing that pistol that was as much a part of him as his Stetson. Still, she was reluctant to accept his offer. "That is kind of you, but I have so much work to do here," she responded loudly, trying to be heard above Bandit's growling.

"I'm embarrassed to say I had forgotten all about the picnic, or I would have asked you when we met. Surely you can spend a few hours at a picnic since you must eat dinner. This will be the perfect occasion for you to meet your new neighbors." Wallace glanced down at Bandit again, hoping she had a good hold on the vicious animal. He would have to take care of that dog.

Victoria did want to get acquainted with her neighbors and become a part of the community. She wanted the boys to belong here, make friends that they would have all of their lives. Her only hesitation was the ride into town alone with Wallace.

Seeing her hesitation, Wallace added, "You won't have to do one thing. I'll have my cook prepare the dinner and I will pick you up later."

"I'm sure Bartholomew will be attending and we could meet you in town," she said, not at all sure Bartholomew planned on going to the picnic, but she knew he wouldn't object taking her.

Wallace waved away her suggestion. "Nonsense, I shall be more than delighted to pick you up. If Bartholomew would like to ride into town with us, he is more than welcome." He intended to pick her up in his buggy and not a buckboard, ensuring there would be no room for another passenger.

Relieved that Bartholomew would be welcome helped her make the decision. "Thank you. In that case, it would be our pleasure to join you. Tell your cook I will bake a pie."

"Delightful." Wallace made another polite bow before settling his hat back on his head. "I will see you in a few hours. Good day."

"Are you two going to the picnic?" Tate asked Colt and T. J. as they rode back to the stable.

"I'm going," T. J. responded.

Both of them looked at Colt. They had been unsuccessful engaging him in conversation all day; his mind was obviously elsewhere. His dark mood was understandable considering they'd just found thirty head of cattle slaughtered on the range.

Only half listening to their conversation,

231

Colt realized they were awaiting his response. "I had forgotten all about it."

"I wouldn't miss it. Since I came home early last night, I reckon I can take a couple of hours for some dancing. About ten of the men can go, but the rest will be working." T. J. glanced back at Colt. "I thought you might have asked Victoria to go?"

Hearing Victoria's name, Colt's mind drifted back to how luscious she had looked last night in that yellow robe. If he had remembered the picnic last night, he would have invited her. Any man would be proud to have her on his arm and show her off. "No, I didn't. Maybe we'll stop on the way to see if she wants to go."

"You do that and you'll get your ears boxed. No woman would be ready on the spur of the moment to go to a shindig like that."

"She doesn't need to do anything to look beautiful," Tate added.

Colt and T. J. looked at the young man, both surprised at his insight. "Are you going, Tate?" Colt asked.

"Heck yeah, he's going. We've been working on his dance steps for weeks so he can ask Alice Detrick to dance," T. J. said. "Now mind you, he still can't hold a candle to me, but he'll do okay."

"You just wait, I bet more of the ladies will want to dance with me," Tate countered.

Colt smiled at their teasing. Having Tate around always lightened his mood. At sixteen he hadn't outgrown his boyish charm. *Sixteen.* His smile faded when he thought about Tate's age. He remembered what he was like at that age. Now that he thought about it, he had noticed Tate talking to Alice after church every week. Had something been developing there and he hadn't paid attention? Tate was of an age when his urges could get the best of him. He figured it was up to him to give him some fatherly advice. "Make sure all you do with Alice Detrick is dance. Stay away from the sparkin' corner. I don't want to give old man Detrick anything else to complain about. I've seen how he keeps a close eye on his girls. And let's pray Alice is not as wild as her older sister."

"Amen to that," T. J. joked. "And remember, young Tate, God is watching that corner."

Tate's face turned red as a beet. "How'd you two know about . . ." He realized he'd just admitted he knew about the little cubbyhole behind the church where the fellows took their gals to steal a kiss.

Colt and Tate laughed at him. "As hard as

this is for you to believe, T. J. and I were young once," Colt told him. "The picnic will be over by the time we get cleaned up and ride to town."

T. J. leaned over and smacked him on the back. "Just in time for the dancing to start! Since you don't seem particularly interested, I will show Victoria why the ladies prefer me for a dancing partner."

Colt ignored his comment about his lack of interest in Victoria. "Wallace and his men are sure to be there."

"Our men will be ready," T. J. told him. "I've already told them not to get drunk."

Colt nodded. "It won't take much to get a fight started. Old man Detrick and I had words last night."

They dismounted at the stable and started removing their gear. T. J. glanced over the back of his horse at Colt. "You don't think Detrick and Wallace would join forces, do you?"

"I hope not. We've got enough trouble as it is." Colt had considered the same thing last night after he talked with Detrick. If Detrick linked up with Wallace and started a range war, he wouldn't have a snowball's chance in Hades of handling that much firepower.

"Wallace has twice the men he needs to

run that ranch. We all know he's hired every man who comes along, just for their guns," T. J. said.

"Yeah." Colt thought about what Detrick said about squatters. "Tomorrow we need to ride out to some of those line cabins to make sure we don't have any squatters. Detrick mentioned squatters on his land."

"I ran into squatters living in that shack at the far end of the western side. I told them to be out by tomorrow morning or we'd burn them out. Your pa burned out his fair share over the years, but it's not something he enjoyed having to deal with."

"I'll do whatever it takes to protect my ranch. Any man who's willing to put in a good day's work will always have a job with me, but no man takes from me what he hasn't worked for, or that I haven't freely given," Colt stated firmly.

There was no doubt in T. J.'s mind that Colt would protect what was his. He'd worked for old man McBride and admired him for what he'd done with the ranch. In truth, Colt drove himself hard making the ranch more successful than it had been under the elder McBride. Colt worked side by side with the men and he worked harder than any of them. He'd proven himself to be a good businessman, and to T. J.'s thinking he was one heck of a lot tougher than his old man. He'd seen Colt in action with his fists and his guns. A wise man didn't take him lightly. There wasn't a man on the ranch who didn't hold him in high regard, because he'd earned their respect. Those same men would follow him straight to the gates of Hell if need be. Wallace had gotten word out that he'd pay higher wages than Colt paid, but every man stayed with Colt. They thought that much of him.

"Would you look at that," T. J. commented when they reined in at the church.

"I can't believe she is here with him," Tate grumbled, sounding disappointed.

Colt glanced up and saw Wallace standing beside Victoria, talking with the pastor and his wife. "He works fast," Colt ground out.

Bartholomew was standing near the rail and heard Colt's comment. "You can say that again. He came by this morning asking Miss Victoria to the picnic. He told her I could ride along with them. Wouldn't you know when that cagey no-account shows up, he's in that little buggy of his. Weren't no room for me in that thing, so I took the buckboard and rode along behind them to make sure he kept his hands to himself."

They laughed, and Colt asked, "So you

were playing chaperone?"

Bartholomew nodded. "Yes sir, I held my scattergun in my lap the whole time, just hoping he would do something improper."

"We stopped to see if she wanted to go with us," Tate told him.

"You youngsters were just too dang late! The picnic was over a long time ago."

"We just wanted to dance anyway," T. J. added.

Victoria was talking to the schoolteacher when the music started, and T. J. approached. "Could I have this dance, Miss Victoria?"

Wallace had excused himself, saying he had business to see to, so she didn't feel it was necessary to wait for him. She allowed T. J. to escort her to the dance floor. After the first dance with T. J., she danced with Rex, and then T. J. appeared again for the next two dances. As he twirled her around the room, she spotted Colt out of the corner of her eye talking with a lovely woman she hadn't met. Each time she glanced in their direction, the woman had her hand on Colt's arm. It didn't seem like Mr. McBride lacked female attention, judging by the way women flocked around him. She noticed his Stetson was absent, but not his gun. He did look boyishly handsome with that black curly hair falling over his forehead. As if he read her thoughts, she watched him rake his fingers through his hair.

When they rode by Victoria's and found no one home, Colt had had a feeling she might be with Wallace. Seeing her beside Wallace at the dance with his hand on her back, he decided then and there that he was through wasting his breath. If she preferred Wallace, then so be it. He'd spent way too much time thinking about her as it was, but no more. He needed to be thinking about ranch business, and that was what he was going to do from now on. He'd still have his men keep an eye on things at her farm. Any good neighbor would do that, he reasoned.

He'd keep his distance from her tonight, and seeing as how several women were already surrounding him, that wouldn't be difficult to do. Mavis Connelly, a lovely young widow with three young children, was one of the ladies vying for his attention. He'd escorted Mavis to dinner and other social events over the years, and he liked her, but the relationship had not developed past friendship. At least, not on his part.

Every so often Colt would look around to find Tate, to see if he was doing okay. He'd danced every dance with the youngest Detrick gal, and it looked like T. J. had taught him well. Just as he predicted, old man Detrick made sure his daughters were never far from his sight.

Even though he was resolved to stay away from Victoria, he'd still managed to notice every man she danced with. He knew this was T. J.'s fourth dance, and he looked like he was just warming up. It also hadn't escaped his notice how lovely she looked in the pink dress she was wearing. Not that it showed off her curves as nicely as that silky robe, but it didn't hide them either.

The dance ended, and T. J. steered Victoria in the direction of Colt and Mavis.

"T. J., you're still the best dancer around," Mavis said after the introductions had been made. She leaned into Colt's side and linked her arm through his. "I haven't been able to talk Colt into dancing tonight."

T. J. picked up the hint. "Would you like to dance with me, Mavis?"

"I'd love to, if your partner doesn't mind," Mavis replied coyly, looking directly at Victoria. She was well aware that Victoria had arrived on Euan Wallace's arm, but when he excused himself, she'd had her choice of dancing partners. She'd also noticed Colt had kept an eye on her all night. She thought she might make him jealous by accepting T. J.'s offer.

"T. J. is not my escort tonight," Victoria replied.

T. J. took Mavis's hand and led her away, and Colt was alone with the one person he promised himself he was going to avoid. When he looked at her, all he could think about was how beautiful she was. "Are you having a good time?" he asked politely.

Colt's question was pleasant enough, yet she thought he seemed distant. "Lovely. T. J. is an excellent dancer," she replied.

"What about your escort?" Colt hadn't seen Wallace dance with her. Come to think of it, he hadn't seen Wallace since shortly after he arrived. He was wondering why the man would leave her alone. "What happened to him?"

It surprised her that he knew she had arrived with Wallace. "He had business that needed his attention."

Over Victoria's shoulder, Colt saw Wallace making his way toward them. "Would you care to see if I measure up to T. J.?" he asked abruptly.

"Are you asking me to dance?" she asked, clearly surprised.

Colt took her by the hand and pulled her into his arms. "Yes." He danced away from Wallace. *So much for staying away from her.*

Victoria gave him a quizzical look. "I didn't think you were dancing tonight."

"Looks like I changed my mind." His large hand engulfed hers in a light grip, and the hand on her back spanned the space from her waist to her shoulder blades. He held her close, too close for comfort in her estimation. She made an attempt to put some space between their bodies, but the muscled arm around her back was immovable. She didn't smell whiskey tonight, just a pleasing scent of soap and leather.

Colt liked the feel of her close to him, the way her soft curves pressed against his ribs. She smelled like she had last night, sweet and feminine, and it made him think of things he promised himself he wouldn't. He lowered his mouth to her ear, and lowered his voice. "I like your hair better down, like it was last night. I bet it would look real pretty in the moonlight."

She felt the brush of his lips against her ear all the way to her toes, and she jerked her head away from his mouth. "This is the latest style," she answered, flustered.

He chuckled at that. "Men don't care about style. They like to feel it."

Before she could form a reply, he asked, "Have you decided when you are leaving for St. Louis?"

The change in conversation confused her momentarily, and she tried to concentrate on what he was saying instead of his warm breath on her ear. "I received a telegram from Mrs. Wellington today. She told me not to come, that she was due for an adventure and was bringing the boys to me. I'm not sure that is a good idea, but she sounded so excited."

"That many miles with two young boys will definitely be an adventure."

"I'll worry until I see them here safe and sound. That is a difficult trip, and Mrs. Wellington is not a young woman."

Colt pulled back far enough to see a frown crease her brow. "No sense borrowing trouble. Don't worry until you have a reason." Good advice. Now if he would follow it himself, things would be perfect in McBride's world.

"Mind if I cut in? I haven't had the pleasure of dancing with *my* date yet," Euan Wallace said.

Victoria felt Colt's shoulders tense and his grip on her hand tighten. He stopped dancing and turned to face Wallace. "Another bad decision on your part."

"I intend to make up for my failing manners." He held his hand out to Victoria.

Victoria saw Colt's jaw muscles start to

twitch, and she tried to remove her hand from his, but he was obviously not ready to release his hold. "Thank you for the dance, Mr. McBride," she said, giving her fingers a slight tug.

Colt pulled his dark eyes from Wallace and flashed her that rakish grin. "It was my pleasure, Miss Eastman." He pulled her fingers to his mouth and brushed his lips across the back of her hand, imitating Wallace.

She wasn't fooled by his attempt at a cordial demeanor; that cold, hard look was back in his eyes. He kissed her hand simply to irritate Wallace, and she was equally sure Wallace was aware of his intent. She had no reason to share Colt's opinion of Wallace, and tonight he'd been a polite companion on the way to town. Of course, it was comforting to know Bartholomew was right behind them. Since Wallace hadn't broached the subject of buying her farm again, she thought Colt was wrong about his involvement in the trouble with the ranchers. So far, the only thing that troubled her about Wallace was the fact that Bandit didn't like him.

Colt saw Tate in line to get punch and he walked in his direction. He figured it was time to go home since they had to get up early in the morning. Before he reached Tate, he saw old man Detrick approach, and from the set of his jaw, Colt knew he was angry. As soon as Detrick reached Tate, he started yelling.

"What's the problem here?" Colt asked, interrupting Detrick's tirade.

Detrick jabbed a finger at Tate. "This here boy tried to take my girl behind the church."

Colt glanced at Tate. He knew the boy wouldn't disregard his warning, so he wasn't going to insult him by asking.

Tate said, "That's not true, Mr. McBride! We just walked over here to get some punch. We've been on the dance floor all night."

"I know," Colt told him. The punch table was located next to the area where the teenagers would sneak around to the back of the church. Colt smelled whiskey, so he figured Detrick was spiking his own punch and spoiling for a fight.

"Detrick, if Tate says he was having punch, you can take his word for it," he said calmly.

"Why would I take his word for it? He's nothing but trash that was living in a wagon before you gave him a job and a home," Detrick spat. "He ain't good enough for my gal."

It didn't matter to Colt if they were on church grounds or in a saloon; nobody was going to talk about Tate that way. He grabbed Detrick by the shirt and lifted him up on his toes. "Apologize to the boy!" he demanded.

The music stopped and everyone turned their attention to the confrontation. T. J. and Colt's other men moved to Colt's side in case Detrick's men tried to get involved.

"Take your hands off me!" Detrick demanded.

"I said to apologize," Colt ground out.

Tate moved to stand beside Colt. "That's okay, Mr. McBride, he's just looking out for his daughter."

Tate was more generous than he was. "Then he ought to have the good sense to ask his daughter what was going on before jumping to conclusions. He's not only insulted you, but Alice too."

"Tate's telling the truth, Pa, we were just having some punch," Alice added in a shaky voice, clearly afraid of her father.

"I've told you to stay away from that piece of . . ." He couldn't finish his sentence. Colt slammed his fist in Detrick's jaw and sent him flying into the punch bowl, splintering the glass and table at the same time.

Detrick was lying on the ground drenched

in punch and broken glass. Colt stood over Detrick, wanting him to stand so he could beat the tar out of him. "Get up!" When Detrick didn't move, Colt leaned over and jabbed him in the chest. "Your daughter would never find a better young man than Tate. Don't ever let me hear you say another disparaging word about him, or call him a liar." With that said, he stalked off through the throng of onlookers. One man slapped him on the back and commented, "Way to go, he had it coming." Colt was heartened that the people of Promise knew what a fine boy Tate was. He couldn't have been more proud of him. He hoped one day he had a son as fine as Tate. He'd never met anyone who didn't speak highly of him. Until tonight. It had been a long time since he'd allowed anyone to make him so angry, but Detrick had managed to do so. He told himself that he hadn't exactly set a good example for Tate on how to handle a dispute, but it sure did his heart good to see Detrick dripping with punch.

T. J. put his arm around Tate's shoulders and followed Colt through the crowd.

"I've never seen Mr. McBride so mad," Tate said. "He didn't have to do that. I don't care what her pa says."

"Colt cares about you, and he takes care

of his own. Detrick insulted you and Colt wasn't about to let that go," T. J. explained.

"But won't that just cause more trouble between them?"

"That won't matter to Colt, and Detrick had it coming."

CHAPTER NINETEEN

"We took care of some more cattle today," Hoyt Nelson informed Wallace when he sat down at the poker table.

There was only one man at the table who didn't work for Wallace, but Wallace was not pleased with Hoyt's careless comment. "Let's not discuss ranch business in here."

"I was just commenting on our cattle," Hoyt snapped. He didn't like Wallace censuring him in front of the other men.

Picking up the cards in front of him, Wallace gave Hoyt a look that said he didn't appreciate any comments when he gave an order. "That may be, but I learned a long time ago it's wise to keep business private." He threw more bills to the table, making his bet. "And when I give an order, I will not tolerate anyone ignoring it."

The men around the table looked from Wallace to Hoyt. They didn't think it mattered much to Hoyt what Wallace was paying him; he wasn't a man to make angry. What they didn't know was that Hoyt had been promised a large bonus when he completed his job, so he'd put up with Wallace to a point. Hoyt stared at Wallace, debating on how much more he would take from him.

Ignoring Hoyt, Wallace looked at the stranger across the table. "I don't believe I've seen you before."

The man glanced at Wallace and figured he was the rich boss man the cowboys had been talking about. "Gage Hardy. I'm new in town."

Wallace nodded. "Euan Wallace. Where are you from?"

"I've been seeing the country," Hardy answered noncommittally.

Wallace's eyes didn't leave his cards. "Planning on staying around?"

Hardy looked at him over his cards. "Why are you interested?"

Wallace raised his bet. "Thought you might want a job."

"You hiring?" Hardy called his bet.

"Are you any good with that gun?" Wallace threw his three aces to the table.

Hardy laid down four eights. "You need to be a gunslinger to work cattle now?"

Wallace cursed at losing the hand and

threw his cards facedown. "We're having some trouble around here. I need men capable of handling a gun if necessary."

Hardy pulled his winnings to him. "How's the pay?"

"More than you'll make with any other rancher."

Hardy had listened to the conversation around the table before Wallace showed up, and he had a good idea who was behind the trouble. Since he'd found Delilah he wasn't planning on leaving anytime soon, and he wasn't one to turn down a job that fell in his lap. "I'm good enough with a gun, I reckon, and I've worked cattle all my life."

"We'll discuss the details when you show up at the ranch in the morning. Right now, let's play poker."

Hardy reached for Lucy's arm as she passed the table. "Darlin', would you bring us another bottle?"

"When you get back, Lucy, come over here and talk to me," Hoyt said.

Lucy stared at Hoyt. She didn't want him using his fist on her again. "You drunk?"

"Now, why would that make a difference?"

"You get mean when you're drunk," Lucy replied.

Face flushed, Hoyt jumped to his feet and snaked out an arm and pulled her to him.

"Look here —"

"Careful, Hoyt," L. B. warned, moving up behind him.

Wallace looked at Hoyt, silently indicating he should take a seat. "No problems here, we just ordered another bottle."

Hoyt's grip tightened on Lucy's arm. "Let's go to the bar, honey."

"Not now, Hoyt." Wallace pointed to the bills stacked where Hoyt had been sitting. "Looks like you've been lucky and the boys want to win some of their money back." He didn't want Hoyt talking too much to Lucy when he was drunk.

The men at the table chorused their agreement. "Yeah, we do."

Hoyt smiled at them. "Later."

Wallace put his hand in his vest pocket, his fingers resting on his derringer. "I think the boys want to keep playing now."

"Lucy, get them that bottle. It's on the house." L. B. pulled Lucy's arm from Hoyt's grip. "Mind if I sit in a few hands with you boys?"

Wallace nodded his approval. "I hope you aren't as lucky as normal."

L. B. chuckled, her red curls bobbing up and down. "Well now, I can't promise that."

Grudgingly, Hoyt took his seat, but his eyes followed Lucy as she made her way to the bar. He wondered if Wallace was intentionally trying to get under his skin. "I guess I'll just have to show Mr. Wallace that my luck is gonna hold all night," he boasted.

"Hoyt, I won't have anyone beatin' on my girls," L. B. told him sternly. She put her hands under the table and discreetly pulled her derringer from her sleeve and aimed it directly at Hoyt's gut.

"I was drunk, but I pay for my time. Why do you care?" That was the second time L. B. had come down on him. When his business with Wallace was finished and he got his money for doing his dirty work, he'd take care of her and Wallace. No one talked to him that way.

Lucy returned and handed the whiskey bottle to L. B. "Go on back to the bar and help Sam," L. B. instructed. As Lucy hurried to the bar, L. B. started pouring a round for the men. She held the bottle over Hoyt's glass, but she didn't pour until he looked at her. "I care what happens to my gals. No one is gonna hit on them, drunk or not." She clanked the bottle to the rim of the glass, muffling the sound as she cocked the hammer on her derringer. She wasn't taking any chances with a man like Hoyt. She knew he was just as likely to kill a woman as a man.

Wallace had told him to stop causing trouble in the saloon, so when Hoyt glanced in his direction he wasn't surprised to find him scowling. "I didn't really hurt her," he said.

L. B. filled his glass and then her own. "If you can't handle your liquor better than that, you better give it up." She pointed to the swinging doors and said, "Out there, you answer to God." She then gave the table a tap. "In here, you answer to me. I'll shoot you myself if I find out you are beating on one of my gals again."

Leaning forward, Hoyt narrowed his eyes at her. "That sure is brave talk for a woman who doesn't have a gun."

"Who says I don't have a gun," L. B. retorted.

"That little derringer you carry in your garter doesn't count as a real gun."

"I guess that depends on where it's pointed. Granted it might not kill a man, but it'll get his attention all the same."

Every man at the table wanted to laugh, but seeing the glower on Hoyt's face, they thought better of it. Gage knew that Hoyt was trying to decide if L. B. was bluffing, and understandably wasn't willing to find out. He also realized Wallace was displeased with his hired hand, and if looks could kill,

Hoyt would be carrion about now. Hoyt seemed oblivious to the look on Wallace's face, or he didn't care. Gage figured that meant Wallace had hired him for his fast gun, and whatever job he was to perform had yet to be fulfilled.

Wanting to put an end to the tension at the table before bullets started flying, Gage threw some bills down. "Are we going to play poker or just talk about it?"

"The man's right. Put your money on the table," Wallace said. The men followed Wallace's lead and started throwing bills to the center of the table. Wallace directed his gaze at Hoyt. "Hoyt, you in?"

Leaning back in his chair, Hoyt grabbed some money and added it to the pile, and glared at L. B. "This ain't over."

Releasing the hammer on her derringer, L. B. tucked her fingers in her bodice and pulled out a wad of money. "Look at it this way, Hoyt. You get to keep your . . . dignity, and play poker." She waited a beat before she added, "Today."

Two hours later, Hoyt had managed to lose all his winnings and more. His mood hadn't improved with liquor. "I don't have much left, so I guess I'll go find Lucy."

Seeing how much whiskey he had consumed, L. B. was about to tell him to leave, but Wallace beat her to it.

"Not tonight, Hoyt. You've had too much." Wallace pocketed his money and stood. "Time to go to the ranch."

Staggering to his feet, Hoyt pushed his chair back. "I ain't that drunk." He rubbed his bleary eyes, trying to focus on Wallace. He blinked, but he kept seeing three men that looked like Wallace. "I ain't ready to leave."

"That's the advantage of being the man who pays the wages. It doesn't matter what you want." Wallace glanced at the other men at the table. "Take him to the ranch where he can sleep it off."

The men rose and gave each other a look that said this was one order they didn't relish carrying out. They'd seen Hoyt draw and he was fast, real fast. He could easily outdraw them.

"Get him out of here," Wallace commanded again.

The two cowboys rushed Hoyt, pinning his arms to his sides, and carried him from the saloon.

"Do they always do what you tell them?" Hardy cut in.

Wallace gave Hardy a firm look. "They'd better. Now you come see me in the morning." He grabbed the bottle from the table and headed toward the bar.

CHAPTER TWENTY

"I'd say there's near fifty head missing." T. J. had met Colt at the house to give him the tally on the cattle lost. "Rustlers."

Colt strapped on his gun belt and grabbed his rifle resting by the front door. "Round up a couple more men. We're going to pay a visit to those squatters on the west side. They might not be responsible, but I bet they know who is behind this. Bring what we need to burn down that cabin."

T. J. had seen that look on Colt's face before, and it didn't bode well for the people on the receiving end of his anger. "If they hadn't had that woman and those two kids with them, I would have burned them out yesterday," T. J. replied.

"If they're not gone by the time we get there, it won't matter to me who's there. I've had enough." Colt stalked toward the barn to saddle his horse. It had been over two weeks since he last saw Wallace at the picnic, and every day since he'd been met with more problems. His losses were mounting, and he wasn't any closer to a solution. His men were exhausted from pulling extra duty patrolling the ranch all night for months. He needed to hire on more men, but he couldn't find anyone who wasn't already working for Wallace. Hearing the count of his losses this morning was the last straw. He was determined to put a stop to this, one way or the other. He'd danced around the situation long enough, trying to avoid a range war. But if a range war was imminent, then so be it. He was going to do everything in his power to protect what was his. If Wallace thought he was the only one who could play rough, Colt was going to show him, the hard way, how wrong he was.

Walking from the cabin, T. J. mounted his horse. "Looks like they've pulled up stakes."

Colt studied the fresh hoofprints around the cabin. "Burn the place down."

"I doubt they will be back," T. J. said.

"We don't have enough men to watch every acre, and I don't want anyone else coming along behind them. Burn it down." He watched as the men threw kerosene around the cabin and set the fire. "T. J., the men can handle this. Let's follow these tracks to make sure they're off McBride land."

While following the trail of the squatters, Colt's mind wandered in several directions. There was no question Wallace was behind all the trouble, even if some people might disagree with him. Like Victoria. It puzzled him why she trusted the man. *So much for female intuition.* He'd even considered that she might be developing feelings for Wallace since she had attended the dance with him. He hadn't seen her since that night, but he'd sent Tate over to her house several times to see if there was anything she needed, and he still had two men watching the place at night. Bartholomew made a point of stopping by the ranch to let him know Wallace had been visiting Victoria frequently, hinting that he was still courting her. Colt felt he was also indirectly suggesting he needed to do something about that. The way he saw it, Victoria was old enough to make her own decisions, and she was making them. The last time Bartholomew was over, he mentioned that Mrs. Wellington and the boys were due to arrive any day.

He told himself he hadn't intentionally avoided Victoria; his schedule at the ranch was demanding. There were barely enough hours in the day for him to sleep, so he certainly didn't have time for social calls. He hadn't even had time to go to town to see Maddie, and that was where he needed to go if he had free time. He wasn't inclined to waste time with a woman he had no intention of marrying. Sure as shootin', Victoria was the kind of woman a man would have to marry. If he got involved with her he'd be saddled with even more responsibility in the form of two growing boys. He'd been so busy he didn't even know what day it was. He looked over at T. J. "What day is it?"

Laughing, T. J. said, "Saturday."

"Huh." *Saturday.* What was it about Saturday? Seems like he remembered something was going to happen on Saturday. *Oh yeah.* Bartholomew mentioned Victoria was having dinner at Wallace's ranch tonight. Did Bartholomew say he was having dinner with them? He tried to recall the conversation, but he'd been so preoccupied at the time he was only half listening to him.

"I thought about going to town tonight," T. J. said.

Colt eyed T. J.'s dust-covered face. He had dark circles rimming his eyes and at least a week's worth of beard. He wondered if he looked as bad as his foreman. "You look like you've been on the range for a week. How

260

are you going to find the energy?"

"You plain hurt my feelings. You're not exactly lookin' your Sunday best," T. J. teasingly replied. He nudged his horse into a gallop and yelled over his shoulder, "Besides, I always have enough energy for the ladies. I can rest when I'm six feet under. I might even keep Maddie company tonight since you've given her up."

There was a time T. J.'s crack about Maddie would have rankled him. Right now, he was curious why he didn't give it a second thought. He didn't even bother to push Razor to catch up to T. J.

"Your home is lovely," Victoria said to Wallace as she and Bartholomew followed him into the dining room.

It wasn't high on Bartholomew's list to join them for dinner, but Victoria didn't want to go without him. He'd told Colt about the dinner, hoping he might find a way to intervene, or at least put a wrinkle in Wallace's plans, but no such luck. Colt was too busy with all the mischief going on around his ranch. Wallace was up to something, and he didn't have to be a genius to know what that was. Not taking anything away from Victoria, but he didn't doubt Wallace's interest in her was more about her land than her. Victoria ignored his warnings about Wallace, but he figured he'd just bide his time. Wallace was sure to show his darker side, sooner or later. He was praying for sooner.

Once they were seated at the table, Wallace placed his palm over Victoria's hand and squeezed. "It's lovely to have you at my table."

Sitting across the table from Victoria, Bartholomew rolled his eyes.

Two Mexican women carrying platters of food walked into the dining room. "I hope you like Mexican fare, my dear." He pointed a finger at the older woman. "That's the only decent food she can prepare. It's been my misfortune to have hired two women that can't seem to learn how to cook true English fare, or become skilled at the English language."

Victoria's eyes darted to the women placing the platters on the table. From the look on the older woman's face, she felt certain she understood Wallace's cruel words. Taken aback that he would be so unkind, she jerked her hand away. "Actually, I've never been particularly fond of English food." She gave the Mexican woman a smile. "I must say that this dinner looks absolutely delicious."

Bartholomew chuckled to himself. He couldn't have been prouder of Victoria if she had been his own daughter. "It sure smells delicious too," he chimed in.

The younger Mexican girl placed a platter near Wallace's elbow, and as he lifted his hand to pick up the plate, the girl flinched as if she expected him to hit her. Wallace waved her away and handed the plate to Victoria.

Victoria saw the frightened look on the girl's face, and glanced Bartholomew's way to see if he noticed. She could tell by his expression that he did.

Wallace continued talking, unaware of their questioning glances. "I lived in Texas for a few years and had my share of Mexican food there. When I moved to Abilene, I found a woman that could cook anything I desired," Wallace told them.

"You lived in Abilene?" Victoria almost choked on her food when he mentioned Abilene. She had thought he looked familiar when she first met him, but she couldn't recall ever seeing him in Abilene.

"I spent a few years there," Wallace replied. "Have you been to Abilene?"

Keeping her eyes on her plate, Victoria stammered, "Ah . . . no, but I've heard about the town." More lies. Would she ever be able to tell the truth to anyone?

Wallace reached over and patted her hand. "I thought not. It's no place for a lady like you. It's a rough, uncivilized cow town."

"That was wonderful food," Victoria said to Bartholomew once they were away from Wallace's ranch.

"Yes, ma'am, it was. Wallace should be grateful he has such a fine cook."

Victoria thought about Wallace's comment to the Mexican women. "Do you think those women understood what he said?"

"They surely did. They don't like him, so they don't want him to know they understand him."

It was the first time Victoria had seen a different side to Wallace. Perhaps she was making too much of his unkind words to the women, but it bothered her all the same. What if Mr. McBride was right and Wallace wasn't all he appeared to be on the surface? Seeing the younger girl flinch when Wallace raised his hand made her question if he was all he professed. She'd seen women at the saloon in Abilene react the same way after years of being smacked around by men. Yet it probably wasn't fair of her to jump to the conclusion that it was Wallace who hit the girl. It could have been another man.

264

Preoccupied with her thoughts, Victoria didn't notice the two men on horseback riding toward them until she saw Bartholomew pull his shotgun onto his lap. When the men drew near, she recognized one of them. Gage Hardy. Slowing his horse to a trot, Hardy tipped his hat to Victoria as he passed the buckboard. Ignoring him, Victoria gazed at the other man, and judging by the insolent grin on his face, she figured Hardy had told him about her.

Snapping the reins, Bartholomew urged the horses to a faster pace. "Do you know that cowboy that tipped his hat?"

Victoria turned and looked over her shoulder to make sure they didn't turn around and follow the buckboard. "He thinks he knows me, but he has me confused with someone else."

"I don't know him, but that other fellow is a gunslinger by the name of Hoyt Nelson. He works for Wallace. You be sure to stay away from them."

Wanting time to think, not to mention question his own sanity, Colt held Razor to a slow pace. If his life depended on it, he couldn't figure out why he was out here on the trail at this late hour, going visiting instead of getting some much needed rest.

He'd slept out on the range more than he had in his own bed for the last two weeks. But asleep or awake, Victoria continued to plague his thoughts. No matter how busy he was, he couldn't stop thinking about her . . . and Wallace.

He was so deep in thought that he was scarcely aware of his surroundings and didn't hear the sound that caught his horse's attention. It wasn't until Razor came to a complete stop that Colt realized he was near Victoria's farm. Razor turned his head toward the trees and when his ears flicked forward, Colt knew something was amiss. Attuned to Razor's habits, Colt snapped his head around in the same direction as that of his horse. He placed his hand on Razor's neck and gave him a pat to let him know he had his attention. Both were motionless as they listened. Colt scanned the darkness around them. From the trees a few yards away he heard a horse whinny. Quietly, he slipped from the saddle and led Razor to the brush. When the moon peeked from behind a cloud he caught a glimpse of the horse tied to a tree. Pulling his pistol, he moved slowly in the direction of the animal. Drawing closer, he recognized the horse as one he had seen in front of the saloon the last time he was in town. There weren't many horses that he couldn't place with their owners. He thought of the men he'd seen in the saloon that night. Then it clicked. Gage Hardy. After checking the horse and finding him sound, he searched the area for the rider. No one was about, and Colt knew the horse had intentionally been left out of view from Victoria's house. He couldn't think of a good reason Hardy would be snooping around Victoria's house in the dark.

Moving Razor a safe distance away, he tied him out of sight. Pulling his rifle from the boot, he took off at a run toward the house. He stopped in the shadows of the barn and scanned the property for any movement. It was dark and quiet. Too quiet. But he had the feeling he was being watched. What about Bandit? Why wasn't he barking? The last time he'd ridden over, he'd heard Bandit long before the house came into view. Maybe Victoria and Bartholomew hadn't arrived back from Wallace's house and Bandit was with them. It occurred to him that Hardy could be inside in the dark, waiting on Victoria.

Out of habit he checked the load in his pistol before he opened the latch on the barn door. Nosing the door open with the barrel of his rifle, he listened before moving. Hearing nothing except the usual sounds of horses in their stalls, he slipped inside. Spotting the buckboard, he knew Victoria was home. He didn't like the look of this. It made the hairs on his neck stand up, but he refused to allow his mind to go to the worst possible scenario. He prayed to God that Hardy wasn't inside the house waiting for her when she arrived.

Exiting the barn, he once again scanned the perimeter of the house. There wasn't a sound, nor a single light from the house. Still, he couldn't shake the feeling that someone was watching him. Out of the corner of his eye he thought he caught a glimpse of something white just a few yards from the front of the house. His eyes remained fixed on the spot, hoping to catch a flash of it again. Nothing. *What was it? The handle of a pistol? Maybe.* The night he played poker with Hardy he'd noticed his pearl-handled pistol. Hoyt Nelson's pistol also had a pearl handle. That was one of the reasons gunslingers usually ended up six feet under; they allowed vanity to get in the way of good sense.

In a crouch, he quietly ran to the side of the house. Ignoring his desire to rush in, he forced himself to remain patient. Inching his way slowly to the back of the house, he prayed the moon stayed behind the clouds a little longer. He waited and listened. Silence. Stepping quietly onto the back porch, he peered through the corner of the window. Nothing but darkness. He squatted beside the window as he contemplated crashing through the back door. That's when he heard a low growl. He peeked through the window again, but this time he made out two figures crouched by the stove. Victoria and Bandit. She was holding his muzzle to keep him from barking. He didn't know if they could see better than he could, but he hoped Bandit would know his voice. He moved to the door and softly called the dog's name. Within seconds he heard Bandit's nails scraping the wooden floor as he ran to the door. Suddenly the door swung open and Victoria and Bandit tumbled into his arms. Victoria was clutching the useless derringer in her shaking hand.

"Why did you open the door?" Colt whispered as he half carried the woman and dog back inside.

"I knew it was you from the way Bandit was acting," she responded softly.

"What happened?" He pulled the derringer from her fingers.

"Not long after we arrived home, Bandit started barking and jumping at the front door. I thought I saw someone at the front window, and I was afraid to open the door. It was his mean bark, so I blew out the lamp and pulled him in here to hide."

"His *mean* bark?" Colt didn't know what she was talking about.

"He barks one way at you, but another way when it is a stranger," she explained. She had first learned the difference in Bandit's bark when Wallace called on her.

Her words tumbled out of her mouth so rapidly that Colt knew she was scared to death, even if he couldn't see the fear in her eyes. "I think Gage Hardy is around here. At least, I think it's his horse tied up in the trees." He had the feeling she wasn't at all surprised that it might be Hardy snooping around.

"We passed him and another man on the way back from dinner."

Seeing her alone with Bartholomew, Colt figured Hardy thought it was an opportune time to follow her home. "You and Bandit stay put. I'll go have a look around."

She grabbed his forearm with a grip more forceful than he would have given her credit. "No, please don't leave. He's dangerous."

He stared at her a long minute, wondering if she had just told him more than she intended. He tucked her derringer in his belt and pulled his pistol from his holster. "Take this. If you shoot someone with that pea shooter it will just make them mad. This one makes a bigger hole." She took the pistol and gripped it with both hands.

"I'll be back," he said, slipping out the door. Hoping to calm her fears, he turned to her and whispered in her ear, "Don't shoot me by mistake."

As if. She wasn't even sure she knew how to use the pistol. If she was forced to shoot, she probably couldn't hit the broad side of the barn, she was shaking so badly. Shutting the door behind him, she leaned against it and held the pistol with both hands. It was much heavier than the derringer. Did she need to cock it before she pulled the trigger? She clutched it to her chest, hoping she wouldn't have to figure it out.

Circling back around to the front of the house, Colt stopped at the porch when he heard a noise coming from the direction of Hardy's horse. He checked the barn one more time before he headed back to where he'd left Razor. Hardy's horse was gone, so he rode back to Victoria's house.

Two hours later Colt was riding back to his ranch after fetching Bartholomew. He ignored Victoria's protests when he told

Bartholomew to stay with her. From now on he'd have one man bunk in her barn at night, but Bartholomew was going to be inside the house with her. He hated to leave them alone, but he needed to get back to the ranch to relieve some of his men. He couldn't expect his men to pull double duty if he wasn't willing to do the same thing. And he couldn't afford anymore dead or rustled cattle. Somehow he would make it work until Victoria's kids arrived with Mrs. Wellington. He hoped once there were more people around the farm, Hardy wouldn't be tempted to harass her.

CHAPTER TWENTY-ONE

Victoria spotted two blond heads popping out the side windows of the stagecoach before it came to a halt. Once the boys saw her, four arms were hanging out the window waving. Before the driver set the brake, the boys jumped from the coach and hurled themselves into her outstretched arms. Bartholomew assisted Mrs. Wellington from the coach, and introduced himself to her. When the boys finally released Victoria, she hugged Mrs. Wellington. She expected Mrs. Wellington to be worn out from the journey, but in truth, she had never seen the older woman looking so vibrant.

"This country is simply beautiful!" she exclaimed, fairly crushing Victoria in her excitement. "I must confess that I have been as excited as the boys! God has truly blessed me."

"Well, ma'am, we've sure been looking forward to your arrival," Bartholomew said, holding his hat in his hand.

Not a man to speak more than necessary, Victoria was surprised at Bartholomew's reaction to Mrs. Wellington. She'd noticed he was particularly well-groomed today, every strand of his usually wild white hair in place. She thought his shirt was new too, and he had even polished his boots. Amazing. When he'd asked some questions about Mrs. Wellington, she assumed it was just natural curiosity. But she was beginning to think he might have another motive for his interest. Perhaps Bartholomew was looking for a wife.

"Are we really going to live here?" Cody asked, jumping up and down.

Smiling, Victoria gathered both boys in her arms again. She pulled back far enough to see their eyes, huge with excitement. "We really are. We have our own home now." She was so glad to see them she found herself near tears. Tonight the farm would truly feel like home with the boys there.

"Does that mean we will have a pa, too?" Cade chimed in.

"What? Well . . ." Victoria was at a loss how to respond, wondering where in the world they had gotten that notion in their heads. Fortunately, she had a surprise for them to redirect their attention. "We have a dog. His name is Bandit and he loves to play."

"A dog!" They both hugged her neck. "Thank you! Thank you!"

"How can you tell them apart?" Bartholomew asked, looking from one towheaded boy to the other and seeing no discernible difference.

"I'm Cody." "I'm Cade," they replied in unison.

Bartholomew chuckled. "That clears it up."

Understanding his confusion, Mrs. Wellington said, "It took me forever to tell them apart. It's just a matter of learning the little things that they do."

The boys grinned at each other, knowing they fooled Mrs. Wellington all of the time.

"Yes, ma'am, I guess it will take some time at that." Bartholomew picked up some of the luggage the driver had placed beside them.

"Bartholomew, please call me Pearl," Mrs. Wellington urged.

Victoria wasn't sure, but she thought Bartholomew was blushing as he headed toward the buckboard.

Seeing the many pieces of luggage, Victoria thought Mrs. Wellington must be planning to stay a long time. "Boys, let's help

Bartholomew put the luggage in the buck-board," Victoria urged. "I'm sure Mrs. Wellington will be anxious to get to the farm so she can relax."

"I wish you would call me Pearl too, dear," Mrs. Wellington said.

"I'll try," Victoria promised. Mrs. Wellington had asked her before to call her by her given name, but she thought the boys would imitate her.

Mrs. Wellington squeezed Victoria's hand. "I simply cannot wait to see your new farm. We have so much to talk about over a nice cup of tea. I brought some tea with me. Oh, how I've missed your desserts with my tea. Though I have lost several pounds since you've been gone."

Eyeing her soft pink traveling suit, Victoria thought she did look considerably thinner and younger. "You look lovely." She leaned over and whispered in her ear, "I think Bartholomew is smitten."

"My word! An old woman like me attract-ing a man?" Mrs. Wellington exclaimed, her face turning as pink as her suit.

"You are not old! How many women could travel across country with two young active boys? And look at you! No one would ever guess you've been on a stagecoach for days."

A glimmer of tears misted Mrs. Wellington's eyes. "My dear, it has been a true adventure. I have you to thank for allowing me to bring the boys to you. I can't remember the last time I've had so much fun. That boardinghouse has been both a curse and a blessing, and I fear I've hidden out there too long. Until this trip, I had forgotten how to enjoy life. I feel as though my spirit has been renewed."

"Oh, Mrs. Wellington, I should be thanking you. You have done so much for me and the boys that I could never repay you." More than anything Victoria wanted to confess all of her lies to her.

"Nonsense! You and the boys are my family. I've fallen in love with this wild country on our trip. If you have no objections I may just stay here permanently. The boardinghouse would be frightfully lonely without the three of you."

Victoria squeezed her hand. "It is so good to have you here. I do hope you decide to stay . . . that would be wonderful. Please do not expect anything as grand as your home. Mr. Barlow and Bartholomew were the only two on the farm, and they had no time for frills. It's quite utilitarian, but it is clean, and the views are stunning."

"I know it will be perfect," Mrs. Wellington

assured her.

The boys resumed asking questions, and it seemed they had stored up thousands on the journey to Promise. They were so excited they could hardly contain themselves, and by the time they arrived at the farm, Victoria was worn out. She marveled at Mrs. Wellington's fortitude on the trip. "Were they like this the whole trip?"

Mrs. Wellington laughed. "Oh my, yes, they chattered like magpies the entire trip. It was question after question. They should sleep for a month once they get settled in."

Gage Hardy was leaving the general store when he spotted Victoria. That old man was with her and they looked like they were waiting for the stage. He previously thought it was a waste of his time when Wallace sent him to town to fetch supplies, but he was now grateful. With that old man by her side he couldn't go over there and talk to her. Unconcerned with Wallace's directive that he come right back to the ranch, he took a seat in front of the store. There was no way he would be leaving before he saw who she was meeting on that stage. Then a thought gripped him, sending a wave of anticipation through him. What if she was getting on that stage to leave? The thought energized him.

He would just mount up and follow her to her destination. If she landed someplace new, she wouldn't have any defenders like that big cowboy last night. Before McBride came along, he'd planned on talking to her last night. Even at a distance in the dark, he knew it was McBride by his size. That man had a habit of showing up at the most inopportune times.

Hardy propped his boots on the rail, but before he got comfortable he heard the stagecoach coming down the road. He couldn't believe his eyes when two blond boys jumped out of the coach and ran to Delilah. There was no doubt in his mind these were the same two boys from that Abilene saloon. Even at a distance he could tell they were twins, and they were about the right age. After the fire at the Lucky Slipper, he'd heard the boys were missing, the same day Delilah disappeared. Everyone speculated that Kitten took them to an orphanage, since that had been her plan. Others speculated that they all died in the fire, as unidentifiable remains had been found in the saloon after the fire burned out. There had also been talk that Ruby and Kitten were suspected of starting that fire. He didn't give much credence to the gossip back then because all he cared about was

Delilah's disappearance. He never believed she died in the fire.

An older woman was traveling with the boys. It definitely wasn't their mother, Kitten. What was Delilah's game? She'd changed her name and pretended she didn't recognize him. Now she had those two boys with her. He didn't know what she was up to, but he was going to find out. If it hadn't been for that cowboy last night, he might have had some answers. What if she was the one who burned down that saloon? He looked hard at the older woman. She didn't look familiar, and he prided himself on his memory. If anyone knew Delilah's secrets, it had to be that old woman. He smiled. Delilah might decide to be real friendly to protect her secrets.

CHAPTER TWENTY-TWO

"Some of the boys were met with gunfire when they moved the cattle to the river," T. J. told Colt, meeting him at the back door as he was washing before going inside for dinner.

"Wallace's men?"

T. J. shrugged. "The cattle scattered in every direction, and the boys took off after them. They didn't have time to chase the culprits down. I came back for more men."

"We know it was his men." Colt grabbed his hat and headed for the stable.

T. J. followed him, motioning for some men to mount up and ride with them.

Tate heard the conversation and came running out the door. "I want to ride with you." He didn't want to stay at the ranch like an old woman if there was going to be a confrontation with Wallace.

"Not this time. Colt doesn't need to be worrying about you on top of everything else," T. J. answered.

Tate wanted to argue, but the men were already riding away.

"Why don't you rustle up some food and keep the coffee hot?" T. J. suggested.

Dismounting in front of Wallace's home, Colt told his men to stay in the saddle while he barged up to the front porch and started banging on the front door.

One of Wallace's servants opened the door, and Colt said, "I want to see Wallace."

"Señor Wallace is having dinner," she replied.

Seeing she made no move to tell Wallace he was there, Colt figured she was either afraid or had been instructed not to interrupt him. Either way, it didn't matter to him. He turned to his men. "Wait here." He nodded to the woman, but walked around her and stormed down the long foyer. He'd been in Wallace's house before, so he knew his way to the dining room. Shoving open the large double doors, Colt stormed through and all conversation at the table came to an abrupt halt.

Wallace jumped up, dropping his fork in the process. In the silence of the room it sounded like a loud cannon going off when it hit the floor. "McBride, what is the meaning of this?"

The Mexican woman appeared at the door. "Señor Wallace, *lo siento* —" She stopped when Wallace signaled for her to leave.

Colt took in the scene before him. Victoria was sitting next to Wallace at the far end of the table with her two boys sitting beside her. Mrs. Wellington was sitting across from her. "Aw, hell," he muttered. *I forgot about her boys arriving. She sure as hell didn't waste any time bringing them over to Wallace's.* That thought made him even angrier. Everyone was staring at him in wide-eyed disbelief. In fact, everyone but Wallace looked scared to death, and he was the one who should be afraid.

In two strides Colt stopped at the end of the table, his spurs clinking loudly on the wooden floor. "My men were shot at today driving cattle to the river."

"What does that have to do with me?" Wallace demanded.

"You know it was your men doing the shooting."

"I know nothing of the sort," Wallace countered.

Colt glared at him. He wanted to take him by the seat of the pants and run his smug face down the length of that long table.

"Then I'll put it this way: I know it was your men doing the shooting."

"If you had proof of anything you would be at the sheriff's."

"That wouldn't do me much good, would it?" Colt barked.

Wallace waved his arm like he was brushing him aside. "You've interrupted our dinner long enough. Now please show yourself out before I call my men to throw you out."

Ignoring his dismissal, Colt stalked around the table toward him. He glanced at Victoria. "I'm sorry I've interrupted your fine dinner, Miss Eastman," he snapped.

Victoria stared at him in disbelief. His anger was palpable, and the murderous rage in his cold, dark eyes truly frightened her. She thought he looked like the evil avenging angel. She stood and moved between the boys, pulling them to her as if she needed to protect them from him.

Colt saw her move and that brought him up short. Did she think he would actually do her boys harm? He forced himself to calm down before he did something really rash. He stopped a foot from Wallace and lowered his voice. "That's how you do things, isn't it, Wallace? Call your men to do your dirty work. Well, you'd best call every hired gun on this place, because that's

284

what it's going to take if I decide to wipe the floor with your sorry ass."

Seeing the lethal look in Colt's eyes, Wallace sputtered, "This is neither the time nor the place. See here, you are frightening my guests."

Colt did feel bad about that. On the other hand, if Victoria wanted to be around Wallace she needed to know the kind of man she was involved with. Now was as good a time as any to see what she was getting. "Consider this my last warning. This is going to stop now, or you will be seeing me again. And guests or no guests, you'd best be wearing a gun." As he turned to leave, he reached up and tipped his hat to Mrs. Wellington.

"You can't come into a man's home and threaten him," Wallace yelled bravely to Colt's back.

Turning around, Colt zeroed those satanic eyes on him. "It's not a threat," he promised in a low growl. He walked out at a leisurely pace with five sets of eyes glued to his back as the sound of his spurs echoed down the long hallway.

Wallace returned to his chair, his face flaming with anger. Colt McBride was going to pay for embarrassing him in front of his guests. "Sorry for the rude interruption.

Let's enjoy the remainder of our dinner, shall we?" He called to the old woman to bring him more silverware.

"He lives here?" Mrs. Wellington asked, absolutely shocked that the man she'd met at her boardinghouse was in the same town as Victoria.

"Is he a real cowboy?" Cade asked before anyone answered Mrs. Wellington.

"He's the biggest man I ever saw," Cody said.

"Did you see that gun?" Cade asked.

"Yeah, and I want a black hat like that. That's a real cowboy hat," Cody said.

"Me too. Can we have one?" Cade asked.

"What were those things clinking on his boots?" Cody asked.

Victoria remained silent. She hadn't mentioned to Mrs. Wellington that Mr. McBride lived in Promise, or the problems the ranchers were having. Colt was obviously still convinced that Mr. Wallace was creating the problems. She wasn't convinced, and from what she had seen, it was Colt acting like a madman. Wallace was a gentleman of some means, not some cowboy that needed to steal land, or create havoc to increase his wealth. He hadn't mentioned buying her land again, and he truly seemed more interested in her than purchasing her farm.

"Victoria?" Mrs. Wellington asked when no one answered her question.

"Mr. McBride owns a ranch next to my farm." She hadn't yet told Mr. Wallace that she had met Mr. McBride before in St. Louis.

Mrs. Wellington opened her mouth to say something else, but closed it when Victoria shook her head at her, silently indicating she shouldn't ask questions.

"Is he an outlaw?" Cade asked. He nudged his brother under the table. "He wears a gun, doesn't he?"

"Yeah. Did you see how tall he was? I bet he has a big horse," Cody chimed in.

"I bet he's ten feet tall," Cade added.

Snatching the silverware from his servant's hand, Wallace impatiently shooed her away. Between McBride barging in, and the incessant jabbering of these boys, he was ready to throw everyone from the room. "Shall we forget the incident and discuss something else?" he snapped. No matter how much he wanted to marry Victoria for her land, he would never tolerate her boys. He wanted his own sons, not the offspring of some other man. He'd asked Victoria if her husband had died and she told him she had

287

never been married. Her admission surprised him, but he hadn't pressed for more information. It displeased him that she wasn't a true lady, but he'd take her for the land. He consoled himself thinking at her young age she probably hadn't had many lovers. He wasn't in love with her; he'd never been in love with anyone. She was a beautiful woman and he would be the envy of every man. He'd put a ring on her finger and the Barlow farm would finally be his. Confident that she was beginning to trust him, he would give her a little longer to bend to his will. Once they were married he would send her boys away and she would have no say in the matter.

One glance at Wallace's icy blue eyes told Victoria he was more upset than he was letting on. She turned to the boys and softly instructed, "No more questions. Let's enjoy this fine meal."

"Yes, ma'am," they said in unison.

Mrs. Wellington made an effort to smooth Wallace's ruffled feathers by plying him with questions about his life in America. It had been her experience that men like Wallace loved to talk about themselves, especially those countrymen who had amassed land and money. Wallace had become a wealthy man since leaving England.

Victoria barely listened to Wallace's responses to Mrs. Wellington's questions. Her mind was on Colt and the threat he issued to Wallace. She wondered if he would really have a gunfight with him. When she heard Wallace mention Abilene, she started listening intently to what he was saying. It was the second time he'd mentioned the town.

"How long were you in Abilene?" Mrs. Wellington inquired, more to keep the boys from talking than any real interest. She'd already taken a dislike to Wallace. She didn't like the way he ignored the twins. She wondered if Victoria realized he considered the boys a nuisance.

"Three years. I thought I was ready to settle there and purchased a ranch. After a while, I decided to see more of the West. I still own the ranch, but I have a man running it for me."

Victoria hadn't realized that he was in Abilene that long. She wanted to ask him some questions, but she didn't want to raise his suspicions by showing too much interest.

"How long ago was that, Mr. Wallace?" Mrs. Wellington asked.

"I left Abilene four years ago. I was particularly fond of a wom . . ." He hesitated, not wanting to reveal the true reason he'd stayed in Abilene so long. The woman he was involved with from the Lucky Slipper had left town without telling him, and he'd left soon after. "I must admit I was fond of the excitement of the wild town."

Mrs. Wellington caught what Wallace was about to say, and she looked across the table at Victoria to see her reaction.

Victoria's hands started to shake. She didn't hear any of the conversation after he said he was in Abilene when she lived there. She took a deep breath, trying to calm her nerves. He'd never given any indication he had seen her before, so there was always the chance he didn't frequent the saloon, or if he did, he didn't recognize her.

"Oh, I've heard some fantastic stories about that town," Mrs. Wellington confessed.

Wallace was barely listening to Mrs. Wellington. He was watching Victoria. Just like the last time he'd mentioned Abilene, a strange look crossed her face. When she glanced up and found him staring at her, he turned back to Mrs. Wellington. "I assure you, the stories you've heard are most likely true."

"Are you planning to stay in Wyoming?" Mrs. Wellington inquired.

"Yes, I'm here to stay." He reached over

and squeezed Victoria's hand and gave her a slight smile. "I have more reason to stay here now."

Victoria didn't know what to say. It hadn't occurred to her that he wanted more than friendship from her. She thought she had made it clear she wasn't looking for a husband since Mr. Barlow died. Now that she had a home for the boys, she no longer planned to marry. By accepting his invitations she'd obviously given him the wrong idea.

After dinner Wallace walked them to the front porch, where Bartholomew was waiting for them. Mrs. Wellington and the boys got into the buckboard, but Wallace reached for Victoria's hand and led her a few feet away so he could speak to her privately.

"I enjoy having you here at the ranch, Victoria." He took both of her hands in his and held them to his chest. "You can't mistake my affection for you."

Victoria couldn't meet his eyes. She had no intention of leading him on, but she wanted to find a way to let him down gently, since the night had already been a total disaster.

When she didn't immediately respond, he pressed, saying, "I do hope you are beginning to feel some affection for me as well."

She could not give him a declaration of affection she did not feel. "I certainly appreciate your friendship, Mr. Wallace. The boys and I would be very lonely in this new town without friends."

"I've asked you to call me Euan." His irritation was evident, and he moved his hands to her shoulders and pulled her closer. "Victoria, I want more than friendship from you." His impatient tone sounded like a man who was used to having his way.

The look on his face made her nervous. "I . . . I . . . This is all so new for me. The death of Mr. Barlow . . . the farm . . . the boys in a new place . . ." She was babbling, but she wouldn't allow him to force her to say what he wanted to hear.

His gaze darted to the buckboard to see if anyone was listening. Seeing they were all watching, he softened his tone. "Yes, yes, you're right, my dear. You've had many changes in a short period of time. But you and your boys are going to need a man to care for you. You will not be able to make it alone out here. This is wild country, not a large city like St. Louis, and I can protect you."

His comment irritated her. Who did he think had looked out for her the last few years? She tried to move away from him, but he held her firmly. "I'm not alone. I have Bartholomew, and Mrs. Wellington is considering staying in Wyoming."

"An old man and woman are not the protection you are going to need," he whispered.

It was obvious he was going to press her for the response he wanted. She took a deep breath. If he insisted on an answer, she would give him one. "I hope you understand I'm not ready for any kind of commitment. I value friendship, but I am not prepared to say things I don't feel."

"Perhaps you will soon change your mind." He released her hand and walked her to the buckboard.

If not for the late hour and wanting to get the boys home and in bed, she might have asked what he meant. Instead she said goodbye and climbed in the buckboard to face the long ride home, knowing she was going to be peppered with thousands of questions from the boys about Colt McBride.

The boys exhausted themselves with their questions, and were ready for bed as soon as they reached the farm. Mrs. Wellington was waiting for her in the kitchen having prepared their nightly tea. It seemed she had stored up her own questions about Colt McBride.

"Have a seat, my dear, let's enjoy a nice cup of tea."

Victoria took a seat and Mrs. Wellington poured the tea. "You failed to mention that Mr. McBride lived here."

"Yes, I'm sorry. I just didn't think of it, and we've had so many other things to discuss."

"He is a stunning man," Mrs. Wellington said.

"Mr. Wallace?" Victoria asked innocently, knowing full well Mrs. Wellington was talking about Colt. That was the same word she'd used to describe him the first time she saw him in St. Louis.

Clanking her cup on her saucer, Mrs. Wellington exclaimed, "I'm talking about that handsome Mr. McBride!"

Victoria smiled. "Oh?"

"Surely you can't think Mr. McBride living in this very town is a coincidence."

She was reminded of what Colt said about coincidences.

"You must believe in miracles now! You mark my words: God has his hand in this."

"I hardly think Mr. McBride is a miracle, and God hasn't had His hand in my life for a long time, if ever. And I'm definitely not interested in cowboys."

Mrs. Wellington gave her a long look, and

shook her head from side to side. "I'm sorry you've stopped believing, Victoria. I hope one day you will change your mind on that subject. I know in my heart the Good Lord has a wonderful plan for your life. Now tell me, have you been to church here?"

"No, I haven't." She needed to tell Mrs. Wellington the truth about the reason she came to Wyoming before Bartholomew blurted out something about her planned marriage. She didn't know where to begin, but she needed to do it soon.

"Perhaps we can go this Sunday." Mrs. Wellington had never been able to talk her into attending church in St. Louis, but she always allowed the boys to accompany her. It was obvious something had happened to Victoria to cause her to turn away from her faith, yet Mrs. Wellington was confident that she would come around in time.

"We'll see," Victoria responded, knowing she would think of an excuse not to go.

"What is the problem between Mr. Wallace and Mr. McBride?"

Victoria related what Colt had told her about the recent events.

"Do you think Mr. Wallace is behind this mischief?"

Victoria thought about Wallace's behavior before she answered. Tonight was the first time she'd seen Wallace angry. Still, she had no reason to believe he was not what he seemed. "He has been nothing but a gentleman to me, showing the utmost consideration and kindness. It just doesn't make sense why a man of his wealth would do such a thing."

Mrs. Wellington wasn't as enthused as Victoria over Mr. Wallace's fine manners. Perhaps it was because she had more years' experience, but there was something in his eyes, a lack of emotion, or at least genuine emotion, that she had detected when he looked at Victoria. He was interested in Victoria, as any man would be since she was such a beautiful young woman. But, after hearing what Victoria told her about the land, she suspected he had other motives for his attentions.

"Do you have feelings for Mr. Wallace?"

Giving a nervous laugh, Victoria said, "Mr. Wallace asked me that very question just tonight."

"Please forgive me if I am being a nosy old woman. It's just that I am very fond of you. I feel like you are my own daughter."

Leaning over, Victoria squeezed her hand. "You've been like a mother to me, and I don't mind your asking. As I told Mr. Wallace, it is too soon for me to make a decision when I'm just now starting a new life. But there is one thing in his favor. He's not a cowboy, he's . . . he's . . ." Actually, she didn't quite know how to describe Wallace. "He doesn't work his ranch like Mr. McBride. He says he has a manager who runs it."

Mrs. Wellington leaned back and chuckled. "My dear, cowboy or not, if the man doesn't make your heart beat faster when you see him, then he is not the man for you. You wouldn't have to think about it, you would just know. The way I knew when I saw my wonderful Wellie . . . did I ever tell you that's what I called my dear husband?" She didn't wait for a response before adding, "All the same, I must say you are in a fine pickle."

Victoria frowned at her. "What do you mean?"

"Two handsome men vying for your attention! I'd say that's a fine pickle!"

"Two?"

"Why, that big handsome cowboy was so angry seeing you sitting at Mr. Wallace's table, I thought he might drag you away."

"You are mistaken about that. Mr. McBride has no interest in marrying."

Taking a sip of her tea, Mrs. Wellington's eyes twinkled over the rim of her cup.

"Really?" She'd seen the look on his face when he looked at Victoria, and if that wasn't jealousy she didn't know what was. *Why can't the girl see what the Good Lord has literally placed in front of her? And twice, for heaven's sake!*

"Yes. I'm quite sure Mr. McBride is content with his life. He's like most cowboys: interested in women, but not matrimony," Victoria replied.

"Many men do not realize they want to marry and they fight the notion. It's up to the women to show them what they are missing. My dear Wellie wasn't keen on marriage, but he changed his mind rather quickly when he thought I was going to marry another man," Mrs. Wellington confided. If she were in Victoria's position there was no question which man she would choose. And it wouldn't be that English fop.

Victoria was surprised to hear Mrs. Wellington would have considered another man after listening to her glowing stories about her deceased husband. "Were you really going to marry another man?"

"Heavens no, my dear! I was crazy in love with Wellie, but I didn't let him know." She looked off in the distance with a wistful smile, as if reliving a pleasant memory. "It was like you and Mr. McBride. We kept run-

ning into each other in the oddest places."
She gave Victoria a reproving look. "I had
the sense to know the Good Lord was telling me something. And you know what? He
was right! We were meant for each other. I
didn't actually tell him I was marrying
another, I just allowed him to think he had
some competition. He came around as
quick as you please!"

"Seeing Mr. McBride here is just a coincidence, nothing more. He's the kind of
cowboy who frequents the saloon on a
regular basis." She said that, knowing Mrs.
Wellington would frown on such behavior.

Mrs. Wellington poured her more tea. "It's
not only cowboys who visit the saloons, my
dear girl. I'd bet that Mr. Wallace does as
well. Many men engage in that behavior
before they figure out what is important."

Her response surprised Victoria, and she
didn't have a comeback, so she said the first
thing that came to her mind. "I would be
remiss not to say Mr. McBride has been
quite kind since I arrived, although I'm sure
he sends his men over to help Bartholomew.
He's very fond of him, and I think he's worried. Mr. Barlow's death has been very hard
on Bartholomew."

The girl was either blind or intentionally
choosing to ignore Mr. McBride's intent.

Mrs. Wellington gave her a motherly look. "You can tell yourself that Colt is being kind solely for Bartholomew's sake, but that doesn't make it so. Just remember, dear, that time passes like the wind on your cheek. You should never waste one minute on the *wrong* man."

CHAPTER TWENTY-THREE

Colt dismounted in front of Victoria's home and tied Razor to the post. Having had only two hours of sleep again last night, he was in a grouchy mood. He'd been going since three in the morning, and his day was far from over. All day, he hadn't been able to concentrate on anything but the look on Victoria's face when he'd stormed into Wallace's dining room last night. It troubled him that she thought she had to protect her boys from him. He couldn't decide if he admired her or wanted to strangle her for insulting him. He'd apologize all right for his bad behavior, but he also intended to make sure she understood that her boys were never in any danger from him. On top of everything else, he'd decided to forgo dinner and make the trip to apologize, and he was starving to death.

Being honest with himself, he was also irritated that every time he turned around she was with Wallace. *Seems like she's gotten over her fear of men. She certainly isn't afraid of Wallace, and if that isn't enough to make me madder than a wet hen, I don't know what is!* One thing for sure, he was going to find out once and for all how involved she was with Wallace.

The boys were playing with Bandit near the barn when they spotted Colt riding in. They stopped what they were doing and stared in disbelief as he dismounted. Bandit ran to him with his usual enthusiasm, begging for attention. Pulling his leather gloves from his back pocket, he gave one end to Bandit and started playing tug-of-war with him. "Looks like you've been eating good, boy. You're getting fat."

"You know Bandit?" Cade asked, tentatively approaching the big man.

"I sure do. He's a great dog," Colt responded, turning his attention to the boys.

"When did you meet him?" Cody questioned.

"The first day I saw your mother in Promise." His gaze moved from one boy to the other, wondering how Victoria could possibly tell them apart. They were handsome boys, yet he could find no resemblance to Victoria.

"You mean Victoria?" Cade questioned.

302

Colt chuckled. "Yes, I mean Victoria." *Odd that they call their mother Victoria.* He stuck his big hand out to one boy. "My name is Colt."

Cade was first to put his small hand in Colt's, then Cody. It wasn't what Colt would call a manly shake from either boy.

"Aren't you men going to be seven years old soon?" Colt asked, squatting down to look them in the eye.

Both boys nodded.

"Well then, it's time to learn to shake hands like men. When a man shakes your hand, make it a firm one. Your handshake is your first impression, and a good one says you are a man to be reckoned with."

The boys traded a puzzled look. "What do you mean?" Cody asked.

Colt took their hands and showed them by giving as firm a grip as possible without hurting their small fingers. "That's how a man shakes hands." He ruffled their blond hair. "Now tell me how to tell you two apart."

"I'm Cade. But we'll fool you sometimes, like we do Mrs. Wellington. It's fun."

"Yeah, unless one of us is in trouble," Cody admitted. "Then it's not so much fun."

"I reckon not." Colt smiled at their honesty. He could see that these two could be a handful. He did hear a slight difference in their voices.

"Are you a real cowboy?" Cade asked.

"Are you an outlaw?" Cody asked.

"Well, if those are my choices, I guess I'm a cowboy," Colt replied, laughing at the rapid-fire questions. He felt the tension of his day disappearing, just like when he was with Tate.

"You said a bad word last night," Cade said.

There were times he would forget that he wasn't on the range with the men. "I did?"

"Yeah, you said aw, hel—" Cody began, but his brother punched him in the arm.

"You better not say it. Victoria will wash your mouth out again," Cade warned.

Colt knew that was a habit of his. "I shouldn't have said that," he told them, making a mental note to watch what he said in the future. He thought he and his men did pretty well with their language since Tate was around. He remembered his mother would never let his father get away with using profanity in the house.

"It might not really be a bad word since Mrs. Wellington said if we're bad we could go there, and the preacher in St. Louis said it all the time," Cody said.

304

"Yeah, and it's supposed to be hot," Cade added.

Colt chuckled. "I think you're safe."

"You could say *aw, heaven,*" one of them suggested.

"Yeah, we're supposed to try to go there 'cause it's a good place. But you also said as —" Cade started, but Cody elbowed him.

"Can you show us how to shoot your gun?" Cody asked.

"I . . . uh . . . we'll have to ask . . ." He didn't know what to say to that, but before he finished his reply they were on to the next question.

Thankfully, Razor caught their eye when he snorted, wanting attention of his own. The boys cautiously approached him. "What's your horse's name? He sure is big!"

"Razor. Yes, he's a big one. Stand to the side so he can get a look at you. A horse can't see you directly in front of him." Colt urged Razor to hold his head lower. "Rub behind his ears. He likes that."

"Why?" they asked, scratching behind Razor's ears.

"Because —"

"Will you teach us to ride?"

"We've never been on a horse."

"Is he the biggest horse in the world?"

"Do you have cows?"

"I have cattle," Colt was able to answer when they took a breath.

"Were you gonna shoot that Mr. Wallace last night?"

Colt figured he shouldn't tell them the truth to that question.

"He didn't even say a prayer before supper, thanking God for our food like Mrs. Wellington says we should. I don't like him, so you can shoot him if you want."

Colt thought it was Cade who made that comment. He wanted to laugh out loud, but refrained. Realizing they weren't going to wait for a response before asking another question, he just listened to their chatter.

"Do you have a ranch?"

"Can we come to your ranch?"

"Do you have a wife?"

"Do you have boys?"

"Boys, give the man time to answer one question before you ask another one. You are forgetting your manners."

Colt rose to his full height and removed his hat as Mrs. Wellington walked down the steps.

Stopping in front of him, Mrs. Wellington smiled. "I didn't get a chance to say hello last night."

Colt twirled his hat in his hands. "Yes, ma'am, that's why I'm here. I came to apologize for interrupting your dinner, and for my bad manners."

Cade jerked on Colt's shirtsleeve. "Aren't you going to shake hands? This is Mrs. Wellington."

"Mrs. Wellington, Colt taught us how to shake hands like a man," Cody announced proudly, grabbing Mrs. Wellington's hand and giving her a hard grip to demonstrate.

Grimacing, Mrs. Wellington tried to pull her hand from the boy, but he hung on.

Colt put a hand on Cody's shoulder, reminding himself he had a lot to learn about little boys. "Wait a minute, cowboy," he said patiently. "You don't shake a lady's hand like that. They're more delicate and you don't want to hurt them. Remember I told you that handshake is just for men."

Dropping the older woman's hand, Cody looked at her with concern. "Did I hurt you?"

"No, you did no lasting damage," Mrs. Wellington assured him. "But listen to Mr. McBride."

"He said we could call him Colt," Cade told her.

Colt gave her his most charming smile. "Yes, ma'am, and you do the same. I am sorry I disturbed your dinner last night."

Mrs. Wellington was as susceptible to that

dimpled smile as a woman half her age. "Sir, no need to apologize. We needed a little excitement last night. I must say, the conversation picked up considerably after your visit."

"Will you show us how fast you draw your gun?" Cody asked.

"No. A man never draws his gun unless he's prepared to use it," Colt said seriously.

Eyeing him, Mrs. Wellington thought he was wonderful with the boys as he responded to their questions without losing patience. Totally opposite of Wallace, who hadn't said as much as two words to them over the course of the evening. Why Victoria was wasting her time with that man was beyond her, particularly when there was a man like Colt right in front of her eyes. "Dinner is about ready. Would you like to join us?"

Colt was in a hurry to get back to work, and he'd already wasted too much time today worrying about everything but his ranch. Thanks to Victoria. "I have a lot of work waiting. I'd best be getting —" Before he finished what he was about to say, Victoria walked out the door. She was looking down, wiping her hands on her apron.

"Boys, it's time for dinn—" She stopped

in midsentence when she saw Colt standing there.

Colt couldn't believe the effect she had on him. Every time he saw her he thought she was more beautiful than the last time.

"Hello," she said, taking in the scene with the boys hanging all over him. Then she noticed how close they were to his large horse. She stepped off the porch at the same time Colt took a stride in her direction.

"I came by to apologize for last night. I didn't mean to frighten you."

Victoria was caught off guard by his apology. Just when she thought he was a madman, he would do something unexpected, like apologize. She didn't know what to make of him. "I, that is . . ." Her eyes shot back to his horse. "Boys, you are too close to that horse."

Colt turned to see what had her so concerned. The boys were gently rubbing Razor's muzzle. "Razor won't hurt them. They're friends," he assured her.

"Yeah, we didn't walk up in front of him 'cause horses can't see too good right in front of them. They can see you better from the side," Cade added.

Colt smiled, pleased that they'd listened. "That's right. And don't walk up behind them without letting them know you're there."

"I see you've met the boys," she said. "I was just calling them for dinner." She looked up at him, thinking he looked very tired. "Thank you for coming by . . . and for the apology."

Mrs. Wellington spoke up. "I've invited Mr. McBride to join us for dinner."

"Please, please, please," Cade and Cody chorused, jumping up and down.

Turning his dark eyes on Victoria, Colt tried to gauge how she felt about their invitation.

She hadn't intended to ask him to stay, but with the boys so excited, how could she refuse? "Of course you should join us if Mrs. Morris isn't waiting with your dinner." The thought crossed her mind that he might be riding into town to visit the saloon.

"No, she knew I wasn't sure when I would be home." He smiled at the boys, who were still begging him to stay. "I guess I can't turn down an invitation like this." He returned to Razor and loosened his girth and started to lead him to a shade tree, the boys trailing behind him.

"Boys, let Mr. McBride tend to his horse while you get washed up," Victoria instructed.

They hesitated, obviously wanting to stay with Colt.

"I'll be right along behind you," he promised them.

Mrs. Wellington hustled the boys away, but Victoria lingered. "I see you haven't given up the notion that Mr. Wallace is behind what's been going on here?"

"No, ma'am, I haven't." He removed Razor's saddle and ground tied him. "And I see you're still spending time with him."

"Yes, and I am quite convinced he is not the person you seem to think he is."

"Are you now?" Colt clenched his molars together to keep from saying something he would regret and be forced to apologize again. He walked to the well and dipped some water into his hat for Razor.

Victoria stayed on his heels. She wasn't going to let the subject drop. "Yes, I am. He's a perfect gentleman."

He walked back to Razor and held his hat while the horse drank. "Well, tell me, Miss Eastman, do you think he might have an agenda where you are concerned?"

Victoria put her hands on her hips. "What do you mean by that?"

Razor finished drinking, and Colt shook the remaining drops of water from his hat. "I mean he's a man and you're a woman. It follows that he wants you to think the best of him so he can make some headway."

Face flaming, Victoria repeated, "Headway?" Her word came out in a squeak.

"Yeah, *headway,*" he enunciated. "It means he's trying —"

"I think I know what you mean," she retorted, then presented him with her back when she whirled around and marched toward the porch.

"And it insults me that you thought I would hurt your boys!" he yelled at her back.

She stopped at the door and turned back to him. "You were the one acting like a madman!"

He had to give her that. "I didn't know you were there," he admitted more calmly. Then he added more forcefully, "But I dam . . . darn sure wouldn't hurt children."

Not knowing how to respond to that statement, she said curtly, "Dinner is ready."

When she was out of sight he turned and patted Razor's neck. "Well, that went well, don't you think, buddy?"

The horse snorted at him.

Falling into bed four hours later, Colt was exhausted. He felt like he'd been in the line of fire with all the questions from the boys and Mrs. Wellington. It was a toss-up who asked more questions. He was disappointed that he hadn't had one moment alone with Victoria the entire evening, to find out exactly what was going on with her and Wallace. It was probably for the best since she seemed hel . . . heaven-bent on defending Wallace in every discussion. Remembering what the boys said about shooting Wallace brought a smile to his face. At least they had good sense, he mused. He liked those boys, and they were obviously hungry for male companionship judging by their many questions. They had pleaded with him to teach them to ride a horse. Seeing as how they were around two women all the time, he figured they needed a man to show them some things, and Bartholomew was getting up there in age. Even though Victoria hadn't seemed too pleased when he promised the boys he would teach them, she hadn't objected. Every boy needed those skills, to his way of thinking, and he figured she understood that, if she was determined to stay in Wyoming.

Being around the boys reminded him of his own childhood. There were so many things he'd learned from his father, whose influence made Colt the man he was today. It saddened him to think those boys had lived almost seven years without a father's love and guidance. They were the perfect age to learn, and he decided what they really needed was their own horse. It didn't make sense to teach them to ride if they didn't learn the importance of taking care of the animal that could help them survive in times of trouble. He decided he'd pick out two of the smaller horses on the ranch for them. He smiled to himself just thinking how they would react to having their own horses. If he knew boys, they would want to spend a lot of time on his ranch seeing to the horses. He wondered if Victoria would object. It might mean she would have less time to spend with Wallace. Now, what could be wrong with that plan?

Chapter Twenty-Four

"Have a drink with me, honey?" Gage Hardy leaned against the bar next to Lucy.

"You want to have a steak?" Lucy asked, hoping he would offer to buy her dinner as well as drinks.

Since the bar was nearly empty, and there was no one around to play poker with, Gage thought why not. "Order up a couple of steaks if you want to have dinner with me." He pointed to a table. "I'll be over there. Bring a bottle back with you."

Lucy returned with the bottle and pulled a chair closer to Hardy's. "I told the cook to make the steaks extra special," she said with a smile. She made more money when the cowboys ordered dinner, and seeing how much Hardy could drink, she was already counting the coins. Pointing to the bottle, she added, "I had Sam give me the good stuff. Wallace drinks this."

Hardy looked at the bottle. "Yeah, I've

noticed that."

She didn't mind spending a few hours with Hardy. He was always nice to her, and he was handsome enough. Admittedly, he wasn't as handsome as Colt McBride, but no man measured up to him in her estimation. The best thing about Hardy was the more he drank the more he liked to talk. The evening wouldn't be boring. "I'm glad you came in tonight before your boss. He never talks to me, he just bosses me around."

"You don't like the boss?" he teased.

"Not much. He thinks he's better than most folks," she retorted snidely.

He thought she had Wallace pegged dead on. "He's a strange one, that's for sure."

"I hear he's sweet on that woman from the Barlow farm," Lucy said, hoping to find out more about the woman she'd seen with Colt. "L. B. said her name was Victoria . . . or something like that."

Gage's ears perked up at the mention of Victoria. He'd glanced down at his glass thinking he needed to pace himself if he wanted to stay coherent. "How did she come about owning that farm?"

"She came here to marry Chet Barlow."

He hadn't heard that bit of news. "How long has she been here?"

"Not that long. I heard she was a mail-order bride."

"When they gettin' hitched?" Gage asked.

Lucy laughed. "The old guy went toes up. He dropped over dead before she even got here. But the strangest thing is, he didn't even know her, but he left the farm to her."

"He left his farm to a woman he didn't know?" He wasn't sure Lucy knew what she was talking about. Now why would a man do something so harebrained?

"He sure did. I never met the man, since he never came into the saloon, but I would have found a way to meet him if I'd known he wanted to leave that land to someone. I can guarantee he would've had more fun with me than with that starched-bloomers I saw with Colt McBride," she boasted.

"Is McBride courtin' her too?" Gage asked.

"I've seen him with her, but the men say she spends more time with Wallace."

"Wonder if her intended knew who she really is?"

Lucy looked at his eyes to see if he was already feeling his whiskey. "What do you mean?"

"I wonder if he knew Delilah before she came here."

"Her name's Victoria," Lucy told him,

thinking he must have had more whiskey than she thought.

"Her name is Delilah, not Victoria," he said firmly.

Eyeing him steadily, she thought he still looked sober enough. "Are you sure? Do you know her?"

"Oh yeah, I know her. Met her in Abilene a few years back. Her name is Delilah."

"Then why does she call herself Victoria?"

"I haven't figured that one out. What makes you think Wallace is sweet on her?"

"He's never been seen courting any woman before she came to town. And you know how cowboys talk when they get to drinkin'. The men say she's been out to his ranch, but then, I guess you would know about that. They also say he wants her land."

Gage had heard from some of the men that a woman had been to Wallace's ranch for dinner. Wallace wasn't the kind of man who confided his personal business to anyone, but he figured Hoyt Nelson would know what was going on. "I don't spend much time around the ranch house." He hadn't been back to Delilah's farm since that night McBride almost caught him. It was his intention to talk to her that night to tell her she shouldn't be afraid of him. He didn't want to scare her off by coming on

318

too strong like he did before. Alcohol got the best of him that night in Abilene, and he wasn't about to make the same mistake a second time. He'd done a lot of thinking since that night, and for the first time in his life he was trying to plan for the future. He figured it was time to settle down, and there was only one woman he wanted to do that with. He'd considered getting a small place of his own and making a go of it. He wasn't afraid of hard work and he was good at cowboying. Not that he'd made enough money working for other ranchers to buy land, but thanks to his poker skills he'd managed to put some money aside.

The cook approached and put the steaks on the table. He glanced at Lucy and thought if he married Delilah he'd have to give up seeing other women. He liked Lucy, she was young and pretty, but she wasn't Delilah. He wondered if Delilah was interested in marrying Wallace. It'd be hard to compete with a man with his kind of money; he could give her anything she wanted. He smiled to himself, thinking that problem might be solved if Wallace continued to give Hoyt Nelson grief.

By the time they finished their steaks and the second bottle of whiskey was empty, Lucy had heard the details of Gage's obsession with Delilah from Abilene. Once the dishes were removed, Gage's head dropped to the table in a drunken stupor. Lucy finished the last of her whiskey as she thought about what he'd told her. There was no doubt in her mind he knew the woman. What man would spend that many years searching for a woman and not recognize her when he found her? The only thing that didn't make sense to her was why Gage hadn't told Wallace about the woman's past. There had to be a way for her to use this information to her advantage. Her thoughts trailed to Colt McBride. She'd bet her Saturday night wages that he didn't know the woman he'd had on his arm that day was a soiled dove from Abilene.

Walking from the stable, Colt stopped when he saw the buckboard coming to a halt near the house. "Hello there," he said to the group in the buckboard.

"Hi, Colt," Cody and Cade said together as they jumped from the back.

"Colt, I hope you don't mind us stopping by, but I need you to take a look at Bandit. He's been really sick and we're worried about him," Bartholomew said as he helped Mrs. Wellington to the ground.

Colt wondered why Victoria wasn't with

them, but he didn't ask. "I don't mind at all." He walked over to the buckboard and saw the motionless Bandit on a blanket. Usually the dog was all over him, so something was definitely wrong. When he lifted Bandit from the wagon he let out a little moan. "Come on, buddy, let's go to the house and I'll have a look at you." When Mrs. Wellington caught up to him, Colt asked, "How long has he been like this?"

"He seemed fine this morning, but it wasn't long after Victoria left to go to town with Mr. Wallace that Bandit became ill. He started pacing around and wouldn't lie down. Then he started vomiting and the poor thing hasn't been able to keep water down. After he vomited several times, he staggered and just tumbled over and wouldn't move."

Colt placed Bandit on the kitchen table to examine him as everyone hovered around.

"We said a prayer for him," Cade said in a trembling voice. "And Mrs. Wellington said you was God's helper."

"Is he gonna be okay?" Cody asked, his lower lip trembling.

Colt smiled at them. "I'll do my best."

Colt pulled the lids of Bandit's eyes wide and peered into them. He wasn't sure of anything. "I sure hope so. He's my buddy, too." He didn't know who looked more frightened, the boys or Mrs. Wellington. "Mrs. Wellington, I think Helen made a cake last night, and I know there's some ice tea. Maybe you could take the boys to the dining room and fix them up."

Grateful for something to do, Mrs. Wellington nodded. "Excellent idea." She took the boys by the hand and led them away from the table. "Help me find that cake and some glasses for the tea."

"Bartholomew, would you get me a quilt from one of the bedrooms?" Colt asked.

Bandit moaned again when Colt pressed on his stomach. "It's okay, boy, we're going to make you better." Bandit licked his hand when Colt looked at his gums, the action bringing a large lump to his throat. Not only would the boys be heartbroken if Bandit died, but he'd seen the way Victoria doted on him. They would all be devastated, himself included.

After she settled the boys, Mrs. Wellington came back to the kitchen. "Do you need assistance, Mr. McBride?"

"Please call me Colt," he told her. "What has Bandit eaten today?"

"I gave him some leftover ham and eggs this morning. That's his favorite. We all ate the same breakfast, so I don't think it was bad." She was quiet for a moment before saying, "Dear me, I had forgotten about the treat Mr. Wallace gave him. I thought it was nice of him since he generally seems fearful of Bandit. Perhaps it was spoiled meat."

Colt didn't comment. Wallace didn't strike him as the kind of man who would even think about a dog, much less bring him dinner. Bandit had all the signs of poisoning.

"Can you help him? We are so fond of this animal. It's the first dog the boys have had," Mrs. Wellington said.

Before Colt responded, Bartholomew returned with a quilt in hand. "Is this okay?"

"Sure." Colt lifted Bandit and Bartholomew placed the folded quilt underneath him. Pointing to a cabinet, Colt said, "Mrs. Wellington, there are some large bowls in that cabinet. Would you fill one up with some water? Can you tell me how many times he vomited? Do you think it was equal to the amount he ate?"

"I think he vomited four times, and I remember thinking the poor thing couldn't have much left in his stomach."

Mrs. Wellington placed the bowl of water next to Bandit. When the dog didn't move, Colt dipped his fingers in the water and let it drip into Bandit's mouth. "Come on, boy, you need to drink something."

Bandit looked at Colt, then at the water. Slowly he leaned over and stuck his tongue in the water.

Colt rubbed his ears. "Good boy!" He looked at Mrs. Wellington and Bartholomew. "We need to keep some water in him, but I think since he vomited so much, he got most of it out of his system. I'll get some bromide from the stable. That should help him rest easier."

"I'll get it, Colt," Bartholomew offered, hurrying out the back door.

"Do you think he will be okay?" Mrs. Wellington asked nervously.

"I think so. He just needs to drink and get some rest. The bromide will help with that."

"I'll go tell the boys. They will be so relieved," she said, hurrying from the room.

When she was out of earshot, Colt leaned over and looked in Bandit's eyes. "Now, don't you make a liar out of me. And from now on don't take any food from that son of a —" He stopped what he was going to say and looked around to see if the boys had slipped into the room. Seeing he was alone, he lifted Bandit's ear and whispered to him, "You know who I'm talking about."

Bandit moaned in response.

After Bandit fell asleep, Colt moved him to his bedroom and placed him on his bed so he could rest without being disturbed. Returning to the kitchen, Bartholomew handed him a cup of coffee. "Thanks. Why don't you all stay and have dinner here? I think Bandit needs to rest for a while."

"Thank you, but I must insist on preparing dinner," Mrs. Wellington told him.

Colt winked at her. "Why do you think I asked? Helen is not coming tonight, and I didn't want to eat my own cooking."

Mrs. Wellington laughed. "It would be my pleasure after what you've done for Bandit. I should tell you, though, my cooking isn't as good as Victoria's." She turned to Bartholomew. "I think you should —"

"I was just going to say the same thing," Bartholomew responded.

Colt looked from one to the other. "What?" He thought the two of them had become fast friends. They were already acting like an old married couple, finishing each other's sentences. His mother and father had done the same thing.

"Victoria should be back soon, and if you don't mind including her in your invitation, Bartholomew will bring her back. I really don't want her staying there alone, especially with Mr. Wall—" She glanced at the boys and decided not to finish her sentence. *Seems like Mrs. Wellington has the same feelings about Wallace as I do,* Colt thought. "Of course she's invited." He glanced at the boys. "I have some chores to do. Why don't you boys come help me?"

"Sure thing!" They were so excited they raced to the door.

"Mrs. Wellington, I'll send Tate in from time to time to check on Bandit and to see if you need anything."

"That's fine. Now you boys mind what Colt says," she instructed. It brought tears to her eyes watching the two boys hanging on to Colt as they made their way to the stable. They adored the man, and she hoped she wasn't wrong in her estimation of his feelings for them and Victoria. Those boys would be devastated if she married Wallace.

Having kept the twins busy to keep them from worrying about Bandit, Colt thought they would be worn out just trying to keep up with him. Their short legs worked hard trying to keep pace with his long strides. Over three hours later they were still going strong and chattering away. Colt was checking on a sick pony and the boys were sitting outside the stall watching his every move.

"How do you know so much about horses?" Cody asked.

"I learned from my pa. He owned this ranch before me and taught me and my brothers everything he knew."

"Your pa sure knew a lot of stuff," Cade said.

"Yep."

"Where are your brothers?"

"One is in Texas, and I'm not sure where the other one is right now."

"Do they ever come home?"

"They haven't been home in a long time."

"Do you miss them?"

"I sure do."

"Are you twins?" Cody asked.

"They can't be twins 'cause he has two brothers," Cade told his brother. "That's . . . uh . . . what's that called?"

"Oh yeah," Cody agreed. "What are they?"

"That would be triplets. No, but we all look alike. You can tell we're brothers," Colt told them.

"Your name starts with a C, and our names start with a C," Cody said.

"That's right." Colt smiled, unaware where this conversation was going.

"Maybe that means you're our pa," Cade remarked.

That pulled him up short. He stopped what he was doing and placed his arm over the railing and looked at them. "Don't you know who your pa is?"

"No."

Colt was puzzled why Victoria wouldn't tell the boys who their pa was. He figured every boy had a right to know who sired him. "Did you ever ask your mother?"

"We don't know our ma."

At first Colt thought they were teasing him, but they weren't smiling. "What do you mean?"

"We can't remember our ma," Cade said solemnly.

"Cade," Cody said in a warning tone.

"Colt's our friend, we can tell him," Cade replied, his small face turning serious.

Colt watched as the two boys communicated with each other without words. "Victoria isn't your ma?"

That made the boys laugh. "No!"

"Well, if she's not your ma, who is she?"

Colt watched as the boys stared at each other.

"She's our . . . sister," Cade answered.

"Cade!" Cody shouted.

He didn't believe for a minute that she was their sister. There was more to the story than the boys were telling, and Cody wasn't happy Cade was sharing the information. When he thought about it, Victoria had never actually said she was their mother. She referred to them as *my boys,* and he'd just assumed she was their mother. "I just thought she was your ma."

"She knew our ma," Cade told him.

"Where does your ma live?"

"We don't know."

"Doesn't Victoria know where your ma lives?" This story was getting stranger and stranger.

"No."

"But Victoria is like our ma. We just need a pa. She said she was going to keep us forever, so we need a pa." Both boys nodded their heads like they were connected.

"Do you think you could be our pa?"

There was a hopeful note in Cade's question that wasn't lost on Colt. He wanted to say the right thing. He wasn't inclined to make their pa look like a no-account in case the man ever showed up, but he wanted to be honest with them. "Any man would be proud to be your pa. But if I was your pa, I would have been with you since you were born. I would never have left you." He smiled at them. "Look how dark I am. I have black hair and you two are blond."

"You would be a good pa 'cause you know a lot of things. Do you think you would ever want some boys?" Cody asked.

Bartholomew walked into the stable, interrupting the conversation. "Mrs. Wellington said to tell you men that dinner is almost ready. She wanted to know if you are at a stopping place, or if she should keep it warm."

"I didn't know you were back," Colt told him. He was relieved that Bartholomew walked in when he did. He needed to have a talk with Victoria so he would know what to say to the boys.

"Victoria was already at the farm when I got there, so we've been here for an hour," Bartholomew replied.

Leaving the stall, Colt lifted a boy under each arm, carrying them like sacks of potatoes. "We've worked up quite an appetite, haven't we?"

"Yep!" the boys chimed in, trying to sound like Colt.

"Victoria made a special dessert for you," Bartholomew told them.

The boys made a game of guessing what they would be having for dessert as they washed up outside.

CHAPTER TWENTY-FIVE

After dinner the boys quickly fell asleep, and Bartholomew and Mrs. Wellington insisted on cleaning the kitchen. They pushed Colt and Victoria to the front porch. Colt had a feeling this was a prearranged plan between the pair in an effort to leave him alone with Victoria.

"Thank you for taking care of Bandit. Are you sure he will be okay?" Victoria asked.

"Yes, he will be fine in a day or two. I'd like him to stay here so I can keep an eye on him." He pulled a cigar from his pocket and held it in front of her. "Do you mind?"

"Not at all," Victoria responded. "I like the smell of a cigar."

"You are an unusual woman. I thought most women just tolerated a man's cigar." His eyes remained on her as he lit his cigar. She always looked beautiful and tonight was no different. No matter how many times he told himself he was going to stay away from her, circumstances kept throwing them together. They chatted for a while before he decided it was time for some truth. "The boys told me they don't know their father."

Her head snapped around to face him. She was stunned the boys had been so open with him. "No, they don't."

"Do you have a reason for not telling them?"

"I don't know who he is," she said honestly.

"I thought you were their mother." She hesitated so long Colt thought she might not answer. He waited.

For whatever reason, she knew she couldn't lie to him and she wanted to stop all of her lies. "No, I'm not."

"You're not their sister." He made the statement as a fact, not a question.

"No."

"Do you know their mother?"

"Yes, I do." She had spent so many years afraid to tell anyone the truth for fear of losing the boys that it was a relief to finally be honest.

Colt noticed her hands were tightly clasped in her lap, a habit of hers when she was nervous. "Why do you have them?"

She raised her eyes to meet his. "Why are you so interested?"

Taking a long pull on his cigar, Colt considered what he wanted to say. "Victoria, it seems to me you wanted me to think you were their mother, and I admit I did at first, but a lot of things didn't add up. For one, you don't look old enough to have boys that age. Then there's the fact that they call you Victoria. And of course, they look nothing like you." When she didn't respond, he continued. "You are a woman with a lot of secrets and for some reason you think you can't confide in anyone. I doubt even Mrs. Wellington knows what you're hiding. I'm interested because I think you need a friend."

Tears welled in her eyes, threatening her fragile composure. She wondered if he really knew how much she wanted a friend, how much she needed a friend. She'd come to Promise hoping to find a friend in Mr. Barlow. It was tempting to confess her whole past to Colt, but how could he possibly understand her life? She didn't want to be judged for her past, she wanted a fresh start. Just thinking about telling him the truth made her want to run away again.

"Does Mrs. Wellington know you aren't their mother?"

"She thinks I'm their sister."

Colt turned his chair so he was facing her

and leaned forward, placing his forearms on his thighs. "I've told you before you can trust me. I know you are not telling me everything. I also know that you have met Gage Hardy before."

That statement drained the color from her cheeks. By the look on her face, he no longer questioned that Gage Hardy knew her true identity. "Am I right about that?" He waited a beat and still she didn't respond. "Well, you need to tell someone your secrets. If not me, why not tell Mrs. Wellington? She cares for you and the boys, and I'd say she deserves the truth." Seeing she had no intention of opening up, he leaned back in his chair. "Well then, why don't you tell Wallace? You're spending enough time with him, he should know the truth if things are serious between you two."

"Things are not serious between us."

"The way I see it, you are making two mistakes. Number one, you should know by now you can trust me. I really don't know what else I can do to make you see that."

She waited for him to tell her the other mistake. When he didn't continue, curiosity got the better of her. "The second?"

"Getting involved with Wallace."

She reddened from the neck up. "I told you we are not serious. He is a neighbor just as you are, and he's treating me kindly as a newcomer to the town. That's all."

Colt stared at her, wondering if she truly believed what she said. "I think you know he has plans for something more. Tell me, do you think he gives one hoot about those boys? Or Bandit?"

She returned his stare. Part of her knew what he was saying was true. Wallace had been more forceful in his attentions for the last two weeks, and had made it clear he wanted more than friendship. He'd put pressure on her to go to town with him today. She'd already told him she couldn't go, but this morning he stopped on his way and wouldn't take no for an answer. Since she needed some supplies from the mercantile, it was easier to give in than to argue with him. She was going to have to deal with Wallace in her own way. Right now she needed to tell Colt the truth about the boys.

"Their mother was going to put them in an orphanage," she whispered.

"She didn't want them?" Colt was shocked. It was difficult for him to believe any woman would just walk off and leave her two boys.

"She wanted nothing to do with them."

Colt moved even closer until his face was scant inches from hers. "Why?"

She pulled back just a bit. "I can't tell you. I just want people to think they are mine so no one tries to take them away."

"Okay, that answers one question, and we need to talk about that. But right now I want to know why you are seeing Wallace."

She wasn't sure she could answer that. She wasn't attracted to Wallace like she was to Colt, but he seemed safe to her. He didn't frighten her as much as Colt. Wallace didn't seem to care about her past; at least he didn't ask many questions. "He seems safe, and —"

"And what?" Colt fairly snapped.

"Well . . . I do want a good future for the boys."

"Safe? Future for the boys?" Colt could barely contain himself from bellowing his response. "You haven't believed a word I've told you about him, have you?"

"I've told you before, he's been kind to me." At least, he had been until this morning. She'd asked him if the boys could go to town with them, but Wallace wouldn't hear of it. He said they needed time alone and refused to include the boys. After they arrived in town, he wouldn't let her out of his sight. But it was when they arrived back to the farm that she became truly concerned. As he was leaving, instead of his usual peck on the cheek, he'd pulled her close and kissed her on the mouth. It was a brief kiss, but she didn't like it. She shivered just thinking about how his mouth felt on hers. She'd made a vow then and there that she would never be alone with him again.

"What?" He saw her shiver.

His question jolted her back to the moment. "Nothing."

"What happened today?"

What was it about him that he seemed to know what she was thinking? "Nothing."

"You're a terrible liar. What did he do?" he demanded.

She could see he wasn't going to leave it alone. "He seemed a bit too possessive today in town."

As a man, Colt could understand why a man would be possessive of her. "Have you let him believe there is more than friendship between you?"

"Certainly not!"

He pinned her with his black eyes. "Has he kissed you?"

She waited too long to respond, and Colt said, "So you have encouraged him."

"I have not!" She turned away from him. "And this is none of your business. And besides that, he's not a . . . cowboy," she blurted out.

Colt couldn't believe she'd said that. "And what's wrong with cowboys?"

"Let's just say they are only interested in . . . let's just say I'm not interested in cowboys and leave it at that," she said with finality.

"Let's not leave it at that!" he said louder than he intended. "I want to know what's wrong with cowboys." She didn't make any sense to him. The men on his ranch were honest and hardworking, men to be trusted, no matter what. She'd just insulted almost every man he knew, including his own father.

"I've seen enough cowboys in my life that I know I don't want one for a husband," she told him honestly.

He shook his head and wondered if she was trying to make him angry. "If that don't beat all. Every good man I know is a cowboy. Are you telling me you would rather have a man like that skunk Wallace?"

"I'm not telling you anything. As I said, it is none of your business what happens between Mr. Wallace and me."

"Maybe not, but I'm making it my business." He rose from his chair, took her by the shoulders, and gently pulled her from her chair.

"What are you doing?"

He glared at her. "I asked you if he kissed you."

Even though he seemed angry, she wasn't afraid of him, and that was a revelation. "This is not your concern."

Colt almost smiled. He gave her credit for standing up to him. He didn't know many men who would have her nerve.

"Has he?" he asked again, this time lowering his voice because he didn't want to frighten her.

She tried to pull away from him, but he was having none of it. "He normally gives me a peck on the cheek, but today he didn't."

"I take that as a yes." She looked into his eyes, but she couldn't deny his statement. Holding her firmly by the shoulders, he lowered his head. When his mouth covered hers she didn't push him away. Considering that a good sign, he pulled her into his embrace and deepened his kiss. It was a long, thorough kiss, and by the time he pulled his lips from hers she was clinging to him.

He held her at arm's length. Her eyes were glazed and her lips were red and puffy from his kiss. He liked the looks of that. "Did he kiss you like that?"

No one had ever kissed her like that. She

was so astonished she couldn't even think of what to say, so she just shook her head from side to side.

"Well, that's how this cowboy kisses." He released her arms. "I didn't hurt you, did I?"

She shook her head again.

"Okay, then." He walked toward the door, then stopped and turned back to her. "Tate and I go to church every Sunday. We'll be at your house in the morning, so all of you be ready."

Victoria found her voice. "I don't go to church."

That surprised him. He walked back to her. "Why not?"

"I just don't."

"Why not?"

The man was impossible. "I'm sure Mrs. Wellington would be delighted to go with you, and she can take the boys."

"Why don't you go?"

She looked at him, thinking he was the most stubborn man in the world. He wouldn't leave without a response, so she said, "I don't believe that God listens to my prayers. And I don't understand why people go to church and pretend to be believers, and then continue to do things they know are wrong."

If what Gage Hardy said was true, she had lived a tough life for someone so young. He could understand why she'd lost her faith. "Why don't you believe God listens to your prayers?"

She turned away from his dark, penetrating stare and looked off in the distance. "I used to pray, and prayed for . . . something, but nothing ever changed. So I stopped believing."

He couldn't see her face, but he heard the pain in her voice. "What did you pray for?"

"Nothing you would understand."

"What if I told you I was at that point in my life once? Try me." His voice was gentle, persuasive.

"One thing I prayed for was a home for the boys," she replied, thinking that was one thing she would share with him.

He took her arm and gently turned her around to face him. She wouldn't look up, so he put his finger under her chin, urging her to look at him. He saw the tears in her eyes, and he knew there was a lot more, but she'd trusted him with enough for now. "And you have a home for you and the boys. Sometimes it takes a long time for a prayer to be answered. I know. I stopped praying when I was young. One day I figured out I hadn't lost my faith; it was just dormant for a while. I've been praying for one thing for years, and it hasn't happened yet, but I'm confident it will."

She wanted to ask what he prayed for, but he asked another question.

"Now what kinds of things do church-going people do that they know are wrong?"

She said the first thing on her mind. "Men like you who go to church and then visit those women in saloons. The preachers say it is a sin to be with a woman and not be married." As soon as the words left her mouth she wished she could take them back. It was none of her business what he did in that saloon. She didn't want to care.

Colt was caught off guard by her response. He'd never really thought about it that way. He saw himself as a man who had needs, as did most men. It wasn't like he was taking advantage of anyone, he wasn't married . . . the women weren't married and they needed to make money . . . so who was he hurting? Priding himself on being a fair man, he really didn't know how to respond to her. The first thing that came to mind was just saying the truth, "I've been in the saloon, but I haven't been with Madd . . . anyone since I met you." He mentally calculated exactly how long that had been. She might not appreciate the significance of that statement, but in his estimation, it was a long damn time.

Victoria was equally surprised by his admission, particularly since those two women in town hinted they saw him frequently. "You mean you haven't seen . . ." She hesitated. She knew she should drop the subject, but couldn't. "Not since I came to Promise?" she asked in disbelief.

"No, I mean since I met you in St. Louis." *That should give her something to think about,* he thought. It sure gave him something to think about. He dropped her arm and walked back to the door. "I will pick you up in the morning for church."

After opening the door, he added, "If Wallace kisses you again, he'll answer to me . . . a cowboy. And don't let him give any more food to Bandit." There was more he wanted to say to her, and one heck of a lot more questions, but he'd pushed her far enough today. That kiss should keep her awake tonight, just as he suspected it would him. *So much for staying away from her.*

Once he'd walked inside the house, she came to her senses and wanted to yell at him that he had no right to tell her what to do. Instead, she sat down and thought about his kiss and how much she liked it, and why she was no longer afraid of him. But the real question was, why hadn't she realized that her prayers had been answered? And what was Colt McBride's prayer?

CHAPTER TWENTY-SIX

Wallace expected to see Victoria's buck-board in town since she wasn't home when he'd stopped by earlier. What he didn't expect was to see her standing in front of the church with Colt McBride, talking to the preacher and a few townspeople. He jumped down from his buggy and pushed his way through the churchgoers.

"What's going on here?" he demanded.

Colt had one arm around the boys and his other arm rested protectively on Victoria's back. His black eyes bore into Wallace. "Looks like you're too late for church."

Ignoring Colt, Wallace directed his attention to Victoria. "I stopped by your place on my way to town, hoping I might buy you dinner today."

"I'm sorry, but Mr. McBride is taking us to dinner," Victoria responded.

Wallace could barely contain his anger. She hadn't informed him she was seeing

McBride. "I'm very disappointed in you, Victoria. I was under the impression we had an understanding."

Victoria didn't know what to say to him. She didn't plan on seeing him again, but she hadn't had a chance to tell him. "Understanding?" she repeated nervously.

"Yes, my dear. I've conveyed my interest to you and you didn't object to my attentions," he snapped.

By this time, all conversations around them had stopped and folks started gathering around to hear what all of the commotion was about. The people had already been buzzing when Colt walked into church with Victoria on his arm.

Victoria was trying to form a response when Colt spoke up. "Obviously, the lady has no interest."

Wallace bristled. "Victoria can speak for herself. You can't possibly know what passed between us. We've been spending a great deal of time together . . . alone. Now, Victoria, if you've been leading me on, say so at once."

Colt didn't want the boys to hear anything Wallace had to say, and he wasn't about to stand idly by and allow the man to insinuate there was a romantic link between the two of them. He turned to Tate. "Take the boys to the restaurant. We'll be there shortly."

As much as Tate wanted to see Colt punch Wallace in the nose, he didn't question his instructions. "Yes sir."

Horrified that Colt felt it necessary to defend her, Victoria knew she had to say something before this situation got out of hand. She wasn't going to allow Wallace to slander her character in front of everyone and not have her say. "Don't you dare hint that we have done anything inappropriate! I certainly have not led you on in any way. I've considered you a friend."

Outraged by Wallace's coarse behavior at church on a Sunday morning in front of all the townspeople, Mrs. Wellington moved to Victoria's side. "Mr. Wallace, remember where you are! This is a house of God! And lest you forget, most of your time with Victoria was spent in my presence, not alone with her. I demand you apologize immediately!"

Colt wanted to laugh. He thought he would be defending Victoria, but Mrs. Wellington, puffed up like a mother hen, was an impressive foe for Wallace.

Seeing his chance with Victoria slipping away, Wallace recognized he needed to back off. "It was not my intent to offend you,

Victoria. I will call on you later."

"No, you won't." Colt delivered his words with a menacing tone.

Wallace ignored the remark and walked back to his buggy. He would handle Colt McBride and Victoria. He would see to it that she never again embarrassed him by being seen with another man.

Lucy was headed to the kitchen when she spotted Wallace sitting at the poker table. This was her day off, but she wasn't going to pass up an opportunity to make some money. She was confident Wallace would pay handsomely for the information Gage Hardy had revealed. Reaching the table, she leaned over and whispered in Wallace's ear, "I have some information you might be interested to hear."

After his encounter with Victoria and McBride, he couldn't concentrate on poker anyway. Lucy piqued his interest, so he threw his cards to the table and followed her to an alcove under the staircase.

"Get me another drink first," he ordered.

Returning with his whiskey, she started relating the story she'd heard from Gage Hardy.

Wallace sipped his whiskey, considering what she'd told him. That was some story, but he didn't know if he believed her. If it was true, Victoria had played him for a fool. He'd believed she was a lady, not some tart who worked in an Abilene saloon. He'd lived in Abilene, and he'd frequented the saloon many times. He felt sure he would have remembered seeing someone like Victoria. On the other hand, he'd been involved with Kitten. She was another woman who had made a fool of him. Kitten was his favorite girl at the saloon, and he'd spent a lot of time and money on her. She left Abilene once without telling him, and it was months before he saw her again. When she returned, he was no longer enamored with her. He considered her just another woman not to be trusted.

He recalled how oddly Victoria reacted the night he mentioned he'd lived in Abilene. Lucy said Victoria wasn't the mother of those boys, and now that he thought about it, she was very young to have boys that age. "I want to know who told you."

"That doesn't make any difference." She was afraid he might have Hoyt Nelson kill Gage.

Grabbing a fistful of her hair, he pulled her face close to his. "Who was it?"

She tried to pull away from him. "You're hurting me!"

"Would you prefer I choke the information out of you? Who would care? Do you think the sheriff will come to help you?"

She knew he could kill her and the sheriff would do nothing. But she was resourceful, so she asked, "Will you give me some money to get out of this town if I tell you?"

"Where do you want to go?"

"San Francisco. I've heard there's a gentlemen's club there looking for girls that are young and pretty. I'm thinking I can make a lot of money there."

"I know the place," Wallace replied. He had been to that club before and it was a definite step up from the L. B. Ditty's Saloon. Lucy was pretty enough, and she might do well if she could learn to keep her mouth shut. "I'll pay your way. Now give me the name."

"Gage Hardy. He lived in Abilene."

"When?"

"Four years ago."

After overhearing the conversation between Wallace and Lucy, Maddie slipped quietly into her room at the top of the stairs. She could hardly believe the woman Colt had been escorting to the hotel that day had worked in a saloon.

Remembering it was Sunday, she walked

to the window, hoping to catch a glimpse of Colt. Every Sunday he walked to the restaurant with Tate and T. J. after church. She pulled the curtain aside and peeked out. She didn't have long to wait before she spotted him coming down the sidewalk, but it wasn't Tate or T. J. at his side. It was that woman. *Is she the reason he hasn't been with me since he returned from St. Louis?* To her knowledge Colt had not been with another woman in years. She remembered asking him one time if he courted any of the women in town, and he told her he didn't want to create problems for himself, he didn't want to risk being forced into a shotgun wedding.

She loved Colt, and because of that one-sided love she was foolish enough to harbor dreams that one day he would fall in love with her. She had known a few saloon gals who were lucky enough to marry customers, and that had given her hope. A few times she even hinted about a permanent relationship, but Colt always said he wasn't a marrying man. She'd taken him at his word, even though one time he mentioned having sons. So she'd waited. And grown older. Now all of her dreams were crumbling because of that woman.

She watched as he opened the door for

Victoria, and when he disappeared inside, she dropped the curtain in despair. Walking aimlessly around her small room, she stopped when she caught her reflection in the mirror. Staring back at her was a woman she almost didn't recognize. The reflection exposed what her lifestyle had taken from her. The woman in the mirror had a pallid complexion that belied her years. If she continued drinking, sleeping all day, and carousing all night with men, in a few short years she would see nothing but a wasted image of what she once was. She'd seen this happen to other women at the saloon. Their demise happened slowly and they had been unprepared, taking their youth for granted. Slowly, their regular customers would seek out the younger, prettier gals and they would no longer be in demand. They would have no choice but to move on to another town where women were scarce. Her future was before her and the thought terrified her. She took a deep breath and told herself to calm down. She had to think.

She walked back to the window and stared at the door across the street. If Colt was escorting that woman to church, then it stood to reason he didn't know about her past. All she had to do was go see him and tell him about her. She knew how he valued honesty. He would certainly end the relationship once he found out Victoria had deceived him. If he didn't come to the saloon, she would go to his ranch. Once he knew the truth, everything would be the way it was before Victoria came to town. She smiled for the first time in weeks, confident her plan would bring Colt back to her.

CHAPTER TWENTY-SEVEN

Victoria made coffee while Colt sat at the kitchen table with two energetic boys clinging to him. Bartholomew and Mrs. Wellington excused themselves to go for a walk by the river. They tried to get the boys to go with them, but the boys wanted to stay with Colt. Victoria couldn't help but smile at the threesome. Cade was on top of Colt's wide shoulders, while Cody was straddling his long outstretched legs. Colt didn't look nearly as formidable with the boys climbing all over him.

She had come to understand that there was much more to him than his fearsome countenance. There was a gentleness about him, never more evident than in moments like this with the boys, or when he played with Bandit. And with her, she realized. He always treated her like a lady. She smiled to herself, thinking of that morning, when they walked into the church. Every female head in the room snapped around to look at him. She couldn't blame them; he was certainly a handsome man. She couldn't fathom why some woman hadn't snapped him up, like that widow woman at the dance, who couldn't keep her hands off of him.

Victoria placed a cup of coffee in front of Colt, and pried the boys from him. "It's time to change out of your Sunday clothes."

"Aw, do we have to?" Cade whined.

"Let us play some more," Cody pleaded.

"Listen to your moth . . . Victoria," Colt said.

"Will you stay?" Cade asked.

"A while longer," Colt promised.

The boys hurried from the kitchen and Victoria sat in a chair next to him. She was grateful for the chance to speak with him alone. "You were right."

Colt gazed at her, thinking how beautiful she looked sitting next to him. His chest had swelled with pride when he walked into the church with her on his arm. "It's not often a woman tells me that," he teased. "What was I right about?"

"About me being honest with Mrs. Wellington. We talked last night. And you were right when you said my prayers had been answered. I do have a home for the boys now." All night she'd thought about what he'd said. Maybe her prayers hadn't been answered on her timetable, but they were answered. "Thank you for the lovely day. It was nice to go to church, and the boys love being with you."

He thought there was something different about her today. She seemed more relaxed, at least before Wallace showed up at the church. "Do you?"

She knitted her brows together, puzzled by his question. "Do I what?"

"Love being with me?" His dark eyes watched her intently. He couldn't deny her response was very important to him.

It was time for honesty. Spending the day with him had been one of the best days of her life. For the first time it felt like she had a real family. Going to church, having dinner at the restaurant, these were the simple things a family would do every Sunday. Even though they'd provided the parishioners with gossip to last a month when Wallace showed up, she didn't mind. It didn't seem to bother Colt, either. He seemed truly happy, laughing and teasing Tate and the boys. Actually, it was when she was watching him at the restaurant that she realized she was in love with him, or what she thought must be love. She had tried to ignore her feelings for him, partly because she was afraid, but mainly because she didn't want to have him reject her when he found out about her past. Like Mrs. Wellington, he deserved to know the truth.

Colt leaned toward her. "Well?" he asked somewhat impatiently.

"Yes, I do," she admitted softly.

Bartholomew and Mrs. Wellington picked that moment to walk into the kitchen before she had a chance to tell Colt everything she intended to say.

"Are we interrupting?" Mrs. Wellington asked, all too aware of the tension in the room.

"I was just going to ask Colt if he would like to take a walk," Victoria responded.

The look on Colt's face said he was clearly surprised, but he recovered quickly. "You want me to get the boys?"

"No, I want to talk to you alone." She looked at Mrs. Wellington, who was smiling from ear to ear. "Would you watch the boys?"

"Of course, dear," Mrs. Wellington replied. "Now go! Take all the time you want."

Colt jumped up and snagged his hat from the peg and opened the door before Victoria was out of her chair. Unsure what she had on her mind, he wasn't a man to kick a gift horse in the mouth. She surprised him again when she didn't stop on the porch but kept walking toward the barn.

Thank you, Lord, he thought. It seemed she was having trouble starting the conversation, so he thought he would ease her into it by asking, "You want me to bring Bandit back tomorrow? He's feeling much better and I think the boys are missing him."

"Um . . . yes, that would be nice. Or we could come to get him, since I know you have a lot of work to do."

They walked past the barn, and when they were far enough away that she felt sure they would have a few moments of privacy, she turned to face him. But Colt took her by the hand and gently tugged her into his arms.

"Um . . . Colt, I want to talk to you about . . ." she said before he could do what she knew he had in mind.

"I know, but I have to do this first." He hadn't planned to kiss her, but when the right moment presented itself, he could think of nothing else. He put his hand under her chin and lowered his mouth to hers. She didn't pull away; instead she looped her arms around his neck and moved closer. Kissing her felt so right and she tasted so good, and he really didn't want to stop. Finally he knew he had to stop before he couldn't, so he pulled his lips from hers. When she rested her cheek against his chest, he placed a kiss on the top of her head. "What are you doing to me?" he whispered, his breathing ragged. No woman had ever left him feeling like he was ready to lose control with a few kisses. He could feel her heart thumping wildly against his ribs, or was it his heart beating like he'd just been thrown off a wild horse?

He wanted to know what she was going to talk to him about, but when he pulled back and saw her big blue eyes staring up at him, all thoughts left his brain. All he wanted in that moment was to kiss her again. And he did. She didn't hold back from him, and when she pressed closer to him, curling her fingers in his hair, his desire was nearly out of control. Both of them were breathing hard, lost in the moment, and when he felt her hand push against his chest, he was momentarily confused by her action. Then he realized someone was calling his name. He wanted to ignore it, but the voice belonged to T. J., so something had to be wrong at the ranch. As much as he hated to stop, he moved away from her and whistled loudly. "T. J., over here."

T. J. spotted him near the barn and turned his horse. "You better come quick, someone killed Ol' Ass Kicker." His eyes landed on Victoria and he nodded in her direction. "Excuse me, ma'am, but that's his name."

"What happened?" Colt asked.

"We found him shot in the head, and they got more steers."

This was terrible news for Colt. Not only was that bull his best breeder and a valuable animal, he was fond of the surly beast. "How many more?"

"About twenty head."

Colt slapped his thigh with his hat. He really wanted to let out a string of curse words that would turn the air blue, but he was watching his language.

"We just don't have enough men. We've pulled double time for months now," T. J. lamented out of frustration.

"I know." He hated to leave Victoria when she wanted to talk to him, but he had to get to the ranch. Not to mention, he wanted more kisses. He turned to her. "I've got to go. We can talk later." He almost kissed her good-bye, but he didn't know how she would feel about that with T. J. watching. "Tell the boys I'm sorry I had to leave."

Victoria understood the demands on his time, and she could tell by the look on his face this news was devastating. "Of course, go."

■ ■ ■ ■

They'd been on the range all day, and it was late when they stopped for the night. It was an overcast night and Colt had to light a lantern to see. After they cared for their horses, Colt gathered firewood while T. J. threw some coffee beans in a pot and added water from his canteen. Once Colt got the fire going, T. J. put the coffeepot on.

"I wish we could find those culprits in the act," T. J. told Colt.

"While I was in town I telegraphed the U.S. Marshals office. Maybe we can get some help, since the judge was killed." Colt had been running on anger and strong coffee for the last several days. He'd hoped to get back to see Victoria before midnight, but it hadn't worked out that way. Every hand was needed to watch the cattle.

T. J. started to respond when Colt held up his hand at the sound of hoof beats in the distance. They moved away from the fire to stand in the dark, and pulled their pistols. A few seconds later, Tate came into view.

"Colt? T. J.?" Tate whispered.

Colt and T. J. walked from the darkness. "What are you doing out here?" Colt asked.

"I wanted to help. You didn't tell me I

couldn't come this time," Tate said sheepishly.

"I couldn't tell you because I didn't see you before I left." Colt figured Tate had intentionally avoided him before he left so Colt couldn't tell him to stay put. He knew he couldn't keep the boy from danger forever, no matter how hard he tried. Tate was getting older and he wanted to ride with the men instead of staying close to the house. Colt remembered being his age and he'd already been cowboying alongside his father for several years. At least the boy had remembered to bring a rifle with him. "Who's with Bandit?" Even though Bandit had recovered Colt didn't want him to be left alone.

"Rex brought Tom and Helen over to stay the night in case of more trouble."

"Good." He wanted to tell Tate to get back on his horse and ride back to the house, but it was a long ride and it was late. Anyone could bushwhack him along the way, and Colt couldn't spare a man to ride back with him. "You can stay with us, but hang close. I don't want you riding off by yourself. Now before you settle in, get that saddle off your horse and give him some water."

Tate flashed that boyish, contagious smile to everyone around him. "Yessir!" He reached in his saddlebag and pulled out a bundle, tossing it to T. J. "Helen sent some sandwiches."

"Bless her," T. J. said, opening the cloth and pulling out a sandwich.

"You can say that again," Colt agreed. It had been a long time since the noon meal. He caught the sandwich T. J. tossed him.

After he cared for his horse, Tate put his bedroll by the fire. "Can I have some of that coffee?"

"I don't know, youngster, you might wet the bedroll," T. J. cracked, but he poured him a cup.

"I ain't no youngster, I'm already as tall as you," Tate responded indignantly, biting into his sandwich.

It was hard to believe how fast Tate had grown in the last few years. "If you're so grown up, then you know not to say *ain't,*" Colt told him.

"The men say it all the time," Tate argued.

"Yeah, but you know better."

"Why do cowboys have to speak good English? That Mrs. Wellington speaks proper English and I can hardly understand every other word," Tate grumbled.

T. J. and Colt both laughed. No argument there, Colt had to admit. Mrs. Wellington occasionally said some words he didn't understand.

"I sure thought she was going to box Mr. Wallace's ears at church," Tate said.

"She wasn't the only one," Colt said gruffly.

T. J. looked from Tate to Colt. "Trouble?"

"Nothing that won't be resolved real soon," Colt replied, throwing the remnants of his coffee on the ground. "We'd best get some shut-eye. Rance is in the south range with five men and we'll need to relieve them in three hours. I want those cows watched twenty-four hours a day." He jumped up and collected some more branches for the fire. After spreading his bedroll, he lay back, rested his head on his saddle, and pulled his hat low over his eyes.

A few minutes later, Tate and T. J. climbed into their bedrolls. The night was quiet and the crackling and hissing sounds of the fire filled the air.

Tate leaned up on one elbow and looked over at Colt. "You gonna marry Miss Victoria?"

Colt flipped his hat off his eyes. "Where in the hel . . . Hades did you get that idea?"

"Well, you never took another woman to church with us. And she sure is pretty. Nice, too." He was quiet for a minute, then added, "She can really cook. Best pies I ever ate."

"You had a lot of experience with pies?" T. J. leaned up on his elbow, taking a sudden interest in the direction of the conversation.

Thank goodness for T. J., Colt thought. He didn't want to think about marriage, much less talk about the possibility.

"I've had a lot of my mom's and Helen's pies. But Miss Victoria's are the best."

"I'm gonna tell Helen," T. J. teased.

"Helen said the same thing," Tate retorted. "She knows Miss Victoria is a great cook."

Colt pulled his hat back over his eyes, smiling to himself.

"Well, are you?" Tate asked.

The boy had a one-track mind. "Not tonight," Colt mumbled into his hat.

"I'm serious. Don't you think it's time you had a family? You're not getting any younger." Tate sounded so grown up it made Colt chuckle.

"Well, don't call me grandpa just yet."

"Well, are you?"

Colt sighed, pushed his hat back again, and turned on his side to look at Tate. "You're going to worry this to death, aren't you?"

T. J. let out a chuckle. "I think that's his plan."

"Maybe she'll wait for me a few years if

none of you men are smart enough to snatch her up," Tate told them.

T. J. curled to an upright position. "Don't lump me in with this stupid son-of-a-gun. I already set my sights on her until this jackass" — he pointed a finger at Colt — "pulled the reins in on that."

Tate grinned at Colt. "So you do like her!"

Finally, Colt figured he wasn't going to sleep anytime soon, so he sat up. "When did I pull the reins in on you?" he asked T. J. Then he looked at Tate. "And yeah, I like her fine."

T. J. started to roll a cigarette, obviously warming to the conversation. "That day I told you I would snap her up in a minute and you told me to stay away from her."

"I don't recall —" Colt stopped midsentence. He sort of recalled that conversation. But mostly he'd been teasing T. J. — at least that's what he told himself.

After he lit his cigarette, T. J. took a draw and blew smoke rings in the dark night. "Well then, if you are too dang stupid, like Tate said, I will start courting her. Since you have no objections and all."

"I didn't say Colt was too stupid," Tate objected. "And you can't court her, 'cause she's sweet on Colt."

Colt wasn't about to mention that kiss

he'd shared with her just a few hours earlier; he wasn't a man who talked about his experiences with ladies. After the way she'd kissed him, he thought Tate was right and she *was* sweet on him, but he wasn't going to admit that to these two knuckleheads. "I kinda thought she was sweet on Wallace," he teased.

T. J.'s loud snort reverberated in the stillness. "You are too dang stupid if you believe that. As a matter of fact, if you are that stupid you don't deserve to court her. I guess it looks like I'm the only man around smart enough and up to the challenge. Not to mention the best dancer. I'm sure she'd have a better time with me."

"Sweet on Wallace?" Tate gave Colt an incredulous look. "Who could be sweet on that . . . nancy boy?"

T. J.'s laugh could be heard for miles. "That says it all."

"Tate, don't ever underestimate Wallace," Colt warned. "He's devious and that makes him a dangerous man."

"Are you gonna answer my question?" Tate pressed.

The boy was like Bandit with a bone; he was going to gnaw this to death. Exhaling loudly to indicate his irritation, Colt said, "I told you I like her fine."

"But are you gonna marry her? I mean, you don't even see Maddie anymore."

That comment snapped Colt to attention. "What do you know about Maddie?"

"Everyone knows about you and Maddie," T. J. interjected.

"That's because all of you talk too dam . . . dang much," Colt said.

"Ma says when a fella starts getting desires for more than kissin', then he's old enough to consider the consequences."

Colt was happy that Tate's mother gave him such good advice.

"What do you know about desires, whippersnapper?" T. J. asked.

"I'm growing up," Tate answered seriously. "I know about all that stuff."

Tate *was* growing up, Colt realized. Sometimes he wished the boy could remain young forever and not have to face any of the hardships life was sure to throw at him. He'd already seen enough difficulty for one so young.

"Those boys are crazy about you," Tate continued. "When I took them to the restaurant, all they did was talk about you."

"They're good boys." Colt smiled, thinking about all of the questions the boys could come up with. He'd asked his fair share when he was a boy, as had his brothers, as did Tate, but he thought the twins set a record.

"You should have more in your life than the ranch. You need someone to share your life with," Tate said. "Ma says men need a woman's touch or they become too predictable."

"All women say that because they all want husbands," T. J. informed them.

Tate sounded so old and wise, it surprised Colt. He couldn't argue the boy had a point. Until Victoria came to Promise, his life had been fairly predictable. Now it was anything but. *Wait a dang minute, I like predictable. I like things as they were before.*

"Ma also told me it's important for boys to have a pa. She says women can't teach a boy how to become a man without a man's help. That's why she's so thankful to you, Colt. She says you're a good influence on me. She tells me all the time that I will grow up to be a good man like you. She doesn't want me to be like my pa. He was drunk all the time and mean to us kids before he took off."

That brought a lump to Colt's throat, and it took him a minute to collect himself. "I'm honored that your ma thinks highly of me. I'm sorry about your pa; a man should live up to his responsibilities." He thought about the parents of the twins. It was beyond his comprehension that both parents could walk away from those boys.

T. J. waited for Colt's answer, and finally he had to ask, "Are you gonna answer Tate's question, or not?"

Colt got up and threw some more wood on the dying fire as he thought over his response. "I hadn't gotten that far in my thinking." He looked from Tate to T. J. "But I guess you two have given me something to think about." He winked at Tate. "Now can we get some sleep?"

T. J. grinned at Tate. "He was always slow in his thinking."

"I guess we can go to sleep as long as you are gonna think about it," Tate responded.

Long after Tate and T. J. fell asleep, Colt was staring into the night sky, thinking about Tate's question. He was attracted to Victoria and he wanted her, no question there. But if he was going to have her, he knew he'd have to marry her. He liked being with the boys and had quickly grown very fond of them. So what was holding him back? He didn't have a lot of free time right now to court a woman in the right way. The ranch kept him busy when there was no trouble. Now, with all of the problems, his workload had doubled and there was no time for much of anything else. And more trouble was coming; he could feel it deep down. He didn't want Victoria and the boys in the middle of whatever was about to happen. He couldn't ignore the fact that Victoria didn't trust him enough to tell him what she was hiding about her past. What would happen if he did marry her and became a dad to the boys, and their real parents showed up and wanted them back? What would he do then? He couldn't see himself turning the boys over to people who had walked off and left them once before. That could mean more trouble. Then there was the fact that he wasn't a marrying man.

His mind drifted from the reasons he shouldn't marry her, to seeing himself teaching the boys to ride and rope, going to church as a family on Sundays, having family dinners, and ending each day in bed with Victoria. He fell asleep with a big smile on his face.

Colt crouched near the dying embers of the fire with his gun in his hand, looking out into black emptiness.

T. J. woke up and saw Colt crouched down, gun drawn, kicking dirt into the flames. "Colt, what the . . . ?" At first he thought Colt must have had a dream and thought they were in danger. But in the next instant T. J. realized it was gunfire that had awakened him. He scrambled to his feet. "Was that a gunshot?"

"Shhhh," Colt whispered, still gathering his wits after being awakened from a deep sleep. "Get down! Yeah, it was a gunshot." Colt looked at Tate's empty bedroll. "Where's Tate?"

"He probably had to go —"

Before T. J. could finish, Colt was running into the darkness. "Tate! Tate! Answer me, dammit!" he screamed.

T. J. didn't know whether to follow Colt or go in another direction. Before he had time to make a decision he heard a heart-wrenching wail, unlike anything he'd ever heard.

"Tate! Oh, Tate! Nooooooo!" The raw emotion of Colt's cry rent the silent darkness.

T. J. ran in the direction of Colt's voice. He'd only taken a few steps when another shot rang out. Diving for cover behind a rock, he waited, listening. Silence. Without a thought for his own safety, he fired three quick shots in the air to alert the men closest to them that there was a problem. He figured the men in the south range were less than two miles away, so they could hear the shots. Belly crawling over the rocky terrain, he moved slowly in Colt's direction. Even though his eyes had adjusted to the dark, he still couldn't see Colt. It was so quiet he could hear the sound of horses in the distance, and hoping it was their men, he fired off three more rounds to direct them.

Scanning the terrain, he finally saw what he thought was Colt on the ground. He wasn't moving. Just as he was going to call out to him, he heard hoofbeats going in the opposite direction. Jumping to his feet, he ran to the immobile form on the ground.

"Colt! Colt!" When he reached him, he realized Colt was lying on top of Tate. As he turned him over, he felt a wet warm spot on his shirt. Blood. He thought Colt was dead until he heard him groan. Instinctively, he knew Tate was dead, but he prayed to God he was wrong. He placed a hand on the boy's chest to see if he could feel a heartbeat. Feeling no sign of life, he attended to Colt, trying to staunch the bleeding of a wound he couldn't see in the dark. He didn't even hear the arrival of the men until Rance was next to him, asking what happened.

"Colt's been shot in the back. Tate's dead," he said solemnly. "Five of you men go after him." He pointed in the direction he'd heard the assailant ride away.

Rance knew T. J. was not thinking clearly right now. "There might be more men waiting for us to do exactly that, and that would give them the opening they need to cause more trouble. We can track better in the morning."

T. J. realized Rance was right. The men couldn't be everywhere at one time. "You're right. Let's wait until morning. Two of you help me get Colt home, and two of you take care of Tate and bring Doc Barnes back pronto. The rest of you get back to the cattle."

CHAPTER TWENTY-EIGHT

Colt was still unconscious when Doc Barnes arrived some two hours later. T. J., along with Tom and Helen, had removed Colt's shirt and had cleaned the wound and slowed the bleeding. They were relieved to find the bullet had missed Colt's spine, if only by the narrowest of margins. They all worked under the watchful eye of Bandit, who hadn't moved from the side of the bed since T. J. and Rance carried Colt upstairs.

Feeling Colt's weak pulse, the doctor voiced his concern. "He's lost a lot of blood. But we can't wait to get that bullet out." He sent Helen to boil more water and get him some clean cloths. After Helen left the room, he spoke softly to T. J. and Tom. "I have to be honest here. I don't like the looks of him, and that bullet is too close to his spine." He looked at T. J. "You say he never woke up, not even for a minute?"

T. J. shook his head. "No, I thought it

might be because he's just plumb worn out. He hasn't had much sleep in over a month."

The doc pulled up Colt's eyelids and looked into his pupils. "I hope I'm steady enough to get that bullet out without damaging anything vital."

"It's probably best he's not awake. If you'd heard him when he found Tate —" T. J.'s voice broke, and he looked from the doctor to Tom. "I never heard a sound like that." The gut-wrenching scream played over and over in his mind. Everyone knew Colt was crazy about the boy and watched over him like he was his pa. "When he gets better, he'll kill Wallace for sure over this," he added.

"If Colt dies, I'll kill Wallace," Tom stated in his straightforward way. Tom had been around when Colt was born and he loved him like a son.

It seemed to take the doc forever to dig the bullet out of Colt. Once it was removed, Helen cleaned the area again so the doc could stitch him up. Tom and T. J. held Colt so the doc could wrap the bandage around him. "I never realized just how big a man he is," the doc commented.

Between the four of them, they managed to get Colt situated in the middle of the bed. When they stepped away Bandit

376

jumped on the bed, claiming a spot right next to Colt's side. Over the next few hours they held a vigil in Colt's room, waiting for him to awaken. Though they were distraught over losing Tate, caring for Colt gave them something to keep their minds off the boy they all loved.

After a couple of hours, the doctor had to leave to see his other patients. "T. J., if you see any change, if his fever worsens, any change at all, send someone for me. If he comes to, keep him still. I don't want him moving around at all," Doc Barnes instructed.

"I'll see to it. I have to go see Tate's ma and ask her to wait a few days before the funeral just in case Colt wakes up. I know he would want to be there to say good-bye. That boy meant a lot to him."

"We could wait a couple of days, but not much longer." He motioned for T. J. to follow him to the hallway. "T. J., I'm not even sure Colt will make it. And even if he does, and even if we wait to bury Tate, Colt won't be able to get out of bed."

Helen overheard what the doc told T. J., but she wasn't about to accept his lack of faith in the man she'd taken care of since he was a boy. When T. J. walked back into the room, she said, "He's going to wake up, and mark my words, he'll be at Tate's funeral."

"I know if anyone can do it, Colt can," T. J. replied. He was worried, but he wasn't about to let Helen know that. He wanted to believe that Colt would survive.

Leaving Tom and T. J. to watch after Colt, Helen headed to the kitchen to cook, since they had all missed breakfast. She knew the men would be coming in to see how Colt was doing, and she needed to make sure they were fed. On her way to the kitchen she heard a soft knock on the front door. When she opened the door she found Victoria, Mrs. Wellington, and the boys standing there.

"Lane came over and told us about Colt and Tate. How is he? What can we do to help?" Victoria's hurried words revealed her nervousness.

Tearing up, Helen could hardly talk. "The doc got the bullet out, but he's not awake yet. And Tate . . ." she murmured, "that poor boy." She wiped her tears with her apron. Victoria and Mrs. Wellington wrapped their arms around her.

"There now, you just have a good cry," Mrs. Wellington told her.

"I've never seen Colt in such a state. He's always so big and strong, but now . . ."

Helen couldn't go on.

"Colt is a strong lad, he will survive this," Mrs. Wellington assured her.

Collecting her emotions, Helen said, "I know he will. I'm just so worried about what he will do when he gets his hands on the man responsible for killing Tate." She gave them a brittle smile. "I'm so happy you are here. I need the company. I was just going to prepare something for the men to eat. Is Bartholomew with you?" It wasn't often Helen had female companionship and right now it was exactly what she needed.

"I will do the cooking. You're done in, and you need to get some rest." Victoria could tell Helen was at her breaking point.

"Bartholomew will be in shortly. He's seeing to the horses," Mrs. Wellington added.

"I don't think I can rest just yet, I'm just too nervous," Helen replied.

"Then we'll fix you up with a spot of tea — that makes everything better," Mrs. Wellington said.

"Is Colt going to be an angel like Tate?" Cade asked.

"Shouldn't we pray to God for him like we did Bandit?" Cody asked.

Victoria wasn't sure if the boys understood about death, since Tate was the first person they knew who died. She'd explained Tate's death by telling them they would no longer see him, but he was in heaven just like an angel. That explanation seemed to give them some understanding. She pulled both boys into her arms and hugged them to her. "No, Colt is going to be here with us for a long time. We must think good thoughts about him getting well. You can say a prayer for him before dinner." She couldn't even entertain the thought that he might die. To her, he was invincible.

"Can we see him?" Cody asked.

"Not right now. Let's give him time to rest." Victoria thought the best way to keep them from worrying was to keep them busy. "We need to help Helen right now. You two can set the table for her."

"Yes, ma'am," they replied together.

"They are such good boys, Victoria. You're an excellent mother," Helen commented.

Victoria exchanged a look with Mrs. Wellington. Now that she had told the truth to Mrs. Wellington, she felt guilty continuing the lie with other people like Helen, who was becoming her friend. Knowing it was not the time for such discussions, she said, "They are worried about Colt. They're very fond of him."

"I daresay they aren't the only ones,"

Helen replied, glancing in Victoria's direction.

Victoria hurried across the room to retrieve an apron off the peg, needing to keep herself busy. "Do you want me to cook enough for all the men?"

"Yes, I'm sure they will all stop in when they have time, to see how Colt is doing." Helen sipped the tea Mrs. Wellington served her, but in a few seconds she was back on her feet. "I'd better take some fresh water upstairs."

"I'll take it," Victoria offered quickly, wanting badly to see Colt. It wasn't only the boys who needed reassurance that he would be okay.

Mrs. Wellington moved to the stove. "I'll take over here. You go ahead." She knew Victoria was distraught over Colt and would worry until she saw him.

The first thing Victoria noticed when she walked into the room with a pitcher of water was Bandit snuggled up on the bed beside a deathly still, deathly pale Colt. The two chairs in the room were occupied by Tom and T. J., and both were snoring softly. She moved quietly to the bureau and poured fresh water into the bowl. As if he knew he shouldn't move, Bandit followed her every move with his eyes. After placing the bowl on the table by the bed, she dipped a cloth in the water and gently washed Colt's face. The cloth snagged on his dark whiskers, and she remembered when he'd kissed her he was clean shaven. It was frightening how things changed in the space of one day. She could have lost him forever, and that was a thought she couldn't face.

Encouraged that he didn't seem feverish, she reached across Colt and patted Bandit's head. "He will be okay," she whispered. Bandit looked from her to Colt and started wagging his tail. She didn't have the heart to make the dog leave, and thought perhaps on some level it might be a comfort to Colt to have him near.

It was difficult for her to see this larger-than-life man in such a state of helplessness. Yesterday when he'd pulled her into his arms, he was so warm, strong, and solid, so full of life. She moved her hand to his chest to feel his heartbeat. It reassured her to feel a strong, rhythmic beat. She leaned close to his ear and whispered, "You need to wake up. The boys want to see you, and you are worrying everyone to death, especially Bandit." She jumped when Colt moved his head toward her lips. He let out a small moan, and Bandit's head snapped up and he looked at Colt. When Colt didn't open his eyes, Bandit lowered his head back down to rest it on Colt's hand and let out his own little groan.

When she finished washing Colt's face, she took his hand in hers and stared at his face. He looked quite disreputable with a day's growth of black whiskers and his long, unruly hair, but he was still the most handsome man she'd ever seen.

Unbeknownst to her, Tom and T. J. had awakened and were watching her. If T. J. had had serious thoughts of courting Victoria, they would have been quickly dismissed when he saw the look on her face as she held Colt's hand. He couldn't figure out two things: why Colt hadn't realized how she felt, and why she was spending so much time with Wallace.

Mrs. Wellington walked in carrying a tray. On seeing Tom and T. J. awake, she said in a direct tone that indicated she would brook no argument, "Get yourselves downstairs and have a good meal and then get some rest. Victoria will call you if there is any change." Both men jumped up and started moving toward the door, not daring to argue with the woman.

"How is he?" Mrs. Wellington asked.

"He doesn't feel feverish, so I think that is a good sign."

Placing the tray of food on a table by the chair, Mrs. Wellington walked to the bed and looked at Colt. "I thought you might want to stay up here while Helen rests for a while, the poor dear. Why don't you eat here and after I clean the dishes, I will come sit with him. Don't worry about the boys; they are already at the table with the men."

"I got him last night," Hoyt Nelson told Wallace.

"What are you talking about?" Wallace asked, settling in his chair.

Hoyt finished rolling his cigarette and lit it as he strolled to the chair in front of the desk. "McBride. I shot him last night."

Lurching from his chair, Wallace planted both palms on his desk and leaned forward. "You did what?"

Hoyt blew smoke in his face. "I killed McBride."

"I gave you no authority to kill McBride, at least not yet." Wallace wasn't angry that McBride was dead; he just wanted to be there to see him killed. He had a score to settle.

Hoyt grinned. "Let's just say the opportunity came for me to expedite matters. I'm tired of this nothing town and it's time I moved on. Besides, you own the sheriff, so it's not like he will come looking for me. Right?"

Wallace shook his head. He was an idiot to think a hired killer could take orders, or be trusted, for that matter. "I wanted things handled more subtly. Do you know what that means?"

Returning Wallace's glare, Hoyt's voice took on a deadly tone. "Yeah, I know what it means. Problem is, you're going about this all wrong. Everyone's noticed you've been distracted by a pretty face. I'm not inclined to stay around here until you finally decide how to handle that woman and get your mind back on business."

"I'm paying you as well as every other man on this ranch to do things my way."

Hoyt dropped the cigarette on the fancy rug and ground it out with his boot. "I'd say I just did things my way. Now I want my money."

If Hoyt thought Wallace was going to roll over and play dead, he didn't know who he was dealing with. Wallace sat back down in his chair and wrapped his hand around the pistol under his desk. "This is not over. I want the Barlow farm. I had a plan for McBride. Since he's dead, I guess getting what I want will be easier."

"I told you, I don't intend to hang around

here forever," Hoyt ground out. "I don't see anyone else standing in your way."

"McBride has two brothers, and I guess you didn't know that. One happens to be a U.S. Marshal."

"I don't see what difference that makes. I don't see him around."

Wallace just shook his head. "No, I don't suppose you do. As I stated in our agreement up front, when I have the Barlow farm, then you get your money." Before Hoyt could respond, he added, "Find Gage Hardy for me and send him in."

"Why do you want him?"

"I have some questions for him."

"There's a man that can't hold his liquor," Hoyt said.

Wallace was counting on that. "Few men can. Just get him in here."

Hoyt stood to leave, but Wallace stopped him. "You're sure you killed McBride?"

"Yep, it was after midnight. No one saw me."

"If it was dark, how do you know you shot him?"

"He's a big man. Hard to miss."

"I thought you wanted to draw against him," Wallace taunted.

"I did, but I shot his foreman, and McBride came running, so I had no choice."

Turning to leave, Hoyt gave him a parting demand. "If I hang around here any longer, I'll expect triple the amount we agreed on. And don't think of asking Hardy to take me out. He's not fast enough or smart enough."

Wallace leaned back in his chair and put his hands behind his head. It amused him to see what went through Hoyt's brain. He had no intention of asking Gage Hardy to kill Hoyt. But maybe he needed to think this through. Perhaps that wasn't such a far-fetched idea. Hoyt was proving to be a problem, and it might not be a bad idea to find a way to eliminate him after he got what he wanted. Killing McBride didn't bother him, except for the timing, and the fact that Hoyt had a habit of bragging about his exploits to the men. Maybe he should hire someone to take him out.

Thirty minutes later Gage Hardy walked into Wallace's office. "You wanted to see me?"

Wallace poured him a large glass of whiskey. "I wanted to ask you some questions."

Chapter Twenty-Nine

Unable to sleep, Victoria squirmed around in the large chair T. J. had carried from Colt's office upstairs so she would be comfortable. It wasn't that she was uncomfortable, she was just nervous. Colt hadn't moved a muscle for hours. She leaned forward and placed her palm on his forehead for what seemed like the hundredth time that evening. No change. After she refreshed the damp cloth on his forehead, she picked up the books on his bedside table. The Bible and a book of Shakespeare's works. That made her think of Mr. Barlow's letter: *I read the Bible and Shakespeare.* She hadn't read the Bible in a long time, but she picked it up and started reading one of her favorite passages to Colt. After a long while, she closed the book and spoke softly to him.

"I wanted to talk to you, to tell you things about my past." She wasn't sure why she felt the need to talk to him. Maybe it was her deep-seated fear he wouldn't survive, no matter how often she told herself otherwise. Somehow it seemed easier to spill everything in her heart without those black eyes boring deep into her soul. "I'm not who you think I am. I'm the daughter of a woman who worked in a saloon in Abilene. The twins are also children of a saloon woman." From there, she spilled every sordid detail of her life. She told him of the night Gage Hardy attacked her, the one thing she hadn't even told Mrs. Wellington. She described the fire at the saloon, and how she took the boys that night and left that life behind. She told him of her ordeal traveling with the young boys, right up to the day she reached Mrs. Wellington's boardinghouse. When she finished telling him her story, she was both exhausted and relieved. Smoothing his wavy hair back from his forehead, she gazed at his strong features. He was an unbelievably handsome man. Everything about him was masculine except those long, dark lashes of his. She wanted him to know how much she cared for him. "I love you," she whispered.

Her story would have to be repeated one day; she owed him that. Leaning over, she kissed his forehead, much as she did the twins every night. Resting her elbows on the bed, she folded her hands together and did something she hadn't done since she was a little girl living with her grandmother. She prayed.

Colt had awakened before Victoria started talking. The room was quiet, and he didn't know where he was or what had happened. His mind was fuzzy and his body ached all over. *And why is my hand so cold?* Events flashed in his mind as he tried to remember what happened to him, but everything was disconnected and confusing. He saw himself standing by Victoria's barn, talking to her. Kissing her. Then . . . *What happened after that?* He was starting a fire . . . T. J. was there. He saw himself near the fire . . . Tate was asking him about . . . *Victoria?* They were laughing. Nothing was making sense; each thought seemed to be disjointed. He heard something . . . *a gunshot?* Then he saw himself kicking dirt into the fire . . . running . . . his gun was in his hand. *What is evading my memory?* Tate . . . where was Tate? What happened to . . . Tate? To T. J.? Suddenly the disconnected scenes of that night assaulted his mind. It was so dark, but he saw a body on the ground. Not . . . oh no, not Tate! No! He reached down to feel the boy's chest to see if he was breathing.

Warm blood was flowing from his lifeless body. Tate . . . shot . . . no, God . . . Tate was dead. He started to drift back to the place where he couldn't feel the pain. This had to be a dream. Tate couldn't be dead.

Someone placed a cool cloth on his face. He was so hot and it felt so good. Maybe he'd caught a fever and was out of his head. Then he heard Victoria's sweet voice. He tried to hang on to every word to remain conscious. He wanted to ask her if he was dreaming, but he couldn't speak. All he could do was listen. He concentrated on what she was saying so he wouldn't drift away. She was telling him about her past. She told him why she'd lost her faith.

Focusing on what she was saying kept his mind off his physical pain and his mental confusion. When she explained how she left Abilene with the boys, he realized she had to have been younger than Tate at that time. How had she survived? What a testament to her strength of character. She had certainly saved the boys from a terrible future. It was amazing that such a young woman had the determination and courage to take on so much responsibility.

Victoria stopped talking and the room was quiet again. Finally, he found the strength to open his eyes. In the dim light he saw her with her head bowed. *Is she praying?* He looked down to see why his hand was wet and cold, and he saw Bandit by his side with his cold, wet nose pressed against his hand. Not wanting to interrupt Victoria, Colt gently rubbed Bandit's paw resting beside him, and in silent understanding, Bandit returned the affection with a lick.

When Victoria finished praying she rested her head on his arm, and after a few minutes he realized she had fallen asleep. Her soft breath tickled the hairs on his arm. He closed his eyes and thought about all she had been through the last few years. Growing up in a saloon couldn't have been an easy life for a young, beautiful girl. In a wild town like Abilene, anything could have happened to her. When she talked about Gage Hardy, he wanted to get out of that bed and track him down and call him out. He figured he would still have his chance. Now he understood why she didn't like cowboys. He also understood why she had lost her faith. What young girl could experience such a past and still believe there was anyone who cared about her? He understood because he'd felt that way when his mother was killed. He'd turned away from his faith, and it wasn't until he returned to church that he realized his faith was an important part of him.

His thoughts drifted back to Tate. He knew it wasn't a dream. He hadn't caught a fever. Tate was dead. That sweet young boy with so much promise was gone. There was no doubt in his mind Wallace was responsible for Tate's death, and he figured Hoyt Nelson just pulled the trigger. Both would pay for killing Tate. He choked up thinking about the boy he loved as much as his brothers. Tate's mother was sure to be devastated. He reminded himself that the young man was in God's hands now. But that brought him little comfort because he knew he'd let Tate down. It was his fault he'd allowed Wallace to have free rein for so long, and now Tate was dead because of his inaction. Well, no more. Wallace was going to pay.

He didn't know how long he'd been thinking about Tate when he finally opened his eyes. Victoria was watching him. "Hello," he said raggedly. He hardly recognized the sound of his own voice, it was so weak.

Relief overwhelmed her in the form of tears streaming down her face. "Hello yourself."

He lifted a hand and wiped a tear from her cheek. "Why are you crying?"

Smiling through her tears, she whispered, "I'm so happy you're awake."

"If you're happy you shouldn't be crying." His words came out in a rough whisper.

"Consider them happy tears. Would you like some water?"

"Please."

She held his head while he gulped the water. "How do you feel?"

"Like I've been shot." He struggled, trying to move to a sitting position.

She placed a staying hand on his chest where he wasn't covered by a bandage. "You shouldn't be moving yet."

Colt looked at her pale hand on his dark skin. It felt like someone shot him again. He glanced at her face and she quickly pulled her hand away. He knew she felt it too.

"Could you put two pillows behind my head?"

She put one pillow behind him. "You can't sit all the way up. I'm afraid you will open your stitches. Can I get you something else?"

He pointed to a table across the room. "That bottle of whiskey over there."

Quickly fetching the bottle, she poured a generous amount in a glass for him.

Throwing the whiskey back in one gulp,

Colt held the glass for a refill and asked, "How long has it been?"

"It's been over twenty-four hours."

He had to ask, even though he knew, but prayed he was wrong. He took a deep breath and when he released it, he said one word. "Tate?"

She brushed an errant curl from his forehead and ran her palm over his cheek. "They're taking care of him," she responded gently. "I'm so sorry, Colt."

He shut his eyes. "He was just a boy. I was supposed to look after him."

She took the glass from his hand and linked her fingers through his. "Don't you even think this was your fault," she told him sternly. "This was the deed of a coward hiding in the dark."

"He was still my responsibility," he said sadly.

Hearing the misery in his words, she wondered if anyone ever looked after him. The first day she saw him at the boarding-house, she thought he was larger than life. Since that day, she learned she was right; he was indeed larger than life, not only in stature but in his strength of character. The schedule he maintained on the ranch would be too much for many men, but she had never heard him complain. He looked after everyone: Tate and his family, Bartholomew, Tom and Helen. He'd taken time to see to her needs when she arrived in Promise. She thought of how he had taken care of Bandit, and the time he spent with the boys. He didn't expect anything in return.

It embarrassed her to think that she had been afraid of him. She took his hand and held it tightly between hers. "You are not responsible for this in any way."

He needed to change the subject or he was going to break down. He would think about Tate when he was alone. Finally he pulled it together enough to speak. "I didn't ask why you are here."

"One of your men rode over to tell us what happened and we came right over."

His gaze moved to the chair that was usually in his office. "Was that your bed?"

"Yes, T. J. moved it up here for me. I told Helen I could sleep anywhere."

Looking at her eyes, he thought she looked tired. "Did you sleep?"

"For a few minutes." Those black eyes were so very hard to read. Without thinking about what she was doing, she ran her hand over his hair. "You need tending, Mr. Mc-Bride."

He liked the way it felt to have her fingers running through his hair. "You want to give me a cut and shave?"

"I've never shaved a man, and I'm a bit groggy. I might nick you."

He stared at her intently. "You could crawl in here with me and catch a nap." He scratched Bandit behind his ears. "See, Bandit thinks it's comfortable."

His dark gaze made her feel warm all over. She pulled her hand away and handed him back the glass of whiskey. "You'd best be concerned with getting better."

He drank the contents down. "Don't worry, darlin', I'm already feeling better." Having her near did take his mind off his pain. It surprised him how much he enjoyed having her in his bedroom talking to him. "What if I told you that you could keep me warm if you were beside me?"

Her hand quickly moved to his forehead. "Are you chilled?" she asked anxiously.

He grinned up at her. "Well, my hand is cold where Bandit is resting his nose."

She pursed her lips, trying hard not to laugh. "You are impossible, Mr. McBride."

"Back to Mr. McBride, huh?"

She turned to leave. "I'm going to the kitchen to get you something to eat since you won't rest."

He reached for her hand. "Don't go. I promise I'll be good."

He coaxed her to sit on the bed beside him. "Now doesn't this feel more comfortable than that chair?"

She shook her head at him, but she did have a little smile on her face.

That encouraged him to say something he never dreamed he would say. "You know, if you married me you would have to sleep with me every night."

Her eyes went wide. "Marry . . . *you*?"

"Yeah, me." By the look on her face, obviously the thought of marrying him was right up there with getting shot. "Is that such a bad idea?" He hadn't exactly planned on asking her to marry him, but once he said it, he was warming up to the idea. It was her response that set him back on his heels. Not that he expected her to jump up and down at the thought, but she sure as heck could do a lot worse in his opinion. Like marry Wallace. He surprised himself, blurting it out like that, and he couldn't even pinpoint when the thought of marriage had wiggled into his mind. There had been times when he would be riding alone late at night and he would envision her waiting for him. Perhaps it was having her in his room that made him realize how nice it would be to have her here permanently. He could have waited until he was healed to ask her in a more formal way, but right now he didn't want to wait, not even another minute. He thought of what Tate said that last night on the range. Tate was probably up in heaven with a big grin on his face. He was going to miss that boy.

"Colt, I can't marry you. You don't even know me. Not really." She tried to move away, but he refused to release her hand.

"I know all I need to know," he said tenderly.

"Before you left the other day, we were going to have a talk. There are things I need to tell you."

He squeezed her hand before she could say more. "I know you need me. The boys need me. Now give me a kiss." He pulled her closer and placed his hand behind her head and gently urged her face down to his. "This will make me feel better," he whispered, and nibbled on her lips. He knew the moment her mind was on the kiss and not on any doubts she was having. He finally raised his head and asked, "Do you care for me?"

She didn't respond right away, and he said, "You can be honest." No matter what she said, the way she responded to his kiss told him she cared. She dropped her head, but not before he saw the tears in her eyes.

"Victoria?"

He can't possibly understand how much he means to me. "Yes, I care, but that doesn't change anything. I can't marry you."

"Do you want to marry Wallace?" It'd be a cold day in hel . . . Hades before he would ever allow that to happen. Wallace was going to be dead.

She was ashamed that she'd ever questioned Colt's warnings about Wallace. "No!"

"Then what is wrong with me? I don't mean to brag, but I hear some women think I'm a fair catch."

She had no doubt every woman in town would think he was more than a *fair* catch. "It's not you, it's me." She couldn't deal with the possibility that he would be embarrassed if there came a time someone recognized her from her old life. Someone like Gage Hardy. "As I told you, you don't really know me."

"You're going to marry me. You can't kiss a man like that and not marry him," he teased.

Even when she wanted to cry, he had a way of making her smile. "You kissed me."

"You kissed me back."

She couldn't deny it. "It's going to be morning soon, and you need to get some rest. If you don't lie back and get some sleep, I'm going to leave you alone."

"Yes, ma'am." He was tired and in pain, so he closed his eyes. After she sat back in the chair, he added, "Don't think this conversation is over."

Chapter Thirty

Victoria awoke to the aroma of fresh bread. She looked up to see Colt smiling over a large plate of food.

"I thought you were never going to wake up," he said. "Come over here and you can share my lunch. But you better hurry; Bandit's already eaten his fair share." At that comment, he handed Bandit another biscuit.

"Colt McBride, you know she wouldn't get more than a couple of bites the way you eat. I'll bring her a plate," Helen told him.

Straightening in the chair, Victoria could hardly believe she was looking at the same man. His face was no longer pale under that dark growth of beard, and his voice no longer sounded weak. She wouldn't have expected him to look this good after two weeks' time. She noticed he had two pillows stuffed behind his head propping him up, and she imagined he'd sweet-talked Helen into that.

Victoria asked, "How do you feel?"

"Like I've been shot." He winked at her.

"You said that earlier," she replied, returning his smile.

"The doc was in after breakfast, and he said he thinks I'll make it."

She couldn't believe she'd slept through the doctor's visit. "Did he tell you to stop moving about?" she asked.

"He most certainly did," Helen responded for him. "But he might as well have been talking to his horse for all the good it did."

When Helen walked to the beside table to turn off the oil lamp, Colt noticed the dark circles under her eyes. He smiled at her. "Don't worry about me. I'm fine. You know it'll take more than one bullet to put me down. Now you need to go home and get some rest." Colt didn't need the doctor to tell him he would recover, he knew he would. He'd spent the night thinking while he watched Victoria sleep, and he'd set his course of action. As difficult as it was, he'd come to terms with the loss of Tate. But the men responsible for Tate's death were going to face him, and soon. He was also going to convince Victoria to marry him. More than anything, he wanted to be a good husband and a father for those two precious boys, and he'd asked God for the wisdom to meet that goal. The way he saw it all he had to do was persuade Victoria that he was the right man for her.

Victoria stood. "I need to check on the boys."

Helen handed her a cup of coffee. "Just sit yourself back down and have some coffee. Don't you worry about the boys. They had a good breakfast, and Mrs. Wellington and Bartholomew took them back to the farm. She said she would take care of things there this morning, and to tell you they would be back tonight."

"The boys came to see me this morning before they left," Colt told her. "We were quiet so we wouldn't wake you." He chuckled, thinking of the boys whispering their many questions.

"Did you say lunch? What time is it?"

"It's almost noon," Helen said.

"Oh, I didn't realize I slept that late."

"You needed some sleep. Now you stay put and I will get you something to eat," Helen said.

"Did you get some sleep?" Victoria asked Helen.

"Yes, thanks to you."

When Helen left the room, Colt asked, "Do you always look this beautiful in the morning?" He recalled the morning he was leaving St. Louis when he saw her in the window. "Never mind, I know you do."

"I wasn't the one who was shot, but thank you." Seeing he had finished eating, she jumped up to take his tray. "I need to freshen up. Is there anything you need?"

"Yes, a kiss."

She shook her head at him. "I can tell you are feeling better."

When she left the room, he closed his eyes and thought about how nice it was going to be to have her there with him every day.

Once she returned to Colt's room, he told her they would be burying Tate the next day. He discussed the boys and the many questions they'd had for him that morning.

"I'm sure they enjoyed seeing you. They've been very worried."

"You know they need a man to teach them how to run a ranch, and all the things only I can teach them." It wasn't a question but a statement, and before she could respond, Helen scurried into the room.

"Colt, there is a lady . . . well, a woman is here to see you."

"A woman?" Colt repeated, trying to think of any woman he knew who would be visiting.

Helen looked flustered. "It's . . . well . . . I

think she's that woman who works at the —" Helen stopped as Maddie flounced into the room.

Colt could hardly believe his eyes. To say he was stunned speechless would have been an understatement. She was the last person he expected to walk into his bedroom. To further add to his shock, Maddie was not dressed for a social call in polite society. The bodice of her dress was so tight her breasts were spilling over the top. Colt figured Bob from the livery must have tightened her laces, since he had the strongest hands in town. He'd never seen her dressed so provocatively, other than when they were alone upstairs in the saloon.

"Hi, Colt, honey. I've been so worried since I heard you were shot that I had to come to see for myself that you were okay."

He didn't know how she'd heard so quickly about him being shot, but right now he would have preferred to be unconscious. "You heard right."

"Are you okay, honey?" Her eyes landed on Victoria sitting in the chair close to his bed. Seeing the woman responsible for keeping Colt from her made her furious. *A real cozy scene,* she thought, *with that woman on one side and a dog on the other.*

"I'll be fine." He wasn't sure whether he

should introduce Victoria, but fortunately for him, Helen stepped in before he had to decide.

"Colt needs his rest now. I'll show you out." Helen didn't like the way the woman had barged in uninvited, and she wasn't about to allow her to upset Victoria.

Paying Helen no heed, Maddie moved to the side of the bed where Bandit was resting. "I'll leave in a minute," she snapped at Helen. "Colt, I haven't seen you alone in a long time, and I hope you don't mind that I came, but I need to talk to you about something important," she said sweetly, all the while glaring at Victoria. "Alone," she added.

When Victoria stood to leave, Colt reached for her hand. "Stay here." Out of the corner of his eye he saw Helen turning to leave, but he stopped her. "Helen, wait a minute. Maddie won't be staying." He turned his gaze on Maddie. He hadn't missed her meaning when she said she hadn't seen him alone. "Anything you have to say to me can be said in front of them." He figured if Tate knew about Maddie, it stood to reason that Helen did as well. Victoria was an intelligent young woman, and having seen Maddie in front of the hotel, she probably guessed his relationship with her.

"It might be best if you hear this alone," Maddie insisted.

"I'll leave so you can have some privacy," Victoria said. It upset her to see that woman in Colt's bedroom. Even though he'd told her he hadn't been with Maddie in a long time, he hadn't really told her how he felt about the woman. He had known her for years, so he had to feel something for her.

"No need." He arched his brow at Maddie and said impatiently, "Say what you have to say, Maddie."

"Are you sure? I mean, it could prove embarrassing for some in this room." Maddie was confident in her plan to change Colt's opinion of this woman.

He'd known Maddie a long time, but right now he was seeing a totally different side of her. He should have recognized how jealous she was when she saw him with Victoria. "I have no secrets."

Maddie moved closer to the bed, but Bandit raised his head and gave a low growl. Keeping a wary eye on the dog, she said, "Really? I thought you and I shared some . . . special secrets."

Colt was in no mood for her games. "Maddie, what did you come all the way out here to tell me?" he asked bluntly. If she thought she was embarrassing him, then she was clearly in for a disappointment. Victoria was willing to share her past with him, and he could do no less than be totally honest.

"Have it your way. I came out here to tell you about this woman." She flung a hand in Victoria's direction. "She is not who you think."

Colt held up a hand. *"Hold it right there!"* He shouted the words so loudly that Victoria and Bandit jumped at the same time.

Maddie continued as if Colt hadn't spoken. "She worked in a saloon in Abilene, and those two brats do not even belong to her. She's the daughter of a sportin' woman. And from the looks of her, she must have started young."

Colt was so angry he tried to get out of bed. Victoria tried to keep him from getting up, but she was no match for his determination. Helen rushed across the room with the intention of dragging this horrible woman from the room by the hair if necessary.

Seeing fresh blood on his bandage, Victoria pleaded, "Colt, you're bleeding again, please lie back." Just as she feared, Colt was placed in the position of defending her to his own detriment.

"Maddie, I suggest you leave now," Colt ground out, ignoring the pain as he struggled to his feet. He hadn't given a thought to what he wore underneath the covers, but when he realized he wasn't wearing much in the way of clothing, he wrapped the sheet around his waist.

Bandit stood on the bed and started barking until Maddie backed away, but she upped her volume to be heard.

"Everyone knows, at least everyone but you. The woman you've been courting and taking to church is a soiled dove," Maddie continued smugly. "Lucy's already told every man that comes into the saloon."

Colt glanced at Victoria's grief-stricken face. She turned to run from the room, but he was faster. He reached out and grabbed her wrist and held her next to him. He glowered at Maddie. "You are speaking about my future wife, so be careful what you say. And you'd best tell Lucy the same thing. Anyone who insults her name will answer to me."

Helen took Maddie firmly by the arm. "That's quite enough. I will show you out now."

Maddie wasn't deterred as Helen half dragged her across the room. "Wife? Don't be stupid! You can't marry that woman. Everyone knows, Colt. Everyone knows you're courting a wh—"

Helen put her hand over Maddie's mouth in an effort to shut her up since she couldn't get her out of the room. Colt couldn't let go of his sheet and he didn't want to let go of Victoria, so he said, "Helen, get T. J. and have him carry her out!" The words had barely left his mouth when T. J. walked into the room.

"You need me?" T. J. asked. He'd been walking to the house to check on Colt when he saw Maddie going inside. He had a bad feeling nothing good was going to come of her visit. As soon as he got to the porch, he heard Colt's booming voice from the bedroom and he knew by his tone things had gone awry.

"Get her off my ranch," Colt told him.

Without another word, T. J. picked Maddie up and threw her over his shoulder like a sack of potatoes and walked out of the room with her screeching in his ear.

"Put me down," Maddie squealed. "I'm not finished!"

"Oh yes, you are," T. J. told her. "Now quit squirming or I'll throw you down the stairs."

Mortified, Victoria didn't know what to say. She looked from Colt to Helen. "I need . . . I need . . ."

"You don't need to do anything," Colt

411

said, sitting back on the bed. He leaned back on the pillows, exhausted from the exertion of standing.

"Did I hear you say Victoria was going to be your wife?" Helen asked, totally ignoring what Maddie had told them.

If he hadn't been in so much pain he might have laughed. It was amazing that out of Maddie's tirade, that was the only thing Helen latched on to. "If I can convince her to have me," he answered with a grimace.

"I can't marry you. That is what I was trying to tell you," Victoria began. "What she said . . . well, it's partially true. I'm not a —"

"Victoria, there is nothing to explain," Colt interrupted.

"Yes, I need to tell you about my past."

Colt wanted to tell her he knew, but he could tell that she needed to get this off her chest.

Helen started for the door. "I'll leave you two alone."

"Helen, I want you to hear what I have to say. I want you both to know the truth." Before she even considered her words, she said, "I have worked in a saloon. I cleaned, cooked, and sewed dresses for the women, but my mother was . . . well . . . she worked there."

CHAPTER THIRTY-ONE

"Oh, he was shot all right, but he ain't dead," Maddie told L. B.

"How do you know? Is he going to be okay?" L. B. asked.

Maddie knew she couldn't tell L. B. she had been to Colt's ranch, so she lied. "I saw T. J. in town."

"One of the men from Wallace's ranch said he was dead," Lucy said, joining the conversation at the bar.

"I think T. J. should know the truth," L. B. said. "Did Colt really find that boy dead?"

"Yes, that's what T. J. said."

L. B. shook her head. "God help the man that killed that boy. Colt will surely put a bullet in him for that. He was plumb crazy over that boy."

A cowboy whistled for Lucy to bring another bottle to their table. When Lucy walked away, Maddie decided to tell L. B. what she knew about Victoria. "I also heard that woman he's courting worked in a saloon in Abilene."

"That's nonsense if I ever heard it," L. B. retorted. "I met her and she's a fine lady. Who told you such a thing? I know it wasn't T. J."

Maddie laughed. "Apparently she's fooled everybody. That cowboy that works for Wallace, the one called Hardy, knew her in Abilene."

"She worked for that Englishwoman in her boardinghouse for a few years, so she would have been too young to be in our profession," L. B. countered.

"I started working in a saloon when I was fourteen," Maddie said. "Lucy started earlier than that."

L. B. wasn't convinced. The young woman she met was a well-bred young woman. "That cowboy was probably just spouting off. His whiskey was likely doing the talking."

"Yeah, well Hardy said she was the daughter of some well-known gal in Abilene. Her name was Ruby."

L. B. gasped, and the color drained from her face as she clutched the bar for support.

"L. B.?" Maddie thought she was going to faint so she yelled for Sam.

■ ■ ■ ■

"You need some help, boss?" T. J. asked Colt.

Colt motioned for him to come into the room. "The doc and Tom helped me get dressed. Is everyone here?"

"Yes, Bartholomew picked up Mrs. Wagner and her children." T. J. could tell by Colt's grim face that he was in pain, so he poured them both a shot of whiskey. "Are you up to this?" The doc already told him Colt shouldn't even be out of bed, but they all knew he wouldn't listen. There was no way he would miss Tate's funeral. At least the funeral was being held on the ranch, so he wouldn't need to travel to town. He handed him the whiskey. "Maybe this will help."

"Thanks." Colt gulped the whiskey, hoping it would numb the pain. "Let's go."

Victoria and Bandit were waiting for them at the front door as they made their way down the staircase. T. J. tipped his hat to her. "I'll be outside at the buckboard so you don't have to walk up that hill."

"I'll walk," Colt responded indignantly.

Victoria reached up to straighten Colt's collar. "You most certainly will not. Doctor's orders. If you are going, you'll ride in the buckboard." She knew he was getting ready to protest, so she added, "I'll ride with you if that's okay."

He liked the fact that she was treating him like a wife. At the same time, it galled him that she didn't think he could walk up that hill like he'd done thousands of times. On the bright side, if he rode in the buckboard she was going to be beside him, close . . . real close. "Bossing me around already, huh?" he teased.

"Someone needs to since you don't have enough sense to listen to the doctor."

"I'll be okay."

"I see you shaved," she said, thinking he looked more handsome than ever.

"Yeah, I didn't want to scare people." He wanted to ask her why she hadn't been in his room much since Maddie's visit. If she thought he'd changed his mind about wanting to marry her, then she'd better think again. If anything, he'd become more comfortable with the idea of being a married man. He admired her because she wanted to make sure he knew everything about her past. Now he knew, and he wanted her more, and he planned to tell her that before the day was over. "Where are the boys?"

"With Mrs. Wellington and Bartholomew.

Everyone is already on the way up there." The McBride family plot was on a hill overlooking the ranch house. "I was up there this morning and it's a beautiful spot," she added.

"I like to go up there from time to time. That's where I do my best thinking. If I have problems with the ranch I always seem to walk away with an answer." He'd never confided that to anyone before.

She envisioned Colt sitting on the bench where she'd sat this morning, overlooking the graves of his parents. "In a way it's almost like you still have them with you. It must be comforting to stay in one place all your life and know that's where you belong." Her voice had a wistful note to it. "That's what I want for the boys."

He wanted the same thing. "I guess some people might not think it's an exciting life. All I ever really wanted was to run the ranch the way my dad did, and die right here." He stopped her before they walked out the door. Perhaps it was losing Tate so suddenly that made him feel the urgency to live life *right now.* He didn't want to put off the important things. Now he wanted something besides the ranch. He wanted her and the boys. And he wasn't going to take no for an answer. He remembered how Tate

418

kept badgering him about his feelings for Victoria the last night they were together. Tate was right when he said Colt needed a wife to share his life. Imagine that — young Tate knew what was important and he hadn't even lived life yet.

He placed an arm around Victoria's waist and pulled her to his chest. "All you have to do is say yes, and you and the boys will always be here with me. We can grow old together, build the boys their own homes when they marry, and God willing, maybe live long enough to see some grand-children."

He made everything sound so easy, so uncomplicated, and she was tempted to ac-cept his offer. Nursing him the last few days had only confirmed how deeply she loved him. Problem was, she cared too much to ever become an embarrassment to him. Maddie had said every cowboy in town had been told she worked in a saloon. She could only imagine the crude comments that men would make to him.

She took his face between her hands and looked into his eyes. "I know that you think you want to marry me now, but what hap-pens when someone says something about your wife's past? How would you feel then?"

"I feel like they would be making a big

mistake," he told her honestly.

She frowned at him.

His tone turned serious. "Victoria, as I told you last night, you have nothing to be ashamed of, and you sure as hel . . . heaven have nothing to hide. Don't worry about things that won't happen."

Helen and Colt had been very understanding when she told them about her background, but she didn't think most people in town would be as accepting. People could be judgmental; she'd seen that firsthand from the townspeople of Abilene. She couldn't live with herself if he got killed defending her if someone like Gage Hardy insulted her. "Let's talk about this later."

He grasped her hands, turned them over, and kissed each palm. "I'm proud of you for being courageous even though you had to be afraid. You're the bravest person I know, and nothing about your past will shame me. And you will marry me." He gazed into her blue eyes and added, "If you love me."

By the end of the funeral, Victoria was amazed Colt was still standing. A sheen of perspiration covered his face, the only telling sign that he was on his feet by sheer determination. She knew his physical pain

420

probably paled in comparison to what he was feeling emotionally. True to form, he remained stoic, but he couldn't hide his sadness from her. She could tell by the way he twirled the brim of his hat, much the way he had at Mr. Barlow's funeral, he was fighting to keep his emotions in check. She noticed T. J. and Doc Barnes hovered close by like they thought he might drop any moment. The boys and Bandit stood silently in front of him, not one sound uttered out of the three of them. They were connected to Colt's emotions and understood his heartbreak.

Colt leaned over to Victoria's ear and whispered, "Will you take Mrs. Wagner to the buckboard? I need a minute alone."

She didn't want to leave him, but she understood. "Of course. Will you be okay?"

"I'll be right along."

Victoria gathered the boys and together they walked to the buckboard. T. J. and the doc backed off to give Colt some space.

Colt stood, with Bandit by his side, over Tate's grave as the other mourners moved away. "Tate, I'm sorry," he started, and a tear trailed down his cheek. Bandit leaned into his leg, lending comfort only an animal could offer. The last night he spent with Tate played in his mind. "I guess you've had a hand in getting me and Victoria together. You were right. I do need something in my life besides the ranch. I just wish you were here to help me with those boys. They could use a big brother like you. Don't worry about your family; I will see to it they are taken care of." He swallowed hard before he added, "Lord, you have a good young man in Tate." He pulled a bandana from his pocket to wipe his tears away. After settling his Stetson on his head, he added, "I'll miss you." He stroked Bandit's head and turned toward the buckboard. "Come on, boy."

Victoria met them halfway, and together they walked to Tate's mother. "Mrs. Wagner, I can't tell you how sorry I am," Colt said, his voice cracking.

"Now don't you go blaming yourself, Mr. McBride. This wasn't your fault. You were always good to Tate, and I know you did your best. No one ever treated him as good as you. You gave that boy everything he ever wanted. He looked up to you —" She dabbed her tears with her handkerchief. "He . . . he wanted to be just like you. I guess God just needed him now."

"I promise you I will find the person who did this," Colt choked out.

Mrs. Wagner touched his arm gently. "I know you will. Now you need to get back to the house. Doc said you had no business even being out of bed."

Colt hesitated a moment, trying to find a way to say what he wanted without offending her. He wanted to put her mind at ease about how she would care for her family with Tate gone. "I don't want you to worry. You will stay on the ranch as long as you want, and still handle the wash for the men if you want."

She choked up at Colt's words. She was fearful with Tate gone that Colt might ask her to leave the ranch. He didn't charge her for the house, but even with her earnings from handling the wash, it would be hard to make it without Tate's income. "You've done so much for us." She looked back at her son's grave. "You already gave us a place to live, and now this" — she pointed to the gravesite — "this beautiful resting place for my boy."

Victoria noticed Colt slumping and getting paler by the minute. She politely steered him to the buckboard. "Mrs. Wagner, you and the children ride down with us."

Back at the house, Victoria said good-bye to Mrs. Wagner while T. J. assisted Colt. "When you have some time I would like you and the children to come to dinner. There is a matter I would like to discuss with you. Bartholomew will pick you up in the buckboard whenever you would like."

Puzzled by what this lovely young woman wanted to talk to her about, Mrs. Wagner said, "I will send word in a few days."

Seeing the concerned look on the woman's face, Victoria patted her arm. "Nothing to worry about. I just have a business proposition for you to consider."

Mrs. Wagner hugged her and Colt. Colt whispered in her ear, "Anything you and the children need, the mercantile will know to put it on my bill."

"But —"

"No arguments. One of the men will ride you back to the house." He glanced at T. J., who nodded his understanding.

"What did you want to talk to Mrs. Wagner about?" Colt asked Victoria as they walked inside.

"Before I left St. Louis I sent a letter and a sample reticule to shops in San Francisco and London to see if they might be interested in placing an order. Mrs. Wellington brought their responses to me when she arrived. Both shops placed several orders, and I need someone to help me sew them. The designs I've drawn require intricate detail work, and I'm afraid Mrs. Wellington is not handy enough with a needle. Tate said . . ." She hesitated, thinking it would only cause him more pain to talk about Tate.

Colt pinned her with his dark eyes. "Tate said what?"

"The first day I met him he remarked on my reticule, and he mentioned his mother would love to make something like that since she liked to sew. Just a few weeks ago he asked me if he could buy her one for a Christmas present." She stopped when her voice broke. Colt squeezed her hand in understanding. She cleared her throat and continued. "I had been working on one for him, but I wasn't going to charge him. He was always so helpful to me . . . such a kind boy."

Colt remembered the bag he'd taken off Victoria's wrist the day she fainted. At the time, he thought the flowers were pretty. "Is that what your drawings are for?"

"Yes," she replied, somewhat surprised that he remembered seeing her drawings that night in her kitchen.

"You are an amazing woman, Victoria." He pulled her to him and rested his chin on her hair. "Tate was a great kid. It will mean a lot to his mom to help support her family. Tate told me she doesn't like to accept charity. That's why she started doing the wash for the men."

"If she wants to work with me, she will not be accepting charity," Victoria assured him.

Colt pulled back and looked at her. "You mean she can support all those children by sewing those . . . what are they called again . . . bags?"

"I'll have you know they are not bags, they are reticules," Victoria corrected. "They are the height of fashion."

"Yes, ma'am." Colt shook his head and grinned. "It's amazing what women buy."

"Women could say the same thing about men and their guns."

"Well, you have to admit they're not big enough for more than that derringer of yours."

"And how many guns can you get in your holster?" she asked sweetly.

Colt chuckled, and he heard the voice of his dad saying, *Never argue with a woman, son. You'll never win.* He'd never heard his father say one cross word to his mother. He loved her so much that after she was killed, he remained faithful to her until his death. Colt knew he would love Victoria like that if she would let him. Not *if . . . when,* he reminded himself. She was going to marry him, and she would wrap his tail in knots just like his mom did his old man. He smiled at the prospect.

Tugging on his arm, Victoria said, "Now, sir, you need to get back into bed."

"She's right, Colt," Doc Barnes said from behind them. "You have blood on your jacket and I know you've opened up my pretty stitches again. I need to have a look."

"I'm not going to argue. I'm going up right now." Colt accepted the doctor's assistance up the staircase.

Hours later, when Helen delivered Colt's dinner to his room, he asked, "Where's Victoria?" She hadn't been up to see him since the doc re-stitched him and changed his bandages.

Helen placed the tray in front of him and sat in the chair beside the bed. "She's putting dinner on the table." Seeing Bandit eyeing Colt's dinner, Helen asked, "Should I get a plate for him? It doesn't look like he's ever going to leave your side."

"He can have some of mine." Slicing off a big piece of his beef, he offered it to Bandit and watched him swallow it in one gulp. Since Victoria was downstairs, he thought it was an opportune time to talk to Helen. "Why do you think she won't agree to marry me?"

Helen considered what Victoria had told them about her past, and while she understood the reasoning behind her reluctance to marry Colt, she disagreed with her thinking. "I think she feels that you might regret the decision if her past should ever cause you problems. I tried talking to her while we prepared dinner, but I don't think she heard a word I said."

Colt had always valued Helen's opinion. "I don't know why she thinks anyone would hold her past against her, or why it would cause me problems."

"That girl loves you, Colt. She wouldn't want anyone to think less of you because of her. I think people have been cruel to her because of her circumstances when she was a young girl. She is fearful that you would defend her if anyone insulted her and she doesn't want anything to happen to you."

He was almost offended. "You mean she doesn't think I could handle any man who insulted my wife?"

She leaned over and patted his cheek, much the way a grandmother would do. "Now don't get your dander up, she's just afraid you might get hurt. And stop worrying. You will have tonight to work on her. I told her I was too tired to stay up tonight, and she wanted to stay."

Colt smiled. "You're as devious as Mrs. Wellington. I'll do my best."

"The boys want to come up to see you before they leave." Helen opened the door and the boys were standing there waiting. "Speak of the devils."

"Come on in, boys." Colt patted the side of the bed and they piled on.

They leaned over Colt's legs to pet Bandit. "We're real happy you didn't die. We didn't want you to be an angel," Cody said, and Cade added, "Yeah."

"I'm relieved to hear you're happy about that." Colt chuckled, thinking to himself that he could get used to this; the boys and Bandit in his bed. Now all he needed was Victoria in there with them.

Chapter Thirty-Two

"I heard McBride is still alive," Wallace told Hoyt Nelson.

Hoyt stopped saddling his horse and turned to face Wallace. "Who told you that?"

"I heard it from that old woman at the Barlow farm. I thought you said he was dead."

"I got a good shot at him. I didn't check to see if he was still breathing," he said defensively. "I was in a hurry to get out of there."

"You told me you killed his foreman, but it was some kid that worked for him," Wallace added.

That piece of information didn't move Hoyt one way or the other. "You want me to finish the job on McBride?"

"No, I have another plan. Laid up like he is, he won't be in the way."

Riding in like the devil was on his heels,

Bartholomew pulled the buckboard to a halt in front of Colt's house. Before he could knock, Helen opened the door. "I heard you coming. Why are you running those horses so hard?"

"I need to see Victoria."

"She's in the kitchen. I thought you were bringing everyone back for dinner tonight."

Not taking the time to explain, Bartholomew hustled to the kitchen.

Victoria had her hands in dough when Bartholomew walked in the kitchen. "Oh, you're early. Let me guess, the boys were driving you crazy to get here to see Colt." When he didn't respond, Victoria looked at him and immediately knew there was a problem. "What's wrong?"

"Victoria, Mrs. Wellington sent me on alone. We can't find the boys anywhere."

Eyes going wide, Victoria asked, "What do you mean?" She had spent the night at Colt's so she hadn't seen the boys since yesterday.

"They were playing by the barn earlier, and when Mrs. Wellington went to call them in to get cleaned up to come over here, they were nowhere to be found. We spent over an hour looking for them before I came here."

Fear gripped her. "The river?" she asked

nervously. They had never learned to swim. If they went in that river they would surely drown.

"That's the first place I went, but I saw no sign they were there," he replied, trying to reassure her. He didn't want to frighten her more than he had already, but if those boys drowned they might not turn up for a few days. He wasn't about to say that to her.

"Maybe they fell asleep in the barn," Victoria said.

Helen was in the doorway and overheard the conversation. "You know how boys are; they are probably off in a field somewhere. I can't tell you how often I had to go in search of Colt and his brothers when they were young. They'd always turn up in the strangest places." She hurried across the kitchen and pointed Victoria toward the sink and started working the pump. "Now wash your hands and go on to the farm to look for those boys. I can handle things here, and you won't rest until you see them."

"Helen, don't tell Colt. I don't want him getting on a horse and riding over there. I'm sure there is nothing to worry about." Victoria's words were as much for her own benefit as Helen's.

"I'm not sure I can keep it from him, but

I will try." Helen didn't know what she would say to him if he asked about Victoria's absence at dinner.

"Tell him I will be back later," Victoria said over her shoulder as she followed Bartholomew out the door.

As soon as Victoria and Bartholomew left, Helen found T. J. and told him what was going on so he could send some men from the ranch to help in the search.

Three hours passed and everyone returned to the house without the boys. Victoria was inconsolable. All reason told her the boys would not run off. A million scenarios passed through her mind, but she refused to allow herself to dwell on those thoughts. It was getting dark outside and the temperature was dropping, which worried her even more. Perhaps one of them was hurt and the other one didn't want to leave him alone to find help. It was the longest night of her life. Before dawn broke Bartholomew drove her to town, thinking maybe someone found them and didn't know where they belonged.

"What do you mean, the boys are missing?" Colt shouted at T. J.

"Bartholomew arrived before dinner last night and told Victoria that they couldn't find them."

Colt moved to sit on the edge of the bed. "Why didn't Helen tell me? She told me last night that Victoria had decided to go home for a few hours. I thought she must have been tired and stayed there instead of coming back here for the night."

"Victoria didn't want you upset; she knew you would ride to the farm."

"Darn right I would."

"I sent Rance and Lane over to help search, and told them not to come back until they found them. Since they still haven't come back, I thought I'd better tell you what's going on." T. J. didn't want to deliver this news, considering everything else Colt was dealing with. But he sure didn't want to face him if he found out everyone had kept something like this from him.

Colt pointed to a trunk in front of the window. "Would you pull out my holster?"

T. J. saw his gun belt on the bedpost. "One is hanging right there."

"I need my other one," Colt said. His entire right side was so sore he wasn't sure he could shoot with his right hand. His other holster held two pistols, if he needed to use his left hand.

"You don't need to be going anywhere,"

T. J. said. "Doc says you are never going to mend if you don't stay in that bed. I'll send all the men we can spare to help search." Watching Colt struggling into his pants, he knew his words were falling on deaf ears. "Hold on a dang minute, I'll get the darn holster." T. J. stalked to the trunk and shuffled through the contents. He found the holster at the bottom of the trunk and handed it to Colt. "Doc's going to have a fit, not to mention Victoria," he muttered.

Colt strapped the holster around his hips, and out of habit he checked the cylinders of each pistol to make sure they were loaded. He cleaned the pistols frequently, so he knew they were in good order. "Do you mind tying them down for me? I don't think I can bend over that far since the doc tied these bandages so tight."

T. J. bent to tie the leather thongs around Colt's thighs. "Mind telling me how you are planning on riding a horse?"

"I'll manage." Bandit jumped off the bed, ready to follow Colt out the door. "You have to stay here, boy." Colt had a feeling Wallace was involved in this somehow, and the time had come to have it out with him.

As they walked down the stairs side by side, T. J. said, "Razor's out front. I'm going with you."

Colt smiled. He should have figured that T. J. knew he would go. "I guess you've been around me too long."

"Yep, and you ain't getting any smarter." He'd told Rex to get Colt's horse saddled before he went to tell him about the boys. "Your head is harder than . . . than your old man's." That was the hardest thing T. J. could think of at the moment.

They were leaving the ranch when Lane came riding in.

"What are you doing back here? Did they find the boys?" T. J. asked.

"No, and now the woman is missing."

"Victoria?" Colt asked, sure his heart skipped a beat.

"Yeah. Bartholomew took her to town to see if someone might have found the boys but didn't know where they belonged. They were gone so long that Rance thought he should ride to town to see if they had problems. He found the buckboard on the road. Bartholomew was shot — he ain't dead, but he's in a real bad way. Rance took him to the farm and that Englishwoman is tending him since it was closer than going to town. Victoria was nowhere around. I rode to town to see if she was there, but it looks like they never made it. I sent the doc to the farm to do what he can for Bartholo-mew."

"Let's ride," Colt said.

T. J. had the presence of mind to tell Lane to round up some men and meet them at Victoria's farm.

"Why did you bring me here?" Victoria asked Hoyt Nelson when he reined in at Wallace's ranch.

He pulled her off the saddle. "The boss told me to."

Nothing was making sense to her. Nelson shot Bartholomew, and as she tried to help him, the gunslinger had forced her on his horse at gunpoint. "Why does Mr. Wallace want me here?"

"I guess he has his reasons. You'll have to ask him." He pushed her in the direction of the front porch. "Now walk."

"Did he tell you to shoot Bartholomew?" she shrieked.

Hoyt didn't respond. The front door opened and Wallace appeared. "Victoria, my dear, do come in."

"I want to know why I am here," she demanded. Pointing a shaking finger at Nelson, she said, "He shot Bartholomew!"

"Now you have all of them," Hoyt said to Wallace.

Wallace took her by the wrist and pulled her inside. When they reached his office, he threw the door open and Victoria saw the twins sitting on the settee. They scrambled down and ran to her. Dropping to her knees, she held them to her and felt their thin bodies shaking uncontrollably. She kissed their tearstained cheeks. "It's okay, I'm here. There's nothing to be afraid of now." She hoped they couldn't tell how fearful she was. "Why did you run away from home?"

"We didn't run away. That scary man with the fancy guns made us go with him," Cade said.

"He pointed his gun at us," Cody added.

Standing, she whirled around to confront Wallace. "Why are they here?"

Wallace didn't respond, so she took the boys by the hand and said, "We're leaving here right now."

Wallace smirked at her. "I'm afraid not." He pulled a pistol from his waistband, pointed it at her, and yelled for his housekeeper. When she appeared, he instructed, "Take these boys upstairs to a bedroom and don't let them out until I tell you."

The boys clung to Victoria. "We don't have to, do we?"

Wallace pointed the pistol at Cody's head,

and Victoria saw in his cold eyes that he wouldn't hesitate to pull the trigger. "Everything will be okay. I will be with you in a little while, so please go with the lady," she said as calmly as she could.

They released Victoria and walked past Wallace. "Colt will come for us," Cody said bravely. "He's going to be our pa."

Wallace laughed. "I'm afraid not."

Cade agreed with his brother. "He will too! We asked God for him."

"He said he would always protect us," Cody added.

They turned around and looked at Victoria, their eyes wide with terror. "He will, won't he?" Cody asked, his lips quivering.

Just as she started to reassure them, she noticed something she had not seen before. Her eyes slid to Wallace. Why hadn't she noticed this before? Cade and Cody's eyes were the same steel blue-gray as Wallace's. They had the same white-blond hair, the same lanky, lean physiques. *No! It couldn't be! Is this what Wallace wanted with them? Were the boys the reason he'd stayed in Abilene?*

"He will, won't he?" Cade repeated his brother's question.

Victoria was afraid to respond; she didn't want them to see her own doubt. "Go with the lady now. We'll talk later." Victoria gazed at the Mexican woman and saw pity in her eyes as she gently took Cade and Cody by the hand and led them from the room.

"So you think you are going to marry McBride?" After what Gage Hardy told him about Victoria, or Delilah, he didn't think any man would want her. He wouldn't marry her now that he knew about her past, but he had plans for her. He would force her to sign over her land to him. If she didn't, he would make sure she never saw those boys again. Hardy made it clear she would do anything for those boys. It would be her choice. The boys would be leverage as long as he needed them to get what he wanted.

"No, I'm not marrying Mr. McBride," Victoria responded as calmly as she could manage. She was frightened to death, but she had to remain strong for the boys. "Now what do you want with us? And why did that man shoot Bartholomew?"

Wallace walked toward her, grabbed her arm and twisted it behind her. "Gage Hardy told me you worked at the Lucky Slipper in Abilene. I've been there plenty of times, but I don't recall seeing you there. I thought you were the mother of those boys, but now I find out they are the offspring of another gal from that saloon. I knew Kitten and Ruby well, so who is their mother?" He didn't really care who they belonged to; they were his ticket to get what he wanted.

He doesn't know! He doesn't know! She was overcome with relief. He'd never really looked at the boys, and apparently Kitten never told him. She wondered why she hadn't recognized the resemblance before now. The similarities were unmistakable. She needed to distract him from asking questions about their mother. "I didn't . . . I cleaned and sewed for the girls at the saloon, nothing else."

"Save the lies, Delilah. Is that your given name, or just the name you used at the Lucky Slipper? Hardy told me all about you. He seems to know you very well."

"What do you want with me?"

Still holding her arm behind her, he wrapped his fingers around her neck with his free hand. "I think you know what I want. Land. That's all that matters to me."

She tried to push away from him, but he held her firm.

"I was going to ask you to marry me. Now I don't have to marry you. I don't want someone like you for a wife." He spat, close to her face. "You are not worthy to be my wife, but you will stay here as long as I want.

And you will sign over your land to me."

"Take your hands off me!" she cried.

His eyes were cold and devoid of emotion. That had to be the reason she hadn't noticed the resemblance to the boys — there was no life in his eyes. He was a monster. What had pushed him over the edge? Did his greed for land make his mind snap? "Haven't you forgotten about Mrs. Wellington? She will alert the sheriff. They will come looking for me."

He squeezed her neck, demonstrating his power to control her. "The sheriff?" He laughed. "I own the sheriff."

She recalled Colt saying the same thing. *If only I had listened to him. What a fool I've been. How many people have been fooled by his good manners?*

"If that old woman comes here, you will tell her you are going to marry me."

"I won't do that. Besides, she would never believe me." She struggled against his hold until she heard the sound of cloth tearing. She looked down to see he had ripped her dress down the front. Thankfully, her camisole was still covering her.

"Don't fight me. I will kill those boys, don't think I won't. I might even kill the old woman. I will get what I want, one way or the other."

She was terrified, more so than that night back in Abilene when Gage Hardy attacked her. Gage Hardy had been nothing more than a drunk, but Wallace was worse. He was a man without conscience. "This is about land? You can't mean you've done all of this for land?"

He fisted her camisole like he was going to rip it from her when a knock on the door stopped him. "What is it?" he bellowed.

A man replied, "The men are here."

"Get them into the stable." He shoved Victoria to a chair, walked to his desk and poured himself a brandy. "This is about my empire. It's all going to be mine. These ranchers haven't the intellect to run an empire. They don't deserve this land."

She didn't think he would listen to reason, but she had to try. "Look at what you have here. It's more than enough for one man."

"It's never enough. Land is power. A man is judged by what he owns, and the wife that he chooses to bear his offspring." Leaning against his desk, he regarded her as he sipped his brandy. "I had chosen you to run my household and have my sons. Pity, you are so beautiful and you have learned the graces of a lady, yet you are nothing but a trollop."

"Gage Hardy lied to you." She didn't

expect him to believe her, not that it mattered to her. "Did you kill that boy and shoot Colt? That boy was an innocent. Was taking a young life worth it to you? Was shooting Bartholomew worth any land?"

"Your concern is touching. Almost like a real lady," he mocked.

If only she had her reticule with the pistol in it, she would surely shoot him for his evil deeds.

He poured himself another drink. "I didn't shoot them, Hoyt did. He assured me McBride was dead, but, alas, I see that he isn't. Don't hold out hope he will come to your rescue. I have plans for him if he doesn't die from Hoyt's bullet. His land will soon be mine."

She wondered if the men who worked for him knew he was crazy, or were they all just hired killers and it didn't matter as long as he paid them well?

"Colt has a family. I doubt you can just take his land without their knowledge."

"You underestimate me, my dear. I already have the papers drawn, and witnesses who swore to his signature deeding the land to me. It's just a matter of time, and Hoyt will dispatch him like he should have done the first time."

CHAPTER THIRTY-THREE

Rance walked to the porch with rifle in hand as Colt and T. J. reined in at the Barlow farm. "Colt, we've looked everywhere for those boys."

"Lane told us. How's Bartholomew?"

Hearing Colt's deep voice, Mrs. Wellington walked outside. "And just what do you think you are doing out of bed?"

He smiled at her concern. "How's Bartholomew?"

"He's in a bad way. The doctor is with him now. It wouldn't hurt for you to come inside and have the doctor take a look at you. You look ready to fall out of your saddle."

He thought he probably looked better than she did, but he wasn't about to say that to a woman. "Don't worry about me," he assured her.

"Do you know what's going on?"

Intuitively, he knew the boys' disappear-

445

ance was linked to him getting shot. Someone thought he wouldn't pose a threat if he was dead. And the only person who would take advantage of his death to get what he wanted was Wallace. Of course, Wallace didn't shoot him, he just pulled the strings. Then his thoughts went to Gage Hardy. The man was obsessed with Victoria. He couldn't ignore the possibility that he took the boys to lure her to him, knowing she would not go with him willingly otherwise.

He didn't answer Mrs. Wellington's question, but asked one of his own. "Mrs. Wellington, did anything unusual happen this week? Did you see anyone hanging around the farm?"

She thought a minute before answering. "Nothing out of the ordinary. Mr. Wallace came by to see Victoria, but I told him that she was at your place looking after you."

"Did he already know I had been shot?" Colt asked.

"I do believe he did, but I had the feeling . . ." She hesitated.

"What?"

"I must say, I had the feeling that he was surprised that you were alive. It wasn't what he said exactly, it was the look on his face when I told him Victoria was tending you. At the time, I thought he acted odd, but the man is quite strange, so I dismissed the thought."

"After Maddie's visit I'm sure anyone who went into the saloon knew you had been shot. You think he assumed you were dead?" T. J. asked.

"Maybe." To Colt's way of thinking, if Wallace or Hardy had anything to do with this, then he would find both men at the same place. "Let's ride to Wallace's."

T. J. leaned over in his saddle, closer to Colt's ear. "Don't you think we should wait on the men, boss? You don't look like you can make that ride, and you know there will be trouble."

"I'll make it." He glanced at Rance. "Stay with Mrs. Wellington, and tell the men to ride on over to Wallace's." Before he reined his horse around, he glanced back at Mrs. Wellington. "That old man is tougher than nails. He'll make it."

"I'm counting on it, just like I'm counting on you to find Victoria and those boys," she responded.

Wallace's housekeeper left the bedroom, giving Victoria her first chance to speak to the boys alone. "Boys, we need to talk," she whispered.

"I want to go home," Cade said.

"I don't like him," Cody said, referring to Wallace. "Where's Colt?"

Victoria hated to alarm them even more, but this might be her only chance to tell them what they needed to do. "Mr. Wallace is not himself. He is holding us here because he wants our land." She pulled them to her. "If you see a chance to leave without being seen, I want you to run as fast as you can and go to Colt's ranch. Do you think you can find your way?"

"Yes, but Colt will come and get us," Cody said, and Cade nodded his agreement. "He told us he wants us to be his boys."

Victoria wasn't surprised by their faith in Colt. "When did he tell you that?"

"The last time we saw him," Cody replied.

Cade added, "He said he wants that more than anything 'cause we are good boys, and he was just waiting on you to decide to marry him. Are you?"

They seemed more concerned about her marrying Colt than being held hostage at Wallace's. "We will talk about that later. Colt is hurt and he can't ride his horse right now. We have to depend on ourselves to get out of here. Besides, no one knows where we are."

"Colt will know," Cade assured her.

"God will tell Colt," Cody confidently added.

"Now pay attention." Her serious tone made them stop talking. "Do you think you could find your way to Colt's in the dark?"

"Without you?" Cody asked.

"Yes, I want you to go, even if I can't go with you. Even if it is dark outside," she replied. "Do you understand?"

Both boys nodded.

The housekeeper came back into the room. "Señor wants you."

The housekeeper seemed at odds with what she was being directed to do, but Victoria dared not trust her since she was obviously too afraid of Wallace to help them.

Hoyt Nelson passed her on the staircase, and she watched him walk into the room with the boys. She started to turn around and go back to the room when Wallace yelled to her.

"Come down here."

"Why is he going into that room?"

"We have visitors riding in. As long as you know he is with the boys, I will have no trouble from you." He walked up the few steps separating them, grabbed her by the arm, and pulled her behind him into his office. Tossing a paper in front of her, he thrust a pen at her. "Sign."

"What am I signing?"

"You're selling your land to me."

"Are you going to let us go if I sign this?"

He tapped the paper on his desk impatiently. "So you can tell everyone that I forced you to sign this document? I think not, my dear."

"Then why would I agree?" The man was mad, his reasoning was not sound. He had truly gone insane.

"If you don't, Hoyt will kill the boys," he stated flatly.

His face and words were devoid of any feeling, and deep down she knew he would carry out his threat. She took the pen and signed her name.

"One of the men said McBride is riding in. I thought his wound made it impossible to ride. If it is him, we will go to the door together and you will tell him we are getting married. You better sound convincing or you can say good-bye to those brats."

As long as the boys were being held by that gunslinger, she would have to do what he wanted. She had to think of a way to get the boys away from him.

Wallace instructed his men to stay out of sight until the two riders were at the house. He looked out the window, and as the riders neared the house he could tell one of

450

them was indeed McBride. He turned back to Victoria. "Stay here until I call for you."

Colt and T. J. noticed there were no men moving about as they rode in. It was certainly unusual for a working ranch to look deserted at this time of day. They knew they were riding into a trap.

"I imagine there are some guns trained on us from that stable," Colt said, and T. J. nodded his agreement.

Wallace walked out on the porch before they could dismount. "What do you want, McBride?" he snapped.

"Send out Victoria and the boys," Colt answered calmly.

"What do you want with my fiancée?"

It surprised Colt that Wallace didn't bother to deny he had Victoria and the boys. Something about Wallace had changed. He had a wild-eyed look about him, akin to a panicked horse. He figured the man had finally snapped. He fought the urge to shoot him where he stood. "The only way you can get a woman is to take her by force?"

Colt knew he hit the right button to make Wallace angry. His face twisted with rage.

Wallace didn't dare pull his pistol on Colt, no matter what the rancher said to goad him. He'd heard how fast he was, and he hadn't come this far to be killed. "I didn't take anyone by force."

"Either she comes out here, or I go in there. With you breathing or not, makes no difference to me."

Wallace shouted for Victoria. When she appeared in the doorway, he told her, "Please tell Mr. McBride our good news, and that you are not here by force."

The boys were right. Colt did come for them. She knew he must be in pain even though he was sitting strong and tall in his saddle. It shamed her to think she'd even considered Wallace above him. Her emotions were at war; she was so glad to see him, yet so afraid for his life. It hurt her to say what Wallace wanted her to say, but as long as Wallace's men were prepared to shoot Colt and T. J., and Nelson was with the boys, she had no choice. Part of her prayed he wouldn't believe her, but she wanted him safe, so she tried to be convincing. "Yes, we are to marry," she said, barely above a whisper.

Colt noticed her visibly shaking hand as she clutched the top of her dress. She said the words Wallace had obviously instructed her to say, but she couldn't hide the fear in her eyes. "When did you decide this?" he asked, not believing one word she said. It didn't really matter what she said, he was just stalling for time, trying to figure out his best course of action.

She stared into his eyes, willing him to ride away and not look back. "Well . . . recently." She hesitated to take a deep breath. No matter how much she didn't want him to ride away, she needed to make him believe her. His life depended on how well she lied. "The boys and I discussed it and we came to this decision."

Colt arched a dark brow at her. "I find that mighty strange since they said they want me to be their pa. Why don't you go get the boys so we can sort this out?"

"That won't be necessary," Wallace told him. "Victoria has told you the way of it. Now get off my ranch."

At the same time Wallace turned to push Victoria back inside, T. J. whispered, "Look up."

Colt casually removed his Stetson and wiped his brow with his shirtsleeve, his gaze casually moving to the window above. He caught a glimpse of Hoyt Nelson standing to the side of the second story window.

"I still want to see the boys," Colt said to Wallace.

He ignored Colt's demand. "As a wedding present to her husband, Victoria signed her land over to me. You can't win, McBride.

It's over. I told you before, I always get what I want."

"You're not going to get Victoria," Colt retorted, his voice deadly calm.

"I've already got her and the land. I'm afraid you have interrupted us in our private time together."

Colt had heard enough. He started to dismount at the same time Wallace raised his hand, and total mayhem erupted. Wallace's men poured from the stable and started firing on Colt and T. J. In unison, Colt and T. J. jumped off their horses and hit the ground with guns drawn. They rolled away from the horses' hooves, yelling *"Ya! Ya!"* The animals ran from the line of fire. Colt hit the ground hard, and thought he might pass out from the pain. He felt blood oozing down his back, and knew he had opened his stitches again. Rolling up on his feet, he crouched low, and along with T. J., returned fire as they ran to the side of the house for cover.

Bullets splintered the wood near their heads, pelting them with sharp slivers. "How many?" T. J. yelled above the gunshots.

"Could be twenty, maybe more. Looks like he hired every man he could find."

T. J. laughed. "Well, that makes me feel a

whole lot better." He saw Colt was returning fire with both guns, ignoring the pain,
and quickly picked off two men. "Guess you
can use your right arm just fine," he said,
astonished at Colt's accuracy in his condition.

"Yeah, but I need to reload." Colt stopped
firing and hurriedly inserted cartridges in
the cylinders.

"We can't hold them off for long. What's
the plan?" T. J. asked.

"Keep them occupied for a while. I figure
the men will be here soon."

T. J. chuckled. "Is that your best plan?"

"All I can think of at the moment."

"I have to reload. I only have enough for
another round." T. J. reloaded and started
firing again. "Wish I'd grabbed my rifle."

Colt looked around for Razor, but he
didn't see him. He handed T. J. one of his
pistols and a handful of cartridges, then ran
to the back of the house. He spotted Razor
some distance away, and when he gave a
loud whistle, the horse quickly trotted over
to him. After pulling his rifle from the boot,
he smacked Razor on the hindquarters to
send him away again.

Colt tossed the rifle to T. J. "Now hit
something besides the barn."

"Yessir. I wish you would teach that trick

to my horse." T. J. handed Colt his pistol, and aimed the rifle, wounding one man with a single shot.

Colt smiled. "You were always better with a rifle. If we make it out of this alive, I'll teach your horse to bring you breakfast in bed."

"Just teach a woman to do that."

"Aw hell."

T. J. stopped firing. "That doesn't sound good."

"They're going around behind us. Stay here, I'll go to the back corner."

They were getting blasted from two sides, but Colt managed to keep Wallace's men pinned at the other side of the house to keep them from advancing from the rear.

"Boss, I'm hit!" T. J. yelled.

Colt turned to see the rifle falling from T. J.'s hands as he slumped to the ground, his back to the house. Colt ran to him, but he couldn't stop shooting to find out how badly he was hurt. He crouched down with his back to T. J., protecting him as best he could while he continued firing in both directions. "How bad?"

"I'm hit in the shoulder, but I can shoot a pistol with my left hand — not as good as you, but maybe I'll get lucky."

Colt quickly reloaded and passed him a

pistol. The odds were getting better since Colt had wounded so many men. Problem was, he was running out of cartridges, and the remaining men were advancing.

Wallace's men started ducking for cover when gunfire erupted from another direction, and Colt turned to see his men thundering in under a rain of gunfire. Perfect timing, he thought, since he couldn't have held Wallace's men off much longer. When a gunshot hit the wood next to his head, he turned to fire, but the man who fired the shot slumped to the ground. A man Colt didn't know stood over the dead man. When he spotted a U.S. Marshal's badge on the man's chest, he nodded his thanks. The man tipped the brim of his hat in response. Colt's men quickly surrounded what was left of Wallace's men. Colt yelled for Lane to take care of T. J. while he stormed up the front porch, stopping short of the large window.

"Wallace, come out now! It's over!" Colt yelled.

"It's not over! I still have what you want," Wallace countered through the door.

Colt ran past the window and a shot shattered the glass, missing him by inches.

"I'll kill her!" Wallace threatened.

"Let them go. This is between you and

me," Colt growled.

"The only way you get her alive is to ride away now." Wallace hadn't considered what would happen if his men were defeated. His only hope now was to use Victoria and the boys to get out of this dilemma.

"So you're not man enough to come out and face me?"

He heard Wallace laugh. "I don't profess to be stupid."

"I'll ride out of here with Victoria and the boys. There's no need for more bloodshed."

The door opened, surprising Colt and his men. Colt backed up a few feet, thinking he was finally going to have his showdown with Wallace. Instead of Wallace, Victoria charged through the door and ran right into his arms. Seeing a shadow in the doorway, Colt tried to push her behind him. But it was Wallace, walking through the door with his hands in the air.

"Well, big brother, do you want me to shoot this son-of-a-buck, or what?"

Colt could hardly believe his eyes. His brother, U.S. Marshal Jake McBride, was holding a gun in Wallace's back. "Jake, what are you doing here?"

"Looks like I'm saving your sorry butt, big brother," he joked. "Cole!" he yelled.

"Right here."

The other U.S. Marshal walked from the side of the house. He was the man who'd saved Colt from getting shot a second time.

Jake shoved Wallace toward Cole. "Will you tie him up since it doesn't look like my big brother will let me shoot him?"

"The sheriff will hear about this," Wallace threatened.

"Well now, that has me real concerned since your sheriff is locked up in his own jail," Jake said. He walked toward Colt. "Your men told us what was happening when we got to the ranch." He pointed to the other marshal. "This is Cole Becker."

"Cole, I'm glad you arrived when you did," Colt said earnestly. He pulled Victoria into his arms and looked her up and down. When he saw that her dress had been ripped, he flew into a rage, pushed Victoria toward Jake, and stalked to Wallace.

Cole glanced at Jake to see if he should intervene. Jake nodded, so he released Wallace's hands and pushed him forward toward Colt. Judging by the murderous scowl on Colt's face, Wallace was about to face a well-deserved, old-fashioned ass-kicking. Wallace fisted his hands as if he intended to fight, but Colt landed his massive fist in his jaw, which ended the fight before it began. The only sound was the loud crack of bones breaking and Wallace flying through the air, landing in an unconscious heap several feet away.

"Why didn't you just let me shoot him? Could've saved yourself some sore knuckles," Jake teased.

Colt grabbed his brother's shoulder with one arm and squeezed. "Not that I'm not happy to see you, but what are you doing here?"

"We were sent here because we got a telegram saying the judge was ambushed and murdered. We have reason to believe Wallace was the one who hired the killer. We've been tracking him for a while. He's left a trail of trouble, and he'll spend the rest of his life in the territorial prison."

"I'm glad to see you." Colt found himself becoming emotional at seeing his brother. He was just like an old woman, he thought. He pulled Victoria to him and looked down at her. "Did he hurt you?"

Clutching her dress to her chest, Victoria knew what he was really asking. "No, I'm fine, but that man . . . he shot Bartholomew."

Her lips started trembling, and Colt said, "Bartholomew is with Mrs. Wellington. He's alive." He saw no reason to tell her Bartholomew was in bad shape.

"He has the boys upstairs," Victoria said.

He didn't need to ask her who. He knew. Hoyt Nelson.

Colt walked toward the porch and Victoria saw the blood on the back of his shirt. "Colt, you're bleeding again," she cried.

"Again?" Jake asked, catching up to Colt at the doorway. "What happened to you? Who is in there? Let me handle it."

"This is my fight, Jake, and it gets settled today."

Jake had seen that determined look on his brother's face before. It wouldn't do a bit of good to argue with him. "Just tell me you're okay."

"I will be when Nelson is dead." Colt stepped inside the house just as Hoyt was walking down the stairs with his gun pointed at the boys in front of him.

The boys tried to run to Colt, but Hoyt grabbed Cody by the back of his shirt. Cade stayed by his brother's side and took his hand. "We knew you would come," Cody said to Colt.

"We told Victoria you would," Cade added.

Their tearstained faces broke Colt's heart. He wanted to pull them to him and tell them no one would ever hurt them again. But he couldn't console them right now; he was going to dispatch Holt Nelson to Hell. He made a mental note to tell Cade later what a brave thing he did by staying with his brother when he could have run. He winked at them. "You're okay now. Go on outside and meet one of my brothers."

His dark eyes turned to Nelson, and he said the one thing he knew would taunt him. "You wanted to see how fast I am. Now is the time — or would you prefer to shoot me in the back again?"

"Outside. I want everyone to see this," Hoyt boasted. He motioned with his pistol for Colt to precede him through the door. "I'm glad I didn't kill you now."

So it was Hoyt who had killed Tate, Colt thought. He was going to pay.

Once outside, the boys ran to Victoria, and Colt said, "Victoria, take the boys to the side of the house and get Razor." He figured that would give the boys something to do and keep them from seeing him kill Nelson.

She was torn between not wanting to leave Colt and not wanting the boys to see what was about to happen. "Please, don't do this," she pleaded softly.

In that moment Colt saw how much she loved him; it was written all over her beautiful face for all to see. He felt invincible, and wanted to pull her into his arms and tell her to have faith in him. But he couldn't be distracted; he needed to stay focused on Nelson. He said three words to her. "He killed Tate." Glancing at his brother, he said, "Jake."

Knowing what Colt was asking, Jake ushered Victoria and the boys to the side of the house. He didn't know who she was, but she was obviously important to his brother and that was all he needed to know. "Trust me, he'll be fine. Stay here," he instructed. She nodded her head in understanding, and he walked around the house to see Colt and Hoyt stepping away from each other until they were some distance apart. He was confident Colt would win any gunfight; he didn't want to even think it might end another way. But if it did, he'd kill Nelson for him.

Watching Hoyt's eyes, Colt knew the moment he was going to draw.

Hoyt hit the ground before his pistol was completely out of his holster, two bullets lodged between his eyes.

"He hit him with both guns! I didn't even see him draw!" Cole exclaimed, totally in awe of Jake's brother.

"I never could," Jake replied.

CHAPTER THIRTY-FOUR

"Colt, there is a . . . woman here to see you," Helen announced.

Colt had been back in bed for two days, threatened by the doc that he wouldn't sew him up again if he broke the new stitches, because he was running out of skin. Colt assured him he wasn't going anywhere. Why should he? Bandit and the boys were on one side and Victoria was on his other side. His brother was slouching in the chair beside the bed. He gave Victoria a sheepish grin at Helen's announcement, and she gave him that wide-eyed innocent look. He knew what that meant. He was certain to catch holy heck if Maddie was visiting again. She hadn't said much about the last visit, but he had the feeling he wouldn't be that lucky a second time.

"I guess T. J. can't carry her out, since he's laid up," Colt mumbled.

Jake looked at his brother and raised a

brow. Out of the corner of his eye, he saw Victoria smile. "What's this about T. J. carrying a woman out?"

"A long story for another day," Colt told him.

"Oh, it's not that . . . woman," Helen interjected.

Colt looked surprised and relieved. "Good. Well, who is it?"

"It's L. B.," Helen answered.

Colt looked at the boys, thinking it was best that they didn't stay in the room for her visit. "Why don't you two take Bandit outside so he can do his business? Then you can give him something to eat." He glanced at Helen, hoping she got his message. "Maybe Helen will find a treat for you."

L. B. was walking into the bedroom as the boys were leaving with Helen. They stared at her with eyes wide, awestruck by her flaming red curls.

Jake was almost as bad as the boys. The woman had the reddest hair he'd ever seen. He quickly jumped up from the chair. "Have a seat, ma'am." He didn't know what this was about, but he was as anxious as Colt to find out what she wanted.

"Thank you." L. B. took the offered seat. "Colt, I hear you are on the mend."

"Yes, ma'am, I'm doing fine."

"T. J.?" she asked.

"He's on the mend," Colt replied.

"And I hear Bartholomew is doing well."

"Thanks to Mrs. Wellington," Colt replied. "He was too afraid of her to die."

"You've got that right. That woman would make one heck of a marshal," Jake added.

After everyone stopped laughing, L. B. said, "I hear congratulations are in order."

Colt took hold of Victoria's hand and squeezed. "Yes, she's finally agreed to make an honest man of me."

"That's a fine thing." L. B. could see they were crazy about each other. "When's the big day?"

"Next week," Colt said. "I can't take the chance she will change her mind."

L. B. was silent for a moment, trying to decide how to go about asking the question she came to ask.

Colt wasn't sure what was on L. B.'s mind, so he said, "Have you met my brother?"

Turning her attention back to Jake, she looked him up and down. "No, but I thought he must be one of your brothers. You look alike."

Victoria thought the same thing when she first met Jake. Their chiseled features, dark hair and eyes, were so similar, but he wasn't as muscular or as tall as Colt. She had been as charmed by his personality as she was by Colt's.

"And here I thought you were going to say I was the handsome one," Jake teased.

"I can see you are like your brother in more ways than looks," L. B. said, thinking he was as appealing as his brother.

Jake grinned at Victoria. "It's a good thing he lassoed Victoria before I arrived. Big brother wouldn't have stood a chance. Now I only have a week to work on her."

L. B. laughed. "You'd best wait on the next filly. These two only have eyes for each other." Then her tone turned serious. "Colt, I wanted to talk to you and Victoria about . . . well, I had a question for her . . . about her past."

Jake turned to leave when Colt stopped him. "Jake, we've told you everything. No need to leave the room." He looked back at L. B. "What is it you want to know?"

Colt felt Victoria stiffen beside him. "Nothing to worry about, honey." He'd already assured her that if anyone came to take the boys away he would fight to his death to keep them. Whatever it took, those boys weren't going anywhere. He squeezed her hand, silently telling her to relax.

L. B. looked at Victoria. "You remember

the first time I saw you, I thought you were someone I used to know. Ruby. That Gage Hardy fellow said that your mother's name was Ruby. Is that the truth?"

Victoria nodded. "Yes."

L. B. dabbed at her eyes with the handkerchief she pulled from her cleavage. "I thought so. She looked like you when she was a young girl. Not as pretty, mind you, but she was a lovely child."

"How did you know her?" Victoria asked.

"We were sisters," L. B. replied. "Well . . . half sisters. We had different mothers."

Victoria didn't know what to say. "I didn't know my mother had a sister."

"When my mother died, my father remarried and had another daughter. Ruby was just a little kid when I left home. A few years later, I heard my father left Ruby's mother not long after I left town. I wrote a letter to see if they needed anything, and to tell them where I was located, but they had moved on. I've looked for her over the years but never found her. She was an unusual child, sort of distant, never really close to anyone. She may not even want to hear from me. Some years ago I heard there was a gal who worked at the Lucky Slipper in Abilene named Ruby. I wrote a letter, but the sheriff wrote me back saying the saloon had burned down and Ruby had left town. Then one day a cowboy came into the saloon and I overheard him talking about a gal named Ruby who was working in San Francisco. I was planning to take a trip there to see for myself if it was Ruby."

"I know my mother always planned on going to San Francisco."

"Why did you want to see her after all these years?" Colt asked.

"I reckon I just wanted to make up for the past, the way my pa ran off and left them. I didn't want her making the same mistakes I made. It's the reason I've stayed in one place so long."

Colt could hear the pain in her voice, but from what Victoria had confided in him about her mother, and what Gage Hardy said, Ruby wasn't the kind of woman who wanted to be burdened with family. He didn't think she would want to hear from L. B., or Victoria.

"A smart woman told me one time that women make their own decisions about their professions," Colt reminded her.

L. B. remembered that conversation. "Yes sir, I guess I did. By the way, Lucy left town with that Gage Hardy. There's no need to be worried about him."

"That's good news." Colt saw the relief

469

on Victoria's face. He hadn't seen Hardy at Wallace's, but he had planned on finding him soon and setting him straight.

L. B. stood to leave and directed her parting words at Victoria. "You let me know if you need anything. Seeing as who you've chosen for a husband, I think he will treat you kindly, but if he doesn't, you come to see me. I hope God blesses you with a big family. That's something I always wanted."

Victoria smiled at her. She'd never thought she would have a large family, but with Colt she thought anything was possible. She left Colt's side and linked her arm through L. B.'s. "Let me walk out with you."

While they were still in earshot, Colt heard Victoria ask L. B. to come to dinner one night.

Colt heard L. B. say, "You can call me Laura Bea." Life was full of surprises.

Victoria left Colt's room to put the boys to bed while Jake was keeping Colt company.

"Jake, I'd really like it if you decided to stay," Colt said.

"You sure you want me to do that?"

Colt had always felt it was his fault his brothers left the ranch. "I made a mistake letting you leave in the first place."

Jake laughed. "It wasn't your call."

470

"I made you and Lucas feel like there wasn't a place for you here."

"That wasn't the reason we left, big brother. You always knew you wanted to run the ranch. Lucas and I needed to find out what we wanted, not what the old man wanted for us."

Colt looked at him thoughtfully. "I always thought I ran you off."

It had never occurred to Jake that his brother was under that impression. "You didn't run us off. We needed to find out what else was out there. This ranch was in your blood from the time you were born. It wasn't that way for us. When you left to search for Creed Thomas you had a chance to see things, other places, and to think things through without the old man pressuring you. After you came back, your future was settled. We were envious of that."

Smiling, Colt felt such a sense of relief. He hoped his brother wasn't just saying that for his benefit. "I guess it was one and the same for me. Yeah, I knew the old man wanted me to take over here and keep the ranch going. But it was an easy decision after I came back. Nothing else would have made me happy."

"Don't get me wrong, I like what I'm doing," Jake explained. "But now that I see what you have, well, I'm thinking I might want to settle down." Jake had already made his decision. All he needed to know was that his brother wanted him to stay. After all, Colt was the one who single-handedly managed the ranch and made it such a success. And that wasn't the only thing on Jake's mind. If he stayed he had to be careful where his soon-to-be sister-in-law was concerned. After just a few short days, he was already half in love with Victoria. He was happy Colt had found someone to share his life, but also envious as hell. Logic said it was infatuation because she was such a beautiful woman with a heart to match, and his feelings would fade with time.

"I can't tell you how happy that would make me," Colt told him. "Now if we could get Lucas back here . . ." His words trailed off as he found himself becoming emotional again.

"I heard he was in New Mexico, so I sent a telegram to a friend of mine to check around for me."

Colt should have known his brother's thoughts were close to his own. "How long ago?"

"Two weeks. My friend will telegraph us here."

"Good."

Their eyes slid to Victoria when she walked back into the room. She sat beside Colt and he put his arm around her and pulled her close to his side.

"By the way, I've heard Creed Thomas is in Colorado," Jake said.

Hearing that bit of news made Colt's senses go on alert. His eyes snapped back to his brother. "How do you know?"

Victoria felt the change in Colt's entire body. She glanced at his face and was surprised at what she saw. Only one other time had she seen that deadly look on his face: when he'd smashed Wallace's face. She wondered who this man was who earned such a reaction from him.

"I've had everyone I know keep a lookout for him for years. I knew you would want to know." Jake's eyes cut to Victoria before he asked, "You going after him?"

"Yes." Colt always knew this day would come. He'd never gotten over his hatred for Creed Thomas, just stuffed it deep inside, knowing that one day he would kill him.

Victoria's mind was racing. Who was this man? she wanted to ask, but was almost frightened by Colt's demeanor. A feeling of doom coursed through her veins.

The room had grown quiet, and Victoria worked up the courage to ask Colt about this man, but Jake broke the silence with another surprising comment.

"There's one more thing I need to talk to you two about," he started. "I was in Abilene right after that fire in the saloon. There was some talk that one of the gals there started the fire. She went by the name of Kitten."

"That's the boys' mother," she told him.

"The owner said she stole some money from the safe and he also suspected she set the fire. We have a witness to the theft. You don't happen to know Kitten's real name, do you?"

"No, everyone called her Kitten," Victoria replied.

Colt noticed Victoria looked lost in thought. "Are you okay?"

She nodded. "I was just remembering the night of the fire."

"You were there that night?" Jake exclaimed.

"Yes, that was the night I left." She hadn't told Jake about the events with Gage Hardy; that was something only Colt needed to know. Her mind drifted back to that night. After the bartender saved her from Hardy, she'd made up her mind to leave. While she was gathering her few belongings, she heard someone screaming *Fire!* She opened the bedroom door and ran to look over the railing of the balcony. Flames were devouring the front of the saloon. She raced down the hallway to the room where the boys stayed. They were alone in the room, so she snatched them up and ran. "I barely made it out with the boys," she muttered.

"You didn't see who set the fire?" Jake asked.

"No, the front of the saloon was on fire when I left my bedroom. When we reached the bottom of the stairway, the ceiling was falling in over the bar, so we got out through the kitchen."

Colt recalled how frightened she'd looked the night of the fire near Tom and Helen's cabin. "Sounds like you were lucky you got out."

"We were very lucky. I was planning to leave anyway, but after . . . well, it was the perfect time."

Colt understood she was talking about what happened with Gage Hardy.

Jake could tell there was something they were not telling him. "Do you think Kitten could have set that fire knowing her boys were upstairs?"

Giving him a level look, Victoria said, "Yes, I do. She didn't have a conscience. She cared for no one except herself, and the boys were going to be taken to an orphanage."

"Do you think your mother was involved?"

"It's possible. They were making plans to go to San Francisco together," she said bluntly.

Jake stood. "I'll let you two get some rest." When he reached the door he turned around to give them a piece of good news. "As my wedding present to you, I will speak to the judge about getting you permanent guardianship of those boys. Their mother abandoned those boys, and this way you won't ever have to worry about someone trying to take them away from you."

Colt's voice broke with emotion when he said, "Thanks, Jake, that's one heck of a wedding gift."

Victoria ran to him and gave him a kiss on the cheek. "I don't know how to thank you."

"Get away from him, or he might think of a way," Colt grumbled. He was only half teasing. He'd seen how quickly his brother had become smitten with Victoria. It reminded him of Tate following her around like a lost puppy. How he missed that boy. He had Tate to thank for making him admit he was in love with Victoria. He knew he'd miss him until his dying day.

"Well, I figure I owe you something for

making you handle all the work around here without our help," Jake teased. "Good night."

Chapter Thirty-Five

Having convinced Victoria that they would not be disturbed at the late hour, Colt coaxed her to stretch out beside him. He gazed into her eyes. "Are you okay? I know it upsets you to talk about your past."

"It does bring back painful memories, but the more time that passes, the fainter they become," she replied softly. Since they were alone, she decided to ask him about Creed Thomas. "Colt, who is this man you are going after?"

Colt had expected the question since Jake had mentioned Creed Thomas. He explained the events surrounding his mother's death, and how he'd left home for a time searching for the man who had caused the events that day. "I vowed I would find him one day and make him answer for what he did."

"Why did you come back before you found him?"

He thought a minute before answering. "I was tired, and I missed my family and the ranch."

"I'm glad you came back," she said softly. "Yet you still blame that man?"

"Thomas goaded Gaines into a fight that killed my mother," Colt said unwaveringly. "He's going to answer for that."

She leaned up on her elbow and touched his cheek. "Colt, I don't have the right to ask . . ."

"You can ask me anything."

She took him at his word. "Please don't go looking for him."

He set his jaw. "You can ask me anything but that."

"I don't want to lose you. And what would I tell the boys if something happened to you? They need you. I need you. I love you."

Her words touched him, but he was determined. "Nothing will happen to me."

"You are a fair and honorable man, and deep down you know this man didn't kill your mother. Do you think losing your mother in such a cruel way has tainted your thinking about him?"

"Victoria, I won't change my mind about this." He spoke with resolve.

She put her head on his shoulder and her arm around his waist. "Just ask yourself if

479

killing that man will make you forget your mother's death, or bring her back. What would your mother want?"

Colt closed his eyes and thought about what she said. He would never forget his mother's death that day, no matter what happened. But Victoria was right; he now had a family to consider, and he knew what his mother would want for him.

He was quiet for so long Victoria thought he'd fallen asleep. She wouldn't ask him again not to hunt down Creed Thomas. She knew the kind of man he was, and had confidence he would come to the right decision. She would always support him, no matter what. "Colt?" she whispered.

"Hmm?"

"I know what you have prayed for all of these years. You wanted your brothers to come home."

It surprised him that she knew him so well. "Yes, I wanted them home. And when Lucas shows up, I'll be an even happier man, if that is possible." He turned his face to her and kissed her forehead. "I have so much more than I ever deserved with you and the boys."

Bandit let out a puff of air, telling Colt in his canine way that he'd excluded him.

Colt scratched him behind his ears. "You

too, boy."

They were both quiet, each lost in their thoughts of the events that brought them together. Victoria came to Promise in the hopes of finding a man she could trust, but she'd found even more than that. "Mr. Barlow promised me a home and to always care for the boys. He kept his promise."

"Chet was a man of his word, and it doesn't surprise me he found a way to keep his last promise." Colt was more grateful to Chet than he could say. "I give you that same promise. You and the boys will always be the most important thing in my life. I will protect you with my life."

"I love you so much, Mr. McBride," she told him, her voice cracking with emotion.

Colt leaned over and kissed her gently on the lips. "I love you, Victoria McBride."

She liked the sound of that. "Thank goodness I responded to Mr. Barlow's letter."

Colt gave her a curious look. "How many letters did you receive?"

"Mrs. Wellington told me after I left for Promise they continued to arrive daily. She said she stopped counting after one hundred."

Colt could hardly believe that many men had responded to a newspaper advertisement. "One hundred? Why did you respond to Chet's letter?"

Recalling how she'd felt when she read Mr. Barlow's letter the first time, it wasn't a difficult question for her to answer. "Besides his promise to provide us a home, I thought he sounded trustworthy. And he was the only man who didn't mention my *wifely duties,*" she added.

Colt laughed. "That would be the first thing on any man's mind." All he had to do was take one look at her to know that would be on the top of his list.

"And, of course, he said he was a farmer and not a cowboy," she teased.

Colt pulled her into his embrace. "What do you think about cowboys now?"

She batted her eyelashes at him. "I think I'm partial to them now."

He grinned. "Not afraid of me anymore?"

She almost laughed. It was difficult for her to remember why he'd frightened her in the first place. "No." She turned serious. "Colt, thank you for showing me I hadn't lost my faith. You were right about my prayers. Having found you, I have everything I've ever prayed for and more. I just needed patience. I should have listened to Mrs. Wellington the night you were at the boardinghouse."

"What did she say?"

"The first time I saw you in St. Louis, Mrs. Wellington said the Good Lord sent you into her boardinghouse for me, but I refused to help Him out."

"I told you before, I've never believed in coincidences," he replied. "I think God has a hand in everything," he added before kissing her again.

When his lips moved to her neck, she curled her fingers in his hair, pulling him to her. Colt pulled back and stared at her. How many times had he thought about seeing her just as she looked in that moment, her face flushed from his kisses and her long hair mussed and falling seductively around her? "You're so beautiful," he told her sincerely. "We're going to be married next week . . ." He stopped talking and started to unfasten the button at the top of her dress. Fearful she might tell him to stop, or that she wouldn't, he said, "But if you want me to stop, I will." His eyes followed the long, long row of buttons and his fingers moved to the second one. While he waited for her direction to stop . . . or continue, he thought his heart might beat out of his chest.

She responded by pulling his face to hers and kissing him again. This time, she was the one to pull away from his lips. Giving him a tentative smile, she whispered, "I love you."

Colt took that as a yes, and he had her beneath him in record time, forcing Bandit to the foot of the bed in the process. His lips were on her neck and his fingers were on the third button of her bodice. All of a sudden his fingers stilled and he stared into her eyes while his mind warred against his passion. When he didn't move for the longest time, she said, "Is something wrong?"

"I love you," he replied, his voice low with desire. He didn't tell her it was taking every ounce of determination to control himself. He wanted everything to be right for her, and more importantly, he wanted to do the right thing. Problem was, he'd never wanted any woman the way he wanted her. "I want to do this right," he said. It was important to him that she knew she meant the world to him. He remembered what she'd said that day about men going to church and then seeking the companionship of the saloon women. He knew what he had to do. On the upside, he only had to wait a few days and they would be married. *A few days,* he mentally repeated. *Lord help me!*

He could actually feel her heart thumping as loudly as his own. When he lowered his lips to hers again he almost missed the sound of the door opening. Instinct kicked in, and he whipped his pistol from his holster hanging on the bedpost, had it cocked and aimed at the door before Victoria could scarcely form a thought.

"Pa, can we sleep with you? We're scared that man is going to come back." Not waiting for an answer, Cade and Cody closed the door behind them.

"Aw . . . heaven," he said, relieved it was the boys and not an intruder but frustrated at the same time. Quickly replacing his gun in the holster, Colt pulled the covers back. "Come on, boys, hop in." The twins scampered across the room and dived on the bed.

"You two don't have to worry about anything. You know I won't let anything happen to you," he assured them.

"We know, Pa," they said together.

"We just feel safer with you," Cady told him.

"Yeah," Cody agreed.

Their words made Colt feel ten feet tall. And every time he heard the word *pa* he got a lump in his throat. "The only thing you need to think about tonight is that surprise I have for you tomorrow." He'd already told Victoria he was giving the boys their horses tomorrow. What she didn't know was he'd picked out a horse for her too. He intended to teach her to ride along with the boys.

"A surprise, for us!" they chorused.

Colt had a lot to learn about little boys, Victoria thought. "Shhh. You need to go to sleep or you don't get your surprise."

"Okay, Ma. Night-night, Pa," they said, settling down beside Colt.

"Good night," Victoria and Colt said together.

Victoria's eyes welled with tears. When she told them she was marrying Colt, they'd asked if they could call her ma since they were going to be a real family. She thought her heart would burst from sheer joy.

"Do you think Mrs. Wellington will keep them on our wedding night?" Colt whispered in her ear.

She loved him all the more because he wasn't upset, he was actually smiling. "I'll see to it, cowboy," she promised.

Five minutes later, Colt found himself in the middle of the bed on his back with Victoria snuggled close, her head on his shoulder. Both boys were on his other side, and Bandit was between his legs, snoring loudly. Not too long ago he thought he liked his life the way it was. He hadn't known what he was missing. He leaned over and kissed

Victoria on the nose, and whispered, "I could get used to this." He couldn't afford to take his good fortune lightly. He had to learn to let God fight his battles. "I won't go after Thomas," he whispered to her.

She hugged his neck and started to cry.

"Now don't cry," he said. "I thought that would make you happy." More than anything, he wanted to make her happy. She deserved that.

"They are happy tears," she sobbed. She pulled his face to hers and gave him a kiss. "Thank you."

He grinned at her. He might not understand her on occasion, but he was willing to spend the rest of his life trying. "I'll be expecting thousands of those kisses," he told her. Victoria settled close to him and he knew he'd never been happier than he was in that moment, his family in his arms. He looked out the window at the glittering stars in the night sky and said a silent prayer, thanking the Lord and Chet Barlow.

ABOUT THE AUTHOR

Scarlett Dunn's fascination with the West began as a child growing up in Kentucky, where a love of horses came with the territory. Always a voracious reader, Scarlett decided to pursue her interest in creative writing after years of corporate work. *Promises Kept* is her first novel. She lives in Kentucky. To learn more, please visit www .scarlettdunn.com.